Merrickville Public Library (OMER)

3 6637 00017025 5

P9-BTY-652

SHOOTING BUTTERFLIES

Due

BY THE SAME AUTHOR

Guppies for Tea
A Rival Creation
Purveyor of Enchantment
Frozen Music

MERRICKVILLE PUBLIC LIBRARY

SHOOTING BUTTERFLIES

MARIKA COBBOLD

McArthur & Company
Toronto

Published in Canada in 2003 by
McArthur & Company
322 King Street West, Suite 402
Toronto, Ontario M5V 1J2

Copyright © 2003 Marika Cobbold

The moral right of the author has been asserted

The use of any part of this publication reproduced, transmitted
in any form or by any means, electronic, mechanical, photo-
copying, recording or otherwise stored in a retrieval system,
without the expressed written consent of the publisher, is an
infringement of the copyright law.

National Library of Canada Cataloguing in Publication Data

    Cobbold, Marika
      Shooting butterflies/Marika Cobbold.

    ISBN 1-55278-352-9

    Title.

    PR6053.O175S56 2003   823'.914
    C2003-900119-9

Printed in Canada by *Friesens*

10 9 8 7 6 5 4 3 2 1

To Jeremy (My son the doctor.)

Light is energy, making visible anything that produces it; also anything that receives and is illuminated by it, such as the moon and virtually any other object we see.

THE REMARKABLE THING ABOUT this morning was not that it was Grace's birthday; after all, that occurred once a year so by the time you got to forty you should have ceased to be surprised. Nor was there much to say about the day itself; she walked down Kensington High Street to get the paper and it was muggy and overcast, the air so heavy with pollution you felt like offering it a hand to rise.

Back home, there was nothing odd about the toaster malfunctioning, Grace's two slices of white bread getting caught and having to be prised out piece by piece, nor about the tea turning cold before she remembered to remove the teabag. And she had expected cards; she had friends, after all, and Mrs Shield. No, what gave the day its unusual quality was that the postman, when he arrived, handed her a present from her dead lover.

She tore open the tattered brown paper parcel with its US stamps, thinking it might be a present from her Aunt Kathleen. Inside was a picture. She lifted it out and turned it the right way, gazing at the painting as if she had found a pink, breathing baby beneath a heap of rags. Outdoors, it was murky; leaden sky, charcoal asphalt, and the dirty white of the 1960s concrete building opposite. Indoors, the picture brought its own light.

There was an envelope hidden in a pocket of the wrapping. It had been opened and sealed again with a couple of bits of tape. On it was written simply *Grace*. It was his writing. She put the envelope down on the table, shook herself and then she looked again. It was still his writing. She picked the envelope up and tore it open. Her heart was hammering in her chest as she read on, but her hands remained steady; it was her training.

My darling Grace,

I came across this painting on my walk this morning. You were working and I was strolling through Chelsea, frightening passers-by with the stupid grin on my face as I thought of seeing you in just a little while. I found it at the back of a small antiques shop and I knew you would love it. I was told it wasn't for sale. I thought I recognised the building in the background and when I saw Northbourne House actually written next to the signature I knew I had to have it. Don't ask me how I managed to talk them round, but I did.

And don't ask me what the sea is doing not far from that house – artistic licence, obviously – but I wonder if the figure at the edge of the painting is your 'ghost'.

I'll send the painting to you when we are far apart, as an emissary of my love. Poor ghost, I know how he feels as he gazes at the girl on the beach; I know how he longs to be with her.

I love you, always and for ever,

J.

She read the letter three times and with each reading her heart beat faster and she grew dizzy and short of breath and had to sit down. She was in her kitchen, surrounded by familiar things; the sky-blue painted cupboards and the old gas cooker that she never got round to replacing because there always seemed to be something more urgent, or at least more interesting, to do with the money. There was the small tray with bottles of olive oil and vinegar, the jars of different teabags, her pot of honey. In front of her was the battered oak table that was too big for the room and on the wall behind hung the double row of black and white photographs, each of the same forlorn seascape, each taken at a different time with the sea in a different mood. She looked at it all, disconnected, floating like a leftover balloon in a factory sky.

The painting was the kind of gift – remarkable and utterly right – that he would send her; but two years after his death? Grace was not one of those people who discounted miracles; she just didn't think them likely. He was dead and, this being life, there would be no resurrection.

She propped the picture up against the back of one of the kitchen chairs. She looked at what he had looked at; there was a time lag of over two years, but they were sharing a view: the house brooding in the background, the dark-haired girl seated by the water's edge, the figure gazing at her with such longing, and all washed in a light so clear it might have been sieved through a fine muslin cloth. The sea was playing in shades of blue and, beyond, the horizon was endless. Grace had seen such light and such horizons in the past, in other places, but never from a window at Northbourne House. And A.L. Forbes, who was he? She had never heard of a painter of that name, yet this was not some amateur effort but the work of a true artist.

She turned the letter over in her hand and it was then she noticed the scribble on the back.

Well, Grace, I found this touching little note and the accompanying 'artwork' while going through the last of his stuff. As I can't believe even the thrift shop will want it, I am passing it on to you. Maybe he had second thoughts about giving it to you; an unexpected lapse into good taste, perhaps. But that we'll never know now, will we? I wish you joy of it.

Sincerely yours,

Cherry McGraw (Mrs)

Grace arrived at her stepmother's in time for tea. Mrs Shield said, 'You look like you've seen a ghost.' Grace laughed so loudly and for so long that Mrs Shield decided her stepdaughter must finally be having that nervous breakdown.

They went for a walk in the grounds, Mrs Shield casting little searching glances in Grace's direction. Mrs Shield could not stand being left out. And Grace was trying to think of a way of telling her about the painting without getting emotional. It was not that Mrs Shield would not understand, because she would. She would cluck and pat and fuss and fret and put the kettle back on, and that was all right for a bashed toe or a mislaid wallet but not for the really serious stuff; for that you needed space and time and silence. So Grace said nothing and Mrs Shield was left to worry as the sun shone across the lawns where rabbits played, not just at dusk but in the middle of the day, in broad daylight.

Evangeline Shield had only recently moved back to Northbourne and the purpose-built development on the edge of the village. The change had been prompted by her discovery, one spring morning, that her windows were a disgrace. The final decision to move had been taken when, at their usual Tuesday bridge tea, her dear friend Marjory pointed out that the little black grains in the cake were not cardamom but mouse droppings. Soon afterwards, Mrs Shield became a resident of the newly opened Northbourne Gardens, modelled on the Golden Agers Village in Florida. What were now sixteen small flats and twelve purpose-built bungalows, all so bright you could smell the paint, and set in grounds as stiffly immaculate as a dowager's bouffant, had once been the home of the Glastonbury family, the stately Northbourne Manor with its stables and extensive grounds. The Glastonburys had departed in a hurry long before Grace was born and for years the once-magnificent house had been left to decay, its famous gardens turned into thorny wilderness. But now it was all part of what the new owners described as *Dedicated Living for*

Active Seniors. Apart from the actual accommodation, there was a cafeteria-style restaurant in the main building *for those days when you're too busy enjoying life to cook,* a swimming-pool, a gym, an arts centre, the *village hall* and a *village store* selling food staples, stamps, newspapers and support hosiery.

Mrs Shield had said to Grace at the time of her move, 'As you can see, it's a world away from one of those *old* people's places.'

Now she said, 'The gardens are looking wonderful, don't you think?' gesticulating at the neatly undulating borders of asters and tea roses. 'Quite restored, they say.' But she still kept her eyes on Grace.

The next morning however, Mrs Shield forgot all about Grace's 'queer look' as she opened the Sunday papers. 'Oh my goodness! Really, I never thought anything would come out of it.'

Grace vaguely registered her stepmother speaking from behind the arts supplement, but it was the fifth time in as many minutes that Mrs Shield had muttered some comment or other so she paid little attention. Mrs Shield, never a respecter of other people's space, reached forward and gave Grace a sharp poke with the index finger of her good hand. 'Grace, you're not listening. *Where Are You Now?*'

Grace assumed a look of infinite patience; she had not realised how old her stepmother was getting. 'I'm here, Evie; right opposite you.'

'Don't be daft, Grace. I know where you are. It's *this*.' She slapped Grace on the knee with the paper. 'There, see for yourself. *Blighted promise: the heavy prize of success.* Prize with a z; it's a pun, I think.'

Grace took the paper. 'Thank you, Evie, for explaining that.'

The shortlist for Britain's biggest photography prize, the Unibank Award, had just been announced and the newspaper's arts editor, Nell Gordon, was taking a look. The prize, awarded every two years and worth thirty thousand pounds, was said to make a photographer's career. Other than in the case of the last recipient, Grace Shield. It's true that for the couple of weeks that constitutes an eternity in the world of the media, Grace Shield had been everywhere and called everything from *shutter babe* to *voyeur*, from

6

remarkable talent to *exploitative pervert*. But after that nothing was heard of her. So whatever happened to all that controversial talent? Let's do a profile, try to find out. August was the silly season. A chunk of misery, a hint of scandal and some promise lost must have seemed like a godsend. It was not as if Grace was entirely unprepared for the attention; she had been contacted by the paper a few days earlier, but she had believed that her short polite, 'I have nothing to say, but thank you for asking,' would be the end of it.

'At least it's a *serious* paper,' Mrs Shield said. 'That's what I thought when they called. As long as it isn't one of those dreadful tabloids, I'm quite happy to help. And they had talked to your cousin Patricia in Ireland already – fancy going to all that trouble – and all sorts of other people. I said to them, "Of course, I know Grace is very clever, but I didn't appreciate that she was *this* important."'

'You talked to them. This . . . this *rubbish* is your doing?' Grace felt a sudden urge to leap at Mrs Shield like a rabid monkey and grab her plump neck and squeeze. Instead she took three deep breaths: in through the nose, out through the mouth. Mrs Shield, a large woman with tiny features assembled close together in the middle of a moon-face, shrank and her pale blue eyes filled with tears as she twisted her broad hands in her lap. 'I'm sorry, dear.'

Grace looked at her and sighed. 'No, I'm sorry, Evie. I didn't mean to be nasty. I just hate it all being raked up again. I can't tell you how much I hate it.'

'I don't think it's at all *unkind*. It's quite sympathetic, actually. I don't know where she got all the information from because I certainly didn't say much.' Mrs Shield paused to blow her nose in a pink tissue she had pulled out from her sleeve. 'Oh Grace, I thought you'd be pleased.'

'It didn't occur to you to check with me first?'

'I was worried you might be . . . difficult about it.'

'How right you were,' Grace said.

'And I thought a little encouragement, a little push, might help you get started again.'

'A little encouragement . . .' Grace waved the paper at Mrs Shield. 'Is that what you call being turned inside out and hung

7

out to dry with your guts flapping? And even if, by some twisted chance, I did find that *encouraging*, do you really think I'd pick up my camera just like that . . . after everything that happened?'

'Grace, please . . . And the picture is nice.' Mrs Shield dabbed at her nose with the tissue. 'I always did like your hair short.'

'I look like an ageing orphan,' Grace said, which, come to think of it, was exactly what she was. That black dress with its round neckline and that awful urchin cut and the eyes all wide and tragic; ironically, she had been truly happy that evening. She sighed once more, shaking her head. 'Evie, don't you see, I wouldn't mind *unkind*. Unkind is fine with me. I've made peace with nasty. But *pity*! That bloody article is holding me up to all the world . . .'

'I believe the readership, that is the people actually reading the paper as opposed to the copies purchased, is two and a half million.'

Although tall and agile with strong hands, Grace was not, by and large, an intimidating person, but something in her expression made Mrs Shield decide to say nothing more for a moment or two. When she felt that Grace had calmed down sufficiently, she concluded, 'At least I'll have something to stick in my album.'

Mrs Shield was not an imaginative woman, nor was she especially creative, but her scrapbook, bound in burgundy leather, was her flight of fancy. She had begun assembling it soon after her marriage to Grace's father, Gabriel, starting with a spare invitation to their modest wedding and following with theatre programmes, admission tickets to special events and exhibitions, little notes from her husband and from her stepchildren, Finn and Grace, the odd pressed flower, a menu or two and, eventually, clippings from newspapers and magazines. Lately there had not been much for Mrs Shield's album.

Grace, having finished reading, folded the paper neatly before getting up and putting it in the bin. Mrs Shield, moving with a speed admirable for a woman her age and weight, retrieved it and clasped it to her chest. Grace looked at her and then she shook her head and went to sit down again. Speaking quietly, she said, 'I really don't understand. There's been sadness, of course there has. But that's life, any life. Compared to most people on this earth, I've been lucky. I am lucky. So what is this?' She waved in the direction of the paper still clasped to Mrs Shield's bosom. '*Tragic, failed relationships, crushed dreams* . . . Well, I ask you, am I the only one? *Unfulfilled promise, thwarted desires* . . . that's what you expect, isn't it? And what about the rest, the good stuff? I've experienced happiness that some go to their graves without ever knowing.' Grace was not the pleading kind, but the way she looked at Mrs Shield just then, you might think she was.

'It's only a newspaper article,' Mrs Shield said. She returned Grace's gaze, eyes round and bright, her head cocked to one side. 'Maybe you're so upset because you think they might have a point.'

'Don't be so bloody stupid!' Grace leapt from her seat, knocking into the spindly-legged coffee table and upsetting a cup.

Mrs Shield said, the way she had always said to Finn or Grace when they were shouting, 'Screaming won't scare the truth away.'

'Screaming might alert your neighbours to the fact that I'm in the process of killing you,' Grace replied. Mrs Shield ignored her, brushing some crumbs of toast from her navy cardigan.

'Anyway, there's no such thing as "just a newspaper article" these days, Evie. Things are downloaded and stored. They don't ever go away; oh no, they hibernate somewhere on a disk, and just when you think you're safe, up they pop, mutated into a columnist's rant or attached to someone else's life, but there, never really gone.'

Nell Gordon was a serious journalist writing for a serious paper. Her piece was not ill-informed; it dealt well with many aspects of Grace's work and when it came to her private life did not rely entirely on gossip. No, the problem was a question of focus, focus and an absence of Grace's living mind on the bare facts of her life.

Mrs Shield shook her head. 'Tragedy lurking beneath the successful façade; it's a common story.'

'And happiness lurking behind the tragic façade is *my* story.'

Mrs Shield gave her a long kind look. 'If you say so, dear. If you say so.'

Grace asked, 'How did a simple phrase like *if you say so* come to mean *I don't believe a word you say*?'

*   *   *

9

On Monday morning Mrs Shield took a tumble as she ran behind the car, waving Grace off.

When she emerged from the surgery an hour later, her voice was small as she told Grace, 'I've cracked three ribs. Oh, I am a silly old woman.'

In the car she said, 'They can't do anything, of course; that's the fashion these days, leaving broken bones just to get on with it, but I will have to keep still. No bending or lifting.'

Back home, she agreed to use the lift. 'At least you're in the right place,' Grace said. 'You have everything at your fingertips and a resident nurse.'

Mrs Shield put a chubby finger to her lips. 'The walls have ears.' Once they had got inside the flat she explained, 'It's different when you really *need* to use it all. It's not good to be seen to be incapacitated in any way. And I've got my commitments. Old Mrs Thompson relies on my Wednesday visits and now I can't drive. And then there are the Lifeboats. I always do the Lifeboats.'

Mrs Shield had known about the rules when she moved to the Gardens. The most important dictated that anyone who became too sick or frail to look after themselves would be asked to leave; Northbourne Gardens was *not* a nursing home. This rule, like most, was popular with everyone to whom it did not apply.

'I'm sure someone else will fill in for you. And a broken rib could happen to anyone at any age, if that's what's worrying you. Look at me, I fall over all the time.'

'You don't break your bones,' Mrs Shield said, sinking down into her chair with a grimace of pain. 'Oh my dear, couldn't you stay just until I'm a little more mobile?' Before Grace had had a chance to formulate her excuses, Mrs Shield went on, 'Please, Grace, you don't understand what it's like. People round here are vultures. They hover round if you're the slightest bit unwell, just waiting . . . I've got a garden view. There's a queue for garden views.'

Grace inhaled on her cigarette as she thought about what to do. She was having four weeks off from her work for a London charity for the blind. She had planned some weekends in the country with various friends and there was any number of people to catch up with and things she had hoped to do with her free time back in London. She was still thinking of a way to get out of staying in

Northbourne when the phone rang. It was for Grace, her agent Angelica Lane. 'There you are.'

'Thank you for the card. And when will you stop sending photographic ones?'

'When you become sensible. Now, what about the *papers*?'

Angelica was surprised when Grace replied that she would like to track down the journalist, Nell Gordon, and ram her fist into the woman's big mouth before turning her inside out like a glove.

'What's the matter with you? It's publicity and you know what they say . . .'

'Yes, thank you, I do know, but that doesn't mean I agree. There's definitely such a thing as bad publicity and this was it.'

There was a pause, then Angelica spoke again with the determined cheer normally reserved for the terminally ill. 'Anyway, great news; I've sold one of the photos in your *Illusions of Love* series this morning. It's been months since anyone bought anything of yours. I bet you there'll be more on the way. And don't tell me the extra income won't be welcome. Daisy phoned; she'd read it too and . . .'

'I have to go,' Grace said and put the phone down. She turned to Mrs Shield, who had been leaning against the sofa back pretending not to listen. 'I'll stay a few days.'

Mrs Shield's pale eyes brimmed with tears. 'Thank you, darling, that's a great relief.'

'And I could pop over to Northbourne House. There's something I want to ask Louisa. She is still there, isn't she?'

'Of course she is. And I meant to tell you, I saw Noah the other day.'

Noah, the Blackstaffs' Canadian grandson, Grace's childhood playmate. Noah, irritatingly cheerful, always busy doing something: digging holes, learning tricks on his bike, running faster than anyone else, riding his pony. Noah, with his shock of wheat-blond hair and those slanted amber-colour eyes, a chunky little boy growing into a lanky adolescent. Last time she had seen him they had both been nineteen.

'I did tell you Arthur Blackstaff died, didn't I? It happened just before I moved back to the village. I missed the funeral. Someone should have let me know. I can't be expected to keep up with everyone who dies.'

'I didn't write to Louisa. I meant to.'

'One always does, dear. But you haven't seen her since you were a girl. She wouldn't expect to hear from you. Anyway, she's almost a hundred. She most likely wouldn't have remembered who you were even if you had written. That's why Noah is here: to sort things out before the house goes on the market. And to write Arthur's biography for the exhibition. It's a retrospective.' Mrs Shield nodded. 'I shall have to go, of course. I can stay overnight with you.' She shifted in her chair, pulling a face and putting her hand to her chest. 'I think I shall have to take those painkillers after all, dear.'

Arthur Blackstaff had been a famous artist in his day. A.L. Forbes had painted Grace's picture at Northbourne House, so the Blackstaffs must have known him. If Noah was writing a biography of his grandfather, then he might have come across Forbes. Finally, she told Mrs Shield about the picture from Jefferson.

Mrs Shield pursed her lips. 'So that's why you were so out of sorts when you arrived yesterday. That man has never been anything but trouble. Even now, after he's been dead for two years, he manages to upset you.'

'Don't go there, Evie.'

'Go where, dear?' Her brow cleared. 'Oh, I meant to tell you, Doctor Llewellyn had read the piece about you and so had Hazel, that's his receptionist; and Percy Witherspoon, he's two flats down the corridor, told me to say how sorry he was . . . you know, about your difficulties. He had no idea, he said. What's that noise? Oh Grace, you've started grinding your teeth again.'

'That's quite enough, thank you. Now, if you'll excuse me I'll just go and make a call to Mrs Williams, my neighbour, to ask her to feed the cat.'

'You don't have a cat.'

'You're right, I don't. So I'll just go and lie on my bed for a while and think about all the people in this world who are feeling sorry for me. Bastards!'

Even as a young child Grace Shield showed signs of the morbid streak that came to categorise so much of her work.

The mother placed the fireguard in front of the dying fire and told the boy to mind his sister. She wouldn't be long, she said, but she was gone for ages and the boy grew bored sitting there with the baby. She, as always, seemed perfectly content just to watch. She was podgy. She was almost four, not really a baby at all, and she could speak perfectly well, but most of the time she chose not to, although you could hear her when she was alone in her room, talking and singing to her toys.

'Silly old baby,' her brother said. She was no fun; difficult to tease because she was too stupid to notice. 'You're just a big silly baby.' He glared at her and was rewarded with a wide smile that lit up her big eyes. Her mouth was like a rubber band, stretching wider than you had thought possible.

He decided to try to make her cry. For such a baby she hardly ever did. He stuck his tongue out, but the stupid old baby just giggled. He jabbed her hard right in the softest bit of her round tummy. Her smile gave way to confusion as the pain registered. But she had soon recovered and was smiling again at her funny older brother. He gave her a shove and she toppled backwards, banging her head on the floorboards. For a second the smile remained fixed on her chubby face, but as she realised he had meant to hurt, her eyes flooded with tears. He thought she looked like a great beetle, her arms and legs waving around as she struggled to get up, and he laughed his high clear choirboy's laugh; she always was a clumsy baby. Now she got on to her hands and knees, her

13

fat bottom sticking up in the air, and next she had poddled off to get her comfort, a brown velveteen puppy called Father. She had barely begun the cuddle when the brother was by her side, making a grab for the puppy. She ran, the puppy close to her chest. Being chased, even in fun, scared her and although she knew, really, that it was only her big brother coming after her, she panicked, scenting a pack of wolves or maybe Red Indians on horseback, whooping and whirling their bows and arrows in the air. She stumbled and fell and, as she lay sprawled on the floorboards, he grabbed Father and swung him round his head, shouting triumphantly as he ran off towards the fire. Dangle, dangle. Father, held by his stubby tail, dangled for his life. His plump little owner struggled to her feet and went to his rescue. Dangle, dangle, close to the fire. 'Hot dog,' the brother laughed. 'Hot dog, hot dog.'

With an anguished yelp, the baby snatched her puppy and swung her little fist at her tormentor, sending him tumbling on to the fireguard and into the fire, barbecuing his freckled cheek on the grid of the guard.

'She's obsessed with that toy,' the father was saying on the landing outside the children's bedrooms that night. 'And why does she call it Father? Why not Daddy or Gabriel if she had to call a velveteen dog after me?'

'I asked her that,' the mother said. 'It's nothing to do with you. She's called him after Father O'Toole because, she says, Father O'Toole is important. It seems to make sense to her.' The mother sighed. 'She'll have to be punished. She's quite old enough to know that what she did was very naughty.'

'I don't expect she meant her brother to fall into the fire,' the father said.

The baby lay trembling in her bed. What would her punishment be? In her brother's fairy-tale books people had their tongues cut out. But the grown-ups kept telling her to talk, so they probably wouldn't want to do that. In those books they also rolled people down hills in barrels of a thousand nails. Her brother had explained that it meant barrels with nails hammered through so that all the spikes were on the inside sticking into you as you rolled. But she was fat and the only barrel she knew of was the barrel of wooden bricks in the nursery. She would never fit and her father always said that they did not have enough money, so they would hardly go out and buy a new one, just for her. In some ways she was clever for her age, so she knew that a thousand nails as well as a barrel would cost a lot. Then she remembered another line in her own book of stories. 'You will lose the thing you love best.'

She yelped in distress and clutched Father to her chest. That would be her punishment! They would take Father from her. She lay stock still, as if by not moving, by staying absolutely silent, they would not be found. Once she heard footsteps approach on the landing, pausing by her door. Then it went quiet. But as the minutes ticked away on her red clock she could bear it no longer. What if she did it herself; the punishment? They might leave it if she got there first. She felt calmer now. When the idea came into her head she felt scared but she knew too that she had found the right thing to do. She climbed out of bed, Father in her arms, and padded downstairs listening out for voices or steps, but all was quiet. She found the right room although it was dark. Once in there she dared to put the light on. The box of extra-long matches lay on top of the mantelpiece. She placed Father on the floor at a safe distance before dragging up a chair and clambering up on the seat to reach. She lit the match at the third strike and only hesitated a moment before putting the flame to her cheek.

Her screams woke everyone up.

At kindergarten, Sister Francis, the youngest and prettiest of the nuns, looked at her with kind eyes. 'Poor wee thing, she looks like an angel who's had a bad landing, so she does.'

'Angel,' Sister Joseph sniffed. 'Have you seen her brother? No, she's a little devil, more like.'

'We don't like Sister Joseph, do we?' Grace muttered in Father's floppy velveteen ear.

Once upon a time up a neat shingle drive there stood a white clapboard house with blue painted window frames and a blue door. The house lay on Brook Street and Brook Street was in Kendall. Kendall was a small town in America, a clapboard and red-brick and ivy town, a place for skating on the pond on winter's days and swimming in the lazy river in the summer, a soda-parlour and neighbourly kind of town where every mother made her child a new costume for Hallowe'en.

In the white house on Brook Street lived a mummy and a daddy and a big brother and a little sister. The mummy was beautiful as a mermaid and the daddy was handsome and strong. The brother was a pain in the butt and the little sister was as pretty as a princess and just as lucky, with her lovely yellow and white room and her own swing in the yard. The mother and father loved each other very much. They always said so. And they loved their children and wanted only what was best for them. The mother's name was Moira and the father's was Gabriel. The brother was christened Finnian but his little sister called him Pigface. The little sister was called Grace, such a good name for a princess. When Pigface wanted her attention he called out, 'Oi, Clothears!' Pigface was at boarding school in England during term-time, which was lucky, although for some reason Grace and her mother cried at the start of each new term. 'Women,' the father said to Pigface and then they both shrugged and drove off in the station wagon towards Boston and the airport. Grace would run as far as the end of the street and wave at the departing car and Pigface would always be

16

waving back with a look on his face like he didn't want to leave all that much.

But now it was the holidays. Grace was preparing for her forthcoming birthday. She liked the word forthcoming; it seemed to make an already important occasion even more so. She used the word often, making the 'o' in forth long and drawn out. She had already decided which pyjamas to wear for waking up on the day; and for later she would be wearing her best dress, of course: the white one with red polka dots and a wide red sash to tie round the waist.

Grace's Aunt Kathleen and Uncle Leslie lived in the same town, but they could not come to the party because they were away. Roberta O'Reilly was there, though. She was Finn and Grace's grandmother, Moira's mother. It was hard enough, the children thought, to believe that Roberta O'Reilly was their grandmother, but to think she was actually someone's mother was close to impossible. She had only been in the house for a couple of days, but already she was causing trouble.

'You spoil her, Moira,' she said, sending a spiteful look in Grace's direction. 'There's nothing good that comes from spoiling a child.'

'Daddy says you think the sun shines out of Uncle Michael's backside,' Grace said, returning the look with a long hard stare of her own. 'That means *you* spoil *him*.'

Roberta O'Reilly was large apart from her feet that were small but so fat that they spilt over the edge of her navy-blue court shoes. She had washed-out fair hair curled tight and brushed away from her face. Her eyes were mean and her fat cheeks looked as if they could slide down her face at any time. Those cheeks turned bright pink and wobbled as she looked at Grace's father and at Moira, *that child's* mother. Then they all looked at Grace. Grace, who sometimes rode her bicycle so fast down the hill that she knew for sure it would end up with her crashing into the hedge; Grace, who had to clamp her hand tight over her mouth in church to stop herself from shouting, 'Bugger, bugger, bugger baby Jesus *and* the Holy Ghost'; Grace, who always walked too close to the edge of the river where it was at its deepest and most wild.

'*Grace.*' Her parents spoke in unison. But Grace was too far gone to heed the warning. 'And it's really funny that you think that about the sun shining out of Uncle Michael's backside, because Daddy says Uncle Michael is a pompous fool who talks through his arse. Arse,' she added helpfully, 'is the same as backside.'

Grace, the offender, the bad girl, a mosquito child all eyes and teeth and knees, got sent to her room, which was absolutely fine with her because she had lots to do. She had to change the sign on her door, for a start. At the moment it read *Trespassers will be persecuted* – 'it's prosecuted, Clothears,' Pigface had said. But Grace had assured him that hers would be persecuted. (She had been reading about Bloody Mary in Finn's schoolbook.) But for tomorrow, her birthday, there had to be a different sign. When it was all done and stuck to her door, it read *Trespassers will be welcome*.

There was a knock on the door. It was her father. He knocked on his children's doors even when he was angry. It was useful because it gave them time to hide stolen goods, stub out cigarettes or blow out small fires. Finn had shown Grace how to smoke during his last holidays. He said that his friend Nathan's little sister could blow smoke rings already. But, for now, Grace was doing nothing worse than work on her sign.

He perched on the end of her bed. 'Grace, you know that what is said within a family should never be repeated outside. Not even to grandparents. In fact, especially not to grandparents. We must be able to trust each other to be discreet. Do you know what discreet means, Grace?'

Grace nodded hastily. 'It's still my birthday tomorrow?' she asked nervously.

'Of course it is. But no more talking out of turn, Grace. Can I rely on you for that? If we can't trust each other, who can we trust?'

'God,' Grace said.

'*Yes.*' Her father dragged out the word. 'Of course we can trust God, but I'm talking about here on earth. So try to be a good girl, Grace, especially during your grandmother's visit.'

Grace hung her head. She wanted to be good. It was just that sometimes she could not help giving things a stir, that was all. Like the time she put the slug on the anthill. She had been very

young, no more than five, and she had regretted doing it ever
since, even having nightmares about it. But at the time, there
had been the slug, all plump and sticky, and there had been the
anthill, all hungry and busy. One thing had led to another. The
slug landed neatly on top of the anthill. Grace wiped her sticky
hands on her dress and squatted down to watch. Her eyes grew
round. Now she really wanted to rescue the slug, but when she
put her hand out to pick it up she couldn't bring herself to touch
it, it looked so horrible oozing desperate slime under a crust of
tormenting ants, so instead she ran away and was sick. Afterwards
she tried to pretend the whole thing had never happened. But as
Grandmother Roberta O'Reilly always said in that satisfied voice
she used for pronouncing doom, 'Sweep a thing under the carpet
and sooner or later it'll trip you up.' Grace's father had explained
that sweeping something under the carpet was a figure of speech
meaning *not facing up to something.*

Grace did not wish to face up to the slug incident so it faced up
to her instead, at night in her dreams and when she sat in church
listening to the things good people did. Putting a poor little slug
on an anthill to be eaten alive was not a good thing. Children,
however, were supposed to be good, and innocent. Grace, and
there was no denying it, was a child. But Grace had also done a
very bad thing which meant that she was not good. After pondering
this seeming contradiction, she went to her father and said, 'To
you I'm but a child but, know this, I am capable of great evil.' She
had read a book where the hero, a little boy not much older than
Grace, had said almost exactly that, only with him it was deeds –
'capable of great deeds' – not evil. But she had particularly liked
the sentence, memorising it for when it would come in useful.

Her father had looked at her, shaking his head and laughing.
Grace had watched him for a while and then she had walked off.
Only the previous day he had whacked her on the thigh for being
rude. Now, when she told him she was evil, he just laughed. There
were times when things just did not make sense.

'Now, try to be the sweet little girl I know you are,' her father
concluded, getting to his feet. He walked out of the room a little
bent, as if he was carrying the trouble that was his daughter on

his shoulders. He was Clark Kent today, his dark hair combed into a neat side parting and his bright blue eyes dimmed behind smudged spectacles. But when he took the lead in the Kendall Players' production of *Guys and Dolls*, he had whisked his glasses off and his dark hair had fallen across his forehead and he had definitely looked a bit like Superman. Apart from her eyes that were sea-green and almond-shaped like her mother's, Grace looked like her other, dead, grandmother. So there they were, Grace's mother looking like a mermaid, her father looking like Clark Kent and a little like Superman, Grace looking like a dead person and her brother looking like a geek.

The evening before her birthday was meant to be a good time, with everyone having little secrets and being nice just in preparation. But this year something was not right. Like her record player dragging the record half a note behind, the tune was recognisable yet wrong.

'Tell me the story of when you and Mummy first met,' she said to her father when they were on their own in the sitting room after supper. But her father kept getting it in a muddle. Grace had to prompt him. 'So there you were, a young man visiting Boston, and there she was, the prettiest girl outside the prettiest doorway in town.'

'Oh yes,' Gabriel said, 'the doorway. Your grandfather had it shipped all the way from Dublin although he couldn't even pay the rent at that time.'

'You thought she was a mermaid . . .' Grace had to prompt again.

'Grace, I can't remember.'

'You always remember.' Grace's voice turned shrill with anxiety. 'You thought she was a mermaid, so you . . .'

'If your mother is a mermaid, then I'm afraid she is the kind who wants nothing more than to paddle in her goldfish bowl with a nice piece of plastic seaweed and a tasteful plaster shipwreck.'

'I don't understand what you are saying.' Grace was close to tears. 'You fell in love with Mummy, then and there, because she looked like a mermaid and the girls you knew back in England all looked like silly Imogen Jones and *she* looked like a horse.'

'If I remember right, Imogen was rather a jolly girl. Fun,

20

always laughing. Nothing was ever difficult. I can't imagine what I thought was wrong with her.'

'She wasn't a mermaid,' Grace yelled. 'That's what was wrong with her. *You wanted a mermaid!*'

She slammed out of the room in search of her mother and tried her. 'Anyway, you were fed up with living with Roberta O'Reilly . . .'

'Granny, darling. You're meant to call her Granny.'

'. . . because she was always yelling and throwing china, even if it was the ugly cheap stuff, and because Grandpa O'Reilly, God rest his soul, told stories that weren't true and never stopped going on about the old country when you were perfectly happy with the new one, so when you saw this handsome young man from England . . .'

Moira looked at her little daughter who stood there, all indignant in her birthday pyjamas, and she sighed. 'Grace, isn't it time you went to bed?'

Grace turned on her heels and walked upstairs. She had given up on the evening.

But her birthday still arrived, right on time, at seven o'clock the next morning. Blue, the red setter, burst through the door first, wispy tail wagging, a big grin on his foxy face; dogs just have to get through a door first. Gabriel followed, carrying a tray with the birthday cup full of sweet milky tea and a vase with a single red rose. Finn came behind, sullen and sleep-swollen. He was on holiday and could not see why he should have to get up early just because it was Grace's birthday. But Grace heaved a sigh of relief and beamed a smile at them. The world had snapped back into its proper shape and everything was as it should be, almost, because where was Moira?

'Where's Mummy?'

Gabriel placed the tray at the foot of the bed and disappeared, returning a moment later with a heap of gift-wrapped parcels. 'She's got a bit of a headache, that's all. She'll be along in a minute,' he said. 'And,' he winked. 'I *might* have forgotten to wake Grandma up, although,' he raised a small parcel wrapped in creased paper with reindeers on in the air for Grace to see, 'I've got her present for you.' Grace winked back with both eyes.

21

First Grace opened Finn's present. It was a red kite. Grace was delighted. 'When can we fly it?'

'In a minute,' Gabriel said. 'Open the rest of your presents first. And you have to get dressed.'

Grace picked up the birthday cup and drank a little. 'When's Mummy coming?'

'I told you . . .'

'Here I am, darling.' Moira was wearing a dress that matched her eyes, a dress Grace especially liked. Her lips were Princess Grace-pink and her hair was piled up in a golden bun on top of her head. It was just that her eyes were swollen like Finn's.

'Is your headache better?'

'Headache? I don't have a headache, darling. I got caught on the phone, that's all.'

Grace turned to her father with her mouth open, poised to speak, but he quickly forestalled her by handing her the next parcel.

Roberta O'Reilly's present was a camera. 'A camera for a seven year old,' Moira muttered. 'And she'll be furious we didn't wake her.'

'She got it free with an electric blanket,' Finn said. 'She told me. Anyway, seven isn't too young for a camera. I'm sure I knew how to use one when I was seven.'

'But Grace is not at all technical.' Moira caught her reflection in the mirror and wrinkled her little nose; the adorable snub nose that was the sure mark of every heroine in every book that Grace had read, a nose that Moira had not passed on to her daughter. She patted the skin beneath her chin. 'What is the point, I ask you? You moisturise and moisturise and you moisturise and still you die.'

Grace turned the small square box in her hands, admiring the frog's eye Finn said was the inbuilt flash. She raised the camera to her right eye and squinted through the lens as her father spoke. 'Can we concentrate on Grace's birthday gifts, Moira . . . dear.' The 'dear' did not match the look on his face. She lowered the camera and now, as she looked at them, her parents were both smiling.

'Do you see the same in the camera . . .'

'Through the camera,' Finn said. 'There's nothing *in* the camera, Clothears.'

'I know that. What you see *through* the camera,' Grace frowned at Finn, 'is the same as you see outside?'

'Jesus, you're thick.'

'Don't take the Lord's name in vain, Finn,' came a warning voice from Moira and Grace raised the camera and saw her mother's smile. Weird, Grace thought, but interesting.

For as long as Grace could remember, her parents had been having 'words'. Those words were either very quiet, seeping out from between clenched teeth, or very loud, jetting out of gaping mouths. But Grace didn't worry because her parents *loved each other very much.* That's what they said, every time after they had had words. 'Now, there's no need to take on so, Grace. It's healthy to disagree and you know that Mummy and Daddy love each other very much.'

But today they did not have words once. First it felt nice but after a while Grace grew uneasy. True, it was her birthday and everyone was supposed to be happy, like at Christmas, but that had not stopped them in the past. Something was wrong. Like a dog, Grace sniffed the air and picked up on an atmosphere thick with unsaid *words*. Even Finn was being OK. (Last time he had been decent to her it turned out that he had dropped her tortoise from the attic window strapped to a homemade parachute. It had been months before they found the desiccated remains, a pretty shell, suspended from the branches of next door's maple.) Only Roberta O'Reilly was the same as always. She sat at the head of the table, in the place that was usually her son-in-law's, having vetoed eating outside in the August sunshine because sun meant sunstroke, and the lazy buzzing of insects meant bites, warmth meant cream curdling and butter melting before they even reached her scones, and the light cooling breeze meant soot coming from next door's barbecue. Roberta O'Reilly's mouth was a downward line of disapproval as her small sharp eyes gazed round at her family. 'I trust that camera won't be wasted on you, Grace,' she said, having had to think for a while to find something new and unpleasant to say. 'Because there is many a child who would give his or her eye teeth for a fine gift like that. Little Patricia was ten before *she* received a camera.'

'I suppose you had to pay for that one,' Gabriel muttered.

His mother-in-law turned her large head with a sharp, 'What was that?'

'I was just saying what a lovely little girl Patricia is,' Gabriel lied and he and Moira exchanged amused glances. Grace loved it when her parents thought the same thing, even if the same thing was that Grace should be sent to her room or have her pocket money docked. She beamed at them over her tall glass of pink soda.

Little Patricia was Uncle Michael's daughter, so Finn and Grace's cousin. Apparently she was as good as she was pretty, sweet and kind and fair of face with blonde hair and a natural wave. To have a natural wave was a great gift bestowed only on those most deserving. Grace's hair was dark and dead straight, poker straight, not a curl, not even the slightest wave to be seen. Grace had never met her cousin, who lived far away in Ireland, but if she ever did she would surely hate her.

'Finn,' Roberta O'Reilly snapped, 'what is that nasty grabbing? Has no one told you that it's rude to reach?'

But even Roberta O'Reilly turned nice, eventually, complimenting Moira on the light-as-air scones and pretending not to notice Finn burping after his second Coca Cola. Her parents continued to smile at each other across the sunlit table, chatting amiably, not having words, not once. It occurred to Grace then that she was dying. It was the only possible explanation. She knew it only too well from her illustrated stories, the dying child surrounded by heavenly light and grown-ups with sad brave smiles across the sickbed. Those leg cramps she got sometimes at night; they weren't just growing pains, as her mother had airily dismissed them, but signs of some terrible sickness. They all knew about it, all of them, other than Grace herself – until now. Of course they had not been able to bring themselves to tell her. She couldn't blame them. How do you tell a child that she is about to die? No one noticed the tear that dropped off her thick black lashes and into her jello. Anytime soon she would be dead and they were all making sure her last birthday was bright and full of joy, just as it had said on Roberta O'Reilly's card. *May your special day be bright and filled with joy.*

The phone rang and Finn slipped off his chair and ran into the

24

MERRICKVILLE PUBLIC LIBRARY

hall to answer it. He returned moments later. 'They hung up when they heard me,' he said. 'I hate people who do that. And it's the second time today.'

Moira stiffened in her chair. 'It's happened before?'

'Yup.' Finn grabbed a chocolate cookie on his way. 'And once yesterday.'

'Well, well,' Moira said, smiling at Gabriel. It wasn't, Grace thought, a very nice smile. They had barely finished tea when the phone went again. Her father looked at her mother. Her mother's eyes widened, but her voice was quiet when she asked, 'Why don't you answer? I'm sure it's for you.' And Grace's father went into the hall so slowly you would have thought he did not want to get to the phone in time. When he returned he looked at no one and said, 'Wrong number.' Grace's mother's eyes filled with tears, but she got to her feet and said something about 'games' in a cheery voice. Grace thought they were all very brave.

Come bedtime, she was beginning to think they were a little too brave. She lay in bed planning her forthcoming funeral. She had never been to one. When Grandfather O'Reilly died, Finn had been allowed to go, but Grace had been considered too young. Try telling her that this time, she thought with some satisfaction, now she was the dead person. She had learnt about funerals from a stack of old children's books she'd found in a trunk in the attic. The books had pictures and someone always died. Grace felt she knew just how a good funeral should be. First there would be her little coffin. The smaller the coffin, the louder people cried. Grace wondered if she could ask to be folded double. Then the coffin would be so small even Roberta O'Reilly would weep buckets. And it should be white with brass handles. There would be wreaths of white and pink flowers and much talk of God preparing to receive a new little angel into the heavens. She closed her eyes in the darkness and imagined it all. Soon her pillow was damp with tears. It was so sad. The saddest thing she had ever thought. Suddenly she got frightened. She did not want to lie all alone in a coffin, folded double or not. She did not want to be a new little angel in heaven. She would miss her mother and father, even Finn. And what about her rabbits? Were there rabbits in heaven?

Finn's room smelt of farts and dirty feet. He was asleep, face down, the blanket and sheet kicked right to the bottom of the bed. She walked up to him and shook him hard. 'Pigface, wake up.'

'What?' Finn's fair hair stood on end and he rubbed his eyes. 'What do you want?'

'Pigface, am I going to die?'

He turned on the bedside light. 'Yes.'

Grace burst into disconsolate tears.

'Don't be silly. Everyone's going to die,' Finn said.

'But I'm dying *now*,' Grace wailed.

'You're not.'

'Am.'

'Not.'

Grace opened her eyes wide, wiping them with the back of her fist. 'I'm not?'

'You're so dumb. Why should you be? There's nothing wrong with you.'

'There isn't?'

'No. Apart from being a typically annoying little brat and usually that isn't fatal.'

'Fatal?'

'Dead-making. Now go back to bed.'

'Promise I'm all right?'

'Let me have your camera all tomorrow and I will.'

'No.'

'Then I won't.'

'You will too. Promise I'm not dying.'

'Let me have your camera all tomorrow?'

'OK then.'

'You're not dying, Clothears; promise.'

Back in her own room Grace was wide awake. She did not trust Finn. His own camera had got broken at the beginning of the holidays and he had been nagging her all day about using hers for some experiment. He might have said she was not dying just so that he would get the camera. She took it out of its cardboard box, turning it in her hand. She had taken two pictures earlier in the day, both of the cake, but she had had help. Her grandmother said that little Patricia, in spite of not even having owned a camera

26

until she was ten, had been taking beautiful pictures from a much younger age.

Grace, still awake, sat on her bed, the light on, fiddling with the loaded camera, when raised voices reached her from downstairs. Instead of hiding her head under the pillow to muffle the noise, Grace wandered outside and downstairs, lured by the comforting sound of her parents having *words*.

She stood in the doorway in her birthday pyjamas, the camera still in her hand. Her parents did not notice her being there. 'I told you it didn't mean anything,' her father said. He said it in that tired loud voice he used when he had to say the same thing over and over again. 'And you said you forgave me. We were starting again, that's what you said. One day, that's all you managed.'

'I tried, you . . . you pig.' Moira's voice was quiet. 'God knows, I tried.' She was still wearing her pretty dress. Gabriel's dark hair was falling across his forehead. Grace was proud of how handsome they looked. None of the other children had such young good-looking parents. And they weren't tearful and good and planning a funeral, they were cross. Grace felt a warm feeling all over as she raised the camera to her eye and clicked the button just as her mother raised her hand. As the flash went off they both turned round.

'Grace, what are you doing up?' Moira snapped. 'Back to bed this minute. And put that camera away.'

Grace padded off happily. Pigface had not lied. In return he used up all the rest of the film. Gabriel took it in to be developed. All three of Grace's pictures had turned out well. She held up the picture of her mother and father for everyone to see. She was proud of herself. 'Look,' she said, 'I managed without help.'

NELL GORDON: *After her mother's death in a single-vehicle car accident, Shield and her family returned to England. When Shield was ten her father remarried and the new family settled in the Home Counties village of Northbourne.*

Grace and Noah Blackstaff were sitting cross-legged on the rug in front of the open fire in Noah's grandparents' house, playing Monopoly. Noah was banker. Grace should really be at home but coming back from school she had paused outside her own house and looked in at Mrs Shield, who was taking a tray of biscuits from the oven. She was wearing extra-long oven gloves on both hands because she burnt herself so often everyone was beginning to get annoyed with her. In the sitting room were the ladies, waiting to be fed. Grace could see poor Marjory and Mrs Daly and two more. All Mrs Shield's friends were really kind to Grace.

Grace had resisted the smell of freshly baked biscuits. Instead she had turned and run down the path and across the road to Northbourne House. Noah, who lived most of the time with his mother in Canada, was over for his holidays already.

'Another station for Blackstaff Enterprises.' Noah stretched across to grab Liverpool Street station.

'Why don't you want to look for your ghost?' Grace nagged.

'I don't believe in her.'

'But lots of people have seen her. That's why you're so lucky. My mother is a ghost but I *never* see her. No one does.'

'So how do you know she's a ghost?'

Grace threw the dice and got a double three. 'Because I don't believe in angels.'

'That doesn't make any sense,' Noah said.

'Oh look,' Grace said, moving her top hat. 'Park Lane.'

They took a break for tea and cake. 'You should be nicer to your grandmother. If you had a grandmother like Roberta O'Reilly, you would know about it.'

'Granny's all right; she's just not much fun. You can't do things with her like you can with Grandpa.'

'She's always looking at you when she thinks you're not noticing and she has this funny expression in her eyes.' Grace thought for a moment. 'It's like she misses you.'

'How can she miss me, dumbo, when I'm right there?'

Grace shrugged. '*I* don't know.'

Poor Mrs Shield had cried so hard there were no tears left for anyone else. Finn was over from Australia for the funeral, but he would have to fly back the next day because they needed him at work. And he was getting married. His fiancée, whose name was Robyn, did not like it when he was away. Grace looked at her tall dark-haired brother, and searched for a way back to the time when they were central to each other's life. 'We need you, Mrs Shield and I.'

Finn put his arm round Grace, awkwardly, as if he was not sure how to do it. 'I know.' His cheeks had gone pink, as they always did when he was feeling guilty. 'I have to get back. There's really nothing I can do.'

Grace shrugged free. She thought, I'm seventeen and no one in the world loves me best.

Mrs Shield had told Grace to leave her 'wretched camera' at home. 'I'm sorry, Grace, but there's something unhealthy about a young girl taking pictures at her own father's funeral.' Grace had put her camera back on the hall table without protest.

The service was about to begin when Noah's grandfather, Arthur Blackstaff, strode in through the church portals and everyone turned to look. His wife had arrived earlier and slipped into her pew, but that kind of quiet fitting in was not for Arthur. There were not many men, Grace thought, who could upstage a corpse at its own funeral. Arthur made much of taking a seat at the back and slowly the congregation settled once more, all eyes towards the coffin. As the first hymn was sung, Grace thought about how all those people, most of whom she did not even *know*, were alive and the one person who had been hers lay dead in front of the altar. 'Excuse me for living' – was that not what people said? Well, Grace thought, looking around her fiercely, I won't, I bloody won't. But wherever she looked she met pity. She wanted sympathy and she wanted love, but pity was for freaks. Roll up, roll up, for the girl who can't stop losing her loved ones. Her angry eyes met the calm blue gaze of Louisa Blackstaff, Noah's grandmother. Until that moment, if you had asked Grace what Louisa Blackstaff looked like she would have said, 'Pale, sort of old,' and shrugged to indicate that that was about it. But now, as she looked into the slanted deep-blue eyes that looked back at her not with pity or curiosity, but with understanding, she would have said that Noah's grandmother was beautiful.

The organ started up and the congregation got to its feet. Grace stood mute as the singing started; it was pretty rude, she thought, expecting an orphan to sing.

The sun was shining. The birds were on the wing and a faint breeze ruffled the feather in Mrs Shield's black velvet beret. Grace was staring down at the deep-dug grave. Any moment now her father would be lowered into that dark hole. Grace would return to the house and who would chase away the pictures in her mind of what each new day would do to her father's body?

Mrs Shield reached for Grace's hand. 'My darling girl,' she said, her voice barely audible. 'Thank God for you.'

NELL GORDON: *First love ends in heartbreak.*

Grace stood outside the house where once she had lived with her mother and father and her brother Finn when she was one of the lucky people. She had returned to Kendall, the eternal small town where everyone was busy but life flowed by slowly, where people sat on their porches on warm summer evenings watching the world go by, where they were born and grew up and stayed to make new families and died to be taken across the river to be buried. Grace was there to try to learn enough to forget.

She was staying with the Singletons, her Aunt Kathleen and Uncle Leslie. Theirs was a big house, a house that was waiting in vain for children to occupy its rooms. But none came and although by now Aunt Kathleen and her husband Leslie had all but given up hope, they could not bring themselves to leave the house for a smaller, more convenient place. That house was their home. There was a closed-in porch where Uncle Leslie went to smoke and a large yard at the back where roses thrived in the dry heat, flowering bright red and filling the air with scent, and in the summer of 1976, here was Grace, their orphaned niece, not exactly a child at eighteen, but messy and noisy enough to make the house seem just right.

Grace had heard talk from friends, leaving school like her, of the need to get away, to break free of the maternal bond and to strike out and find yourself. But it was easy for them; they knew from whom it was they were trying to cut loose. Grace remembered a sea-green frock and eyes to match, coral lips, and a cool hand across her hot forehead. How little that was, she had realised only when her father died.

32

She had tried to explain to Aunt Kathleen that it was as if she had lost her mother all over again when Gabriel died. While he was there she felt secure in the knowledge that she could visit her mother through him, so consequently she seldom did. Now it was too late.

'I know what you're saying.' Aunt Kathleen nodded. 'Everyone goes on and on about the Monument across in Vermont, but have I been there? No, I have not, because I live just round the corner, that's why.'

'Something like that,' Grace said and all at once she remembered hearing, a long time ago, her mother being discussed and someone saying how she was a really sweet woman but not very clever.

There weren't many photographs; Grace's father had not been one for taking pictures and the one Grace had taken herself with her first camera had disappeared. In the few she had seen, her mother looked different from how she did in Grace's memory. Grace had tried in vain to get the memories and the photographs to add up to one whole person, but it never worked. How do you let go of memories? Memories entwined themselves in your thoughts and stole into your dreams at night. They could go everywhere and anywhere, they travelled with you, invited or not, and they never grew old and slow enough to leave behind.

Aunt Kathleen was said to look quite like her late sister. Same transparent pale-freckled skin, same sea-green eyes, same soft voice. It was Kathleen who had first given Moira the brand of indelible lipstick she used right until the day she died. Moira had even named her only daughter Grace after her favourite shade; a soft shimmery coral called Princess Grace. You couldn't get that brand of lipstick any more, not since it had been discovered that its unusual staying power was due to harmful chemicals. Kathleen told Grace that Moira had been lucky not to suffer the effects, as for months, even after the banning of the cosmetic, you could see women walking around with lips that were swollen and purple, as if they had just gorged themselves on blackberries.

'I know I was the one who got her on to it, after I found it at the drugstore in West Lebanon,' Aunt Kathleen told Grace as they sat together in the kitchen, fanning themselves with the straw placemats and drinking iced tea. 'But then I told her, "There's no such thing as an easy option. Lipstick just doesn't stay put and, if it does, then you should probably be worried about it." No, she was lucky she didn't suffer any ill effects.'

Lucky, Grace thought. Was her mother lucky to have crashed her car before her lips had had time to swell and turn purple from over-use of her stay-put lipstick? Now, there was a new way of looking at it. 'I wish someone had thought of keeping a tube of the stuff,' she said. 'Full of chemicals or not, it was such a part of my mother, and me too, what with the name and everything.' Most of Moira's belongings had been cleared away soon after her death. It had been thought best by the helpful friends gathered around, as the little girl in particular was given to almost unstoppable floods of tears at the mere sight of a familiar frock or the whiff of scent from a pretty glass bottle.

Grace did remember looking at the leftover bits of her birthday cake and wondering how it could be that her mother was gone for ever whilst a strawberry cake was still there. Roberta O'Reilly called things like cakes *perishables*. That, her father had explained, meant they did not last very long.

'Your mother is an angel in heaven,' one kind lady had told Grace.

'No, she is not.' The little girl had shaken her head. 'She is a *perishable*.'

Now Grace asked Aunt Kathleen, 'Do I look like her?'

Aunt Kathleen put her glasses on and studied Grace before saying, 'At first glance you favour your father – you have his height and his dark hair and square chin – but I can see Moira there too, in the cheekbones and the freckles and the eyes, although hers were kind of misty, misty-mild, and yours are very clear. And you're a strong athletic-looking girl. There's nothing fey or fragile about you, which is a great good thing as far as I'm concerned.'

'I can't help thinking if only I had paid more attention to her when she was alive.' Grace sighed.

Kathleen said she thought that was an odd way of looking at it. Children as young as Grace had been, back when her mother was still alive, did what they did. It was up to the parents to pay attention. She brought her photograph album to the kitchen table for the two of them to look at while they finished their iced tea.

The photos of Grace's parents showed two people who, although standing side by side, would have preferred to have been in separate pictures. Grace could not say exactly what it was that made her think this; maybe the stiffness of their arms crammed up against their sides, the way their shoulders just missed touching, or their tight smiles as if someone was counting to ten. 'I thought they were happy,' she said.

Aunt Kathleen leant over Grace and paused to gaze at the pictures in the old album. She gently tucked back the lock of hair that flopped across Grace's forehead. 'They were, dear.'

Grace tilted her head to look up at her. 'No. No, they weren't. Of course I wanted to believe they were, but I think I always knew what it says here.' She jabbed her finger at the photographs.

After that she looked out for people who, although physically close to one another, were actually a world apart; and also for their opposites: people who, although at the other end of the room from each other, were connected in a way you could almost see. She thought she would very much like to meet someone to whom she could feel connected like that. Up in her room, the never-used nursery, where little blue fish still swam along the ceiling borders, Grace drew a picture of a matchstick woman and a matchstick man each at opposite ends of a piece of paper, but with a cord running from one stomach right to the other.

The days grew hotter and there was no cooling breeze. Aunt Kathleen stayed inside with the air conditioning, but Grace, who swore she had her own body thermometer that kept her just right whatever the temperature outside, was out most days exploring with her camera. Aunt Kathleen noticed that Grace had little to say about what she had seen during her excursions other than a shrugged 'You know, stuff,' until she brought home the developed photographs and then she talked and gesticulated so that you had trouble stopping her. 'It's like she only just saw it all,' Aunt Kathleen said to Uncle Leslie. 'And then I look and I think, yes, there's more to this place than you see at first glance.'

'I keep telling you,' Uncle Leslie lit his pipe and leant back in the rocker, 'you won't find anywhere better.' He spent his life fighting to be allowed to stay just where he was while Aunt

Kathleen kept glancing around looking for something better. Luckily for Uncle Leslie, she never settled on where that better thing might be for long enough for them to go anywhere very much, even for a visit.

Already Grace had a second roll of film developed. 'Who is that?' she asked Aunt Kathleen. 'That boy standing on the corner lighting a cigarette.'

Aunt Kathleen put on her reading glasses and peered at the picture of Main Street on a Sunday morning. 'Well, firstly he should have been in church, as should you, although I know better than to try to force you. And second, his parents would be none too happy to see him with a cigarette in his mouth. They're always boasting about what an athletic boy he is.'

'Who? I want to know who he is.'

Aunt Kathleen smiled to herself. 'You sound mighty interested in someone you've never even met.'

'Of course I'm interested. He's beautiful.'

Aunt Kathleen looked again at the tall blue-eyed boy with his loose broad shoulders and brown hair that was a little too clean, too shiny, to be entirely fashionable. 'Jefferson; yes, I suppose he is a good-looking boy. He could do with a good hair-cut, though.' She glanced sideways at Grace. 'I happen to know from his mother that he's nursing a broken heart. And don't you go taking that as a challenge.'

The McGraws, Jim and Gene, played Kathleen and Leslie at doubles, although Gene, Kathleen said, could not serve to save her life. 'Mostly we go along for her baking. No one bakes cookies like Gene McGraw.'

And, Grace thought, her son was handsome enough to be a film star; handsome enough never to be interested in someone like Grace Shield. It wasn't that she was bad-looking; she was just that bit too tall, and she was angular. There was no softness to her, no curves to speak of, and she was aware that she looked fierce a lot of the time when all she was doing was concentrating. Mrs Shield always told her that she had the kind of looks that older, more sophisticated men would like. She had meant it as a comfort, but it hadn't worked. Older and more sophisticated meant forty at least. What use did Grace have for the admiration of men like that? No, what she wanted was to look like the girl standing next to Jefferson in the second picture. 'Who is she?'

'I don't know. This might be a small town, but that doesn't mean I know everyone.'

'She's pretty.'

'Sure, she's pretty,' Aunt Kathleen said.

She was of medium height, a little plump but nicely so, with loose dark curls falling to her shoulders, pouty lips and an upturned nose. Aunt Kathleen must have noticed Grace's wistful look because she quickly added, 'But so are you. Maybe not in such an obvious way, but you'll see, your time will come.' Grace told her she sounded just like Mrs Shield.

'Anyway, I want to be obvious. And I don't want to wait for this mystical day when my kind of looks, whatever they are, suddenly become everybody's cup of tea. I want to be obvious and I want to be obvious right now.' Aunt Kathleen just smiled and shook her head.

Grace took to walking down Main Street at least twice a day hoping to catch a glimpse of the boy.

'A hamburger? In this heat!' Aunt Kathleen raised both eyebrows; auburn and pencil thin like her dead sister's. She and Uncle Leslie had not believed Grace when she told them she had never been to a McDonald's. 'There's a Wimpy but no McDonald's in our nearest town. They've got them in London, but I haven't been.'

'No McD?' Uncle Leslie had sounded like a missionary who had discovered a place where no one had heard of Jesus; incredulous but excited all the same. 'Well, someone's standing to make a lot of money over your way,' he said.

On her own, Grace dawdled, looking into nearly every shop window on her way downtown. She went inside one of her favourite places: the small electrical-goods store with its shelf of photographic equipment. She bought herself a photograph album that she had admired for some time now. It was matt-black and squat, requiring little stick-on corners that you bought on a reel, an old-timer surviving amongst the shiny red and green ones with their pockets and self-adhesive pages. She walked on down Main

Street, thinking there were more people than usual about, although none of them was Jefferson McGraw. But she did not want to give up just yet so she went into the last shop on the street, Andersen's, just to eke out the time and get some more air conditioning. The shop was having a pre-summer sale. There was a poncho in the window, knitted in bright red wool, its voluminous hood trimmed with dark fur. Grace thought of how snug that would be in winter and how becoming; Little Red Riding Hood wearing the wolf.

It turned out that the poncho was reduced to less than half its original price. The assistant, a heavy-set girl with long perm-bleached curls and a smile that showed she was relieved to finally see a customer, said, 'Mr Andersen had planned to keep the fur stock over to the next season, furs being classic and always just right, but it looks like he might not stock any fur items no longer so he thought he'd get them into the summer sale.'

'Hardly the weather for it,' Grace said.

The assistant shrugged. 'That's the time to buy,' she said. 'Come the season, you won't find something of that quality for even twice the price.' She went on to explain that there were two of the ponchos: the red one in the window and a white one with white fur at the back. 'I reckon the white one would be really neat on you with your dark hair and all. You know Abba?'

Grace nodded. 'Sure.'

'Well, the dark one has a poncho just like this one. I saw her wear it on TV the other night. It's, like, really cold in Finland even in the summer.'

'Sweden,' Grace said. 'Although she's actually Norwegian.'

The girl looked at her blankly for a moment. 'Whatever. I find them European places real hard to remember. You're British, aren't you? I know about Britain.'

Next she made Grace try on the white one, telling her it looked great. Grace asked to try the red and the assistant told her that too looked great. Grace asked her which of the two looked the greatest. The girl said there was nothing in it. Grace decided on the red, thinking that although it was half price it was still an expensive item of clothing and as she tended to spill quite a bit and sit in things it made sense to be practical and go for the darker colour.

She had been aware, for minutes now, of people gathering

outside the shop, but she had put it down to the sale. As she waited for the girl to wrap the poncho, however, she realised that these were not shoppers. Fists were raised and there was shouting, although she could not hear what exactly.

'Lord.' The girl returned from the back, handing Grace a glossy pink and white paper carrier with the handles tied with a pink ribbon. 'Mr Andersen won't like this.'

It was a demonstration, by now that much was clear to Grace. 'But the war is over,' she said. 'Anyway, what does it have to do with the shop?'

'Nothing. But this isn't about no war. It used to be all about that, but this here is about skin. Fur-skin. I don't mind tellin' ya that Mr Andersen has had about as much as he can take of that kinda thing. His blood pressure's shooting up. He's at the clinic right now, as a matter of fact, and it's not as if they're making any sense.' She nodded towards the crowd outside. 'I mean, them animals are dead anyway, so I say you might as well turn them into something pretty like a collar or a hat . . .'

'I suppose the point they're making is that if there weren't shops selling fur and people like me willing to buy, then the animals wouldn't be dead in the first place.'

'I don't agree with you there. I mean to say, there would be no point to them in the first place if it weren't for that you could turn them into something nice and useful. Take them minks; I mean, yours is rabbit, but take them minks.' She gesticulated towards a loose fur collar draped round the shoulders of a shop dummy. 'No one in their right mind would have them breed if it wasn't for what you could turn them into. Same with rabbits. You ask my Uncle Kirk what he thinks of rabbits. Darned pests, that's what they are. As I see it, none of them critters would be allowed to be born if it wasn't for folks like Mr Andersen. Anyway, you come with me and use the back door and that'll bring you out right by the pizza parlour with no one being the wiser.'

Grace told her she disliked the idea of sneaking out the back as if she had something to be ashamed of. The girl shrugged and said, 'Suit yourself,' before unlocking the door and closing it the second Grace was out.

At first no one took any notice of her. They all seemed too busy managing their placards and shouting slogans. 'He's your brother not your coat,' one guy yelled right in Grace's face, but Grace didn't think he even saw her. It was just as well, as she had a bag full of bunny brothers in her hand.

An elderly woman walking her basset hound came down the sidewalk. The woman was fat and slow, but the dog was fatter and slower still as it pattered along behind, its stomach trailing the ground. Its tail was wagging in a lazy fashion. Maybe the hot tarmac felt good against its belly. Seeing the commotion, the woman prepared to cross the street, but by now the dog was getting nervous, circling its owner, entwining her trunk-legs with the lead. Grace had taken her camera from her crochet bag, about to take a picture of the troubled animal in the midst of the demonstration. In photography class at school, one of their visiting lecturers had talked a lot about irony. Grace reckoned that this was just what he had meant. She raised the camera and took her shot just as the basset hound lunged in panic, sending its owner tumbling, her white straw hat down over her face, her mouth open in a wide O. Grace's shot turned out extra ironic.

She was trying to help the old woman to her feet when a girl, her hair styled in a hostile bob, blocked her way. She made a grab for the carrier bag and yanked out the poncho with a triumphant shriek. 'Blood-stained bitch,' she yelled. Grace was slow to react as she was still trying to reach the old woman who remained sprawled on the pavement, the panicking basset hound pulling the lead ever tighter around her thick ankles. Grace, on her hands and knees now, dirty sneakers and frayed denim legs marching all round her, managed to reach out and grab the dog's collar, unclipping the lead before getting to her feet and grabbing the old woman by the wrist, pulling and yanking until she had got her upright. The basset hound ran free; its high-pitched barking could be heard going down towards the river. 'Dog went that way,' Grace said.

After that it took her a few minutes to locate the demonstrator who had stolen her poncho, but there she was, still swinging the bag over her head as if it was the enemy standard.

'Give that back,' Grace said. 'Give that back immediately.' She made a grab for the poncho – sale or not, it had cost her forty dollars – but the woman was too quick and with a flick of her shot-putter's wrist she had sent it flying across the wall into someone's front yard. 'Now what good will that do the poor creature?' Grace wanted to know. 'It was a dead rabbit in there, not Lazarus.'

The woman raised her fist in a triumphant gesture. She was shouting and her wide-open mouth was inches from Grace's face. She was carrying on as if she'd done something brave, something special, rather than chucking away forty dollars' worth of clothing. For a second Grace hated her and that second was enough for her to punch a fist straight into that inviting mouth. By the time her knuckles made contact with the woman's teeth she was already regretting hitting her.

At the police station there didn't seem much point in trying to explain that she had not, in fact, been part of the demonstration but an innocent shopper caught up in the hubbub. So she sat quietly with the others on the benches lining the walls of the small station, waiting for her turn to be processed. It was all taking such a long time. It had been a year since the last anti-war demo and, apart from a few domestic disputes and a guy caught speeding in his father's car, not much in the way of crime occurred in Kendall. Grace supposed the police were unused to the sheer volume of suspects. She must have nodded off, and when she woke up the throng had cleared and there were fewer than ten people waiting. Amongst them was the boy she had been looking out for these last few days: Jefferson McGraw. Grace stared at him. She had a habit of staring which always annoyed Mrs Shield. But as Grace said, 'What is the point of people if you can't take a good look at them?'

Jefferson McGraw must have noticed that stare because his cheek, the one turned towards her, turned pink. Seconds later he sat down next to her on the bench. 'Pigs,' he said.

'Oh no, I'd never wear *them*,' Grace, all of a twitter, assured him. His eyes were the bluest she'd ever seen on any human being.

He looked puzzled at her reply, but was not at all fazed by the way she could not take her eyes off him; he was probably used to it. He said he did not recall seeing her before; was she from out of town? Grace told him she was from England and that she was staying with her aunt and uncle, the Singletons. Sure, he knew the Singletons, or rather his folks did. Grace said it seemed that everyone knew everyone else in Kendall, which, she added, was fine with her. It was cosy. 'I used to live here, when I was a kid. Then my mother drove into a tree.'

Jefferson, it was obvious, was the kind of person who gave you his full attention, taking in every gesture and listening as if each word spoken was new to him. His eyes, as bright as if they'd had a good rinse and polish in the morning, grew concerned. 'Jesus, that must have been tough.'

People said that kind of thing to Grace all the time. Usually she paid no more attention than she would to the tears people shed in front of a cinema screen; all second hand with no echo in their hearts. But Jefferson seemed, for that moment, as stricken as if it had happened to him. His shoulders hunched and there was real pain in his eyes, as if he was sharing her loss, not just watching it with interest.

It was dinnertime and the police, bored by now, let the rest of them go without even taking their details. The girl in the punch-up must have decided against making a complaint and Grace realised she was disappointed; she wanted to stay talking now she had finally found him. 'They aren't doing their job properly,' she complained as they lined up to leave. 'I even punched someone. I don't know why it hasn't been reported. I should be charged.'

Jefferson hushed her as they got up to go. 'They'll keep us here all night.'

Suits me, Grace thought, but she knew enough to keep that to herself.

'Was it a cop you punched?' Outside it was hot and humid as if the very streets were sweating.

'Sure,' Grace said. 'I wasn't going to be pushed around.'

'That's so cool; the way you're prepared to really do something. Most of the girls I hang out with aren't into issues. They say they are, sure, but they're into other stuff, you can tell.'

She felt bad lying, pretending to have been part of the demonstration when actually she was the enemy. She considered owning up – she had a thing about honesty. In fact Mrs Shield had taken her to see the school nurse because, in her view, you could take honesty too far, as Grace had – way too far – on several occasions.

Grace had confided to the nurse that she believed bad things would happen to anyone who did not tell the truth. The school nurse had smiled a soothing smile and explained that, although telling the truth was *very, very good* and *very, very important*, it was not always appropriate. Grace had stopped listening and was counting the hairs on the mole on the nurse's left cheek, only tuning back in when the session was drawing to a close. 'Your mother –'

'Stepmother.'

'– your stepmother told me that you believe that God will punish you if you tell a lie. Of course I'm not saying telling lies is a good thing . . . as such . . . just that you should remember that there are times for telling the truth and times when, well, when it's wise to keep that truth to yourself; to think of it as your little secret.' By now the nurse herself seemed a little confused. Looking at Grace who sat so still in her chair and with such an attentive expression on her face, the school nurse took a deep breath and tried again. 'Let's take an example. If someone had spent a lot of time and effort cooking you a lovely meal but you didn't like it, what would you say? Would you say, "Yuk, that wasn't very nice"?'

Grace was not stupid and time was wearing on. Soon the lunchbreak would be over and she would have missed the chance of a smoke. 'No, I would probably keep it as my little secret.'

The nurse looked pleased, giving Grace a friendly pat on the shoulder. 'I hope you've found our little chat helpful.'

The answer to that, Grace decided, was best kept her little secret.

She went back for a follow-up a couple of weeks later. 'Your mother –'

'Stepmother.'

'– stepmother tells me that you've been much better since our little chat and that you haven't upset anyone . . . much. That says to me that you have been using your *judgement*.

That's good.' The nurse smiled, pleased. 'And nothing bad happened, did it?'

Grace told her, 'My dog died.'

Jefferson McGraw thought she was cool. So maybe she would keep the facts about what she was really doing at the demonstration her little secret.

'I'll walk your way, if that's OK with you?'

Grace nodded. 'Sure.' She looked away to hide her smile.

'What's on your mind, Grace? You've hardly said a word all evening.' Aunt Kathleen was peering at her as if she was trying to read a manual.

'Grace shows absolutely no interest in boys,' Mrs Shield had complained to Grace's father. 'It's not right. Girls her age should be in love.'

Gabriel had muttered something non-committal before asking his daughter when she was going to bring home a nice young man for them to meet.

'When I find one,' she had assured him.

'See, she's avoiding the issue as usual,' Mrs Shield had complained. But she knew as well as Grace that this suited Gabriel very well. Gabriel had lost his shine of late. His life back in England with a new wife had turned out to be much the same as his old life in America with his first wife. He was still doing what others expected of him, still doing work that bored him, still seeing people for dinner to whom he did not wish to speak, still mowing the lawn on Saturday and washing the car on Sunday, although grass made him sneeze and he cycled to the station. To Grace he said, 'The moment you know what to do with your life, do it and let nothing get in your way.'

Grace felt anxious, as if she had heard heavy sighs behind each word. 'What did *you* want to do?'

Gabriel looked at her, head tilted. 'Now, you mustn't laugh at your old father, but I wanted to go on the stage.' As so often, he looked sadder when he smiled than when he was serious and Grace had not felt in the least like laughing. 'I nearly made it too.' He shook his head as if in disbelief. 'I was invited to join a travelling

44

theatre company run by a man who slept every night with his head propped up on a hardback volume of Shakespeare's tragedies, but it was not to be. I had responsibilities.'

'Why?' Grace had asked. 'Why would he want to sleep like that?'

'It was so that he would never forget that great art is forged through suffering.' At that both began to laugh. Sad eyes met sad eyes. 'Oh Gracie, we are the same, you and I.'

Gabriel, who never got away, became a man who wanted a quiet life above all else. This taught Grace to hang on to her dreams. In conversation her father's words skimmed the surface like daddy-long-legs on a pond. He liked everything to be pleasant, he said. Keeping things pleasant meant no one getting cross or exercised and everyone agreeing. Everyone agreeing meant no one bringing up anything disagreeable. Never bringing up anything disagreeable meant never being contentious. Never being contentious meant always being pleasant. Always being pleasant was very trying. Grace had grown accustomed to silence. Poor Mrs Shield never did. When they were meant to be talking about her stepdaughter's lack of teenage ways and she met only vagueness in return once again, she got so provoked that she said something about Grace maybe preferring girls. Grace had not minded. You could take pleasant too far, she had been thinking for some time. As her father fled the room, red-faced and upset, she explained kindly to Mrs Shield that, as she had never kissed a girl let alone slept with one, she could not be absolutely sure, but thought that, on balance, it was boys she liked. Mrs Shield had apologised, saying she didn't know what had come over her. Grace had told her not to worry; having to be so damn pleasant was a strain on everyone.

At the time of her father's death Grace had still not brought back a nice boy, or girl either for that matter. She had friends, quite a few, but as for falling in love; well, it seemed not to be for her. Anyway, she had other things to do.

At just after eight o'clock the following morning Grace was woken by Aunt Kathleen knocking on her bedroom door and telling her 'that McGraw boy' was downstairs waiting to see her. Aunt Kathleen did not approve of visitors dropping in before nine in the morning or after nine at night. Before and after those times she wore her curlers and her housecoat and wished to be private; everyone knew that.

Face to face again, they became shy. He kept looking at his feet, shuffling like a ten year old. Grace started to sweat although it was still cool inside. 'I thought you might want to go for a walk or something,' he said finally. 'I could show you around the place.'

Aunt Kathleen had appeared behind them on the stairs. 'Grace has been here for two weeks already,' she said. 'I'm sure she knows her way around by now.'

'No, I don't,' Grace said firmly and without blushing. 'I have a truly shocking sense of direction.' When it came to telling lies she was coming on a treat.

Much later on Aunt Kathleen told her that she had watched the two of them walk down the path and out of the gate that morning and then she had gone into the bathroom where Uncle Leslie was shaving and said, 'I expect that soon they'll think they're in love. They're young and good-looking and we're going through a hot spell.' And she had worried that Jefferson might not yet have got over Cherry Jones, who had upped and left for Europe in the late spring. But she had kept her concerns to herself as she had an idea that a negative thought, once let out, would spread and take hold.

They lay in the deep grass, gazing at the sky. He was wearing nothing but his old cut-off jeans; his shrunken tie-dye T-shirt was suspended from a low-hanging branch of a maple and his mucky sneakers lay upside down on the ground. Grace, in her khaki shorts and a white cotton shirt, was chewing on a blade of grass. He reached out and took her hand and then he raised himself on one elbow and leant down as if he was about to kiss her. Instead he said, 'Do that again.'

'Do what?'

'Smile.'

'Why?'

'Because.' He turned away, but not before she could see the colour rise in his tanned cheeks. 'Because you could light up a room with the wattage of that smile.' Then he turned back to her.

Grace's grin widened. God he was corny, but still it felt good.

'You're special.'

I'm dreaming, she thought.

'This girl, Cherry, is travelling in Europe. She's in Greece right now. Could you believe that, Greece?'

'I've never been,' Grace said. 'Mrs Shield always yearned to go to Rhodes but my father refused to go because of the junta. He played Theodorakis records instead, but that just made Mrs Shield yearn more. "I will not compromise my principles because my wife wants a holiday in the sun," he said.'

'He was right.' Jefferson sat up. 'I couldn't believe it when Cherry said she was going. It's like there's no consciousness.'

Grace sat up too. 'Jefferson.' She took his rough boy's hands in hers. 'I bought fur . . . once. I never got to wear it but I might have if . . . if something hadn't got in the way. So you see,' she lowered her eyes, 'I'm not . . . conscious either, not the way you mean it.'

Jefferson looked back at her, his brow furrowed. 'That's different,' he said finally, pulling a chunk of grass up by its roots. 'It's OK, Grace.' He was smiling and she could feel his warm spearmint-gum breath. 'You're different.' Grace did not ask him how, or why. Instead with a little sigh of contentment, she lay back down in the grass.

A while later she took pictures of him asleep in the shade, resting on his front, one knee drawn up and his arms above his head. He was nineteen and perfect and she, who was eighteen, wept because, in her experience, that which was perfect came back to haunt you from the far side of loss. She knelt down and brushed her lips against the soft hollow of his young boy's neck, tucking a lock of dark hair behind his ear. 'Come, wolves and giant birds,' she whispered, 'come, storms and angry winds. I'm here and you can't hurt him.' The dappled light from the branches and leaves above formed shifting patterns across his sleeping form. She got to her feet and shot close to a roll of film.

Grace and Jefferson were jumping, laughing and as naked as God had created them, into the cool water of the wide, lazy-flowing river that divided the town from the woods beyond. She twisted round in the water, dived and surfaced right by him, shaking the

47

water from her hair, sending a cascade of droplets like a spinning wheel around her head. She dived again, swimming beneath him slinky as a seal, stretching her hand up and touching the soft slippery skin on the inside of his thighs. This time they surfaced together, wide-eyed and out of breath. Without a word they swam towards land. He lifted her up and she wrapped her legs around his hips and leant back against the bank, closing her eyes against the bright sun.

'And Jefferson always such a *good* boy.' Della Parker was complaining to her friend Jan Miller while they were in the queue at the mart. Della was shocked and she was angry and she didn't mind who heard what she had to say, and that included Aunt Kathleen blushing by the cereal aisle. 'You would think a person would be spared that kind of sight, practically in their own back yard and in the middle of the morning with the kindergarten walking by on their nature ramble. I tell you, it's that girl. We've all heard about the way those Europeans carry on.'

Aunt Kathleen had responded by saying loudly to her friend Susie, 'It's good to see the boy so happy. There was no end to his moping after that Cherry Jones went away.'

But to Grace she said, 'It's not that I expect you young people to be angels, but did you have to be so . . . well . . . public about it?'

Grace was too proud of her happiness to be embarrassed, although she was sorry to have upset Aunt Kathleen. She wanted to ask her if it was common to feel holy when you made love, but she did not know how to go about broaching the subject. She made a very pretty apology in the form of a photograph of the house framed with freshly picked roses. 'I know the roses won't last,' she said. But Aunt Kathleen had already forgiven her. Grace was in far worse trouble with Jefferson's mother. She too blamed Grace, that English girl with the unfortunate mother, and she told Kathleen all about it. 'But I shall keep my opinion to myself, Kathleen. As Jim pointed out, the more you fuss the more they go their own way. No, Jim says let him go on seeing her – in a decent manner, of course – and it soon won't seem so interesting. She leaves at the end of the summer, doesn't she?'

Aunt Kathleen thought that Gene McGraw, in spite of her cosy small-town ways, was a frightening woman. She tried to warn Grace, but love had turned the girl, if not blind, then deaf. But it seemed that a week later Mrs McGraw too had forgiven her. Jefferson had organised a picnic for just the two of them. He turned up, looking slightly embarrassed, with a coolbox and a red and blue picnic rug. He'd brought cans of Coke and even some candy-coloured chocolate buttons because he remembered that she had told him she missed Smarties. There were sandwiches and some cookies his mother had baked specially. It was that which made Grace think she was forgiven. After all, why make cookies for someone you don't like? Who cared what the oldies thought, said Jefferson, and anyway his mother blamed what had happened more on the 1960s than on Grace. Mrs McGraw blamed most things on the 1960s and wished with religious fervour that the entire decade could just be rubbed out as if it had never been. She herself remained firmly in the 1950s, with her gingham apron and her neat blonde curls.

Jefferson and Grace unpacked their basket by the pond at the edge of the woods. The air vibrated with heat, the stagnant water was covered in soft green suds whipped up by the tiny insects scuttling along its surface. Even insects stayed close to home in this heat.

Once they had eaten they lay down in the shade, only the tips of their fingers touching for now. The air smelt clean. Every now and then, just as they began to say the heat was getting too much, the wind listened and, eager to please, stirred up a faint breeze to cool them down. This was a good moment to be alive.

And that, as far as Grace was concerned, was the trouble. Good times were made to pass. Happiness existed to keep the pain alive. She grabbed her camera and sat up.

When he was little, Finn had a box of treasures. It was really just an old cardboard shoebox with some discarded buttons, a few pieces of coloured glass polished smooth by the sea, a nugget of golden amber with a tiny insect trapped for eternity, a dried seahorse, some fool's gold, bits and pieces. Finn used to show his treasures to people if he really liked them and when he felt sad he would go and look through the box to cheer himself up. Grace had tried to make up her own, but though she ended up with a nicer shoebox and much the same kind of bits inside, she could not help feeling that it was just an old box filled with tat. Years later, when sorting through her albums of photographs, good times pinned down like butterflies on the page, she remembered Finn's box of treasures and thought that finally she had her own.

'Enough.' Jefferson pulled a face like an awkward schoolboy and raised his hand to shield his eyes. She looked at him sitting in the tall grass, tousle-haired, a sullen pout to his mouth. 'No one sees exactly what I see.' She pointed the lens at him and pressed the shutter. 'There; you're mine.' She smiled as, now she had her picture, the anxiety melted away.

When everything was tidied up and stowed away, he pulled her close, smiling down at her, blue-eyed, wild-haired, and kissed her. She thought she might faint with love. He released her, looking up at the sky. 'It's cooling down a bit. What about a walk? There's this place I want you to see.'

To Grace it felt hot enough for the devil to sunbathe, but she said she would love a walk; the longer the better she added, never knowing when to draw the line. They wandered further into the great woods; he told her they stretched all the way to Canada. The buzzing of insects got louder and Grace admired their manners. They seemed to understand that they were best heard and not felt, because they didn't bother either of them, not even for a seat on an arm or neck. Above, the branches of the trees reached towards each other tangling and entwining, letting in just enough of the sunshine to cover her and Jefferson in a veil of soft green light. From a distance came the chuckling of water running across the stones of a nearby stream. Grace let go of his hand and ran towards the sound. She stumbled on a half-buried twig and, as she straightened up, a cascade of tiny yellow butterflies rose, a spray of colour on the faint breeze, hovered, then fluttered off into the deeper recess of the woods.

'I used to come here all the time when I was a kid,' Jefferson said. 'I imagined I was the only person in the world who could get here; that the place existed just for me and vanished the moment I left.' He grinned at her as if he was a little embarrassed at this earlier, dumber version of himself.

'Like Brigadoon,' she said.

'Brigawhat?'

'A Scottish village that appeared and disappeared just for Gene Kelly.'

'Really?'

She took both his hands as if inviting him to dance. 'No, no, not really.'

It was coming to the woods, this part especially, that had made him decide to dedicate his life to the care of animals. His father and his uncle were lawyers and his grandfather had been one too, so he was set to break with a family tradition.

'It's the most beautiful place I know and yet all around animals are suffering with no one to help them. When the bluebells come out in the spring, it seems all the more obscene. I found a raccoon once, with its hind legs crushed. He had dragged himself along to die by the stream, one small raccoon paw feebly whisking the water. I've seen a fox caught up in a snare. It had chewed through the flesh and bone of its own leg to try to get free. That's when I stopped pretending the woods were mine.' He shook his head slowly and Grace thought she saw him blink away a tear. She thought he had cub eyes; wide, slanted, watchful. 'I tell you, he was so tiny he wouldn't even have made a decent-size collar.'

'Don't.' Grace took a step back, her hands in the air.

'I plan to earn my money tending to rich people's pets and then for the rest of the time I'll make it known that anyone can bring in sick and injured wild animals for free treatment.'

She cradled his face in her hands and looked deep into his eyes. 'I think that's a good plan.'

He kissed her, a slow sure-of-itself kiss. 'I knew you'd understand,' he said. 'I knew that you would be the girl who understood.'

He was as beautiful inside as he was out and she loved him; so what was there to understand? She wandered off, kicking her feet, rolling her neck, shaking out her arms; she was so full of love she had to shake some of it off before it became too much to bear.

'These six weeks have been the longest of my life,' Grace said to Jefferson.

'Don't you say that when you're bored or something?' They were lying side by side on the musty mouse-nibbled mattress stored in the Singletons' attic.

Grace turned her head. 'Don't play the coquette with me; you know perfectly well what I mean.'

Jefferson rolled on top of her, pinning her down. 'No, I don't. You have witch's eyes and soft lips, and you don't make a lot of sense.'

'I do.' She wriggled free and sat up. 'I'm known for making sense. At school my essays were praised for it. *Grace's essays are very clear*, they said. I'll be doing English at Cambridge. You have to make sense for that. So they say.'

'You're better with a camera. So what was it you were telling me so clearly?'

'Just that days filled with significance weigh heavy in the scales of time.' She bent down and kissed his rough tanned cheek. 'Oh, and I love you.' Turning pink, he failed to meet her eyes. She frowned. 'Don't you want me to love you?'

He got to his feet and pulled on his T-shirt. 'Sure, I want you to. It's a bit intense, that's all. I'm not used to it, girls being up-front like that. But it's cool. I like it.'

'That's big of you. But don't worry; right now I don't even *like* you.'

'What's that supposed to mean?'

'Not clear enough?'

'Not five seconds after you told me you loved me.'

'So I changed my mind when you didn't love me back. I don't take rejection well.'

'I didn't reject you. It's a big thing, that's all.'

'And maybe I mistook good sex for love.' Grace zipped up her jeans.

'Are you saying that's all this is about, just sex?'

Grace settled herself cross-legged on the floor a few inches away from him. She leant forward and looked into his eyes. 'There's nothing "just sex" about it.' But next thing she had thrown herself face down on the mattress. He heard her muffled voice. 'Shit, I'm so embarrassed. Shit, shit, shit. Why do I say these things?'

She felt his hand on her shoulder. He was smiling and the look in his eyes was as tender as if she had been an injured cub. 'You're funny, Grace. But kinda nice too.'

Jefferson was playing his father at tennis in spite of the heat. When he saw Grace approach he stopped halfway through his serve and grinned and waved. 'Here comes my girl.'

'Are we playing or not?' his father called across the net.

'I'll have him beat in no time,' Jefferson assured her. 'Then we'll go for a swim.'

Grace was fine with waiting. More than fine. Watching him do his thing was relaxing. She could just sit there and enjoy their love, enjoy being near him but not right up there having to worry about sustaining the miracle. It was hard work being in love. So it was a rest, just sitting back and watching him, knowing that, like the ball he batted over the net, he would return to her. His shiny hair curled damp with sweat was held in place by a white towelling band, just like the one Björn Borg wore. And like Björn Borg his shoulders were wide and thin at the same time and his legs were strong and lean. His father was panting and red-faced.

I know parts of him that his parents don't know, she thought. That's grown-up love.

Jefferson had guessed right; the game was over in no time. 'How many pictures did you take down there?' he asked as he joined her, towelling himself, wiping the sweat from his eyes.

She pulled him close. 'Love's funny,' she said, 'the way it makes you positively like things you'd run a mile from usually, like sweat and saliva and all manner of bodily fluids.'

'Nothing weird about it. It's natural. It's when we're in love that we're most like other animals and that's the kind of stuff they go for.'

*   *   *

On their way to the river Grace spotted a tiny bird in the middle of the road. 'Look how sweet he is,' Grace said at first. Then she saw the wing trailing on the ground as the bird tried to move to safety. They were right up close now and the bird, having taken a faltering step, gave up and just sat there resigned, its round eyes unblinking. Its feathers were scruffy as if it had just had a bath, but there was no water in sight; the dry spell had seen to that. Jefferson knelt down close. His voice was a soft whisper. 'You are in a bad way, little guy, aren't you?' He looked up at Grace. 'His wing's broken.'

Grace blinked. 'That's awful. What shall we do? Shall we take it to the vet?'

'There's nothing a vet can do, not for a tiny wild bird like this one.'

Grace took a step back. 'But he can't move. We can't just leave him sitting there waiting for a cat or a car to come along.'

'No, we can't.' Jefferson reached out and scooped the bird up into his hands. He bent low as if whispering. Grace, almost without thinking, went for her camera. It was the sight of the tall boy cradling the injured bird in his rough hands. Through the lens she saw Jefferson grip the bird's neck with both hands and twist. She lowered the camera, hands shaking, heart pounding, and said, 'You killed it!'

Jefferson looked up at her, the whites of his eyes shot through with red, the dead bird in his left hand, cradled against his midriff. He drew in his breath and wiped his eyes with the back of his free hand. 'And what were you going to do about it? Take its picture?' He walked over to the side of the road and scraped a shallow grave in the dry dirt. When the bird was covered with soil and twigs he got up and took Grace's hand, blinking at her in the strong light. 'Let's go swim.'

One step to the left of wrong; that's how the world seemed to Grace. The weather didn't help. For weeks it had been so dry that you were scared to light a match in case you set the air on fire. There were constant warnings on the news for people to take care with anything flammable, never to flick cigarette butts from car windows or even think about grilling hot dogs in the woods; then, overnight, it turned humid and after that not a day or night went by without it pouring with rain. Aunt Kathleen said the humidity was turning people a little crazy. Two old-timers from the nursing home had all but killed each other in a fight over a woman friend. Children were scrapping in the playground. Next thing, a woman Kathleen played bridge with on the first Wednesday of every month had run off with the local baseball coach, leaving her poor husband with nothing but a brief note of goodbye and a freezer full of TV dinners for one.

So was it the humidity that had got to Jefferson? He had made excuses not to meet a couple of times now, leaving it so late on each occasion that Grace was all ready and waiting in the hall, teeth brushed, hair freshly washed, by the time the phone rang with him cancelling.

When they did spend time together she might as well have been sitting there dragging her nails up and down a blackboard the way he twitched and frowned. When she snuggled close he acted embarrassed rather than loving, although if she looked up at him at those moments there was a kind of smile on his face. When she asked if something was wrong, he said, 'No.'

'I'd die for you, do you know that?' she said early one evening as they were parting outside the Singletons' gate.

He took her hands and his cheeks and ears turned pink. 'You shouldn't say that.'

'Why?'

He pulled her close. 'You give too much away,' he muttered against her shoulder. 'It scares people.'

55

She shrugged free. 'Do I scare you?'

He smiled and stroked her cheek with the back of his rough boy's hand. 'A little.'

Another time, up in the attic, they were lying silent in each other's arms staring at the whitewashed ceiling. Grace was wondering what it meant when a man makes love to you one moment only to look past you, as if he was alone, the next.

'I can't believe I'm going in two weeks,' she said, attempting to make her voice as light as dust.

'Uh-uh.'

She sat up. He had his eyes clamped closed like someone pretending to be asleep. 'Is that all you have to say? I mean, what'll happen about us?' She knew she shouldn't demand and fuss and be all needy. She knew that would only make matters worse. But since when had knowing that made anyone stop?

He opened his eyes. 'Look, Grace, there's no point in getting all stressed.' He zipped up his fly and, sitting up, pulled his T-shirt back on. 'I mean, we always knew you weren't staying for ever.'

'*I* didn't,' Grace shrieked. Her heart was beating so hard she thought it might break free, bolt off down the sunbeam on the dusty floor. She took a couple of deep breaths. 'What I mean to say is, I'd put that to the back of my mind.' He turned his bright-blue eyes on her, his brows raised in a question. She got to her feet and handed him his shoes. 'I'll miss you, that's all,' she said stiffly.

'Sure, I'll miss you too,' he mumbled.

'What's wrong?'

'What d'you mean, what's wrong? Nothing's wrong. It's you who's acting all weird.' She looked at his handsome face that was flushed and angry. It was as if he was on the other side of a thick pane of glass; she could see him, he was there, close, but she couldn't reach him and she did not have the power to break through. So she turned away, saying more to herself than to him, 'I don't believe you.'

'I'm telling you, nothing's wrong other than you hassling me.'

The right thing, Grace thought, would be to stop pushing and to smile and brush the dust off her knees and leave things be. But she said, 'That's not true. There's something, I can feel it. Tell me what it is . . .' And with a 'please', she crashed like a suicidal pigeon headlong into that pane of glass.

He shot her a look close to dislike. 'All right, you asked for it. Truth is, I'm fed up with you always being on my case.'

Grace flinched but she put her hand on his shoulder so lightly that he would hardly feel it. 'That's not fair. You know that's not fair. Look at me, Jefferson.'

He shook himself like a dog with a flea. 'Cut it out, will ya. I mean, that's the thing. You seemed really cool, easy-going. But you've changed. Take it easy, Grace; I can't deal with all this heavy shit.'

Panic made her angry. 'You can't deal with it. You can't deal with anything. You're weak. And don't you turn your back and don't you, don't you . . .' Running out of words, she picked up his sneaker and threw it at him, hitting him hard on his backside. As he swung round, she met his glare with her own, defiant one.

He lowered his eyes and shook his head. 'You're a child, Grace. Grow up.'

'Jefferson . . .'

'Yeah?'

She gave an inaudible sigh. 'See you tomorrow?'

'Sure.'

They patched it up, but it was pretty obvious to Grace that they would come apart at the seams at the slightest tug. So she was very quiet. She did not laugh or speak too loud or get excited and flay her arms about. She did not skip and run. At all times she trod carefully, but when she woke in the mornings the sheets in her white-painted young-girl's bed were damp with sweat and her jaw was clamped together so tight it took real effort just to be able to open her mouth again.

The following Saturday, her second to last, he worked as usual in the hardware store at the edge of town. Mostly she spent an hour or so keeping him company. This time she had debated whether or not to go. But it was not in her nature to play hard to get, so in the end she went, traipsing the whole three miles in the heat, a flask of ice-cold lemonade in her rucksack. Jefferson had just come in from stacking some asbestos panels out the back. They sold a lot of them, for use in barn roofs and that kind of thing. He was brushing himself down, the sunlight catching the dust rising in the air around him. 'Oh, it's you,' he said, seeing her standing in the doorway. 'You didn't have to come all that way in the heat.'

She handed him the flask. 'Aunt Kathleen made it. She thinks that's what mothers do: make lemonade on a hot day.'

'Well, they do.' He drank some and passed the flask back to her before turning to sort through a box of screws, placing them according to size in myriad little drawers behind the counter. Grace sat down on a stool on the other side, opening her book, trying to read and not look at him. He dropped a screw and disappeared for a moment, scrabbling on the floor to find it. When he reappeared a few seconds later she felt as if the sun had risen after a long night and she couldn't stop grinning.

'What's the matter?'

'Nothing. I'm just happy to see you.'

He shook his head. 'You're weird.'

She knew she should leave him be. She knew that the best thing she could do was to stay just a few minutes more and then put her book away, slip down from the stool and say, friendly but casual, 'I'm off. Call me when you're free.'

Instead she was a gadfly and nothing put her off her gadding. She chatted and picked at the sleeve of his T-shirt. She asked him if she could help when it was obvious he just wanted her to go and sit quietly and let him get on. She told jokes that she knew he would not find funny. The more he wanted her to leave him alone, the closer she went.

It was about noon when the girl turned up. She looked about Grace's age and she was dainty. Her white T-shirt was so brightly clean Grace could tell her mother washed it for her in that powder with blue specks, and her jeans were pressed. Grace had never met anyone before who pressed their jeans. Her hair was blonde and tied back in a high ponytail and her fringe was short and curled. Her features were delicate. Her eyes were small with long curly lashes heavy with mascara. She had a button nose and her mouth was painted bubblegum pink.

'Hi,' said the girl, looking straight past Grace at Jefferson. The *hi* was slow and as soft as a caress. This time he dropped a whole

58

handful of screws. They clattered to the floor, the last one hitting the lino just when you thought they were all done, like popcorn. 'Cherry.'

Cherry Jones, it turned out, had returned from Europe a whole three months earlier than planned. She had been back for a couple of weeks already, mostly just taking it easy on her parents' farm a few miles outside town. Having been introduced, she shot Grace the kind of smile that killed at five paces.

'I kept asking Jeffy to bring me along to meet you.' She opened her eyes wide. 'He did tell you about me?'

Jeffy? Jeffy! Grace did not even attempt a smile. 'Not that you were back, no.'

'Oh, I thought I had,' Jefferson said, looking shifty. 'Must have slipped my mind.'

'The way these things do,' Grace said in a tired voice.

He gave her a wary look. 'Yeah.'

'So you didn't care for Europe, then?' Grace said to Cherry.

Cherry shook her blonde ponytail. 'No, it was great, really. I just missed this place. I'm just a little ole homebody, me. My mom says she'll never get rid of me.' The way she leant on the counter and laughed at her own words, Grace thought that it would never really occur to Cherry that anyone might want to get rid of her, not even for a moment. People like that were lucky. They occupied their space in the world with the assurance of ownership. Grace inhabited hers feeling like a squatter.

It was decided, although Grace could not remember being asked, that the three of them should go to the movies that night.

She walked over to Jefferson's house just ahead of time, around six that evening. A smell of home-baking and vanilla reached her from the wide-open back door. She knocked on the bug-screen and stepped inside as Mrs McGraw, standing by the stove, turned round. Cherry was with her, her tiny hands made to look massive inside a pair of gingham oven gloves. 'Grace,' Mrs McGraw said in the voice you use to say 'rain'.

Cherry gave a wave with one glove. 'Jeffy isn't back yet. He had some stuff to do.' She turned to Mrs McGraw, sniffing the air like a Bisto kid. 'Oh Mrs McG, I can't wait to taste those cookies.'

'Well, you have to hold yourself back a little while yet.' Mrs

59

McGraw smiled indulgently at the girl. Grace felt Mrs McGraw needed reminding that she liked her as well, so she thanked her for having made scones for tea the other day. Mrs McGraw called them 'British scones'.

'You've thanked me twice already,' Mrs McGraw said.

Grace hung around by the door, unsure of whether to sit at the kitchen table or wait until she was asked. In the end, when Mrs McGraw still had not invited her to sit down, she did anyway. She had learnt a valuable lesson: if you wanted to be liked by your boyfriend's mother it was better to bake cookies with *her* than swim naked in the river with her son.

At the cinema Jefferson sat between Cherry and Grace. They each had a Coke and he held the popcorn for all of them. They were watching *Don't Look Now*. Grace did not think that Cherry was paying much attention, but boy did she scream when the dwarf showed his face. After that she needed a lot of calming down. Jefferson was really patient with her. Grace was glad when the film was over and they could go home. They stopped at Cherry's front door listening to the still night.

'Cicadas don't usually come this far north,' Grace said.

'Oh yes they do,' the others said in unison.

'Shall I take you home or do you want to do something?' Jefferson asked Grace as they drove off, having waited to see Cherry walk safely inside.

'Sex,' Grace said.

'Wow, you sure are to the point.' He had said that to her before, but then there had been an admiring note to his voice. Right now he sounded more like his mother's good son. Still, he didn't say no.

They made love in the tall grass behind the sports fields. He had good manners so insisted Grace keep on top rather than get damp from the wet ground.

It was the absence of love that made her feel exposed lying there in the open, not her lack of clothes.

They were swimming in the river, Cherry, Jefferson and Grace. This time they all wore costumes. Cherry was wearing a tiny blue and white-spotted bikini. Grace had to admire the way she looked, as if every part of her was wrapped up tight in her polished golden skin. Grace was wearing Aunt Kathleen's old bathing costume. It was a dull brown and sagged at the bottom where the elasticity had gone. She had ripped her own bikini and had no money to replace it, having spent so much on film and the two albums to stick her photographs in. She thought of those albums now. Jefferson might not want her any more, but nothing could change the loving way he looked at her in those pictures. She dived beneath the surface and came up for air, feeling stunned as she repeated the thought in her head: *He might not want me any more.* It was so clear all of a sudden. No ifs and buts. The water collected in the seat of her baggy suit, weighing her down. But she was a tall strong girl and it took more than a swimsuit heavy with water to drag her to her death. Anyway, what would be the point of dying? It wasn't as if anyone would care. Finn didn't see her from one year to another. Mrs Shield would mind for a bit, but Grace wasn't her own child. Aunt Kathleen and Uncle Leslie would get over it; Grace had started out well but there was no doubt she had proved to be somewhat of a disappointment in the end. And Jefferson; well, he would probably be relieved. She hit a cold current and shivered. Truth was she really did not matter very much to anyone. At that point she began to cry. She was not the crying type, but this once she made an exception. It was too hard, really it was, to know that the boy she loved so dearly, the boy who had made eleven weeks weigh as much as the entire eighteen years gone before, would feel nothing more than a shrug of regret at her death.

The good thing about crying in the water is that no one notices. You can turn up as red-eyed as you like and everyone will assume it's the swimming that has caused it. Grace had been treading water for a while, calming down as she did so. Maybe all was not lost. Maybe he was just a little confused, what with his one-time love turning up so unexpectedly. She hurled herself back on to her front and swam back to shore. Lifting her face out of the water, she watched as Jefferson scooped Cherry up in his arms and ran right up to the water's edge, pretending to throw her in. She wriggled and shrieked and kicked her little feet and Grace thought how ridiculous those games seemed when you yourself were not a part.

61

All three of them were in the water now. Grace swam up to Jefferson and faced him, doing her best to smile, wanting to be kissed. He smiled back without looking her in the eyes and disappeared beneath the surface. She decided to get it over and done with. Walk away before they see the hurt in your eyes, that's what she always thought. So she helped things along, carrying on in a way she knew would best annoy him. She thrashed and splashed in the water so that no one would want to get near her for fear of getting sunk. She made snorting noises like a sealion, and laughed out loud and alone at how funny she was being. She jumped on Jefferson's back and pushed his head underwater and while he was under she climbed up on his shoulders and hung on there like a rodeo rider while he thrashed and bucked. When she got bored with that she yelled, 'Fuck, I'm cold,' and threw herself backwards into the water and swam for land. Back on shore she shook herself like a dog making everyone's clothes wet. Jefferson looked at her as if he didn't know her. Cherry was very kind and that was when Grace knew it was all over. So she lay back in the grass, the sun hot on her face, at last allowing herself a rest.

For once in her life Grace behaved the way Mrs Shield and the nuns had always wanted her to behave: speaking in a quiet voice, laughing just enough and not too much, holding herself well and keeping her legs and arms and hands under control, not knocking anything over with a wild gesture, or throwing herself down into the furniture.

Nothing had been said; there was no need. She was leaving and in the meantime he just kept slipping out of reach, waiting for the week to be up, visiting one day, sitting on the porch on the edge of the hammock with one eye on his watch and getting to his feet with a relief he could not hide when Aunt Kathleen called Grace into dinner and he had a good excuse to go, phoning a few times but only to say he was busy. She did not push to hear him say it: *It's over. I don't love you.*

The day before she was due to leave he dropped by to say he would not be able to see her off; he was needed at the store. He hoped she understood? Grace nodded. She understood long enough to hear him promise to write, to let him give her a brotherly hug and to watch him walk down the path and out of the gate and disappear down the street. Then she walked inside, holding herself straight. 'Is everything all right, honey?' Aunt Kathleen asked as Grace passed.

'Fine,' said Grace as she went up the stairs to her room. Once there she walked up to the window and put her fist through the glass.

The rest of the day passed quickly, what with the drive to the clinic to be stitched.

Grace persuaded Aunt Kathleen and Uncle Leslie not to wait with her for the bus that was taking her to Boston and the airport. She told them that she hated drawn-out goodbyes. They took quite a lot of convincing, Aunt Kathleen saying it didn't seem right for them just to leave her there, Uncle Leslie asking if she had thought about how she would manage with two heavy bags *and* her hand still bandaged. Grace said she would manage fine, just the way she would at the other end. She said that unless they wanted a scene right there in the middle of the bus terminal in Kendall they'd better be off. That did it. There had been enough scenes. Grace got a long tearful hug from Aunt Kathleen and a loose awkward one from Uncle Leslie and then they were gone. They had barely turned the corner before she missed them, but she had her reasons for wanting to be alone those minutes before the bus arrived. She was waiting for Jefferson because, against all reason, she hoped he'd turn up to say it was all a mistake, that it was Grace he loved and that all he wanted was for her to stay so that they could be together. And when this happened, or maybe when it didn't happen, she did not want Aunt Kathleen and Uncle Leslie to see her cry. She had said it before and she would say it again: she was not the crying type. It was just that sometimes she forgot and cried anyway, and the less people around then, the better.

Grace had a theory. There were certain things you knew, but could not be allowed to believe, or you would not get up in the morning. God realised that he had made people a little too clever, so in his infinite wisdom he gave us the Dumb-chip. Without it people would give up before they began and *He* would have no one to play with. The Dumb-chip helps us to believe, against all

63

the evidence, that we matter. One of the prime examples of the Dumb-chip at work is death; however many funerals you attend, you *still* do not believe, deep down, that one day it will happen to – yes *you* over there with the private health insurance and a lifetime supply of multi-nutrients; *YOU!*

Right now, as she stood waiting at the bus station, Grace's Dumb-chip was hard at work, making her say over and over again, *He can't not come, he simply can't.* The way he had looked into her eyes when they made love, the way he had a special voice, low and loving, just for speaking to her, the way he had smiled when she entered a room, as if she was a wonderful surprise delivered to his doorstep; all that could not simply vanish like steam in the air? No, he was on his way driving towards the station in his father's silver Dodge. This is how it would happen: she would hear the engine of the bus as it approached. Her heart would sink; time was running out and she despaired of ever seeing him again. The bus would pull in, doors hissing open. Passengers would alight to be greeted by friends and family. Grace, dying inside, would turn to look for him one last time and then . . . then she would glimpse the silver car and she would be revived, love seeping into every shrivelled part of her heart until it was red and plump again and she could smile. He would burst from the car, his face anxious, pause for a moment, looking around. Then, when he saw her still there, his frown would clear and he would run towards her, reaching her just in time.

It happened almost like that. She heard the engine of the bus as it approached and she felt sick with fear that this could be it and that she would never see him again. It pulled in and stopped, the doors hissing open to let out a couple of passengers who were greeted by hugs and smiles from those waiting for them. She turned, and that was where it got to be different. There was no silver Dodge driving up the road towards the terminal, no sign of a tall anxious boy running towards her. So she stepped on to the bus.

Grace returned home to The Gables. Everything was as she had left it. Only Grace had changed. Mrs Shield had met her at Heathrow having come all the way in a taxi. She cried when she embraced Grace, wiping her eyes with a lace handkerchief, delicate in her big red-chapped gardener's hands. Sad – happy: the words were opposite but we cried at both, which, Grace thought, was actually pretty odd.

'I expect you're longing for a nice cup of tea,' Mrs Shield said. At that Grace too burst into tears.

Two weeks before she was due to start university Grace discovered that she was pregnant. She told no one. Who should she have told? Jefferson, so that she could ask him for money or, given the old-fashioned ways of his family, shame him into a shotgun wedding? Mrs Shield? Yes, she could tell Mrs Shield and the reward would be her stepmother's clumsy yet determined support, but the price would be fifty-five per cent of Grace's mind and soul and right then she couldn't afford that. A helping hand from Mrs Shield made you feel like a glove puppet.

So Grace kept quiet, turning all the taps on in the bathroom when she was being sick and saying only that she had decided not to take up her place at Cambridge but was moving to London and getting a job instead. Mrs Shield was greatly upset. She had told everyone who was interested, and many who were not, that her stepdaughter was going to Cambridge. Grace tried to reason with her.

'You must realise that I can't go to university just because you've told your bridge group and your hairdresser and poor Marjory Reynolds.' Mrs Shield looked as if she realised nothing of the sort.

Grace got the job in the Adam and Eve photography gallery through her friend Angelica Lane, whose mother owned it. Grace unlocked the doors in the morning and locked them at night. She dusted the pictures and sometimes, when there was no one else available, she hung some. She spent those days of early pregnancy surrounded by moments saved in time: Marilyn Monroe stepping out of a limousine, as radiant as if she'd swallowed a light bulb; a man reverently lifting out a book from the shelves of a blitzed library; Audrey Hepburn laughing on the set of *Funny Face*; James Cagney strumming a guitar. And always sunbeams shot through the roof of Grand Central Station.

In her spare time she pored for hours over her snaps of Jefferson and the two of them together; photographs that proved that for a while, at least, he had smiled as if there was nowhere in the world he would rather be than right there with Grace.

She went nowhere without her camera and she saved every spare pound to buy a better one. She learnt to develop her black and white films in a makeshift darkroom, really no more than a large cupboard, in the flat in Bayswater she shared with two old friends from school. Angelica was at secretarial college and Daisy worked in a casino, an added bonus as it made Mrs Shield feel that *things could have been worse*.

Grace had still not seen a doctor. She hadn't put on much weight, but she kept being sick in the mornings and there were days when she was so tired that she would gladly have handed over her last ten pounds to anyone who would take her place in the world. She kept waiting to be overwhelmed by a sense of Jefferson; after all, the baby growing inside her was the mix of him and her. Instead she resented this tiny someone who, although they had never even met, was controlling her physical wellbeing, her ability to do her work, her moods, what she ate and drank: lots of dairy products and no alcohol and an apple once a day. She could not even smoke.

When she finally did see her GP he asked her if she wanted to keep the child. Grace looked as if she hadn't known she had an option so he explained that very soon she would have to decide. On the Saturday she walked into Mothercare. She had almost convinced herself that an abortion would be the right way to proceed, but still she spent an hour wandering around, trance-like amongst the cots and prams and baby clothes, bottles and sterilising units, potties and nappies, singing mobiles and chimes. She found herself at the till, paying for a tiny white

Babygro, and only then did she realise that she must have decided to have the baby after all.

She fretted about the price of things, about how her friends would react to sharing the flat with an infant, about childcare and how to compensate the baby for having no father. She asked how she could be everything to this stranger when she meant not very much even to herself.

But some days were spent happily dreaming. Would her child have bright-blue eyes like his father or green ones like Grace? And what would be his talents and interests?

'What are you doing sitting there grinning to yourself?' Angelica asked one evening.

'I didn't know I was,' Grace said.

'You were. You were looking into the distance with a dreamy smug smile on your face.'

Grace gave her friend an affectionate look. She had known Angelica since they were both fifteen. She was lucky to have a friend like that who she could depend on. When they were younger Angelica had been a left-wing radical who left her washing with her father's housekeeper, she was a rebel who abhorred the use of the F-word. Now she was a young woman who wanted a career and knew it was her right to have a child, who did not believe in men but was forever on the lookout for the one true love. In a changing world Angelica's perpetual state of contradiction was a comfort.

'I'm pregnant,' Grace finally told her.

'You're pregnant. How? No, don't answer that. Who?'

'Him.'

'Oh, *him*. That little prick in America. Does he know?'

'No.'

'It is his baby too. Don't you think he has a right?'

'No,' Grace said. 'He left me.'

'Be fair, he didn't know you were pregnant.'

'Did he ask?'

She lost the baby. She got up in the night to have a pee and found blood pouring out of her instead. Angelica drove her to the hospital. Grace was told that she was no longer pregnant. The baby that had grown inside her without as much as a by your leave had left with the same quiet determination. Once again someone had come into Grace's life, made themselves matter, and left. The doctors told her that a miscarriage at this stage was fairly common and often for the best as it could mean the baby had been malformed or sick. Grace could not help thinking that those early weeks of not being made welcome might have had something to do with it.

In her mind she called the baby Gabriel. Gabriel Jefferson McGraw. Such a big name for a baby small enough to rest in the palm of a hand.

For years afterwards Grace searched the faces of children the age hers would have been, if he had been born, not just dislodged.

And you complain that I make your life out to be miserable. Grace, lying in the narrow camp-bed in Mrs Shield's spare room with the seconds ticking by on the old-fashioned wind-up alarm clock, could hear that journalist, Nell Gordon, like some busybody imaginary friend.

This is an interior monologue, Grace said. *That means I speak and you don't, so bugger off out of my head.* She turned on her stomach and put the pillow across the back of her head, folding the sides down like flaps over her ears. At last she slept.

But sometime in the early hours of the morning she sat up with a start, not sure what it was that had woken her. Her head felt heavy and the room was stuffy. She got out of bed and, pulling back the curtains, opened the window wider, breathing in the night air. She slept well through the constant noise of a London night, but the countryside was different, its thick silence suddenly pierced by branches hammering on your window, an owl hooting, a fox crying out like a child in pain. And if you slept through that there was always the cockerel who, contrary to popular opinion, has no idea of time but just likes to pass the lonely hours crowing. Grace had not spent more than four consecutive nights in the country for twenty years. 'Don't you miss it?' Mrs Shield was always asking her. 'No,' was Grace's answer.

Grace was about to go back to bed when she spotted a pale figure moving out from the moon-shadow cast by tall oaks. Sleepy still, Grace lit a cigarette and leant against the window looking out. Somewhere a dog barked and the figure turned round and vanished back into the darkness, leaving Grace with an impression of silver moonshine rippling down a slender back. Grace stubbed out the cigarette, having waited in vain for the figure to return.

'Could be Edna,' Mrs Shield said the next morning when Grace told her. 'And I don't mind telling you that I didn't sleep a wink myself, not one wink.'

'I'm sorry. How are your ribs?'

'Not good. I'm in considerable pain.' Mrs Shield did look pale. As Grace searched for the painkillers, she raised her hand, grimacing. 'I've taken them already. They don't help, not one bit. Anyway, Edna's hair is dark – and short. I keep telling her that very dark colour is all wrong for an ageing face, much too harsh, but she won't listen; oh no, she goes and gets all huffy instead.'

'Maybe it was Noah's ghost?'

'And combined with such a deep shade of red lipstick she's beginning to look like Baby Jane. The older you get the less make-up you should be wearing, that's what everyone says. Although in your case, Grace, I think you could do with some more. You look awfully pale.'

'I *am* awfully pale. I always have been, remember? That's why all my childhood you used to run after me and feel my forehead saying, "Are you running a temperature, Grace, you look awfully pale." Anyway, I do wear make-up; I'm just subtle about it.'

'Well, there comes a time in a woman's life when subtlety isn't the answer.'

'You're contradicting yourself.'

'Am I, dear? I don't think so. I would love another cup.'

'Have you seen him, Noah? What is he like these days?'

'We saw each other in the churchyard the other day. He looks just the same to me. Then you all do. He was putting flowers on his grandfather's grave and I was visiting your father. Of course he didn't recognise me, not at first. But when he did he asked after you. Anyway, you'll see for yourself. I've arranged for us to go over there today so that you can ask about your artist. Some people seem to have nothing better to do than lie in bed all day; he was really quite offhand when I called earlier on.'

Grace glanced at her watch. 'It's only eight o'clock now. Anyway, you should rest, shouldn't you, not run around the village.'

'I'm perfectly all right if we take it slowly, dear. And you have the car anyway. As long as I don't have to bend or lift.'

'I still think it was Noah's ghost I saw.'

'Of course you don't.'

Grace got to her feet. 'You're right; I don't.'

*   *   *

70

But for his eyes, an amber colour not easily forgotten, Noah Blackstaff looked nothing like Grace remembered. Had he been a photograph, she thought, she would have suspected him to have been a composite. There was Pete the Poet's sensitive delicate face on Steve the Strongman's body. The effect was far from unattractive, just a little unusual. They made as if to embrace and ended up shaking hands. Grace thought, I don't know if you are married, if you have children. I don't know what you do for a living, how you decorate your home, yet I've hugged you when you cried. I know that shellfish makes you puke and once, when we were scared, we shared a bed. She said, 'You've grown.'

He looked sideways at her and grinned. 'Come into the kitchen.'

'I'm sorry about your grandfather.'

'Thank you.' There was the kind of embarrassing pause that occurs between two people who know they should have a lot to talk about but actually have nothing to say. Then Noah thought of something. 'I hear Finn lives in Australia.'

'Yes, yes, he does. Married, two kids. Sadly, we hardly ever get to see each other.'

'It's not as if Australia is that far away,' Mrs Shield said from her chair. The sun shone in through the window, warming her face. She sighed happily and closed her eyes.

'I read about you in the paper; well done.'

Grace frowned. 'What do you mean, well done? Or is public humiliation, and being described as a pathetic loser, quite a coup where you come from?'

He looked at her in a measured thoughtful way, as if he was inspecting her for faults. 'No,' he said, 'no, that was not what I meant. I was congratulating you on winning the Unibank. It's an important award. I never knew you'd won it.'

As it happened Noah was a journalist: politics, mostly television. 'I can see you being very popular with female viewers,' said Grace.

'That's a pretty sexist comment, don't you think?'

'I'm sure it was just Grace's clumsy way of paying you a compliment,' Mrs Shield said. 'She hasn't really changed very much since you were children.'

Noah looked at Grace. 'Oh, she's changed, all right.'

Grace remembered that she was there to ask a favour. 'Then again, some of my best friends are journalists.'

'In fact,' Noah said, 'one could say that you are one yourself. You have done photo-journalism.'

'I stopped,' Grace said.

'She still has the most awful chip on her shoulder,' Mrs Shield said. 'I can't understand why. She comes from a loving family.'

Grace smiled stiffly. 'I hope you don't mind, Noah, but I've brought my own Greek chorus.'

'You know, Mrs Shield,' Noah said pleasantly as he switched the kettle on, 'you're right: Grace hasn't changed. She's just as rude. Coffee, Mrs Shield? Grace?'

'Tea would be lovely, thank you so very much,' Grace said.

For such a big man Noah was surprisingly light on his feet as he moved round the kitchen filling the kettle, decanting milk, outing cups on saucers.

'A mug will be fine,' Grace said.

'I'm afraid we don't have any.'

'And what about you, Noah?' Mrs Shield said. 'Are you married?'

'No.'

'Well, I suppose it's all right for a man. You have time on your side. Grace of course had to go and waste herself on the one man who wouldn't marry her, and I don't mean her husband. No, I'm talking about that American: Patterson. And here she is, in her forties and no family.'

'Thank you, Evie,' Grace said. She turned to Noah. 'When it comes to information, Evie is a communist, private ownership being strictly against the rules.'

Mrs Shield ignored her. 'Six years; that's a long time in a woman's life if she wants a family.'

'You just wait until we get home,' Grace said to Mrs Shield, who laughed delightedly. 'He died,' Grace told Noah. 'I always think that gives him an excuse.'

'And that was not the reason, as well you know.' Mrs Shield turned her attention back to Noah. 'So tell me, why did you never marry?'

'I'm like Grace, I'm afraid; I lose people.'

Mrs Shield assumed the alert look of a dog who knows its dinner is on the way, but if Noah was about to expand on the subject Grace stopped him. 'It's wonderful to see you again after so long and all that, but, as Evie probably explained, I wanted to ask you something. Just the other day a painting came into my possession. I fell in love with it. If I know anything, and as it happens I do, it's a serious work of art, yet I've never heard of the artist. I've checked my reference books and looked him up on the Internet but nothing – oh, apart from a man in Milwaukee who carves animals out of bone. I was going to take the picture round the shops in Chelsea – it was bought there apparently – but then Evie had her accident.'

For several minutes the conversation dealt with Mrs Shield's fall and the painful night she had passed, then Grace managed to get the subject back to her painting. 'I thought you might know something, especially if you're doing all this research on your grandfather. It's dated Northbourne House, 1932 and I absolutely recognise the gardens and bits of the house; give or take the sea and a beech tree, it's unmistakable. It's odd that he's painted in the sea but then it's not that representative a picture. But why is there no information about the artist? He can't have done just one painting and nothing else, before or after.'

'Maybe your grandmother knew him.' Mrs Shield made them both turn round to look at her.

Noah raked his fair hair with his fingers, making it stand up in a cockscomb and said, 'She might but the problem with Granny is that she wasn't very *aware*. Of course I'm fond of her, but if ever there was a person with her sights firmly set on the household minutiae of life, it is she. I can't remember her ever showing much interest in Grandfather's work.'

The biography had been Noah's Aunt Lillian's idea. She had been talking to the son of Donald Argyll, Arthur's old agent, about a retrospective exhibition. The book had grown from there. Lillian's next good idea was to contact her nephew in Canada. As a journalist and fond grandson, Noah was much the best person for the job. 'People seem to assume that because you write for a living you can toss something off just like that. I've had to take two months off work to do all the research. She of course decided that she was needed back at the mission and off she waltzes back to Tanzania leaving it all to me.'

'Diddums,' Grace teased.

'And you want me to help you find out about your artist.'

'Did I say diddums? Absolutely not. Anyway, if you really don't want to do it, just tell your aunt she'll have to find someone else.'

'It's not so easy. Lillian had already told Arthur about her plans. He, the old show-off, got incredibly excited. He even went up to London and ordered a suit.' Noah smiled and shook his head. 'He died before it was finished.'

'Oh dear,' Mrs Shield said. 'I do hope they didn't charge him.'

'So it ended up being a bit of a deathbed promise.'

'Now I'm here I would still like to say hello to your grandmother,' Grace said.

'I'm sure she'd like to see you too, although, well she *is* very old. She'll probably remember you . . .'

'That means you think she might not, and why should she? Some kid that hung around the place a quarter of a century ago.'

'I should have come to the funeral, your grandfather's that is,' Mrs Shield said. 'But I was still in Selbourne. I know it's not very far, but by the time I read the obituary it was too late. Of course if someone had thought to tell me. Your grandmother must be quite lost without him. She was never one to be out and about or get involved, was she? I always thought of them as a pair of birds, him all showy colourful plumage and her the little dull-feathered female at his side. Although she isn't little at all, is she?'

Noah took Grace upstairs to his grandmother's sitting room on the first floor. He went in on his own to warn her that she had a visitor. Louisa told him she would be glad to see Grace Shield again. Grace paused in the doorway, surprised by the stark simplicity of the room. The walls were white and there were no curtains, just white-painted wooden shutters. There were two upholstered armchairs in striped bleached-blue linen, a round table and some lamps, a bookcase filled with books and several framed photographs: snapshots, the kind you found on the mantelpieces of most family homes. She recognised Noah in several, and Arthur. There was a sturdy frowning girl who grew up to be a sturdy frowning woman; Noah's Aunt Lillian? And a young man who might have been Noah but for the clothes and a hair-cut that dated from an earlier time. Noah's father, Grace thought. Most surprisingly, for the wife of an artist, there was not a single painting on the walls.

Louisa sat in a high-backed wooden chair close to the artificial gas fire with all bars burning; like all old people she felt the cold as keenly as a bud. The light from the tall north-facing windows bored into every line and wrinkle, highlighting the spider veins that lay like a fine mesh across her face. But there was beauty too, if you bothered to look: in the shape of her eyes, and in the structure beneath the sagging skin. 'Seeing Noah again, being back here in this house, I can almost smell my childhood,' Grace said.

Louisa smiled and bid her sit down as if their last meeting had been yesterday. 'Noah tells me you have some questions. I don't know that I'll be much use. I have no idea why they built it; ugly old-fashioned-looking thing.'

'What's that?'

'The Dome, Grace.'

'Oh, the Dome.' Grace sat down. 'No, I can't say that I do either.'

'So what else did you want to know?'

'It's about this painting, I have been given a wonderful painting, and wondered if you knew the artist, A.L. Forbes.' There seemed to be no flash of recognition in Louisa's eyes and next thing she had turned her head, looking around, asking where her cup of coffee was. 'I always have a cup of coffee and a biscuit at eleven.'

'Noah said you probably wouldn't know, but I thought I'd ask anyway. You see, it's such a wonderful painting. I'll bring it down to show you next time I'm here.'

'You say Noah didn't think I'd know this Forbes?'

'He just said you didn't mix that much with your husband's artist friends.'

'He is right. I never got on with them.'

Louisa

FROM MY WINDOW I can see Grace Shield get into her car with her stepmother. I remember Grace, Noah's friend. She has grown up to be beautiful, but otherwise she has not changed much. She is still asking questions. It used to be about the ghost. Now she asks did Arthur, did I, know a painter called Forbes?

The dramas of our lives, Arthur's and mine, were played out in different times. Now my grandson wants to write a biography and he has asked me, most solicitously, how I feel about the prospect of our story being told. I said to him that he must do as he wishes. It doesn't do to stand in people's way when they wish to create something. And Grace Shield talks of her artist. She loves his work. When you get very old you tend to run out of tears, and pain comes to you muffled, bundled up against the years, but after Grace Shield left I cried.

BACK AT MRS SHIELD'S flat there was a bundled-up newspaper left on the doormat. Grace picked it up and handed it to Mrs Shield. A green Post-it note in the shape of a Christmas tree announced it had been left there by poor Marjory Reynolds. Another Post-it marked the page.

Inside, Grace helped Mrs Shield off with her lace-ups and handed her her Doctor Scholls. 'I'll make us a cup of tea,' she said, disappearing into the kitchen as Mrs Shield settled down to read. 'Oh dear,' Grace heard. 'Goodness me, now that is unfortunate.'

Grace appeared and put the mugs down on the coffee table. 'What did Marjory want you to read?' She looked over Mrs Shield's shoulder. 'What the hell . . .' She snatched the paper.

There was a photograph accompanying this piece too. They had used the old trick of choosing one that cast their villain – Grace – quite literally in a bad light. Whereas in the picture alongside Nell Gordon's article Grace had looked simply wan, here she looked mean. Her pale face showed up flour-white and, unusually, she was wearing the kind of bright-red lipstick that suggested she had just had a sip of human blood. Her straight brows were knitted together in a frown and there were dark circles under her eyes.

Sandy Lodge-Archer was a tabloid columnist known for her brisk proud-to-be-British, great-to-be-northern, can't-stand-whingers, roll-up-your-sleeves, tighten-your-belt, ready-with-a-quip, spirit-of-the-blitz, Old Mother Brown views which she shared with the nation twice a week on Mondays and Thursdays. Lately she had been posing this question: *Is the New Woman turning into Yesterday's Man?* Grace had read one of the pieces and found the question at least worth debating, until this particular Monday. The entire column, apart from a couple of lines in the bottom right-hand corner dedicated to the wonders of a 95-year-old actress who still put on her make-up every day just to let the cat out, was about Grace. Grace by name, but not by nature. Ungrateful Grace. Disloyal Grace. Immoral Grace. Calamity Grace. Disgraceful Grace.

Sandy Lodge-Archer referred to Nell Gordon's piece as *a recent article in a Sunday broadsheet;* it doesn't do to give credit to a rival. And Sandy herself had got to work, digging up an old newspaper cutting from Grace's first ever exhibition where, aged twenty-five, she had spoken with all the humility and wisdom of youth and most definitely not knowing how her words would be stored and used against her when life was very much more serious. 'The picture is the only thing that matters,' the young Grace had said. 'My aim is to take perfect photographs of our imperfect world.' She had finished by paraphrasing Faulkner's words on writing. 'Everything goes by the board: honour, pride, decency . . . to get the right shot. If I had to rob my own grandmother to get the work done I would. The picture is worth any amount of old ladies.'

In the light of what happened years later, those words were the last ones Grace would have wished to see reappear in print.

Sandy Lodge-Archer had also spoken to Robina Abbot, Grace's one-time mother-in-law.

It seemed that she too had objected to the portrayal of Grace as a sad victim of unhappy circumstances, but for quite a different reason. Under Sandy Lodge-Archer's heading of *Daughter-in-Law From Hell,* Robina explained that she did not blame Grace for her son's misery nor for the humiliation she had visited on the Abbot family, since it was obvious that Grace was mentally unstable. You only had to look at her work. Here Robina went on to describe in surprising detail (Grace had never thought her mother-in-law paid much attention) a series of photographs, a commentary on cosmetic plastic surgery, that Grace had exhibited towards the end of her marriage. *Decomposing bodies with surgically enhanced lips and pert silicone breasts* . . . 'I didn't use real bodies, you foolish woman,' Grace muttered.

Mrs Shield said, 'I have to admit, I never really liked those photographs either. I know they were much admired, but personally I prefer something a little less morbid, shall we say? But then you always did have a morbid side to you, even as a little girl. I remember I couldn't get you away from that book of photographs of people with leprosy. You had to know every detail. "Did their noses really fall off? How did they walk without toes?" The poor nuns didn't know what to make of you.'

79

Grace tried to concentrate on the paper. Robina Abbot went on. She accused Grace of having caused a rift between Robina and her daughter Kate, *only recently healed.*

'I can hardly help it if Kate took my side,' Grace said. 'I was her friend.'

And then there was the final, the great betrayal! She made us, her own family, a laughing stock, Robina told Sandy Lodge-Archer.

'You did poke the most awful fun at poor Robina.' Mrs Shield could not hide a little smirk of satisfaction. 'For someone who is as serious as you, you always did have a humorous side. A little too humorous sometimes, perhaps.'

'And didn't she deserve it?'

She only bothered with her work, her so-called art, but cared nothing for her husband's career nor did she join in the community and she never lent a hand with our charities. Sandy Lodge-Archer added her own comment. *Of course we remember the words 'The picture is worth any amount of old ladies' when we see this ruthless commitment to her career repeated over and over again, culminating in the grossly exploitative pictures that won her the prestigious Unibank Award but also condemnation from the Church and this newspaper in particular.* Grace took a deep breath and counted to ten as she looked out of the bay window and on to the muddy field beyond.

'At least she's not feeling sorry for me,' she said. 'No, really, it's not so bad.' She picked up the paper to read the last paragraph. *A lonely recluse with her career and personal life in tatters, Grace Shield has paid a high price for her mistakes.*

Grace sat with her head in her hands. She didn't look up when she felt the paper being pulled away. I'm not going to cry, she told herself. I'm not the crying type and, anyway, it would provide Mrs Shield with far more excitement than is good for her. She felt a hand on her shoulder. 'Pay no attention, dear.' Mrs Shield's voice was quieter than usual. 'Really, it's not worth it. Everyone knows that people say all kinds of things they don't mean when they're listened to. I always think that's their greatest gift, journalists, being able to listen as if they really care.'

Grace looked up. She was smiling but there was hopelessness in her eyes and in the way her shoulders slumped. 'I know all that.

And I don't really give a damn what a load of strangers say or think of me. Or I know that I mustn't. Define yourself through the opinions of others and you'll never be defined at all, you'll just be this hapless weathervane. But I can't stand pity. And I can't help . . . well, you were right, Evie, I can't help wondering if they've all got a point.'

'But, Grace, you always seem so sure . . . of everything.'

'Just because I'm not walking around with a big sign saying *Hard-nosed Bitches Have Doubts Too* doesn't mean I don't. I even have feelings. And what am I, just some blank wall waiting for graffiti?'

The phone rang and Grace reached across to answer. It was poor Marjory asking if they had seen 'that dreadful piece'.

'What piece would that be?' Grace asked, her voice all innocent enquiry. Mrs Shield frowned at her, snatching away the receiver and putting it to her ear. 'It's me, Marjory. Of course we've seen it. It was good of you to bring it across. Yes . . . yes . . . yes . . . absolutely . . . I know, I know, God only knows; yes, you have, Marjory, you really have. Thank you, dear . . . bless you . . . yes . . . bless you . . . byee.' She handed the receiver to Grace who hung up.

'I don't know *what* you have against poor Marjory! You've never liked her and she's such a sweet person.'

'Sweet, Marjory?' Grace said thoughtfully. 'You remember Jake, Finn's pet snake? Finn always said we just didn't know Jake. "Jake is so sweet," he said. And maybe he was, but personally I always found the sight of him devouring live mice kind of off-putting. And don't say, "Don't be silly, Grace. Poor Marjory's never eaten a live mouse in her life," because I won't believe you.'

'Now you're just being childish. Marjory is a very dear friend, and she hasn't had an easy life.'

'And, boy, do we all know about it. It's amazing, isn't it, that someone so sweet nevertheless manages to let everyone know how hard-done-by she is. Funny how we all seem to know that her husband was a philandering bastard and that her children are heartless money-grabbing ingrates.'

'I think you're very unkind, Grace. And Marjory only called to say how very sorry she felt for you . . .'

Grace shot to her feet. '*Poor* Marjory Reynolds is feeling sorry for me! I'm going for a walk. I'll take an umbrella, shall I? Just in case any more of your friends want to weep all over me.'

The sun was shining. The bright red and yellow tea roses on parade in the newly dug borders were on their second flowering. Those roses, said the brochure for Northbourne Gardens Golden Agers, were a *feature with a thought*, the thought being that a second flowering can be just as beautiful as the first. Overhead a bird was singing in the still air.

'Fuck you, Nell Gordon,' Grace said. 'Fuck you very much for making me the object of pity of a woman whose sole purpose in life is to make others say, "Well, at least I'm not Marjory Reynolds."'

The bird answered with a peal of notes ending in a drawn-out melancholy A flat.

NELL GORDON: *In her late twenties a hasty marriage and a move away from her creative hinterland put the pause button on a promising career.*

Grace had been living in her top-floor studio flat on Talgarth Road for five years. She felt protective of that flat of hers. When Angelica Lane asked her what she saw in it – all right, so it had once been an artist's studio, so the windows were large and the light was good, but the building was not far off derelict and the street was a mess – Grace told her a story her father had told her when she was a child.

Once upon a time there was a poor maiden in faraway Persia who, though as beautiful as the golden dawn, was as lonely as the sky once the sun had set and the moon refused to play. It was her smell; beggars and noblemen alike would stop and marvel at her beauty, but their ardour soon vanished as her foul stench reached them. And it wasn't as if she didn't wash, Grace's father had explained. Oh no, the poor girl was as clean as spring water, washing and scrubbing her poor lovely limbs; but to no avail: the smell, like that of rotten fish, remained, as much a part of her as her radiant wasted beauty. But one day the prince himself rode by and, catching sight of the lovely young woman, dismounted. The poor girl stood, her head lowered, waiting for him to shy away. Instead he remained standing not one hand away, showing no sign of wanting to be anywhere else. Surprised, she looked up into his face that was as beautiful as her own and, forgetting everything but the warmth of his smile, she smiled back and when he spoke to her she spoke back in a voice so sweet the birds in the trees above ceased their singing to listen. The prince fell in love and vowed then and there to marry her. What about the smell? Don't you mind it? All around people were asking the question.

83

But the prince said that all he noticed was the most beautiful girl he had ever seen smiling at him and speaking words sweeter than the sweetest music.

'So let me see if I got this right,' Angelica said. 'You see yourself as a beautiful prince and your flat as a lovely though malodorous damsel in distress?'

'No. I'm saying that you need to look further than your nose to appreciate this place. In fact, even the estate agent tried to talk me out of buying it.'

True, the building was on a busy road where the air was so bad that however hard you scrubbed at the sills and surfaces, a dusting like black snow returned almost as soon as you were done. True, people left their rubbish out any day of the week, regardless of whether it was collection day or not, and stepping out of the building it was advisable to look out for vomit and worse. Pity Aurora, goddess of dawn, who had to wake and show her rosy cheeks to streets like that, but Grace was all right, tucked up inside her bright light room with its high ceilings and tall arched wrought-iron windows and the memories of artists' dreams permeating the walls.

Grace, not exactly a goddess of dawn, nevertheless greeted most mornings with quiet satisfaction. Between her and each new day there existed the kind of comradely cheer of co-workers engaged on a mutually satisfying project. The project, now as it had been for the best part of ten years, was photography. Photography to Grace was a roof over her head and bread in her mouth. It was a pick-me-up and her dreams at night. It was her point of reference and her interpreter. It was her pride and joy and, quite possibly, her one true love. Taking pictures was making love.

She had relationships with men, the longest lasting just under a year, but she remained, stubbornly, living on her own. All but once she walked away. A couple of times it had been a matter of jumping before she was pushed and once it was about jumping just because. She had a streak in her of making big decisions for next to no obvious reason. Angelica said she was probably following her inner voice. Grace thought she did not have so much an inner voice as an inner jester. But mostly she simply woke from the dream, rubbed the stars from her eyes and saw that the man by her side was just a trick of the light, a projection of her hopes and longings.

'Men,' Mrs Shield said to her. 'You have to take them as they are or someone else will.'

'Let them,' Grace said.

'You're like a cat,' Angelica said. 'It's your home you care about; the people can come and go.'

Grace objected; she wasn't overly fond of cats. Essentially it was a matter of trust; she did not trust them. 'I care a great deal about people,' she said. 'I just don't need to live with them. Look at that light.' She gesticulated at the window. 'Northern light; the best.'

'You go on about that light,' Angelica said, 'but you're hardly ever here in the daytime.'

'But I know it'll be back. That's one thing you can trust in life; by morning the light will return.'

'Is there some profound message hidden in that statement of the obvious?' Angelica asked.

'No.' Grace shrugged. 'But people are so worried about stating the obvious that in the end someone needs to, or the obvious will be obscured by the unusual.'

Grace's work was gaining attention but she never turned down a commission. To be able to live almost entirely off the work she loved (she supplemented her income with weekend work at Harrods' photography department) was a luxury; she never forgot that. Her old flatmates, Angelica and Daisy, were both married. Daisy had moved away to Oxfordshire and disappeared beneath the weight of compost heaps, herbaceous borders and babies. Angelica, who had taken over the running of the Adam and Eve Gallery from her mother, had married Tom, a bond dealer. Tom was a big man, tall and broad, a rugby player with coarse black hair and the pink and white complexion of an old-fashioned schoolboy, the kind who played outdoors. He was loud and jovial. Grace thought that he had a mean set to his mouth. Tom told Angelica he liked career women and treated her work as a joke. He liked jokes. 'When I first stepped out with Angelica she didn't wash from one week to another. Ask me why, c'mon ask me why.'

'Why didn't Angelica wash, Tom?'

'Because she was scared I'd call while she was in the bath.'

Alone together in Angelica's kitchen, Grace said to her, 'You're like a negative when you're with him; white is black and black is white. Is that what it takes to be married?' Angelica had soapsuds on her nose and looked as if she might cry. Grace dabbed the suds off Angelica's face with a dry corner of the tea towel. 'There.' She smiled. 'I'm sorry. If you love him it's worth it, I suppose.'

'I do love him,' Angelica said. She looked straight at Grace. 'And there are times when I hate myself for it.'

To Grace, returning home used to be like walking into a pair of welcoming arms. Closing the front door was like pulling up a drawbridge: she was safe from the world, its questions and demands; no one could get at her. Alone in her flat there was no one nudging her for food or love or conversation. Her time was hers to do with what she pleased. There was no one to disappoint. No one to let her down but herself, no one needing what she could not give, or giving her what she did not want. For a long time, this suited Grace perfectly.

But lately she had been feeling lonely, lonely and tired to the marrow. She was even questioning the nature of her work and, as she said to Angelica, once that happened she was on the slippery slope to asking what was the meaning of life, and that, as everyone knew, was the most dangerous question of all.

'You haven't really tried love,' Angelica said.

'Of course I have.'

'You haven't given anyone a chance because you're still obsessed with that great teenage romance, which is sort of sweet but pretty pathetic too.'

'Don't be silly. I haven't given Jefferson a thought for years.'

'How do you know I was thinking of him?'

'Because, Rumpole, he was my only teenage romance.'

Angelica contented herself with a knowing smile; so much more annoying than any words.

Now when Grace arrived home, she found herself restless and picky, seeing flaws, muttering about the lack of cupboards and the temperamental heaters, and that one large room did not spell airiness but emptiness. Nowadays she lifted her pale face from the pillow and asked for at least one good reason why she should bother to get up. Maybe it was the work that was finally getting to her. The problem was that the nature of her work was very much the nature of her. She went out with her camera looking for light and invariably returned with the dark side. She was not a gloomy person; it was just that black seemed to stand out more to her than any other colour. Mostly that was all right. Her work was good and true to what she saw: the cloud around the silver lining, the sadness of a smiling face, a world that held such beauty and smelt so bad. Like everyone else, she was dying to know the hows and whys, but even dead there was no guarantee that she might become better informed. So, in the absence of answers, she documented the view from her small corner, hoping at least to get a glimpse of the bigger picture. By now, though, she felt she could really do with a change of view.

The night was still as Grace left her flat. The lone saxophonist on the sixth floor of the tower block at the back of her street was filling the air with longing; saxophones made her melancholy, always had. But hell, she thought, she should be happy. She had it all; the pretty flat in the run-down area, no one to love, no one to love her and autumn was coming; the season of mellow fruitfulness and slow death.

She was on her way to a preview at a new gallery on Mount Street. She often went to previews but this one was different; this time Grace was one of the exhibitors, showing portraits she had originally taken to accompany a series of newspaper features: black and white pictures of actors and artists and authors, long exposure, no artificial light and the lens pointing straight into her subjects' eyes.

She walked down the road on her way to the tube in her one good suit, black with a hip-length jacket nipped in at the waist. Smart-looking girl from a run-down street. Smart-looking girl with smart-sounding job and a broken boiler and damp creeping up her sitting-room wall like a vine.

Her work received attention. Four sold that night alone.

'The picture,' she said, striking an attitude before an admiring young journalist. 'The picture, Steve, is the only thing that matters.'

She stood, smoking her cigarettes, listening to praise, not

bothering to hide her delight. By nine she was one of only a handful of people still at the gallery. Even Mrs Shield, up from the country, had left. There were trains to catch, dinner parties to go to, families to attend to, babysitters to be relieved. Grace, in her smart suit, took the tube home alone and walked the last few hundred yards down the road where dustbins cast their shadows in the lamplight and goodness knows who lurked in the deep wells beneath the basement steps.

She reached the safety of her front door and stepped inside, switching on the light. She paused on the threshold.

'I know you're dying to hear all about my evening,' she called into the empty flat, 'so I'll tell you; I was a huge success.'

She was wearing a coat over her pyjamas and carrying the news-papers when she walked straight into him, about a block away from her flat. It was Sunday morning. She was sleepy. Without looking up, she told him to mind where he was going.

'I know you,' the man exclaimed. It sounded as if this was the best news he had heard all week. Brushing a strand of hair from her eyes, she looked up at him, a stranger as far as she was concerned. He looked to be in his early thirties and had the curly blond hair of a cherub and a grown man's strong nose and chin. He was carrying a large cardboard box filled with marrows.

'For me?' she said, nodding at the box. 'That's just so sweet of you.'

He looked as if he was about to hand it to her, then his brow cleared and he laughed. 'They're for my sister. She's unaccountably fond of marrows. Mum grows them. But honestly we have met, at Tom and Angelica's party last month. You're Grace.'

Grace made a great show of inspecting her arms and legs before saying, eyes wide, 'My God, so I am.'

His cheeks turned pink but he laughed, which was good of him, Grace thought. She added, 'I'm sorry, I don't remember. There were an awful lot of people at that party; about two years' worth of return invitations, I think. Or maybe I was drunk.'

'Oh no, not at all. No, it's me; I have an instantly forgetta-ble face.' He was not particularly tall, but he had the kind of build that made you think he might be good at forcing open jammed drawers and moving furniture. He balanced the box in the crook of one arm and extended his right hand. 'I'm Andrew Abbot.'

She took his hand. She liked his gaze. It was steady. She had met too many men whose eyes darted round continuously when they talked, as if they were scared that life might sneak off and leave them behind while they weren't looking.

Around them the street was coming alive with Sunday walkers. The sun was appearing after a night of heavy rain and the city had that pristine feel to it as if overnight its soul had been washed clean. 'Have you had breakfast?' Andrew asked.

Grace said she hadn't. Andrew nodded towards the café across the street. 'Would you like some?'

'I shall have to keep my coat on.'

'I'm sure they've got heating.'

She flashed open the coat. 'Pyjamas!'

As they sat down at a table at the back, he asked, 'Coffee?'

'Tea, please. With honey. And milk.'

'Toast?'

'Please, and two poached eggs, bacon and tomatoes.'

Andrew Abbot taught Latin and Greek at a private girls' school in Devon. Apart from three years at Durham University and two years living and working in London, he was, he said, a Devon lad born and bred. 'I like being near my family,' he said. He paused, looking at her with a half amused, half embarrassed expression, and she put a cigarette to her lips to hide her smile. 'I suppose that makes me some kind of freak.' He picked up the packet of matches left on the table and lit her cigarette. She could see from the way he flinched when the smoke billowed across his face that he disliked the habit of smoking so she appreciated the courtesy all the more.

'A freak; not at all,' she said. 'No, it makes you refreshing. If we're honest, most of us probably wish we had a family we would want to live close to.'

'I don't know. It's hopelessly uncool.' Grace did not point out that wearing tweed jackets and corduroy trousers, and being a Classics master at a private girls' school probably disqualified him from serious *cool* anyway.

'What about you? Do you have family nearby?' he asked her.

'Mrs Shield, that's my stepmother, lives in Surrey. I have an aunt and uncle in the States. All grandparents are dead. Parents are dead too, although, so the vicar assured me, they're ever present.' She leant closer. 'Between you and me, I think they're overdoing the low profile.' She straightened up and gulped down some tea. 'I have a brother in Australia; he tried to get further away but realised he was swimming in circles.'

He smiled and shook his head. 'You're pretty flip about it.'

She looked up at him from under dark lashes. 'I could cry if you prefer.'

'No, I don't prefer, not at all.' She was flattered by the way he seemed to see only her, not even turning for a look when a waiter dropped a tray full of glasses. 'Are you close to your stepmother?'

'I take her for granted so I suppose that means yes.'

Andrew looked concerned. He had only known her . . . Grace looked at her watch . . . thirty-five minutes and already he worried about her.

'It's all right. I'm a big girl now. And it's not all bad being on your own. It makes you less scared.'

'I would have thought it made you more scared.'

'Oh no. The worst thing is losing someone you love and I don't have that worry any more; I've lost them already. Apart from Mrs Shield.'

'So what happens if you marry and have children?'

She laughed. 'Good question.'

'And?'

'Oh, I expect I shall have to start worrying all over again. Maybe I can't stand the thought.'

It was half-term and Andrew was staying with his sister and her husband and baby in Earl's Court. Before they parted Andrew asked Grace if he could see her again.

They met up three times that week. Wherever they went they seemed to get involved in conversations with perfect strangers, little joking exchanges or conspiratorial smiles. It was to do with attention, she thought. When Andrew looked at you or spoke to you his full attention was on you and no one and nothing else. It was hard not to respond to all that warmth and interest beamed in your direction. When it was removed from you, you felt bereft as if the music had stopped suddenly or the television had gone fuzzy during your favourite programme. Grace thought Andrew might be addictive.

The last day of his stay she showed him her work, nervous like a mother introducing her darling children to a prospective step-father, but proud too and so very anxious for everyone to get on. 'Here they are,' she said with a mock modest gesture at the wall. 'I hang my own work. Some consider that bad form but, as I see it, if *I* don't want my pictures on the walls why should anyone else?'

He liked what she did. He said, 'Wow! I'm impressed,' and, 'This is really beautiful.' He paused for a long time before the tatty old man sitting on a park bench in the pale winter sun with a smile on his crumbling face as if he had seen an angel.

'Show me everything,' Andrew said, looking deep into her eyes. 'I want to know everything about you.' But he averted his gaze from the prostitute, with her skinny knobbly-kneed child legs beneath the scratched leather mini, and her dead eyes, black-rimmed like a card of condolence, in a child's round face. He felt better when he could turn to the picture next to it, the one of children as he knew children to be, laughing, crying, tugging, jostling in the queue to Santa's grotto.

'So, he doesn't quite get some of my work,' Grace told Angelica as they were trawling through the charity shops for cashmere and old crocodile handbags. 'I can't blame him, actually.' She paused from rifling through a box of knitwear. 'Truth is, I don't much like it myself sometimes.'

'So what? No one likes what they do all the time. You'd be weird if you did. Or deluded.'

'No, I don't mean it like that. I mean I know it's good work, those pictures he doesn't like, but it's work that *hurts*. I know one has to be true to one's vision, but I can't help wishing sometimes that mine would be a little more Bacardi on the Beach and less Hell is a Place Near You. I point my lens at the Andrex puppy and end up with a shot of the vivisection lab. It's not what I want. I want the puppies alive and happy and dragging rolls of pink loo paper for half a mile the way they should be doing, while Doris Day sings that somewhere in this fucking world there's a fine day.'

'I don't think she said fuck.'

Grace said, 'Not so we'd hear it.' She thought for a moment. 'I think that's what I love about Andrew. Andrew is light. Andrew is normal. Andrew is wholesome. He is where I want to be.'

'I'm allowed to get drunk; it's my thirtieth birthday . . .'

'Twenty-nine, darling, you're twenty-nine today.'

' . . . next year. I was going to say; it's my thirtieth birthday next year. I'm allowed to get drunk on the birthday before my thirtieth birthday.'

Andrew pulled her close and whispered, 'You, my darling Grace, are allowed to do whatever you like. But, having said that, we are getting some funny looks. Maybe we should be thinking about getting you home.' He looked around the restaurant, empty but for one other couple and the waiters gazing at their watches and clattering tomorrow's china. Grace smiled delightedly at the pair of him. She managed to get to her feet unaided, one lit cigarette between her fingers, another clamped between her lips. Andrew took the lit one and stubbed it out in the ashtray that was whisked away within seconds. 'You're thoughtful,' Grace slurred. 'I like that. You don't want to keep those poor waiters waiting and I don't care because I'm a horrid selfish person who thinks only of herself and reckons they've charged ridiculous amounts for second-rate food while looking down their noses at their customers and therefore they should be punished by being kept waiting for as long as possible. You see,' she walked unsteadily to the door, 'I'm horrid and you're nice; that's why we get on so well.' She turned in the doorway and looked at him hard, managing to focus for several seconds by opening her eyes very wide and keeping them that way. 'One could say that we complete each other.'

Grace remembered being sick in the basin and Andrew stroking her hair away and rubbing her back with his free hand. She remembered him running a bath and helping her undress, and that she was not shy but busy concentrating on keeping her balance as he knelt in front of her peeling off her tights. She watched him from the bath as he folded her clothes in a neat little pile with her tights rolled up on top, and finally helped her out of the bath and wrapped her in a large pink fluffy towel she did not even remember she owned.

Next thing she knew she was woken by a little man inside her head pounding her brain with an anvil. She had trouble fitting her tongue inside her mouth and she would have paid every pound in her wallet for a glass of water. But as she lifted her head from the pillow, groaning with pain, Andrew appeared in the doorway with a tray. On it was a glass of freshly squeezed orange juice, a tub of live yoghurt and a vase with a single yellow rose. Grace tried to smile but gave up. It was her tongue again, getting in the way. She stretched out her hand for the glass of juice and drank it up, every last drop. Able finally both to speak and smile, although weakly, she said, '"Drink up, darling, every last drop," – that's what my mother used to say. Or at least that's what my father told me my mother used to say.'

Andrew perched on the side of the bed, having placed the tray on the bedside table. 'That's a mother kind of statement. Mine always said that too; in fact, given half a chance, she still does.'

'All right, all right, so my mother wasn't the first one to say it. Cut her some slack here; she died young. She didn't have time to branch out into something more original.'

'Have some of this.' Andrew handed her the pot of yoghurt. 'It's full of good bacteria. Apparently those are just the chaps your stomach needs after a night like we've just had.' He adjusted the pillows so that she could sit up more comfortably and she smiled at him for saying *we* – a night like *we've* just had – when it was clear that there had been no *we* about it. *He* had been perfectly sober while *she* had been throwing up all over the basin. 'I'm sorry you had to see me puke,' she said. 'It's not a nice end to an evening for anyone; watching. Doing it is kind of fun . . .'

Andrew, his head tilted to one side, looked at her as if she was a newborn child, precious and delicate and his to care for, not a tall strong 29-year-old with a hangover. He put his hand out and stroked a tendril of damp hair from her forehead. 'You're very beautiful,' he said.

She stared at him. 'Beautiful? Right now?'

'Hmm.'

'I think I have some cleaning to do.' Grace threw off the duvet.

'You stay where you are. It's all done.'

'You shouldn't have. I believe in two things: world peace and cleaning up one's own puke.'

Andrew smiled at her with that tender look. Tears came to her eyes as she thought of all the times there had been no one around to gaze at her that way.

'I like looking after you, Grace,' Andrew said. He gave a little laugh. 'You seem so capable, tough even. Much more so than the women I usually fall for.'

'And now you've seen that I'm just like any other sweet old-fashioned little thing after all; passing out after my fifteenth double vodka martini.'

'The others usually stopped after two, but all right.'

'What's your mother like?'

'My mother?' He looked a bit surprised at the sudden change of topic. 'Robina, well, she's, you know, my mother.'

'Wow. That's the kind of intimate detail most men don't divulge until at least six months into a relationship. And, no, I don't know. And what about your father? I suppose he's just your father?'

'Sort of. But they're really nice. You'll like them. And they'll adore you.'

'Why? Why should they adore me? I'm not at all an adorable person.'

'Do you always get so combative when you're hungover?'

'I don't know. I usually wake up on my own. Do they love each other?'

He looked as if he had never given the matter any thought until that moment. 'Yes, yes, I think they do.'

'How did they meet?'

'I thought you were feeling sick.'

'I am. I need something to take my mind off *how* sick.'

'OK, my mother was up at Oxford visiting her elder brother. Apparently my father, who was at the same college as my uncle, had a bit of a reputation for being rather pompous; so, anyway, after this party my uncle and some of his chums decided to play a prank on my father so they went outside and substituted his bicycle with one looking quite like it but much smaller. They reckoned that as it was dark and . . .'

'I used to love hearing about how my parents met,' Grace said, and next thing she was fast asleep, the half-eaten pot of yoghurt still in her hand.

'This is a man who deserves the best,' she said to Angelica that evening over the phone.

'No man deserves that.'

'You're bitter.'

'You will be too. You're just a slow learner.'

'He wants me to meet his family. They're all down in Devon. Apparently they're very close.'

Robina Abbot wore her hair piled up on top of her head. A magpie's nest, Grace thought, with shiny pins and Chinese-lacquer painted skewers weaved through the mass of steel-grey. She met Grace at the front door of the white-painted Victorian house high at the top of the steepest hill in a town of hills, her arms wide open ready for an embrace. Grace looked left, then right, and finally, after a quick glance over her shoulder, realised the embrace was aimed at her and stepped forward feeling awkward and gratified both at once. Strong arms and soft bosoms beneath a loose-knit jumper, and a quick decisive, 'My dear!' She was ushered inside the hall that smelt of cooking and wet fur, Robina calling all the while for what Grace thought was the cat but turned out to be Andrew's father. 'Timmy, Timmy, Timmy, where are you?' Robina trilled. 'I know you are there somewhere.'

Timothy Abbot appeared from the back with a fast forward-leaning walk, his hand outstretched way in advance as if he did not want to take any chances. 'Grace,' he said, finally shaking her hand up and down. 'Grace.'

Next Grace was introduced to Kate, Andrew's younger sister. No one seemed entirely sure whether or not to expect Leonora, the sister who liked marrows and lived in London. 'It depends on Archie,' Robina said. 'He's a dear boy. We love him to bits but he works too hard.'

They had drinks, sherry, in the drawing room that was just the right side of shabby and had a deep bay with tall sash windows looking out across velvet-green hills. Lunch was in the large kitchen. Grace sat opposite Kate. It was as if every feature that suited Andrew so well had been rearranged in his sister by some malevolent goblin. On Kate, the golden curls had turned into ginger frizz and the family chin had gone from firm to jutting. Whereas Andrew's high-bridged Roman nose was in proportion with the rest of his face, Kate's features seemed to have been assembled around hers. And yet, and yet, her smile was about the sweetest Grace had ever seen. When Kate realised she was being studied, she blushed a deep pink that went badly with her ginger hair.

'I'm sorry, I was staring. Habit of work,' Grace said. 'You see, I just love faces, so I stare; no excuse, I know. You do have a wonderful smile. Smiles are a real challenge to photographers, much tougher to catch than people think. Or you catch one but it's in full flight or clamped into place and nothing like the sweet thing you glimpsed only moments before you pointed your camera.'

'Kate has the kind of face artists love,' Robina said.

'*Mother!*'

'Be glad you have a mother to embarrass you,' Grace said and, when Kate looked even more unhappy, obviously aware of Grace's orphaned state, she added, 'because you can't always rely on strangers to do it.'

Janet, a friend of Robina's and a neighbour, arrived, apologising for being late and muttering about a sick kitten. She was introduced to Grace.

'I always have Sunday lunch with dear Robina and Timothy,' Janet said, accompanying her words with such a belligerent look that Grace was about to say that a) there were several spare chairs around the table, and b) she, Grace, did not eat all that much. In the event she said neither but just smiled and nodded.

'We're so excited to finally meet Grace,' Robina said.

Andrew searched for and found Grace's hand under the table and gave it a little squeeze. Their eyes met and they smiled at each other. The autumn sunshine coming through the windows hung on the steam from the pudding boiling on the stove, giving the room and everyone in it a hazy dreamy appearance, the kind Grace had to work hard to achieve in her photographs.

Timothy had a puzzle for them. Grace, who found life quite confusing enough without further complicating it with made-up puzzles, sat back and sipped her red wine while the others tried to outwit each other and be the first to find the solution.

'Kate,' Robina said. 'What do you think? You're usually so quick.'

'I'm not. You know I'm not. I never get Dad's bloody puzzles.'

'Don't swear, dear,' Robina said, but she was waving at the glass-fronted back door where another visitor had just turned up. Neil was a lecturer in economics at the college where Timothy was bursar. Neil was about Timothy's age and as tall, but his head, which narrowed at the crown, was bald and shiny, as if it had received a good buffing with Mr Sheen. He shook Grace by the hand and nodded at the others. Kate got to her feet and brought out an extra plate and cutlery. Grace admired the way Robina served lunch so effortlessly. She had roasted a couple of chickens and made a huge bowl of salad. Once everyone was seated she just carved the birds in the tin and piled all the meat on a dish which was passed round the table. There were two homemade loaves of bread as well, and a dish with butter. Everyone helped themselves and when Neil joined them he sat down and did the same. Mrs Shield, on the other hand, was a stickler for proper serving, with everything planned and arranged. The conversation grew louder but Grace, with the sun of an Indian summer on her back and a glass of wine in her hand, could still distinguish the buzzing of a late bee. She felt sleepy and that meant she was comfortable. 'Grace usually brings her own pin-cushion,' Mrs Shield always said, but not today she hadn't, not today in the woozy, hazy, noisy calm of the Abbots' kitchen.

Robina Abbot did not have a profession as such unless you counted sainthood. She was, it appeared, a one-woman bastion in a local community perilously close to being diluted into Everytown, its dairy and butcher's shops, its greengrocer's and small independent bookshop making way for estate agents' offices and handy branches of the big supermarkets; its old people dying off, its young people sloping off to the cities making room for rootless newcomers escaping from those same big cities and bringing most of the big-city ills with them like a persistent odour. Without Robina there would be no choir for the church, not a note sung, not so much as a B sharp on Sundays and highdays. There would be no Evergreen club and no Living Crafts fair, no carol singing at Christmas and God only knows how many more old people in Africa would be without spectacles. No, as far as Grace could tell by the end of lunch, no one got born, baptised, married or buried without Robina giving a helping hand.

Just as the sticky toffee pudding was being served on bright pottery plates, each different from the other, each made by Robina herself and fired in her own kiln at the bottom of the garden, there was a commotion as the dogs, all three of them, all rescued from shelters, rushed to greet yet another arrival. It was Leonora, the sister in London. She appeared in a flurry of shawls and lace and everything impractical for train travel, and a bundle that turned out to be a baby, Rory, in her arms. Robina got to her feet and disappeared into the back porch, returning a moment later wheeling a large old-fashioned pram. She took Rory, covering him in kisses before putting him down. Grace turned her attention on Leonora. She was magnificent. Her hair was as curly and golden as her brother's but hers was long, reaching almost to her narrow waist. Her eyes, close-set like her mother's, had an intense look that seemed to take in everything around her and want most of it. But when it came to eating Leonora just toyed with the plate of bread and salad offered to her and refused even to contemplate the sticky pudding. Neil was complaining about the year's new intake at college when she spoke straight out, cutting through as if no one in the room was talking right then, as if everyone was waiting just for her to begin. 'None of you have any idea what it's like for me.'

Grace thought Leonora must have a habit of saying things like that because no one took much notice. Robina dolloped some more pudding on Neil's plate. She had such a soft voice, Robina, almost a little too soft to be heard without the listener straining. She looked at her eldest daughter across the table. 'You do tend to dramatise, dear. Only last week you were like a lovesick teenager.'

'You only see what you want to see. I know you all think he's Mr Perfect in our Mr Perfect world but he's not like that.'

'C'mon you love him really.' Andrew got up, walked round to his sister and planted a little kiss on top of her curls before filling her glass. He turned to Grace. 'Archie and Leonora are just made for each other, we all know that.' Rory, in his pram, let out a howl.

'Who's for coffee and who's for tea?' Robina asked. 'You all go into the sitting room and I'll clear up here. No, Grace, I mean it, I like doing it. You just go and relax. That's what you're here for.'

The others had gone for a walk. The sofa was soft. Old down-filled seat cushions plumped up and sunk down upon, plumped up and sunk down upon. Grace was dozing, her head on Andrew's shoulder, when Robina came in wheeling a trolley with mugs and both a tea and a coffee pot.

'Milk?'

'Please.' Grace nodded.

'Sugar?'

'Grace likes honey.' Andrew got to his feet. 'I'll get some.'

'There's no need,' Grace assured him, eager not to seem fussy, but he was already halfway to the kitchen.

'No, of course you shall have some honey if that's what you like,' Robina said, sitting down next to Grace and turning towards her. 'Now, I want to know everything about you. I can see Andrew is smitten.' She took Grace's hands in hers. 'I want us to be really good friends, you and I.' Her peppercorn eyes went from alert to concerned and she gave Grace's rough-skinned hands a little squeeze with her own soft ones. 'Andrew told us your mother died when you were just a little girl.'

Grace nodded. 'But I got Mrs Shield, my stepmother, soon afterwards and she did her very best.'

'Still, it's hardly the same. And then your father died.'

'He had a heart attack.'

'Oh dear. How dreadful.'

'It was. Personally, I think he was exhausted from trying to reconcile the man he was with the man his wives wanted him to be.' But Grace was beginning to feel faintly ashamed, as if she had been careless somehow in losing so many relatives.

Robina pulled her hands away. 'Oh my dear, I've upset you. I'm too direct.'

Andrew had come back into the room. 'Grace doesn't like being pitied,' he said. He had decanted the honey into a tiny glass bowl and Grace smiled up at him, trying to remember when a man had last decanted anything for her.

'No, no, your mother is being kind. Compassion I like. I would have been really pissed off if, through the years, I hadn't had any. It's just sometimes I feel as if I'm defined by what I've lost rather than what I have or who I am. I like to think I'm appreciated for myself, not only my uncanny ability to have people die on me.'

There was a pause, then Robina said, 'Quite right too.'

Andrew smiled fondly and said, 'Oh Grace.' She liked the way he said that; it made her sound troublesome but cute. It made a nice change; she did not usually appear cute. 'You were doing so well,' he went on. 'A whole sentence about your feelings with no crap joke in sight and then you go and spoil it all. Stop fighting for a moment. Allow people in.' He leant over the sofa back and kissed her cheek, his lips close to hers, and she turned towards him, forgetting all about Robina until there was a clatter of china followed by, 'Go and find the others, would you darling, and tell them coffee's ready. And I promise; no more pity.' Andrew gave them both an indulgent smile and did what he was told. His mother looked at his disappearing back. 'He's such a dear boy,' she said. 'A little weak sometimes, but then that's all down to a soft heart.'

'Weak? He doesn't seem weak to me.' Grace was surprised at how insulted she felt on his behalf. A little smile played at the corners of Robina's wide unmade mouth. 'You like him, don't you?'

'Yes. Yes, I do.'

'Good. He needs someone like you.'

Grace was so surprised to hear this that she forgot to pursue the point about Andrew being weak. 'In my experience mothers often think I'm exactly what their sons don't need. I'm not sure why. Maybe they sense that I'm bad at nurturing. And I have to say that they are right about that.'

The knowing smile was back. 'Well if you are, it's because you haven't been taught. I suspect you haven't had much nurturing yourself.'

Grace knew that was not true, she had been a loved child. But she thought of what Andrew had said, and she decided to let it go. She felt calm, happy in the moment, like a cat being stroked just the right way – not too soft, not too hard and right along the fur – so she allowed the misconception, the seed of a lie, to drift right on past. She had worn it like a cape – her strength, her independence, her reliance on no one but herself. Now she was tired and longing to take it off and stand there, lighter, smaller, weaker and rather more herself. 'It wasn't so bad,' she said.

'You're a brave girl, I can tell,' Robina said.

'I wouldn't say that,' Grace mumbled. She felt ashamed of how good she felt in the warm light of all this interest and approval. 'Do you mind if I pour myself another cup of tea?'

'And you're a photographer. Such an interesting line of work. And flexible too.'

Grace straightened up, alert suddenly, smiling as if her dearest friend had just walked into the room. 'It's what I do.'

They were joined by the others. Grace took some pictures of them all and Andrew insisted on taking some of her, perching on the armrest of the sofa next to Kate, laughing with Robina, puzzling over Timothy's quiz.

Afterwards, when she was back home alone in her flat, she could not stop staring at those photographs, at the way she looked in them. Was that her, that girl with the rounded face where she was used to seeing sharp angles? Was that her, the woman with the placid smile? From where had she sprung, this younger, happier, relaxed self, the self that she always hoped to find in the mirror but never did? Most astonishingly of all, she appeared to belong.

'I just love his family,' Grace told Angelica. They were drinking tea sitting in the window seat by the open window. Grace was smoking.

'Do you never feel the need for *fresh* air?' Angelica complained. 'And what about him? Forget his family, do you love *him*?'

Questions, always questions. Grace had questioned to death a great many relationships in the past ten years. She knew too that once there had been a love to which she knew all the answers, but she did not expect ever to find that kind again.

'You really love that boy?'

'I love him so.'

'Would you like tea or coffee?'

'I don't mind; I love him so.'

'So what's your view of the US withdrawal from Vietnam?'

'Thank God he's safe; I love him so.'

'Left or right?'

'He lives just to the left of here. I love him so.'

'And animal rights; where do you stand on the issue?'

'Animals just adore Jefferson and he adores them; and me, I love him so.'

'So what are your thoughts on the future of mankind?'

'Well, his grandparents are all alive and fit although in their eighties, so if genes are anything to go by he should be around for a long time yet, and I love him so.'

'Do you believe in God?'

'God, I love him so.'

'So do you love him?' Angelica insisted.

Grace turned her face from the window. 'Who? Oh silly me, Andrew; of course I . . . It's so . . . soft. Andrew, his family, it's this soft place to land and, Angelica, I need one. You know those photographs of big happy families gathered round the table or the open fire, the kind of families we wanted when we were children in our neat little nuclear pockets? Well, with him, with them, it's like I've stepped into one of those photos.' She put her hand on Angelica's arm, a little embarrassed. 'I'm tired, Angelica. I'm thinking, why should I be the one shouldering all the burden of living with myself? Let someone else try it for a change. And how nice it would be to know that if I died, something other than the increasingly unpleasant smell seeping out from under my front door would alert the world to my fate. The last time I was away I forgot to cancel the milk. Each day there was another bottle standing on my doorstep. By the time I got back there were nine. How many bottles would there have to be before anyone noticed or cared that I was gone?'

'Grace, do you *love* him?'

'What is all this talk of love? People didn't go on and on about love in the old days.'

'Remind me to write a note to John Donne about that,' Angelica said.

'I mean . . . what is love?'

'At least you're asking that before you're engaged,' Angelica said. 'Anyway, as far as I see it, if you felt it – love – you wouldn't have to ask. If you need to ask . . . well, brainy; draw your own conclusion.'

'Do you love Tom?'

'I know what you think about him.' She raised her hand. 'No, don't protest. And yes, I do love him. I'd have to . . . wouldn't I, to still be there?' Angelica turned wide blue eyes on her. Grace held her gaze, wanting to take her friend's hand but lighting another cigarette instead. 'Anyway,' Angelica said, 'don't change the subject. Andrew?'

'I believe I can make him happy.'

'Virtue does not become you.'

'All right, so I believe we can make each other happy.'

'Silly ass.'

A year later, Grace, a married woman, lay in her bed, lazy and warm, the summer sun shining a path along her face and chest. Slowly she opened her eyes: a crack at first, then wider. Her gaze took in the faded rose sprigged wallpaper, the heavy mahogany chest of drawers and, as a final treat, Andrew. It was Sunday morning, not yet eight o'clock, but already he was up and dressed. He was going to his parents' house to help with the solar-heating panel; it had gone again, whatever that meant. Before leaving he bent down and kissed her tenderly, lingeringly, on the lips . . . and one more time.

Moments later the front door closed followed by his steps on the gravel. Grace buried her face in the pillow that smelt faintly of him: clean sweat and lemon shampoo. She liked his hair that was golden and curly, mostly brushed tidily to one side in a left-hand parting. She liked it best when it got messed up on a walk or in bed. There was something so appealing about an escaping lock of hair, like the materialisation of a naughty thought. She had taken photographs of him with his hair like that, pictures she would not show his mother.

'My mother-in-law. My husband,' she said out loud. Next she changed the emphasis on the words. '*My* husband. My *husband*. My husband and I. My husband says . . . needs . . . likes . . . is . . . my husband . . . he and I.'

These days Grace, the woman whose soles had not touched grass from one year to another, could go downstairs in her thin nightshirt and walk barefoot into the garden where only the birds could see her, yet if she dropped dead she would be missed pretty damn quickly.

She had an appointment at ten. A friend of Robina's was having her young granddaughter to stay and she wanted the child's photograph taken. Grace was developing quite a reputation for her children's portraits. Robina was proud of her. 'Have you met my new daughter-in-law?' she would say, with a look at Grace as if she had made her herself. 'She's a *photo-grapher*.'

The little girl coming to have her picture taken was called Arabella. In Grace's recent experience it was quite difficult finding a little girl who *wasn't* called Arabella, or at least Fenella, Lucinda or Melissa. And all those little people with names ending in *a* wore smocked dresses that were so long their tiny Start-rite sandals got caught in the hem with every other step they took. Fringes were out that too was obvious. Instead their wispy hair was parted neatly and held in place by a clip with a flower or a tortoise or a kitten as decoration. Grace looked at the photograph of herself as a child that Mrs Shield had given Andrew. Her straight dark hair was cut in an unforgiving fringe above straight dark brows and she was wearing a black dress with brightly coloured raggedy patches sewn on it. That dress had been her all-time favourite item of clothing and had been made by Aunt Kathleen. Aunt Kathleen had always been good at keeping in touch with her dead sister's family in England, sending picture postcards when she and Uncle Leslie travelled around America and little gifts for birthdays and Christmas. Grace sent her drawings. She had sent one of her favourite rag doll, Maude, who was wearing a black dress with raggedy patches. On the back of the picture she had written several unsubtle and badly spelt hints about how much she would like just such a dress for herself. And five weeks later, for her eleventh birthday, a perfect copy of Maude's dress had arrived from America. The dress was not only black but quite short too. Maude's dress had been short, more like a long shirt all the better for her striped odd stockings to be seen. It had been a source of great disappointment to Grace that Mrs Shield had not allowed her striped stockings. She had to content herself with one navy and one white knee-length sock. When Robina Abbot saw the photograph – Andrew kept it in an oval silver frame on his desk – she had looked at Grace and said, 'What a funny little thing you were. And to put you in black.'

'I put myself in black,' Grace pointed out. 'Anyway, I think I looked rather sweet.'

'Heaven help any child of yours.' Robina let out a peal of laughter.

But little Arabella wore the softest baby-blue Viyella and whiter-than-white ankle socks. Grace smiled as the little girl twirled unsteadily, one eye on the large hall mirror. 'I feel so pretty,' Arabella said.

'You *are* pretty,' Grace told her. 'And if you go out with me into the garden and sit on the little wooden bench beneath the cherry tree and think of what you like doing best, we shall have a very pretty photograph as well.' The grandmother pulled a hairy brush from her large bag and started tugging at the child's baby-fine curls. 'No, leave it as it is,' Grace said. 'I don't like children looking too *done*, if you see what I mean.'

'I simply can't abide untidy hair,' the grandmother said as the brush got caught in a curl. She gave a tug and then a backward yank so that Grace thought Arabella's head was going to snap right off the stem-like neck. The child squealed and Grace shot her a sympathetic look; give women of a certain age a hairbrush or a damp cloth and no child was safe.

The grandmother left to go to the post office, and once outside and released from her grandmother's beady eye, Arabella turned out to be a born model. Most little girls were, until someone came along and told them about the sin of vanity and the importance of being good *deep down*. Grace took some close-ups of Arabella twirling her hair, pouting her dark-pink rosebud lips, smiling, showing her perfect pearl-barley teeth. She changed the lens and shot some of the little girl standing by the stream at the bottom of the garden, her whole body arched as she pointed skywards at a bird, and of her bending forward looking at her own extraordinarily pleasing reflection in the water and almost tumbling over as she tried to catch a passing dragonfly. Grace ended up with three rolls of film: two black and white and one colour. People usually preferred colour shots for children, but Grace favoured black and white and always hoped to change their minds.

Arabella wanted to see her picture as soon as the session was over and cried for a bit when told that was not possible. She drank a glass of Ribena without spilling a drop on her pretty blue dress and ate three sponge fingers. Grace retied the bow at her back and brushed the crumbs off the smocked front. Together they listened to the buzzing of a bumble-bee and marvelled at what

106

a surprisingly loud noise it was for such a small creature to make. Arabella said she could make an even louder noise and growled like a lion.

When her grandmother took her away Grace was sorry to see her go, but she knew that soon another little Arabella, Fenella or Lucinda, or a James, Jonathan or Charles, would come to have her or his picture taken.

She had no more work on for that day. Since marrying Andrew she had cut down gradually in order to have time to do things like taking clothes to the drycleaner's and ironing shirts and shopping for groceries and cooking: all those wifely tasks Grace had confessed to Angelica she found strangely enjoyable. 'It's all right,' Angelica had said. 'You're not alone in this strange perversion; I quite like it too. Well, I used to, back when he was grateful.'

'What do you think it is?' Grace asked. 'I used to hate all that stuff.'

'It's nature having its wily way; it's nesting, so they say.'

'Nesting; that expression makes me cringe. Anyway, isn't one supposed to be pregnant for that?'

'It's preparation. Some of us prepare for longer than others. I bet you sniff his shirts.'

Grace laughed. 'I never. I did once stroke a pile of freshly ironed ones, but that's as kinky as I get.'

And there was all this family life to get used to. Today, as always on Sundays, they were having lunch with her parents-in-law. Before she left the house she saw to some of Andrew's ironing. She liked that expression: *saw to*. It sounded so breezy and competent. She picked a blue shirt from the basket and as she smoothed it across the ironing board she smiled at the thought of her conversation with Angelica. Blue was Andrew's favourite colour. She wondered if their child, when they had one, would be good in blue like its father or more suited to black like its mother. Then, as she folded the shirt, she remembered that, actually, Andrew was not really that fond of blue. It was Jefferson who liked blue of every shade. He had been just a little vain and aware that the colour brought out the deep cornflower of his eyes.

*   *   *

107

'Some of the front gardens around here are amazing,' Grace said as they sat round the table at Hillside House. 'Roses with heads the size of cabbages, phlox and peonies; has no one told them the best-kept Devon town award has gone already?'

'You should take some pictures,' Robina said. 'Send them to the local paper.' She had made a huge untidy pie and was serving it along with young carrots, new potatoes and home-baked wholemeal bread.

'I don't shoot flowers much,' Grace explained.

Robina and her friend Janet stared at her. 'But why?'

It was not a question to which Grace had given much thought. 'They just don't stand still for long enough,' she said airily, holding her plate out for carrots.

Robina looked at her for a moment then her brow cleared. 'Oh, one of your little jokes.' She turned to Janet. 'Grace's people on her mother's side were Irish-American.' Robina was a woman who needed a reason for everything. Lately she had seemed very keen to find a reason for Grace who kept trying to tell her that looking for reasons in this world could send a person mad. In Grace's view, if God had wanted people to have reasons He would *not* have given them religion.

Baby Rory was staying the weekend while his parents had some 'grown-up' time, Janet and Neil were there as usual on a Sunday and a young man called Stuart. 'One of mother's waifs and strays,' Kate had said. Sixteen was a cruel age. Stuart Wright was a pupil at the nearby boarding school for disabled youngsters. Stuart's parents were both dead and his closest relatives, an uncle and aunt, lived in Yorkshire, so on hearing that the boy spent almost all his weekends at school, Robina had stepped in and 'adopted' him.

Stuart had been blind from birth although he could sometimes distinguish very bright light. When Grace was little there were times when she had played at being blind, walking with her arms theatrically stretched out before her, fumbling and stumbling, comfortingly aware that all she needed to do for everything to be well again was to open her eyes. But the reality of a sightless life scared her like little else; to live in darkness and never know when someone might be watching you. When she fell in love with photography the fear of blindness became an obsession. If she went blind, photography would have no meaning; and neither, Grace imagined, would life.

She wanted to know if Stuart formed pictures in his mind.

'I have no visual references,' he said. 'And I don't know if what I think of as a picture is what a sighted person thinks of as one. But I do build pictures in my mind – from touch; from the feel of the sun, rain and wind; from scents and atmosphere; I'm especially good at sensing tension.' A small smile spread across his lips. 'Of course I do use other people's descriptions, but that comes last. It's my experiences I draw from, no one else's.'

'Any news on the little-grandchild front?' Robina who had been trying to change the subject for a while now turned to Grace.

'Is that what babies are known as these days?' Kate said, rolling her eyes. 'Grandchildren.'

'Sharp as a tack, aren't you, my dear,' Robina said. 'In fact it gets her into trouble sometimes. She's seen as very much a leader amongst her peers, you know.'

'*Mother!*' Kate protested, but just then Leonora arrived, surprising them all.

'I wasn't expecting you today, darling,' Robina said, calmly bringing out another plate. 'Weren't you and Archie supposed to be going away for the weekend?'

'Well, we changed our plans. Hi, Grace; hi, Stuart; hi, everyone.' Leonora, looking as if she had slept in her hippy chic, nodded towards Janet and Neil.

'Take a look at this . . .' Timothy pushed a piece of paper towards Leonora. On it was a drawing he had been busy with during most of lunch, depicting four little men with tall pointed hats and some other men pointing guns. 'Now,' Timothy said, expanding with the sheer excitement of the problem, 'one of these little guys will be in a position to warn the others . . .'

'Draw a rose for me,' Grace said, tearing a clean piece of paper from Timothy's notepad and putting it in front of Stuart. She found a Biro in her pocket and put it in his hand. 'Here,' she plucked a stem from the bowl of dusky pink roses at the centre of the table and beheaded it, handing him the flower that was just a bud. 'I'll float it in some water on a saucer when we're done,' she reassured Robina. 'I won't waste it.'

Stuart sniffed the rose that had no scent. He touched each petal delicately with the tip of his middle right finger, then he stroked the outer ones. Next he put it down by the side of his plate and began to sketch.

Baby Rory, excited to see his mother, was bobbing up and down in his wooden seat that looked so uncomfortable compared with the new padded manmade ones, but Robina hated anything plastic and swore by natural materials. 'Me, me, me.' He stretched out a podgy hand, wanting his own flower. Grace looked around and caught sight of a nodding daisy right outside the open back door. Excusing herself, she nipped out and picked it, then handed it to Rory who tried to eat it. Leonora took it away and gave him a rusk instead.

'For future reference,' Grace said, 'Feed Baby *rusks*, not daisies.'

'Don't you worry, my dear,' Robina said. 'Motherhood will come naturally. In fact, I always say that Baby brings his own sense with him. And Grace, Stuart is gravely visually impaired; I don't think he wants to play at drawing.'

Stuart's rose was a jagged mouth inside an outline like a pansy and set in a V-shaped cradle. Like all good abstracts, it had captured the essence. Grace was tempted to ask him to draw a portrait of Robina, but thought maybe that would be best kept to later. Instead she deheaded a second stem and handed it to Stuart, saying, 'Tell me what you see now.'

Robina cleared her throat. Stuart explored the second rose. This one was open other than for a small tight bud at its centre. 'Moist,' Stuart said, his index finger prodding at the closed centre of the flower. He smiled dreamily. 'Flesh-pink.'

'That's just a word,' Grace said. 'What makes you think it's that colour?'

Stuart handed Grace the rose, taking her finger and tracing it along the same path as his had wandered a few moments earlier. Grace too began to smile. When she felt the tight bud at the centre of the rose she laughed. Then Stuart laughed too.

Robina, who was like Mrs Shield in the way she hated being left out of *anything*, wanted to know what was so funny. Timothy wanted to know if anyone had solved his puzzle.

'Actually, all the little fuckers can get shot, for all I care,' Leonora said. She had been unusually quiet until then.

The others all began to talk and, knowing they weren't over-heard, Kate spoke to Grace. 'You know, it really bugs me the way Mum keeps saying I'm so smart and everyone loves me and I'm a leader. She knows it's not true. I'm really unpopular. I'm not in anyone's group. Some people are scared of me, that's all. But try telling her that.'

'You're her daughter,' Grace said. 'She's proud of you.'

'She's *ashamed* of me, more like.'

'Why would you think that? She never stops praising you to anyone who wants to listen.'

'If she really was proud of me she'd see me as I am: a frizzy-haired dumpy girl of reasonable intelligence, not some beauty with a brain the size of a melon and a lorryful of charisma.'

Grace stared at her. Then she laughed. 'You're funny, and clever enough for anyone. So, maybe your hair is not at its best right now . . .' They both burst out laughing.

Kate grew serious again. 'But it's true. I'm right, aren't I? Making someone out to be better than they are is not love; it's not being proud, it's being selfish. They're saying, both Mum and Dad, in their different ways, that the way I am is not good enough so they have to embroider the facts to make me more to their taste.'

'I've never looked at parental boasting in that light before,' Grace said. 'And I'm still not sure you're right. Have you tried talking to them?'

'Father only likes abstract problems; anything personal and he bolts to his study. And Mother. You try telling her that her world isn't perfect.'

'I take it she gets upset?'

'You could say that. She takes it as a personal insult.'

Grace nodded. 'Mankind loves to be deceived. I remember when Mrs Shield told me that Father Christmas didn't exist, I hit her.'

'Stuart's very nice,' Grace said to Robina over the washing-up a little later when the others had gone for a walk.

'He's a dear boy,' Robina handed her a tureen to dry, 'not a performing seal.'

'Of course he isn't,' Grace exclaimed. 'Whoever said he was?'

'I'm not the one who made the poor boy draw silly pictures, at the lunch table.'

'They weren't silly pictures, they were fascinating,' Grace protested, sounding even to herself like a ten year old who had been caught drawing willies in her exercise book. 'I was interested in him. How can that be wrong?'

'He might like to talk about other things than his handicap, have you thought about that? He might just like to be treated like everybody else.'

'I did treat him like everybody else, that's the point,' Grace said. 'I asked him about himself. I didn't talk about a handicap. I asked him how the world appeared to *him*.'

'You're splitting hairs,' Robina said. 'The tin goes under there.' She pointed to the drawer by the side of the huge gas stove. 'Now, what were you and Kate so busy talking about?'

'Oh, this and that.'

'And . . .' Soft voice, steely eyes; Grace could see why Kate did not want to confront her mother. Saints were notorious toughies.

Grace leant against the sink, tea towel thrown over her shoulder, her eyes locked into Robina's. 'She feels that you and Timothy need to make her into something better than what she actually is because who she is isn't good enough.'

Robina looked at her, measuring. 'Nonsense,' she said finally. 'I'll talk to her. I won't have such negativity in the house.'

As they walked back home to their cottage by the harbour, Andrew put his arm around her. 'I'm so proud of you,' he said. 'Look how well Kate relates to you. She has been really difficult lately and there she was opening up to you. Everyone really responds to you.'

Love may not be blind, Grace thought, but it sure is short-sighted. Yet she could not help but be pleased that he was so pleased with her. She had learnt, over the weeks and months of her marriage, that having someone think her so good, so pretty and so clever made her a little more of all those things. They had happened gradually, those little changes. Andrew believed that Grace was kind-hearted – he told her so over and over again – so she began to perform little kindnesses even when it went right against her instincts to do so just because she could not bear to see the light of adoration dim in his eyes. Andrew believed her to be forgiving, thoughtful and magnanimous. She sent a birthday card to a one-time friend who had called Grace's contribution to a book on the human form 'depraved' in a review. He said she was a country girl at heart and that she had a way with animals. She was certainly brought up in the country, though her heart was paved with asphalt. Yet when Timothy's dogs put their snouts up against her crotch she did not give them a surreptitious shove in the stomach with her knee, but smiled and patted their curly heads. And she would glance up and see the warm approval in her husband's eyes, the proud look that said, *See, see how she is loved by every living thing, see how sweet, how special she is.*

Grace remembered long ago standing in the doorway of Mrs McGraw's kitchen, an unwelcome presence yearning to be part of the kitchen-cosy and to have Jefferson's mother smile at her the way she was smiling at Cherry, the wanted one, the one who belonged. She looked up at Andrew and mouthed a silent thank you.

According to Andrew, she also had a woman's touch coupled with a rare logical mind. She had her priorities right, he said, putting their marriage and their home before her career. Now, Grace was meaning to speak to him about that. It had been nice not working so hard for a time, but soon she would have to get right back there and fight for commissions or she would be left behind.

They sat down for a while on the soft grass of the riverbank because the afternoon was too beautiful to take at speed. She leant against him. He had the kind of shoulders that really felt as if they could take your weight. 'I was so tired until I met you,' she said. 'I told myself I was all right but no one ever tells you how tired you get, being fine all by yourself.'

She remembered how Angelica had said, on her last visit a few weeks ago, 'You've bought the whole deal, haven't you? The husband, the big jolly family, the rose-covered cottage; like you

113

walked into a shop with a vague feeling that you needed a pair of knickers and came out with a suit and shirt and stockings and shoes as well.'

'So I got a lot for my money,' Grace had said. 'Anyway, you bought it too.'

'I tried. Maybe I haven't got your eye for a bargain.'

'Angelica.' Grace touched her hand. 'What's wrong?'

'Some wrinkles, that's all. It's part of marriage, the positioning and repositioning. Nothing to worry about. We have some negotiating to do, that's all.'

'Negotiate, schmosiate; does he make you happy?'

'It's all about compromise. Anyway, I'm pregnant.' And for the first time that day Angelica was smiling.

'We shall be such perfect parents,' Andrew said now.

'I know,' Grace agreed. 'I shall not die young and you shall not withdraw into your study. The baby will grow up safe in the knowledge that she . . .'

'He . . .'

'. . . it can wear whatever colour clothes it likes because I shall be taking its picture mostly in black and white anyway. We will give it several names so that it can decide itself which one suits it best in mood and extravagance. A girl might be Hester Abigail Tennessee so that she can choose between strong and capable, unobtrusively pretty or downright theatrical.'

'Isn't Tennessee a boy's name?'

'Both,' Grace said.

'I like Amanda,' Andrew said. 'And Charles if it's a boy.'

'OK,' Grace said. 'But I'd better get pregnant first.'

Andrew shot to his feet and held his hand out, hauling her up. 'Let's go,' he said and they looked at each other and laughed. I'm blushing, Grace thought. I can feel it, me, Grace, blushing and simpering before my husband and enjoying every moment.

There was a party that night given by Lady Katherine Ellen School where Andrew taught and Kate was a pupil. Grace was rooting around in her wardrobe for something to wear that wasn't black or grey. Andrew never criticised; he just said how nice she looked when she wore colour. Marriage was all about give and take. Andrew had accepted that Grace was an indifferent cook, a reluctant hostess, a tiddly guest, a smoker, someone who liked looking at gardens a lot better than digging in them, someone who ate horse (it was in France, she was young, and it was quite good) but would never ride one. The least she could do was try to please him, a little, in how she dressed.

In the end she did the best she could and put on a knee-length straight black skirt and a white shirt with a red chiffon scarf tied round her waist, for colour. She felt as if she was still at school. In her last year the new music nun had decided to liven up their usual concert uniform of black skirt and white blouse, telling them excitedly to add 'a dash of colour – any colour, girls' by tying a scarf round their necks. Grace, who played the flute, badly, had worn a snuff-brown tie that had belonged to her father.

'You look lovely,' Andrew said as they walked out of the house.

'Just don't ever make me wear one of those smelly green jackets you have to polish.'

The party was given in honour of Lady Ruth Russell, a long-time benefactor and one-time student. Lady Russell had surpassed herself, donating the funding for an entire art block. The new building was called the Bernard Withering Hall in memory of her father who had been killed in the First World War. He had been twenty-four years old, a lieutenant, when he was injured at Ypres and had died of his wounds three weeks later, leaving behind a young widow who never recovered from his loss and a baby daughter who had just learnt to say Papa but was never to see the face behind the word. This child was now a crooked, lined old woman, childless and a widow herself; a husk propelled by a jet engine. In order to hear what Lady Russell was saying you had to bend low, but once you looked into those eyes, pale blue, a little protruding, alert and laughing, you were hers. She lived with a middle-aged male companion called Colin in a large Victorian stone house at the edge of town. Robina had often spoken of Lady Russell whom she greatly admired. They sat on committees together.

Robina had been washing up glasses, sighing that there was

never enough of anything at these functions, and now she was helping the staff pass round the platters of canapés and pink and yellow iced fairy cakes made by the girls themselves. Grace took the heavy plate from her hands and said that, for once, Robina should be a guest and just relax and enjoy herself. Robina did not exactly snatch the plate back, but her shoulders hunched a little. She looked, Grace said later to Andrew, like a would-be martyr on hearing that there had been a general amnesty declared on Christians.

Lady Russell sat at a table placed there especially for her at the front of the room. She was flanked by Colin and a pretty young woman dressed entirely in red. Robina said she wanted to introduce Grace. 'Lady Russell, you haven't met my new daughter-in-law.' As she moved forward, pushing Grace ahead of her, her face took on a look of concern. 'Are you sure you're warm enough, Lady Russell?' Grace could see how Robina's right hand was twitching to adjust the shawl around the old woman's shoulder. Don't do it, Grace thought. She is not the kind of woman who wants her shawl adjusted for her. Maybe it was telepathy but Robina's hand was stilled. Instead she said she thought Lady Russell's father would have been very, very proud. Lady Russell turned to the young woman in red and whispered theatrically, 'Joanna, dear, do we *know* this woman?'

Robina fled. 'Don't worry about it,' Grace said, having caught up. 'She's probably a bit senile.'

'Senile, my foot,' Robina spat and secretly Grace agreed. There was nothing senile about Lady Russell, not one cell. Robina continued in a voice Grace had not heard her use before, shrill and aggrieved. 'No, she's just a nasty vicious old snob who delights in making other people feel uncomfortable.' She took a few breaths and seemed to calm down. 'When I think of how sweet my old dears at the Evergreen are. Always so pleased to see you, always *so* grateful for everything one does.'

'It must be awful to be old *and* have to be grateful as well.'

'They don't *have* to be anything, Grace.'

Next they were joined by Leonard Brown, the school chaplain and a friend of the Abbots. Grace and he had not got on so well since Grace told him her views on St Paul, but he was giving her a friendly enough smile right now. That was the comforting thing about men of the cloth: they were paid to love and to forgive.

'I've just been told that you're quite the photographer,' he said.

'You could even say that I am *a photographer*.' Grace tried to smile politely but she did not do very well.

'Take it seriously, do you? Good, good. Anyway, I thought you might be able to help us with the new-look school magazine. At the moment a very disappointing proportion of our student body actually reads us.'

'You want me to take some pictures?'

'It was your mother-in-law's idea, actually. Clever lady.'

Robina smiled modestly. 'It was nothing really; I just thought that, girls being girls, some fashion shots, how to pep up your uniform, that kind of thing wouldn't go amiss; and wouldn't it be fun to do some reportage from the girls' homes, *House and Gardens*-style? Nothing intrusive, just a bit of fun to bring in the readers. I just knew you'd love to help, Grace.'

'I would like to, but I have to check my diary,' Grace said. 'I've got quite a busy period right now.'

Robina raised her eyebrows. 'Too busy to help?' Leonard Brown said again what a valuable unselfish member of 'the team' Andrew was.

'I *will* try,' Grace said, spotting Andrew out of the corner of one eye. He was talking, gesticulating, smiling, at ease, surrounded by a group of pupils and their mothers. Grace could see that he was making them have a nice time. As usual he was giving his all. It was not fair that he should be let down by her. Who wanted to be known as that charming fellow with the mean wife?

In the early months of their marriage Andrew's unfailing helpfulness and consideration towards others had made her feel good second-hand. Lately she had begun to feel inadequate. When Doris Leighton, the most boring woman in England, locked herself out of her cottage, Andrew had suggested they ask her to join them for dinner at the exact moment that Grace had reached for the switch to turn the light off and pretend they were not at home. When Jenny Howard told them her Uncle Joe from the States would be so disappointed that she had not managed to get tickets for *Phantom of the Opera*, Grace had barely had time to say, 'Try *Cats*,' before Andrew had handed over theirs. Grace hid the best bottle of red when guests called. Andrew found it and opened it.

But the great thing about being a human was that, unlike other animals, you did not have to take your God-given traits lying down. You could change, play around with your perceived limitations, and stretch and pull into an altogether different shape; you could act against your instincts: this was the gift given to humans. Grace decided to act against her instincts and be nice to Leonard Brown. 'I'll fit it in, somehow,' she said with a big smile that she knew from experience to be winning. Leonard Brown smiled back, a genuinely friendly smile, before hurrying off on busybody legs to pass the news to Glenda Shawcross, the headmistress. 'Grace is a helpful young woman,' he would probably be saying.

So Grace had behaved well, decided to do a tiny bit of good for someone other than herself, even changed someone's perception of her, yet remained, at heart, a selfish woman. What exactly did that mean? Was there no reality, only perceptions? Did it matter as long as the job got done?

When they lay in bed together that night, Andrew said, 'It was really nice of you to say you'd help with the magazine. Leonard seemed quite surprised but I wasn't. It's like you have this front and I'm the first person to have seen through it to the soft sweet person you really are.'

Grace smiled to herself; boys just loved being first. She asked him, 'Do you think it's possible for your actions to create your feelings?'

'How do you mean?'

'Well, you are nice and helpful so you act nice and helpful. Now, what about if you're actually rather a bitch but sublimate it and act nice and do good? Might the feelings catch up with the actions so that actually you become nice?'

'Oh darling, it's late.' He rolled on top of her, kissing her neck, caressing her breasts, and whispered, 'Showtime.'

IT WAS RAINING, SOFT insistent summer rain that soaked you before you knew it. Noah Blackstaff answered the door to Grace looking like a man who had just been asked to choose between his wife and his mistress; his shirt was buttoned the wrong way, his wheat-blond hair stood on end and his amber eyes had a wild look. 'I can't do this. I'm trained to destroy the reputation of people I *don't* know; this is different.'

Grace left her umbrella on the porch and stepped inside. 'I take it you're talking about the biography.' She pulled out two cigarettes from the packet in her bag. 'Here.' She put one in his mouth. '"A well-written life is almost as rare as a well-spent one." Thomas Carlyle.'

'That's *so* helpful; thank you.'

Grace grinned and lit his cigarette, then her own. 'You're welcome. Anyway, you could just *not* do it; have you thought about that? The poor old boy's dead. Of course he'll haunt you for the rest of your days. Your dreams will be full of whispers of broken words and betrayal and any money you make from his paintings will be cursed, but that's OK; at least you would have got out of a boring job.'

'It's not about it being boring. It's about decency and truth and, as so often, the two are not compatible. How, while Louisa is alive, can I write a creditable biography of my grandfather? I would have to write things that would be grossly offensive to her. I'm sure you've heard about Jane Dale.' He led the way into the kitchen.

'No.'

'He, the old devil, would have loved everyone to know what a ladies' man he was, but Louisa; you know how private *she* is.'

Grace shrugged. 'I suppose.'

'Precisely. But there was a sea-change in her relationship with Grandpa, that much I know. They developed an understanding. They became quite close, in the latter part of their marriage. I

119

have this enduring image of the two of them strolling in the garden hand in hand, him leaning on her, both as unsteady as children who have just learnt to walk. It was odd but endearing: he an artist, an extrovert, a man who saw ghosts and loved women; and she so withdrawn, a woman who saw laundry lists, the only six-foot-tall woman in the world who manages to remain invisible. He was completely dependent on her, like a man leaning on his shadow.'

'Mrs Shield maintains there's a lot to learn from laundry lists ever since poor Marjory found a pair of champagne-coloured French knickers itemised amongst her husband's shirts. Still, have you tried talking to Louisa about it? Maybe she wouldn't mind as much as you think. Most of what you would write about – the work that mattered – is from long ago anyway. I fear Arthur's one of those people of whom you say when you see their obituary, not "What! *He's* died!" but rather "Goodness, I didn't know he was still alive."'

'Well, it's time for a revival,' Noah said, pouring the water. 'Always take the pot to the kettle not the kettle to the pot, that's the secret of a good cup of tea.'

'Everybody knows that.' Grace got up and fetched the honey from the shelf above the cooker.

'As I said, try, talking to her.'

He smiled at her. 'Of course. Which is why you should admire me even more for my moral scruples about selling Granny down the river . . .' He stopped and looked at her. 'What's the matter? I'm not serious, you know. The money would be great but . . .'

'It's OK. You just reminded me of why I stopped taking pictures.'

'Actually, I wanted to ask if you might make an exception.'

'No.'

'I had this idea to document this place – the house, the gardens – in still photos, before it's sold and goodness knows what is done to it. Stately homes aside, not many houses have remained in the same family for close to a hundred years. My great-grandparents moved here in 1903 and very little has changed since. My great-grandmother Lydia installed one of the first central-heating systems in the county, and it's still working,' he mock-shivered, 'in parts. I can still ring for the servants from any room in the house – no one will come, of course, so that has changed – but look at the light sockets, this kitchen, the bathrooms . . . it would be a great social documentary. Look at the wallpaper . . . on second thoughts, best not to.'

'No.'

'I can't afford to pay, which is why you would be perfect.'

'No.'

'So why should I help you look for your artist?'

'Because if you don't I'll beat you up. I always could.'

'I wasn't a black belt back then.'

'I've got a shotgun.'

'OK. Go talk to Granny. She's upstairs.'

'Do you ever talk to her? I mean, really talk to her?'

'I say good morning and ask her if she's slept well. She says yes or no, and then we discuss what we will have for lunch before we turn our minds to the latest plot development in *Neighbours*. She watches both the lunchtime and the teatime instalments. That's about the level of intimacy we achieve, my granny and I; the imaginary goings-on of imaginary families. It's not just that she's old. I never found her easy to talk to. I don't see what Arthur and she ever had in common. Then again, I know how it can work; one moment you're with this fun-loving, tender, forgiving and giving creature who seems to share all your interests and enthusiasms; the next, you wake up with some gimlet-eyed sergeant major with a biological clock and an unhealthy preoccupation with giving dinner parties.'

Grace gave him an amused look. 'I think we've left the subject of your grandparents here. Anyway, it's not our fault; women are just too adaptable for their own good sometimes. We've had to be to survive. A woman falls in love, heedless, headless; she wants a soulmate, poor sod. There aren't many of those so she makes one up. She wears his tastes and opinions so she can tell herself and the world, "Look how alike we are, how much we have in common." Then real life sets in; it's back into the old gear: roll-up-the-sleeves-and-get-on-with-it time. Women start off romantic and end up realistic. Men start off romantic and end up wondering what the hell happened. One of those things, I'm

121

afraid. I think men see only what they want to see. Usually that's their reflection in the eyes of an adoring woman.'

Noah had been raking his fingers through his hair as he stared at the piles of papers and notebooks in front of him. 'You're like a troll with your hair standing on end and that wild look in your eyes,' Grace told him. 'A *nice* troll, but a troll nevertheless.'

'Thanks,' he said, his mind on other things. 'You see, I don't know. That's the point; she's my grandmother and I don't know her. She's just always *been there*, like the wallpaper.'

'It can't have been easy for her. When the sun is up you don't see much of the moon.'

'Well, she's been looking forward to your visit. She was quite animated this morning.'

'Most living things respond well to attention. I can't see why your grandmother should be any different.'

Noah frowned. 'You make her sound like a pot plant.'

Louisa

I NEVER GREW FOND of my mother-in-law, but sometimes I remember things she said and I find myself agreeing. 'Always keep something back that they'll want; that's how not to be lonely in old age,' she said to me when she was as old as I am now.

Grace Shield wants answers. She was here not long ago; yesterday she tells me now. 'I'm being a bore,' she says, 'but I just thought I'd ask again if you might have remembered something . . . about Forbes.' And she waits, her hands folded, good-girl fashion, in her lap. Large hands just like mine. Like most young people she has no patience. 'He produces a painting as fine as the one I've got and that's it; nothing more. No one's heard of him. There's no record of him anywhere. No mention, not even an A.L. Forbes Appreciation Society on a small island outpost off Newfoundland. It doesn't make sense. The more I think about it, the less sense it makes.'

I want to tell her to give me time. Everything takes longer when you are old. It seems unfair, as time is what you have so little of. I know what she wants from me, but I have tried for so long not to remember; and now, when nature is on my side, she wants to rake it up again. In any case, I need answers too. 'How did you get your painting? Where did it come from? Do you know who owned it last?'

'It was bought for me in an antique shop, actually. By someone I loved a great deal. He died before he could give it to me but eventually it reached me, two years after his death, on my birthday, although the person who sent it to me didn't know that.'

'Do you know the shop?' I ask.

She shakes her head. 'He said it was in Chelsea although his geography was pretty shaky. As soon as I get back to London I'll go there, ask around.'

We sit in silence for a while. Long-buried feelings stir and flutter. I've been cold for so long.

Then Grace says, 'Did you see the Sunday papers?'

I tell her I prefer the television. 'There's a man I quite like. He used to be funny. Cold over England.'

'There was a piece about me. A very stupid piece. Then there was another one yesterday. This time they had asked my ex-mother-in-law about me. Talk about not giving someone a chance.'

'If my mother-in-law had been asked to sum me up,' I say, 'I believe she would have done it in one word: disappointing.'

Seventy years ago, years that have vanished like small change. There she is, Lydia, tiny in her vast bed, 'Louisa, remember that now you are someone.' Impossible, I thought when I first saw her, that she could be Arthur's mother, he who has the height and strength of a Viking. But I have come to learn that what she lacks in stature she makes up for in resolve, so I imagine that she simply willed her frail body to produce the big bouncing baby boy who had grown up to be my husband. She had used her nine months well, getting the most out of the time. She hated waste, even the waste of breath. 'I shall call you Louisa,' she said when we first met. 'I can't be bothered with fancy double-barrelled names.'

And now I am to remember that I am *someone*. It is a new thought. *Nuisance. Anyone. Nobody*: all of these I was suited to; but *someone*. There are people who draw attention towards themselves as effortlessly as a window draws daylight. Such people have the right to consider themselves someone. But I was like a glass of water on a hot afternoon; worthy of notice only by my absence.

But maybe it has all changed since I met Arthur. He spotted me in a room full of people and did not leave my side that evening. And the strangest thing, or as strange at least as this wondrous man giving me all his attention, was that suddenly I became visible; people who had walked past me in corridors and lecture halls or at parties now found me worthy of notice.

I knew people who could make others laugh three times or more during a conversation and I had always thought what a fine thing it would be to have that gift, the gift of being able to make someone's face crumple up in merriment, sending lines from the corners of the eyes to the cheekbones like rays of sunshine, to make them throw their heads back in helpless laughter. I told Arthur and he took my hands and looked at me so intently that my cheeks coloured as if I had been sitting too close to the fire. 'You are my funny serious girl,' he told me. 'Don't try to be like everyone else. Always just be yourself.' He grinned and, big bearded man that he was, he looked like a boy. 'Anyway, I make enough good jokes for two, don't you think, my most perfect, my most solemnly delightful young friend?' Then he laughed and all around us people turned and looked and *saw* me.

And here I am, Mrs Arthur Blackstaff: *someone*.

'Don't slouch, girl. You're tall; you can't pretend otherwise. Whole county's turning up just to meet you. Make the best of yourself. No need to look like a startled rabbit.'

It was too early yet for me to decide whether my mother-in-law was plain mean, or just bluff with a kind heart underneath. It was the same with the house: Northbourne House, my home now. This evening as I descend the wide oak staircase I find it benevolent. I feel welcomed by the mulled-wine papered walls, embraced by the oak panelling, drawn to the many leaded windows. Other times, when the light comes in bright from the south and west, I shiver in the warmth and feel, great tall woman that I am, afloat in unfriendly seas. Maybe it's the house that can't make its mind up about me. What had previous brides done to pacify it? A sacrifice perhaps; a son and heir to all these contradictions, all this light and dark.

Arthur is calling me. The guests have started to arrive. I suspect that, however much Arthur is admired for his success, his charm and handsome looks, and my mother-in-law is feared for the sharpness of her tongue, most of our guests have come tonight because word has got round that the bride is unaccountably *plain*!

Arthur tells me he has an eye for hidden treasure.

I have uncommonly good hearing. I hear them; the county matrons with their floury cheeks and braying voices. Try as they might, it's not in their nature to speak in anything less than these loud assured tones. It was bred into them, the confidence of knowing they were born to the best seats in the house of life.

'But who *is* she?'

'One of those bluestockings. Apparently he found her in some dusty lecture hall at Cambridge. Both parents dead. Quite a scandal. I expect she's one of these *clever* gals.'

'What a refreshing change.' The speaker has a soft voice with an edge of laughter and I want to see to whom it belongs. Until now the guests had not seen me standing there, just outside of their circle, so when I appear amongst them their faces are too comical; I might have materialised through the sturdy walls, stepped out from the wallpaper like a ghost. I am introduced and I watch the women arrange their lips into tight little smiles, all but she with the soft voice and the kind words. She is much younger than the rest, shorter than I – but then most women are – with dark brown hair cut squarely at the chin and a straight fringe cut short across her wide forehead. Her eyes are brown, almost black. She puts her hand out to shake mine. 'I'm Viola Glastonbury.' I smile at her and take her hand.

We are joined by my mother-in-law. 'So you gals have met? I'm pleased. Viola is the kind of friend I want for you, Louisa. Viola paints. Sweet little pictures.'

But now I'm looking towards the windows where Jane Dale is standing, her gaze fixed on my husband's tall figure some distance away. 'A treasure. Good family. Bad luck. Straitened circumstances,' my mother-in-law explained to me when I first arrived. 'Great help to Arthur. I want you to be kind to her.'

My husband is undressing before me and I do not take my eyes off him. 'You were a great success, my dear,' he says.

I cannot stop smiling; not so long ago he was my dream and now here he is, flesh and blood, naked before me, his chest and legs covered in soft golden hair, his penis rising from the tangle of darker curls just for me. 'I did meet someone I liked.'

'Later,' he says, taking me in his arms. 'Later.'

126

NOAH GLANCED UP AS Grace returned to the kitchen where he was working through a stack of letters. 'You took your time. What have you been doing up there?'

Grace paused by his chair, her index finger on her chin. 'Now, let's see; what could we have been doing? Flown a kite? Played Cluedo; hide and seek, perhaps? All those, of course, but mostly I've been having what is known amongst us women as a *conversation.*'

'You always were facetious. So did she remember your Forbes?'

Grace shook her head. 'No.'

'I told you. And I don't mean because she's senile. I suppose she's getting that way, but I bet you it would have been the same had you asked her ten years ago. She probably never met the guy, or if she did she paid no attention.'

Grace lit a cigarette and blew smoke from her nostrils like a languid dragon. 'Why are you so mean about her?'

'Oh, *I* don't know. Maybe it's because I know I've never really given her a chance. A bad conscience does it for me every time. It was always about Grandpa. It sounds so shallow, I know, but he was *fun.*'

'Maybe she'll perk up now he's gone.'

'And why are you so down on him?'

'Maybe it's a girl thing.'

'No one forced Louisa to be the way she is, you know.'

Grace got to her feet. 'I should be off to be a good stepdaughter. Thanks for everything.' As she gave him a quick kiss on the top of his fair head, Noah glanced up. 'Are you all right seeing yourself out?'

'Sure.'

Outside, the sun was settling into comfortable late afternoon. The strong wind from the north had died to a soft breeze and she stopped for a moment to draw in the scent from the tobacco plants. In the upstairs window she could just glimpse the old lady, straight-backed in her chair. As she walked back to Northbourne Gardens, she thought of the adoration the young newlywed Louisa had shown towards her husband. Godlike: was that the word she had used? Grace smiled to herself. It was the secret of a happy marriage, an adoring wife. No wonder Grace's marriage had ended almost before it had begun.

NELL GORDON: *Baby heartbreak ended the marriage idyll.*

'Oh, I would advise anyone to try marriage,' Grace said. 'It usually starts so well.'

Angelica, seven months' pregnant was down for an advent weekend visit. Tom, her husband, was skiing.

Grace reached for a lollipop. 'Guess what? I'm pregnant too, twelve weeks.' Angelica moved as close as she could with her big stomach and gave her friend a hug. She had tears in her eyes.

Grace hugged her back. She grinned and waved the lollipop in the air. 'See how good I am, how responsible, how very virtuous. I don't smoke, I hardly drink and as for fornication I'm told it's positively beneficial.'

'I'm glad *you're* happy,' Angelica said.

A week later Grace lost the baby. Andrew was disappointed but he coped better than she had expected.

Angelica drove down that weekend, barely able to fit behind the steering wheel. 'I feel like an affront,' she said, embracing Grace, and Grace felt the tiny foot of her friend's baby against her own empty stomach.

Grace freed herself gently. 'Don't be silly.'

Later, as they finished lunch in the kitchen, she asked, 'Angelica, how does he cope so well?'

'By being a bloke,' Angelica said.

'I expect he feels it as much as I do but just doesn't know how to express it.'

'That's no reason. *You're* not usually a master of emotional

129

displays yourself, but it's pretty easy to see that you're not feeling too good right now.'

Grace did not reply directly. Instead she said, 'He's my rock.'

'Stone wall, more like,' said Angelica.

Everyone agreed it was sad, of course it was, but that it was probably for the best: nature's way of telling her there was something wrong with the baby; that it was not meant to be. All Grace knew was that there was another empty space in the world where a child of hers should have grown and thrived, another should-have-been birthday that she alone would acknowledge. She fervently hoped there was such a thing as reincarnation and that her incomplete babies had been able to return to base to be told, with a smile and a slap on the back, 'Better luck next time.'

Angelica asked her to be godmother to little Michael. At the spring-time christening in London, Grace looked at Angelica standing by the font in her cream skirt and coat, the infant in her arms. You never know the measure of your decency, she thought, until your best friend has what you want most in the world. 'I'm so glad for you,' she whispered inaudibly. She kept saying it over and over in her mind: *I'm so glad for you.*

Grace lost the next baby too, at sixteen weeks this time. She had been for a walk, and had sat down for a while beneath the weeping willow at the bottom of the garden. She watched the sun set behind the hill, telling the baby what a sunset looked like, and dawn too. 'Aurora; if you're a girl I'd like to call you Aurora, but I probably won't in the end because I'll be afraid of seeming pretentious, and having people think you are the child of some second cousin of an earl or a half-forgotten pop star.'

It was such a mild evening for mid-October. The wind had been coming from the south for a while and everyone was talking about another Indian summer. The leaves on the trees had not yet changed colour, but there was such a dusty tired look about them you almost wished for them to turn, so they could fall to the ground and get some rest.

It was while she was sitting there, talking to the baby, that the feelings of unease began. She brushed her worries away, staying where she was, enjoying the birds and the fresh air. Suddenly she went cold and her heart skipped a beat. She knew something terrible was happening. She clutched her stomach, begging, praying, as she got to her feet and made for the house.

It is often assumed that people like Grace – people who are not *obviously* cheerful, people who appear to have a slightly darker view of the world than others – are not, as a rule, hopeful. But that is wrong. Grace was one of the most hopeful people she knew; she just kept it to herself. Not to do so would make her even more vulnerable when the worst happened, when the blow fell and she stood there, fool that she was, smiling up at the descending fist, her own hand outstretched as if she had expected a handshake. So when she lay in the hospital, waiting for her scan, having been told that the procedure would probably show that the pregnancy was terminated, she nodded and said she understood. But in her mind was quite a different story; secretly she hoped that the scan would show up a tiny being, still miraculously there, alive, growing. 'Would you believe it?' the technician would say, straightening up, beaming. 'There's a heartbeat.'

By the time Andrew arrived it was all over. Her doctor had just told her, very gently, 'I'm afraid it's as we thought, you've lost the baby.' Grace kept her eyes very wide as she said, 'It's what we knew all along.'

Back home, afterwards, she had spent a lot of time wandering back and forth beneath the weeping willow as if she was looking for something.

Andrew changed. *He* said that it was Grace who had changed, although that was all right, considering what she had been through.

'What *we* have been through, surely,' she corrected him.

He who was so kind, helpfulness itself, always there, a shoulder to cry on, a friend to so many, a man to be counted on to give of himself and of his time and effort, he was curiously absent in those weeks after the second baby was lost. He stayed late at school. He went to see his old friend Ed, who had just lost his job and had no one else to talk to. He spent almost every weekend rehearsing the junior drama club's Christmas production. 'Those girls have worked their little guts out to get this play right; surely you're not suggesting I let them down now?'

'Too right I am. I don't give a flying fuck about the girls' end-of-term play or any other of their beastly little activities.'

He looked at her, incredulous. 'I shall forget you said that.' He stalked off. Even his steps sounded offended.

Grace ran after him, arms flailing, shrieking, unable to contain her pain and rage. 'Don't forget it. *I* need you, Andrew. I, me, Grace, your wife. *I* hurt and *I* need you! Why can't you be with me?'

Andrew went to stay a weekend with Leonora and Archie in London. Their marriage was in difficulty. Mainly, it appeared now, because they weren't actually married. Grace had only just found this out. 'Tell them from me,' Grace had yelled after the departing Andrew, 'that if it's broke, don't bloody mend it.'

Before he left for London, Andrew had told Grace that she had a very odd, narrow view of the world. There were other people to consider, did she not see that? Grace seemed to be concerned only with her own problems, whereas he took a broader view and she would just have to learn to respect that.

Angelica was down for the second weekend in a row, not saying much about the lost baby but being Grace's friend, silent or chatty, smiling or serious, whatever was needed, leaving her own baby with Tom's mother on the pretext that 'the old trout demands her pound of baby flesh and you know how carsick he gets'. Grace had not protested. Seeing her little godson, she thought she might either resent him or run away with him clasped to her bosom, and neither was a good idea.

'So what if you are selfish and possessive right now?' Angelica said. 'You've had a shitty time. You're allowed. But it's typical men; always there when you don't want them, never there when you need them. A problem once removed is so much easier to deal with than one that's right up close, one that is there, with you when you wake in the morning and when you go to sleep at night. People once-removed are so much more grateful and when you've finished being good to them you can leave them where you found them and go back home.

132

You, Grace, *are* home; you're not grateful and there's nowhere else to put you.'

Grace looked at Angelica and gave a little laugh without a trace of joy in it. 'You're saying everything I've tried not to think.'

Angelica leant across the table and took her hand. 'What are friends for?'

'I thought he was a safe harbour. Silly old me. Every sailor knows that when a storm brews you set sail for open waters.'

'How is work? We could do with something new at the gallery. Mother thought she'd found the Georgia O'Keeffe of photography but, as I told her, the point about someone like O'Keeffe is that she's unique.'

'I don't know, Angelica; for the first time I can remember, work just doesn't seem that relevant.'

'I've had moments like that; when I first met Tom, when I was pregnant and for the first months after Michael was born. Maybe it's a woman thing, it's as if a fog descends, of contentment or despair, hiding everything else from view. But the fog does clear, Grace, I assure you, and then you need your work.' Angelica gently stroked Grace's hand. 'I'm not saying that work will make up for what you've lost, but it is the one thing that will give you a fighting chance of getting your life back.'

Before Angelica left, Grace asked her to bring Michael down next time. 'I have to get used to it. It can't go on for ever, this hiding of offspring as if they were illegal substances.'

Yet friends continued to be wary. When Grace was around they changed their conversations about first words, breast versus bottle and the rising cost of magicians for other, child-free topics. They stopped weighing up the advantages of the village school over the private kindergarten – learning to mix with *everyone* – and the advantages of the private kindergarten over the village school – not *having* to mix with everyone. Instead they spoke of teething, of overflowing nappy buckets and the exorbitant cost of toddler shoes. They did not want to flaunt their riches so instead they dressed down their lives for her benefit. They meant well.

Andrew carried on, Grace complained to Robina, as if the main criterion for deserving his support was not to be his wife. Robina told Grace not to be too hard on him. 'You can't expect him to feel this the way you do,' she said. 'Men don't.' Grace was too weary to argue the toss on behalf of the entire species. 'I'd settle for pretend,' she said. 'But he whistles little ditties and avoids my eye. He's busy-busy. He's tired. He's *slippery*, Robina. He ducks and dives. Of all people, I thought he would be different.'

'Men don't feel the need to talk about things. He can't change what happened. He can't get your baby back so he feels useless and that's what makes him withdraw; it's not unusual.'

'I know, I know; men are from Mars and on Mars they *do* stuff and when they can't they go off whistling. But women know that talking is *not* the antichrist of doing. Talking to me about what happened, letting me talk to him, might bring *me* back, at least. And I'm beginning to fear that I won't get back on my own.'

'There'll be other babies,' Robina said. 'I promise.' Robina had a problem accepting that sometimes life did not behave according to her rules.

'I know you've talked to Mum,' Andrew said. 'And you're wrong if you think I'm not upset. But it happens. It happens a lot. Lucinda Baker had at least five of these early miscarriages before Chloe was born.'

When she told him how much she needed him he looked pained. When she got upset he said he had always thought of her as so strong and brave. He had a way of showing his disappointment that involved his whole body; his eyebrows rose above the question in his eyes, his shoulders hunched just enough for you to notice and his arms grew stiff, refusing to extend into a hug.

Mrs Shield came to stay. For two weeks Grace was fussed over and commiserated with. 'I understand,' Mrs Shield said. 'I lost a baby too, at six months.'

Grace had stared at her. 'You were pregnant? You never told me.'

'You were only little. I had not long married your father and I worried that you and Finn might feel even more insecure than you already did, poor little mites. I kept putting off telling you and neither of you noticed anything different.' She smiled and shook her head. 'You probably just thought I was getting fat. And after I lost it; well, there seemed no point in upsetting you.'

'Evie.' Grace put her hand out. 'Exactly how horrible was I?'

Mrs Shield laughed. 'Oh Grace, you weren't horrible. A little challenging, perhaps, but never horrible.'

'I hate it when you are different from how I decided you are,' Grace told her. 'It's too confusing when one's parents start being people in their own right.'

Mrs Shield burst into tears. It was the first time Grace had ever referred to her as her parent.

There seemed to be a tariff of grief allowed, made up according to weeks of gestation. Twelve weeks allowed you fourteen days or so of dignified sorrow and a further fourteen of 'not being quite yourself'. After that you were supposed to pull yourself together and get on with life. Another loss so soon after the first, and at sixteen weeks, allowed you to scream at your husband and his family in an uncontrolled manner and to burst into tears for no reason. ('Hormones still all over the place.') After a few days of that a longer period of withdrawal from activities, even family events, was allowed, if not encouraged. But grieve too hard and too long and they would start to whisper of hysteria and ghoulishness and lack of a sense of proportion and remind you of the value of knowing how lucky you are, really, to have a loving husband and family, friends eager to help, enough money and a nice home.

One day she overheard her father-in-law say to her husband, 'For God's sake, it was a *foetus*. My mother lost three between your Uncle Douglas and me. But in those days people were expected to get on with it.'

Andrew replied, 'I know, but the way she is right now I can't reason with her. If I try to suggest that she might be getting this a little out of proportion, she looks at me as if she wants to kill me.'

They stood talking in the hallway of Hillside House and Grace, next door in the sitting room with Kate, heard every word. Kate looked at her, her face turning pink then ashen. 'It's OK,' Grace said to her. 'It's OK.' Then she got up from her chair and left, brushing past the two men in the hall. She stomped through the wet streets in her thin-soled shoes, the wind sweeping the tears across her face. Back home she went straight upstairs to the bedroom, but before she got to the bed her legs gave way and she ended up doubled over on the floor crying until her face ached and her eyes were so puffy there was just a slit for her to look through.

She thought that the time it took a man to come after his wife, once she had fled in distress, was indicative of the state of the marriage. In the early days when love was both raw and tender he would follow hard on her heels, all concerned looks and anxious hands yearning to comfort and wanting to know what was wrong. Time passed stretching sympathy thin. This was when he would amble along a good half hour or so after the upset – concerned of course, but mostly hoping that a quick hug and a kiss and a soothing word or two would get things back to normal, fast. Then came the day when his eyes would follow his wife way ahead of the rest of him. 'What *now*?' he would ask himself. Finally, and unable to suppress his boredom, he would go off to get the whole business over with. 'What have I done now?' he would ask. And without waiting for an answer he would continue, 'Do you have to make such a big deal out of everything?' He would place his hand on her shoulder, gingerly, as if she had come hot from the oven. 'Calm down . . . Stop being hysterical. You're getting shrill again.'

When Andrew did return home, coming upstairs with steps so reluctant it sounded as if his soles were made of Velcro, the worst of it was that she had ceased to care if he came back at all. He stood looking down at her and asked why on earth she had run off and what she was doing sitting in a heap on the floor. Grace raised her head and looked at him for a moment before answering. 'The bed was too comfortable.'

'There, my point exactly; you revel in your moods.' Then his expression softened and he put his hand out wanting to help her to her feet. She had to stop herself from snatching at it with her teeth. Instead she hugged her knees tight, refusing to budge.

Andrew kneeled at her side, impatient and concerned both at once. 'What's the matter?'

'I heard what your father said.'

'Oh.'

'And I heard you agree with him.'

'Oh!' Andrew jumped up and started pacing the room. 'I was humouring him. He's an old man, he's of another generation. You can't expect him to see things your way.'

'No.' Grace got to her feet and picked up her dressing gown from the bed, searching the pockets for her cigarettes. 'No, I suppose not.' She lit, one, blowing a perfect smoke ring. 'My problem is that I thought there was this thing called *our* way. But there isn't, is there? And that's what frightens me.' Now she looked at him. Whatever it was he read in her eyes made him flinch and take a step back.

'I do love you,' she said, her voice matter of fact as she stubbed out the cigarette, grinding it into the ashtray, then lighting another. Andrew winced; he hated her smoking. 'At least I think I do. And I still quite like your parents. But I wonder about you all, more and more. I wonder what you see from your kindly perky Abbot eyes. I do know that whatever it is it's far away; it's not me or Kate or Leonora; it's not those of us up close. Perhaps I shouldn't blame you. Up close is not very comfortable, is it? I know your mother would rather I wasn't the sort of woman who keeps losing the grandchildren before they are even born. I know you wish I wasn't taking this so badly but that I would bounce back and stop being so tiresomely needy, so inconveniently and thoughtlessly sad. So go on, distance yourself elegantly, go off and be there for those once-removed. It's messy around me, I know.'

Andrew's complexion, ruddy and freckled from weekends spent outside, turned a deeper pink. 'I had no idea you felt like this. You're so . . . so bitter. I don't believe I know you any more, Grace. Really, I don't think I can take this for much longer . . .'

She looked at him, at the pained expression in his eyes, at his jaw muscles working, and she realised he did not concern her much any more. He was too removed to make an impression.

Another month passed. Could Grace please, Robina asked her one day, wear something other than black? She had invited Grace over for tea and a chat, pretending she needed help with choosing curtain materials but really just to get her to step outside the cottage.

'What do you want me to do? Say "Hey, I just recently lost another baby so why don't I go and shop for some fuchsia?"'

'Of course not, Grace,' Robina said in the voice she used when telling Rory that Rodney the pet rooster had gone to heaven. 'All I'm *trying* to say is that you're not the first woman to have suffered a miscarriage.'

'Three times, Robina.' Grace had not meant to say that. No one knew about the first one all those years ago. 'And by the way,' she added, her voice conversational, 'I take honey, not sugar, in my tea. I have done for the whole time that you've known me.'

Robina was staring, her mouth wide open enough to fit in a fist. 'What do you mean *three times?*'

'Nothing; it's nothing to do with you,' Grace said. 'I'd better go. I've got things to do.' As she walked past on her way to the back door, Robina grabbed her by the arm. 'Grace, please tell me, what's all this about three times?'

Grace looked into Robina's keen eyes and saw the concern. She felt bad suddenly. It could not be easy to have Grace as her daughter-in-law, Grace with her black moods and black clothes and lost babies. She opened her mouth about to speak, to say something, anything to show that she was sorry too and that she wanted to be friends. But Robina spoke first. 'You should have told me. You both should. I assume Andrew does know?' She still had her hand on Grace's arm.

'Not entirely,' Grace said.

'What *do* you mean, not entirely?'

'He knows about what concerns him.'

'Are you telling me that you've been pregnant before . . . before Andrew? Did you not tell him about this?'

'No. I didn't think it anyone's business but mine.'

'How can you say that? Andrew is your husband. We're your family. We love you.'

Grace thought for a moment before saying, 'No. No, I don't think you do. And I don't believe the fact that I have had other relationships would come as a complete surprise to Andrew. Then

138

again, in the happy-clappy warm and woolly world of the Abbot family maybe he did expect to marry a 29-year-old virgin.'

'I know you're upset, so I'll pretend you didn't say any of that.'

'Actually,' Grace looked at Robina steely-eyed, 'I really would rather you didn't. I'd really rather you listened to what I'm saying and remembered, just for once.'

But Grace stopped being angry with Andrew. Instead she looked at him like someone waking from a long sleep to find all that was left of the dream was an indefinable sense of loss. She tried to remember how it was that he had come to be her husband.

Louisa

GRACE SHIELD HAS BEEN up to see me again today. I enjoy her company. We tell each other things. 'I don't usually talk to people about things I care about,' she says with a smile that is embarrassed and pleased both at once. 'Maybe if you knew someone back when you were a child, you have that childish trust that they wish you well. Maybe when you've known someone when they were a child, you don't feel the need to dissemble because children use information as stories not weapons. Maybe that's it; us having known each other all those years ago.'

'Or maybe you need to speak to someone and you know that I will probably have forgotten what you said as soon as you've said it.' Grace looks up at me with such a shocked expression that I start to laugh. 'My mind works differently these days. I know that I sometimes make connections where none should be. I know I remember as if it were yesterday what happened half a century ago, while what happened yesterday is covered in mist. But it's quite normal, you know, when you're as old as I am.'

I tell her about Georgie. About how my son died. The seeds of the tragedy were sown long before it happened, by his father and by me. One of the reasons that he settled in Canada was for the wilderness. He would go off for days on end and reappear, so his wife told me, with a new calm that would last a few months before the old restlessness took over and he disappeared once more. Even with a young wife and a new baby, he still felt the need to withdraw, to walk far beyond any human contact. He was found floating face down in a quiet bay of the great lake. It was assumed that the ice had broken beneath his feet. I had

141

to find out every detail of his last long walk, every detail of his dying. No one understood my seemingly unquenchable thirst for information, anything to do with my son's disappearance into the vast winter whiteness. At first even I didn't quite understand but eventually I knew: while I was busying myself finding answers to the questions, I was busying myself with my son; and while I was busy with my son it was not yet over and he was not quite gone.

So I look at Grace Shield with compassion. She thinks I hold the answers to all her questions but soon enough she will realise, as I had to, that the one answer she needs she knows already: the one you loved is gone and will not return. But for now I let her have her head, although it isn't easy. I tell her as much as I can bear to, although I have to take it slowly. It hurts, having grown tough skin over the wounds of the past, to tear them open again.

And downstairs Noah grunts and frets about his book. When he came to see me last night he told me a quote he had come across. *Writing is easy; all you do is sit down at your desk and open a vein.*

Remembering is a bit like that.

'You mooch, child.' How does she do it, Lydia, my mother-in-law; how does she, tiny birdwoman, make me feel small when I tower over her? 'Can't stand mooching. It's high time you took over some of the running of the household. Responsibility, tradition, duty. Arthur needs everything to be just so or he won't achieve the calm he needs, the peace to do his work. It's our task to make sure he gets that peace. I won't be around for ever.'

You don't really believe that? I know you are quite incapable of imagining the world without you, of truly, in your heart of hearts, believing that there will be a time when there is no you. Women like Lydia Blackstaff are never truly gone. Their spirits live on in the anxious glance of a clumsy maid or the nervous laughter of a poor relation and in myriad rules designed to make life uncomfortable: no hot water in the mornings, jam with the bread for the children's tea only on Sundays, no log fires after the first day of the fourth month no matter what the fickle April weather turned up. That same mean spirit reigns in the fruit-cages in the garden where nettles stand guard around the raspberry canes so that you are lucky to get half a punnet of berries before your hands start burning from the stings. Oh no, Lydia Blackstaff would never truly be gone from Northbourne House.

I am told to take over doing the flowers for the main rooms. 'Find my trug and the secateurs, and you may take my gloves.' Here she glances down at my hands that I hold folded across my middle like a schoolchild, and adds, 'No, I think you had better ask Jenkins for a pair of his.'

I don't know many of the plants by name, other than the obvious ones like dahlias and asters, but I know what will look pleasing and find more than enough for every main room of the house and a couple of the bedrooms too. I gather plenty of foliage. I'm especially taken with the shrub whose small leaves glow in the sun like old Madeira. I arrange those branches with the golden-orange asters and the deep-yellow and pink dahlias and some late-flowering dusky pink roses in a blue jug for the drawing room. The colours of a slow sunset, I think to myself, as I stand back admiring my handiwork.

'No sense of colour.' Lydia leans on her son's arm and points an accusing finger at my arrangement. 'And that jug, it's a kitchen jug, child. Have you no idea?'

But soon I find myself useful even by my mother-in-law's standards; I am expecting.

The baby appears, a bruised fruit prised from its shell, and I look down into his unfathomable eyes and swear I will not let him down.

Arthur glances at his son before kissing me tenderly on the forehead, saying I have made him the happiest, the proudest man in all the world. He does not stay long. There is a smell of blood around still and Arthur has an uncommonly sensitive stomach. But for months afterwards the villagers talked about how Mr Blackstaff had come running from the big house with no coat and only his sheepskin slippers on his feet, shouting out the news and standing everyone a drink at the Dog and Hound.

When he next comes to my room, two days later, he presents me with a prettily carved cameo pin before going over and inspecting his sleeping son. 'Ugly little brutes, aren't they, babies?'

143

I barely glance at the brooch and ask him instead why he has not been in to see us both, his son and I, since the birth.

Arthur looks displeased. He was a man who expected more thanks for his efforts. 'Don't you like your pin? It's very fine.'

'Yes, Arthur, I like it very much.'

'I've been in my studio. This little fellow,' Arthur nods towards the infant in its crib, 'inspired me. I couldn't bear to leave the canvas even for a moment.' He bends down and pecks me on the cheek. 'I'll let you rest. I can see that you are still a little out of sorts.'

I watch him go and place the brooch back in its velvet-lined box. My son is awake now and looking at me with eyes the undecided colour of the newborn: a deep mysterious hue that is neither brown nor grey nor blue but a mix of all three and others too, like the water in the glass where Arthur rinsed his brushes. I smile at my son and then I cry from the sheer weight of all the love I feel.

Jane enters as quiet as a draught. She bends over the cot and coos, 'Your grandmama is most pleased with you, little man.'

'And is my son pleased with his grandmama?'

Jane perches at the foot of the bed. 'I know it's not my place to interfere . . .' she pauses but although I say nothing to contradict her she continues '. . . but I feel that as an old friend of Arthur's, and I hope a new friend to you . . .' I still say nothing. Jane's sallow cheeks colour but her pale eyes maintain their mild expression. 'Arthur is a great man, a great artist; we all know that. And he must not be upset or worried with the trivia of everyday concerns. Aunt Lydia has been wonderful; she knows him so well. And . . .' Jane puts her cool hand on my strong one, 'Of course you try as well. It's just that sometimes . . . maybe you don't quite see. This morning, just as an example, he has been so distracted by your bad humour that he has not touched his brushes. He cannot understand what it was he had done to vex you. And he's at a very delicate stage of his new painting. Of course you've only just delivered. Don't think I don't understand that it must be an emotional time for you too, but Arthur is not like other men. And we . . . well, it's up to us not to upset the careful equilibrium that makes him able to create. We have a duty, don't you think, to smooth his path and leave him free to take flight on the wings of creation?'

'Why should he need a smooth path if he has wings?' I ask.

Grace Shield listens and then she says, 'Men are precious, particularly artists; every little distraction puts them off their stride. Then, to be fair, I don't know how good my work would have been if I had had children. Not being able to, sent me mad for a while, but it forced me to walk down a different road than I would otherwise have done.' She pauses, smiles and shakes her head. 'Of course that way too ended in a bit of a disaster, but a different kind. It's the usual choice, isn't it? Turn left for a little bit of love and happiness, some pain and certain death, or go right for . . . well, what do you know . . . a little love and happiness, some pain and certain death. But what I'm saying is: to do the really good work you need to be single-minded. Women are supposed to be good at multi-tasking; and maybe that is the true enemy of promise.'

GRACE WAS PRETENDING to be asleep, her face buried in the pillow. Andrew pretended to believe her as he tiptoed from the bedroom and down the stairs. She heard the front door close followed by his footsteps on the gravel. It was seven o'clock on a Sunday but he was off to help his father with some fencing.

She could not tell what kind of morning it was. She had fitted black-out blinds to shut out the light. She slept badly these days. The merest noise or movement would be enough to wake her: a rattling windowpane, Andrew turning, a bird taking flight from the shrubbery. Wide awake and nothing to be awake for, she would lie rigid on her back staring into the gloom, too exhausted to get up and read or listen to the night-time radio, too fretful to go back to sleep, wondering at the way time slowed at night, the hours dragging along like beasts in chains.

Yet when morning came her bed ceased to be a prison and turned into a refuge that she was loath to leave. This morning, like every morning, she had to prompt herself just to get up. 'Sit up – one leg over the side of the bed . . . then the other. Now you rise. There you are: standing – upright! Ready to hit the shower?' She liked that expression, *hit the shower*; it sounded confident and dynamic. Washed and dressed, she walked across to the windows and opened the blinds. The sunshine steamrolled its way inside, flattening everything with glaring light. Outside the apple tree blossomed, the branches strong and fresh enough to hold a hanging body. Next door's roof was being tiled. A tractor with a clattering trailer rode across the field. The usual gang of ducks waddled towards the river, one leaping, two leaping, all of them leaping, quacking, flapping into the glittering snake of water. The day was happening all around her and she just wished it would stop so she could go back to bed. Another Sunday. Cunning days, Sundays; they took their time arriving for those who most yearned for them – those exhausted by work, commuters, mothers who longed for relief – but rushed towards those who dreaded them:

those whose colleagues were their family or those, like Grace, who found their family the hardest work of all.

There was a knock on the front door. Grace had locked the side-gate into the garden so that there was no way to the back door. Having an accessible back door implied an acceptance of informal visits and people letting themselves into your kitchen and shouting a cheery hello, so she had barred the way. But there was still the front door and behind it, she could see from the landing window, stood Jenny, the smile ready on her long face where all the features crowded into the bottom half, leaving a high forehead perpetually lined with concern. Even when she smiled, Jenny looked doleful, as if really she knew better. She was married but she and her husband had no children, and now she had passed forty it was generally assumed that there would be none. This, it seemed, qualified her as the perfect person for Grace to spend time with. Jenny did everything Robina Abbot expected of her, including making regular visits to cheer up Robina's difficult and, it had to be said, ungrateful daughter-in-law. Grace liked Jenny. She just did not want to see her, not today, not any day, not anyone. Truly, if it were an angel standing on her doorstep, Grace would have opened the door just a crack and said, in her tired, tired voice, 'Thank you, but not today.'

So she got down on to the floor, out of sight from the windows, and crawled back to her bedroom. There she threw herself on to the bed as exhausted as if she had lived a whole full day. Ten minutes later the phone rang. Grace put the pillow over her head.

The windows were closed, the curtains were drawn and the phone was disconnected. She lay curled up beneath the bed-clothes; no one could see her. She was not due at Hillside House until one.

At noon she dragged herself off the bed, and went downstairs. She would see to the household bills. Seated at her desk, she stared at the pile of unanswered letters, unpaid bills and unopened envelopes, before picking one at random. She read that unless she wanted her gas supply to be cut of she should have paid the bill last week. If she was able to make a case for genuine hardship she should call the number at the top of the letter – last week – and the gasboard would try to help. Was there genuine hardship? Did having to locate the chequebook and write the cheque, then find a stamp and go to the letterbox count as genuine hardship? Probably not. She paid that bill and the one for the phone too and wondered idly if these companies made a point of making their payee names as long as possible. Nothing snappy and quick to write like S.E.E. or S.G. or B.T. Oh no, for those boys the adage was always the longer the better: British Telecommunications Plc was Grace's particular bugbear. The pile of ready-to-go envelopes was growing and a kind of calm crept over her. Slit tear open write lick write and lick again. Slit tear open write lick write and lick again.

A woman had written to ask if she could reproduce one of Grace's photographs for a school magazine without paying. Sure. Go ahead. Feel free. Glad you like the picture. Write stamp lick: done. One foot in front of the other, do doing done, that's the way. You feel like shit, like death, or worse, alive, but if you just get the job done that was something, was it not?

She looked around for whatever else might need doing urgently enough to allow her to be late for lunch. Her gaze fell on the pot plant on the sill of the west-facing window; Jenny had said it was the perfect spot for it. She had given the plant to Grace when it was just a cutting and, although by now Grace had forgotten its name, she had grown fond of it. It was a valiant little plant surviving days of neglect, of drought and of great floods, of cold draughts and dry heat, and lately it had begun to flower. Grace felt touched. Shy-looking little white flowers with a soft honey scent had appeared from amongst the plump shiny leaves overnight the week before. But now something was wrong. She walked over to the window. The leaves had gone slack and lost their shine and the flowers had begun to drop off and lay scattered across the windowsill like tiny white stars. She poked her finger into the soil to see if it was dry. No, it was moist. She lifted it from its outer pot but there was no stagnant water rotting its roots. Why was it sick? Robina had given her several gardening books but amongst them not one dealt with houseplants. Robina thought houseplants common unless they were azaleas or hydrangeas. Until she met her mother-in-law, Grace had not realised that there were social categories for plants. Mrs Shield kept aspidistras.

'Don't die, little plant,' Grace said now, tears welling up. She wiped her eyes. This was ridiculous; she was not the crying kind and she most certainly was not the type to cry over a pot plant.

It was gone one already by the time she walked up the long rise to Hillside House, gazing through windows into the stage sets of other lives. It was a habit, that's all, looking, staring. There was some kind of plant in most rooms she could see; plants of every shape, size and social class. In the kitchen window of Meadow Cottage was a potted rose. The buds were tight and tinged with brown, doomed to drop, never to open up and flower. It made Grace sad again, all that early promise brought to nothing. Further on was a small 1930s house with a tumbledown lean-to with a glass roof. The lean-to was full of plants. In the corners were the sturdy taken-for-granted ones with sweaty leaves and blooms that just kept coming. Those plants grew in plastic containers whereas the highly strung orchid stood brightly lit centre-stage, its roots embedded in a fancy no-expense-spared Chinese pot. And Mrs Warner, in the house next door but two to the Abbots, had a plant in her kitchen window that spread further than it ought to, its leafy tentacles reaching far from its roots. It had a sly look about it as it crawled across the sill and up against the wall. Grace thought no one dared cut it back in case it took it badly and decided to die out of spite. It made her angry just looking at it. Had she had some shears, she would have gone in there and cut it back herself and damn the consequences.

Then the rain started. It was the kind that came suddenly from a darkening blue sky, surprising everyone including the sun that just kept on shining while the drops fell. It was a proper downpour and Grace, wearing only a sweater, sheltered beneath the spreading branches of an ash. A man walked by, an unremarkable-looking middle-aged man, and as he passed he lifted his head to the heavens and laughed. Grace wanted to throw something at him, or shout something vile; what business did the damn fool have laughing at the rain?

Something borrowed, nothing blue, something inherited, nothing new. When she first visited her in-laws' home she had liked the slightly scruffy but cosy look of old pine and polished wood, watery landscapes and dog baskets, of heavy pottery and woven

149

rugs. To Grace the mud on the carpets and the powdering of dust that covered the surfaces of occasional tables and the knick-knacks was a liberation after Mrs Shield's constant polishing and dusting and checking of the soles of shoes. Mrs Shield, after an earlier visit, had declared Grace's parents-in-law a health hazard and Robina an incompetent housekeeper. She had sworn that she had received nasty flea bites on her legs and, anyway, what was the point of those rugs in shades of beige that lay everywhere tripping a person up?

For her part, Robina had let it be understood that dear Evangeline was sadly lower-middle-class in her tastes and would do better to spend less time buffing and more being of help to others and her community. Mrs Shield, on the other hand, had confided to Grace that in her book charity began at home and that exposing one's family to damp doggy patches and unhygienic kitchen surfaces might seem charmingly bohemian and unworldly to some but to her it was plain sluttish.

Grace had at first sided with Robina, then taken Mrs Shield's point and asked if it might be possible to be a saint *and* do some occasional dusting.

Robina tried to set Grace a good example by always using a fork, not a spoon, when eating her pudding. Once Grace had set her a test, serving fruit compote one evening when her parents-in-law were visiting, and Robina had still used her fork. Grace had watched and marvelled and then she had decided that there were demons at work behind that calm exterior of Robina's. Then there was the problem of paper, the loo paper. It had to be white at Hillside House, as did the Kleenex tissues. Mrs Shield experimented, choosing honeysuckle one week and rose another, or bluebell, perhaps, and even apple green, and the tissues that she scattered around her like large petals from some tropical bloom were always multi-coloured. The other Sunday Robina had talked almost the entire lunch about the fact that there was only peach loo paper in the shop that day, no white at all. Grace had thought that Robina was not as strong as she had assumed. No, she felt, you had to go gently with a woman whose entire day could be ruined by the presence of coloured toilet tissue.

There was a bigger than usual gathering around the table that Sunday. Leonora was staying, and Rory, although right now Leonora was upstairs having a rest. Neil and Janet were there, of course, and Leonard Brown the school chaplain and the headmistress Glenda Shawcross and finally Debbie, Stuart's replacement. Debbie was profoundly deaf and, Kate whispered to Grace, 'Unlike Stuart, profoundly grateful. She worships Mum.'

Grace sighed. 'So many people do. I come across them all the time. They stop me in the street and say, "Isn't she wonderful!" and "The world would be a better place if there were more people like her."'

'No one ever says that about me,' Kate said with grim satisfaction.

'Me neither,' Grace said. They exchanged a smile.

'Are you going to try for another baby?'

'No.'

'Why not?'

'Because I've lost enough of them.'

'And because you don't love Andrew any more.'

Grace stared at Kate. 'Why do you say that?'

'Because it's true. Don't deny it, don't smooth it over and pass by, don't you dare get like *them*.'

'But, darling Kate, it's not true. I admit we're going though a difficult period right now, but that's to be expected.'

'Why?'

Grace paused before answering. 'Because all relationships do. I'm sure that, happy as they are, your parents' marriage has had its rocky periods.'

Kate shrugged. 'Not really. They don't spend enough time together for that.'

'But they're always together.'

'They're in the same place at the same time. But you tell me, when did they last look at each other for long enough to have a row?'

Grace looked at the cross girl before her, the funny angry girl with her frizzy ginger hair and small bright eyes. Or at you, she thought. Or Leonora or Andrew.

'Mum is like some priest, so busy doing greater good that she can't be held back by the narrow constraints of family. I can't complain. How could I? My mother is a saint, my father is a character and I'm lovely and clever and a natural leader with friends beating down my door to spend time with me.' Kate looked like she was going to cry. Grace touched her hand under the table. 'You don't know what to say, do you?' Kate said. 'But you're all right. You're not stuck with us.'

Grace looked startled. 'Yes, I am.'

'Only if you want to be.'

Robina, her hair piled high and decorated with at least five pins and clips, was handing round plates of pheasant and burnt chipolatas. Pink-cheeked and smiling, she looked younger than her sixty-one years. As she always said, there was nothing she liked more than having a large group of friends and family gathered round her table.

'Don't like,' Rory said, waving his spoon and fork in the air.

'You do,' Robina said. 'It's like chicken. Tweet-tweet bird; your favourite.'

'Tweet-tweet bird?' said Rory, his eyes widening.

'That's right, darling,' Robina cooed and she pointed to the sliver of meat on Rory's bunnikins plate. Rory looked at the meat and then up at his grandmother. His eyes were round with alarm. 'Tweet-tweet bird,' he shrieked, waving his little arms as if he was warding off a swarm of bees. 'Tweet-tweet.' Kate did her best to comfort him, whispering in his ear and stroking his sweaty blond locks. Robina told him briskly that tweet-tweet birdies liked nothing better than becoming food for hungry little boys. Rory, quite rightly, did not seem convinced.

'Cheer up, old chap,' Andrew said from across the table.

'Ghastly racket,' Timothy complained. 'I always say there's no dealing with children until they can recite Greek verse.'

Kate gave Rory a hug with one hand while she lifted a fork with a small piece of meat to his wet pink lips. Rory in his agitation smacked Kate's wrist away so that the fork flipped from her hand and down on to the tablecloth which was white and embroidered and took hours to iron.

Glenda Shawcross looked aghast. Grace thought that maybe Rory was the only non-girl and the only child below the age of eleven that she had ever seen close-up. Rory was banging his spoon wildly on the table, leaving gravy smears all over the cloth.

Andrew's face had turned bright red when suddenly he leapt to his feet and strode across to where Rory sat in his all-natural-materials highchair, his baby mouth forming a perfect O of horror at what he had done. Andrew grabbed the boy by the arm and lifted him up in the air as if he weighed no more than a kitten. Before anyone knew it Rory had had his bottom smacked and found himself on the wrong side of a closed kitchen door. They could hear him howl. Grace looked at her husband and thought that maybe the babies, his and hers, had guessed what was in store and decided it was wisest to stay away.

Apart from Kate, who was telling her brother that he was a maniac, and Debbie, who was staring at Andrew with a look on her young face as if it was she who had been hit, everyone else carried on as if nothing had happened. Andrew had returned to the table red-faced and out of breath, smoothing out his white linen napkin and asking his father to pass the salt. Glenda Shawcross said something about the value of a firm hand early on and Timothy asked Neil if he had come across this absolutely fascinating little brainteaser; he had the diagram right there.

The wailing of the little boy turned into sobs. Grace looked around her at them, but apart from Kate, who slouched sullen in her seat, they were just eating and chatting. The sobs became hysterical. Grace put her napkin on the table, placed her knife and fork neatly together like a pair of ladylike legs on her plate, and got to her feet. She returned a few moments later with Rory clasped to her neck, as he slowly ran out of sobs. He stayed that way, clamped to Grace, while she ate the rest of the meal.

'I don't think it was your place to interfere,' Andrew said as they left the table. Grace was still holding Rory but now the child eased his grip round her neck, pulling away enough to turn his head. The look in his big damp baby eyes as he stared at his uncle made Grace feel sick. Well done, Andrew, she thought. Well done, you complete, you utter bastard, because now this two year old knows how to hate.

'What are you looking at me like that for . . . darling?' Andrew added the last word to lessen the impact of what looked perilously like a public argument. 'Someone has to discipline that boy.'

'I think it's *his* looks you should worry about,' Grace said.

'And how is the collection going?' Robina asked Glenda. She turned to Grace to explain. 'Glenda and I have initiated what we provisionally call the Right to Play. It's just a little idea I had. We are collecting unwanted toys and redistributing them to those poor little mites who have nothing. So many children are completely over-indulged with toys these days when everyone knows that a saucepan and a wooden spoon is just as much fun . . .'

'I know I'd prefer a Fisher-Price cookery set with inbuilt fried eggs and beans any day,' Grace said.

'You're not a child,' Robina said. 'Anyway, my little idea, which Glenda has been kind enough to agree to sponsor through the school, is to have pupils bring in what they themselves see as surplus toys and books and for us to send them to children who truly need them.'

No one could argue with that, not even Grace, but she did her best. 'Give them an old saucepan and a wooden spoon,' she said.

Robina ignored her and Andrew shot her a furious glance, twitching his head towards Glenda Shawcross in a meaningful fashion.

'I have a whole box of old Barbie stuff,' Kate said.

'Good for you.' Robina beamed at her daughter. 'I never approved of you having the dreadful things in the first place, but you made such a fuss I gave in and children do seem to love them.'

Coffee was served in the sitting room in front of the fireplace. There was a fire lit in spite of the mild weather. It was one of Robina's little sayings: *The family's heart is by the hearth.* Grace said she would make herself a cup of tea. She carried Rory back into the kitchen with her, his little legs circling her hip, his damp hot face buried in her shoulder. She stood by the kettle, waiting for it to boil, humming to the baby, rocking gently from foot to foot. Now and then there was a small snuffling sound from Rory and then, as he grew heavier, she realised he had fallen asleep. She freed his legs and cradled him in her arms, gazing down at his face, so calm, so innocent and peaceful, as if nothing bad had happened. Suddenly there was a clattering of heels on the stairs and Leonora burst into the kitchen. She looked right at Grace and her sleeping son but did not stop. Instead she made for the sitting room. Grace, still with Rory in her arms, followed.

'Look at me,' Leonora yelled. 'She told me, no she suggested, that I stay away.' She pointed at Robina. 'We don't want anyone to get a look right up close, do we?'

Rory started to cry again, wanting his mother, but Grace whispered in his ear and held on to him.

'I think you should see, get a good look.' She turned and they all saw how her cheek was bruised and swollen, the black eye and the cut lip. Robina got to her feet, as did Andrew, but they kept their distance. Leonora put her arms out for Rory and Grace handed him to her. Looking round her, Leonora said, in a quiet voice now she was holding Rory, 'I told you he was a bastard, the Honourable bloody Archie Watchfield. I told you, but you didn't listen. Too busy, were you, Mum, being all things to all bloody men and women and fuck-all use to us.'

Timothy had been busy showing Glenda Shawcross his recently acquired edition of A.A. Milne's *When We Were Six* in Latin, now he dropped the book. To Grace it seemed to take ages to fall, like a leaf on a slow wind rather than a whole book. He too stood up and made to go to his daughter but Robina got there first, taking Leonora by the arm and ushering her and Rory out of the room. It was like a magician's trick, Grace thought, it happened so fast. Now you see them, now you don't; amazing! She stared at the door. There was silence.

Then Glenda Shawcross asked, 'Did her husband do that to her?'

'Actually, they're not married,' Andrew said.

Grace lay awake, too tired to sleep. She listened to the ticking of the clock. She could have sworn that ticking got louder as the hours passed. She wanted the night to be over but she dreaded the morning.

Much later she heard the front door open and close and Andrew's steps on the stairs. She turned on to her stomach and buried her face in the pillow, pretending to be fast asleep. He tiptoed into the room pretending to believe her, undressing in the dark, edging into the bed, keeping to his side.

On the third Monday of June Grace woke up and did not wish herself dead. Instead of struggling to keep the curtain of night shut against the break of dawn she opened it wide and said, 'Good morning, all.' At breakfast she ate her toast and had some more. Later, on her way to get the papers, a stranger smiled at her and she smiled back. She had thought of herself as a felled tree, drying up inside the rough bark, then, when she had all but given up, a small green shoot burst forth and reached towards the sunshine. Surprise!

She studied the work she had been doing in the past year and tried to figure out why the photographs were dead. She spoke to Andrew about it not because she thought he would care but because he was there. 'Look,' she pointed at the pictures in the album from her summer in New Hampshire, 'I took those, way back. I knew nothing about photography and yet those shots have more life to them than anything I've been doing lately.'

'Who's the bloke?' Andrew pointed at Jefferson McGraw.

'Oh, just an old boyfriend.'

Andrew took the album from her and leafed through the pages, pausing now and then to study a particular photograph. 'You never looked at me that way,' he said, closing it and chucking it down on the table.

'What's that supposed to mean?'

Andrew looked at her, his eyes opaque. 'I'm just saying that, if you had, maybe we wouldn't have the problems we have now.'

'I won't even dignify that with a response,' Grace said. Because I have none, she thought. 'Anyway, I was talking about my work.'

'You usually are.'

'And you don't talk about yours?'

'I'm not obsessed.'

'You knew what photography meant to me when we met. How important my work was to me. You didn't mind then. I cut the work down; I did all the wifely stuff. And see what that got me? No, be true to yourself. It's high time I was.'

Andrew sat down. He looked at his hands and then he looked at her and her anger evaporated. That small sad smile of his, that little-boy-lost look, never failed to touch her, to make her want to go up to him and make everything better. But she stayed where she was as he said, 'I didn't mind because I expected you to change and to love me more than any work. But it was the babies we didn't have you really loved.'

'That's not true.'

'Isn't it?'

'You're a grown man; you should understand about other loves and not see them as competition.'

'Maybe I should.' He shrugged.

Grace placed an ad in the local paper offering her services as a portrait photographer and she spoke to the editor asking him to consider her for work. Within three weeks she had photographed two brides-to-be, one actual bride and four small children, two of them twins. Then the editor called up to say that the nearby zoo at Crichton Manor was threatened with closure and a group of local councillors and animal-welfare people were meeting on site. Would she cover it? The staff photographer had gastroenteritis. A colleague of Andrew's was coming for supper with his wife that evening. Grace looked at the shopping list – four red peppers, anchovies, garlic, four duck breasts, strawberries, cream, ice-cream – then she went to the phone and called the school leaving a message for Andrew. *Got a job on. Please get Chicken Kiev from M&S plus two cheeses.*

'Be sure to get the lions,' the editor had said.

The zoo was not threatened with closure because of any lack of care for the animals but because accidents kept befalling its staff. Two years earlier, one had been kicked to death by an ostrich and only the other day a black bear known to be friendly and loving had gone for its keeper who only just escaped serious injury. The keeper, Ben Hawkins, was there today pleading the case for the zoo to be kept open. The animals were not only happy and well cared for, but practically tame as well. To demonstrate he asked the visitors to accompany him and the owner, Lord Crichton, to meet Sonia the black bear for themselves. The group stayed at a distance while Ben Hawkins went inside Sonia's enclosure. Grace moved up to get a shot of the chairman of the council and the other visitors. She was backing up towards the enclosure, the camera to her eye. It looked to be a great shot. Whatever was going on in that enclosure it kept the visitors riveted. They stared, they mouthed, what *were* they mouthing? She pressed the shutter and let out a cry of pain.

Sonia's daughter had been curious. Grace should have moved face first, not backing in the way she did. Yes, a bear's claws were vicious but the bear was not. Maybe the enclosure should have been shut? Why? The bears weren't going anywhere, not while Ben was with them. The photographer should not have walked inside, backwards or otherwise. She didn't mean to. An ambulance? Not necessary, Grace said, just something to stop the bleeding until she got to the hospital. One of the animal-welfare people drove her.

Grace phoned the school from casualty and left a message for Andrew. *Might have to start dinner without me.*

'It's been one of those bad bear days,' Grace apologised as she joined Andrew and their guests for cheese.

In the kitchen Andrew hissed, '*Everyone* serves Marks and Sparks Chicken Kiev.'

Later, working in her darkroom, seeing her pictures emerge, she felt as if she had fought her way out from under a sticky grey membrane into the light once more. She smiled to herself and thought, I might be a hopeless bastard most of the time, but I do take exceedingly good pictures.

'They need all the help we can give.' Grace, moving the telephone receiver a fraction further from her left ear, asked Robina who *they* were. 'You mean Leonora and that sod Archie?'

'The *children*, Grace. The Right to Play. I told you all about it the other day.'

'Oh yes, you did.'

There was a pause. 'Well, the girls at Lady Katherine Ellen are being marvellous,' Robina said finally. 'Now, what I need you for is the grand auction.'

'How *is* Leonora? Have you reported him to the police yet?'

'Police? No, no, of course I haven't. I had a long talk with them both and he's agreed to go to counselling. And Leonora isn't entirely without blame. I've always said to her, "Love is an act of will. You work and then you work some more." I'm convinced this was a one-off. He's a good man, Archie.'

'If you say so.' Grace had met him three times and on each occasion she had had to ask Andrew who he was. It was those quiet sandy little men you had to watch. 'Although if someone had beaten up a daughter of mine, I might think that person not at all a good man.'

'You do see things in black and white, Grace. And there is Rory to think of. He needs his father. Archie has asked her to marry him. As you know, I've never been happy about this living together and not being married. Not because I'm old-fashioned – you know I'm the last person to worry about things like that – but because I think it signifies a deeper lack of commitment. Sir Dennis and Lady Barbara called me up and said how thrilled they were that our children were finally taking the plunge. You've never met Archie's parents, have you? Charming people.'

'He beats the shit out of your daughter and you're planning their wedding . . . have you gone mad?'

'Hardly "beating the shit" as you put it, Grace. They both lost their tempers. Anyway, our auction. I want you to do something.'

Grace gave up trying to understand her mother-in-law, asking in a tired voice, 'What?'

'A photograph; something really special for the auction. It was Andrew's idea. He's so proud of you, Grace, if only you knew.'

Andrew came in through the door just then and Grace turned, receiver in hand, frowning at him, pointing at the phone. 'It really was good of Andrew to offer my services but I'm doing a project of my own right now. I've been invited to exhibit at the McLeod Gallery and I don't have much time.'

There was another pause before Robina asked, 'What do you mean, you might not have time?'

Let's see, Grace thought, what could I have meant? She said, 'I might not have time.'

'Please don't make difficulties, Grace,' Andrew said.

'I'm sorry, but as I explained I've got an important project on right now.'

'I didn't know about any project,' Andrew said. He sounded aggrieved.

'I told you about it,' Grace said, turning away from the receiver. 'Then it's not that you're particularly interested, is it? You just hate to think you have been kept in the dark.'

'You mean you won't *help*?' Robina wailed at the other end. Grace, it seemed, still had not learnt the rules. Smack small defence-less child and throw him out of the room: A OK. Refuse to do 'one's bit': descend to hell without passing Go. Grace was feeling strangely light-hearted. How bad becomes me, she thought. How neatly nasty fits.

'But we counted on you.'

'Maybe you shouldn't have,' Grace said evenly. 'Maybe just occasionally you should ask before you start counting. And, if you don't mind me saying so, I think you should pay more attention to your children and less to mankind. Mankind, on the whole, can manage without you. Your family should not have to.'

The conversation ended.

'It's as if I never even knew you,' Andrew said.

Grace looked at him. '*Now* you notice. Of course you never knew me. You weren't interested in knowing me. You had decided what you wanted me to be and then you looked no further, or rather you just kept on looking past me at all the relative strangers you could dedicate yourself to, be a friend to, be good old Andrew to.'

'And you knew me? If you did, how come you're so disap-pointed? No, you're as guilty as I am of projecting your favourite images on to a willing surface.'

Grace turned round. 'You know, you're absolutely right, I am.'

'Well, at least we know where we stand,' Andrew said. 'So what is your precious project about, anyway? And can't you combine it with doing something for the auction?'

'It's up to you. It's about plastic surgery. Silicone and fake bone matter and some kind of fabric surgeons use for enhancing lips which

160

actually is the same stuff used in ski suits. As far as I know, most of these materials aren't biodegradable; well, not as rottable as flesh anyway. And I had this vision of rows of decomposing bodies, all with perfect pert breasts and luscious kissable lips and cheekbones to die for, and I thought it would be a great idea for a series of pictures.'

'So now you're going to rob graves,' Andrew said.

Grace, mock-patient, assured him, 'I won't use real dead bodies, promise. I'll go to my friend Rob. You remember Rob? Does props for films. He's very successful. He'll have bodies and in all stages of decomposition too. I'm not aiming at an exact replication of what actually happens to a body in that situation, but to make people pause and think about the absurdity of what we are doing to ourselves.'

'It's obscene,' Andrew said.

'And, Andrew, that's exactly what I'm saying. All this surgery *is* obscene.'

'That's not how I meant it,' he said. 'As you well know.'

Andrew ate his supper of sausages and mash. In the early days Grace had refused to cook such food as it was so obviously bad for him, but lately she served up whatever he wanted. For a while she had even stopped putting out his vitamin supplements. It used to be a little game between them, she portioning them out for him every morning saying it was important he take them and him protesting that it was all faddist nonsense but taking them anyway; for her sake. Then the day had come when she left them in the cupboard. It was not planned. It just happened that as she was groping round for his multivitamins and his fish-oil capsules her hand came out empty and clenched in rage.

But when, on the third day, he looked at her with hurt eyes and said in a little-boy's voice, 'Where are my vitamins? I thought you said I had to take them,' she had felt bad and had put them out again although she could not, in all honesty, say that her heart was in it.

Grace was arranging her books. She had got to her collection of biographies; row upon row of teachers and role models, line upon line of inspiration and accumulated wisdom. She sank down on to the chair by the desk, a Diane Arbus biography in her hand. How long since she had read any of these books? Had she been frightened of what they would tell her, these lives lived truthfully and in the light of conviction? She had been lost; lately her life had been a half life lived by less than a person. Less-than-Grace had stalked the streets and the meandering lanes. Less-than-Grace had bargained with the truth and negotiated with her feelings. Less-than-Grace had been miserable and pretty damn useless.

The phone rang. It was Angelica. 'I was just thinking about you,' Grace said. 'I need more work.'

'You've lost a lot of contacts. You need to get out there, network. What are you doing right now?'

'I'm arranging my books.'

'Now, that's useful. Beats taking photographs for getting back to work.'

'I'm thinking about whether I should give my marriage another chance.'

'Really!' said Angelica, who had just got divorced and wanted all her friends to be divorced too.

'Oh, Angelica, I don't know. It must be one of the most common delusions of our times; that we can make marriage work. But when the sum of two people makes less than one . . . Then again, Robina was banging on about love being an act of will. Maybe she's right. Maybe if you will yourself to act lovingly the feelings will follow. In fact, I think that's how Mrs Shield came to care about me and Finn.' Mrs Shield was a good woman and when she married Gabriel Shield, she knew that it was her duty to love her little stepchildren, however hard that might be. And she knew it could not be done if you brought the mixed emotions of an adult, of a second wife, to the party. 'She just went ahead and acted the good mother,' Grace said. 'Whatever her actual feelings. She picked me up when I fell over and gave me a hug when I was sad. She took up the hems of my school tunics when short skirts became the fashion, and let them down again when I seemed to have grown an inch overnight. She practised cricket in the garden with Finn and she took us off for our inoculations and cheered us on at sports day. One Christmas she queued all day outside Selfridges to buy us each a Beatles doll, and she did get two although by the time she got to the front of the queue there were only Ringos left. At some time during all that

162

acting the part, she actually came to love us. So maybe I should give it a go; act loving and happy with Andrew and then I might wake up one morning and feel it too.'

'Bullshit. You either love the man or you don't. There is a bit in the middle where you deceive yourself and everyone else, but that's all it is: deception.'

'You're bitter.'

'I was married for longer, that's all.'

'I just think it would be good if we could get it to work again.'

'Why?'

There was a pause. 'Ah, well there you've got me.'

Angelica was phoning from her small office at the gallery. She was busier than ever these days, acting as an agent for several of her past and present exhibitors, Grace included. At the beginning Grace had said, 'What about the rule that says don't mix friendship with business?'

And Angelica had replied, 'If I had to choose I'd rather have you as a client.'

'Thank you. And I mean that,' Grace had said.

But now on the phone, Angelica complained, 'Not that there's been much business from you lately.'

'That's changing,' Grace said. 'It's like all the best romances; through all the turmoil of the past years work has been there, steady, faithful, patiently waiting by my shoulder for when I would be ready. Finally I turned round and saw it for what it is; the love of my life.'

'So why are you arranging books?' Angelica said. 'Why aren't you out there working?'

'I can do both in a day,' Grace said. 'And I need to get some order: in my head, in my house.'

'I've got clients who do more work in a week than you do in a year.'

'Good work? As good as mine?'

'Some of it is better. You've lost your edge, Grace. Your energies have been sucked in other directions.'

'I suppose marriage and fitting into a new family and a couple of miscarriages can do that to a person.'

'Do you talk, you and Andrew? Does he know how you feel or is he

163

walking around convinced that he's really happily married; they can do that, you know. If only Tom and I could have talked we might still be together. That and if he hadn't been a complete arsehole.'

'We talk,' Grace said.

'Andrew, are you busy?'

'I'm going over some papers for work. What is it?'

Grace stood in the doorway of her husband's study. 'It's about the new project.'

'What about it?'

'I don't like talking to you while you're reading.'

Andrew put the pile of paper covered in columns of figures down on his desk.

'You know Angelica's acting as my agent.'

'No.'

'I told you. Anyway, this work I'm doing for the council . . .'

'What work?'

'I told you about it. I also told you I didn't think you were listening.'

'If you got on with it, I would listen.'

'I'm trying to, but you're either reading or you interrupt.'

'Do you want to talk to me or not?'

'Just forget it, Andrew.'

'Grace . . .'

'Yes.'

'Where are you?'

'In the darkroom.'

'Are you planning ever to come out of there? Only asking.'

'What did you want?'

'Have I got any clean socks?'

'I don't know. Look in your drawer.'

'Andrew . . .'

'Yes . . .'

'Do you ever think about the nature of light?'

'Why do you ask such bloody stupid questions? Can't you see I'm busy?'

164

'Grace . . .'

'Yes . . .'

'You never take the initiative any longer.'

'I don't feel like it.'

'I knew it. I just knew it. So what's wrong? I mean, there's obviously something wrong.'

'Of course there's something wrong.' Grace sat up in bed and turned the light on. 'How can you even ask if there's anything wrong?'

'So something *is* wrong.'

'What's wrong is that I feel too angry and frustrated and mean-spirited to have an orgasm. I can lie back and let you get on with it, but that's about as far as it goes.'

'You really are a disagreeable woman. And coarse.'

'Now I *really* feel in the mood.'

'Bitch.'

'Don't ever talk to me like that.'

'Oh, just belt up.'

'Andrew . . .'

'What?'

'Stop bullying Rory.'

'The boy needs a firm hand. It's ridiculous the way Leonora spoils him.'

'I dread to think what kind of father you'd make.'

'Luckily, we're not likely to find out now, are we?'

'Luckily?' A smarter man than Andrew, or, Grace thought, one who gave a damn, might have taken heed of her tone of voice and stopped there.

'Anyway, who are you to talk? What kind of mother would you be?' Andrew's open boyish face had turned pinched and mean-looking. 'I've seen sides of you that make me think it wasn't such a bad thing after all, you losing those babies, not if they were going to take after you.'

His fist in her face would have hurt less.

Robina was thrilled when Grace asked if she could take some

shots of the family and Hillside House for her contribution to the auction. 'I haven't quite worked out how I'm going to do it, but I'm thinking of something along the lines of a series of family life shots, 1950s-style possibly.'

'Of course you can. Any time. Just let me know. I want to make sure my flowers are at their best. Though I say it myself, not many homes could sport such an abundance of home-grown flowers at this time of year. And as I always say, flowers make a home.'

'Oh, that was *you*, was it?'

Grace Shield's contribution to the auction at Lady Katherine Ellen School for the Right to Play consisted of a photographic collage, mostly in black and white but for the rainbow. There was Andrew, straight and handsome, a captain at the helm of his good ship, his eyes fixed on the horizon as Grace swam helpless before the bow. He was there too, staring, a puzzled look on his face, at the broken bits of Grace that had toppled from a marble pillar in Robina's conservatory. Timothy sat serene in his favourite armchair by the fireplace, *The Times* crossword on his knee, while the flames spread from the hearth to the curtains and his house burnt down around him. Kate walked through the fields in a white veil that covered her from head to foot (Kate had been a willing participant but no one ever knew). Finally there was Robina, a light round her magpie's-nest hair, stepping across the river towards the rainbow on the horizon, the heads of them all – Timothy, Andrew, Leonora, Rory, Kate and Grace – neatly laid out as stepping-stones.

Andrew said, 'This is the end.'

'Good,' said Grace, although her last night in the cottage in the small Devon town she cried most of the night and then some more when she collected the mail before leaving and saw the letters still addressing a lost partnership. Andrew and Grace Abbot. Mr and Mrs Andrew Abbot. Mrs Andrew Abbot.

As Angelica had said when she saw the collage, 'Good, you're getting your edge back.'

In spite of this, Grace's contribution did not sell at the Lady Katherine Ellen School auction.

Louisa

IT WAS ELLIOT HUMMEL who made Georgie the carved wooden horse. He drove all the way from London with it strapped to the roof of his motor car, thereby earning my eternal friendship. I am a good friend. So is Arthur; it's just that sometimes he forgets people. When Elliot falls on hard times and has to sell the car, making it difficult for him to visit, Arthur is sorry but what can he do? 'People have to live their own lives.' He says that a lot: people have to live their own lives. Of course they do, we all do, but you can dip into each other's now and then, can you not? 'People don't like charity,' he says. 'You really don't understand, do you? You have no idea how the artistic mind works. With you it's all the material – a new toy for Georgie, next week's menu, logs for the fire, the latest creation by Madame Schiaparelli; you can't help it. Some of us, people like Elliot, live for the spirit. He doesn't want your hampers.'

'Madame Schiaparelli *is* an artist!' I tell him. 'And I don't recall Elliot returning my hampers.' But later, alone in my bedroom, I stand for a long time in front of the glass. What had Arthur seen in this thin face with its long nose and sharp cheekbones? I have a good complexion, if you do not mind its pallor, and fine eyes, but I don't smile nearly enough and my hands and feet are large and bony; there is little that is graceful about the way I move. Gentlemen like softness; round cheeks and rounded shoulders and arms, soft little hands. I was clever when it came to studies, but that was not the kind of cleverness admired in a woman. So what had he seen in me that was enough to make him love and marry me, he who had women offering themselves like merchandise on a market

167

stall? At the time he came into my life I had been content. I had my friends, other young women like myself with little money and few admirers, happy to spend time on our studies and the occasional afternoon out by the river. I had no expectations to be loved. You don't when your parents leapt to their death, hand in hand from a high-backed bridge, with no thought for the child they left behind. But suddenly, there he was, this man made out of sunshine, an artist, a genius some say, who made me laugh and believe in him both at once. He wanted *me*. When he asked me to marry him I stopped breathing for a moment and in that moment the world stopped with me. I felt it: a collective holding of breath at the miracle of someone like me getting her heart's desire. 'Yes,' I said, 'oh yes.'

When we stood side by side in front of the altar in the small church, I thanked God for his goodness and assured him that I would not ask for more because at the age of twenty-one I had already had as much happiness as a woman could ask for in a lifetime.

But of course I became greedy. Maybe if you live in the shadows for long enough you manage to get by out of the sun, but once you have basked in its warmth you can no longer thrive without it, and there is never enough. But the more I crave his warmth, the less he gives. I ask myself over and over again what it was that he had loved and what had changed. Now I am more likely to draw a frown than a smile from his face and his caresses are portioned out as meanly as if he were the warden of an almshouse and I a beggar. But I cannot blame him. The more I aim to please him, the more I seem to drive him from me. He is an artist and I understand little of that world. When he finally allows me a glimpse of his work in progress I offer an opinion. 'Whisper, dear,' I say, pointing at a stroke of carmine. 'Whisper, don't shout.' Arthur, my beautiful husband, turns oh so slowly and looks at me as if I were the smallest creature imaginable. 'Thank you, my dear, for that priceless piece of advice.' When speaking the word *priceless* the corners of his mouth turn upwards as if in a smile but his eyes are stones. 'Coming as it does from such an acknowledged authority on the subject of fine art.'

I do not interfere again. I spend my energies on our child, and on our home. My husband and I are like two pebbles washed up next to each other then edged apart, little by little, by the shifting sands.

I go downstairs to do the flowers and see that Jane has been there before me. She means to help, although I have told her many times that I enjoy this particular task. But you have to be careful because almost anything will make her tearful. What was I to do but give in? Jane is small but she forces her flowers and foliage into postures that nature never intended. Every time I pass one of her arrangements I feel for those tortured blooms and long to free them, but any interference might bring forth those tears. Jane calls herself insignificant but I have learnt that upsetting her causes a murmur of discontent that echoes through the household for days. Today, however, I cannot help myself but lift the stems from the vase and shake them loose before returning them, dripping but unrestrained, to the water.

Arthur finds me in the nursery, astride the dapple-grey rocking horse with the flowing silver mane. Georgie sits on my lap. The horse's name is Dobbin. 'Have neither of you even the slightest imagination?' Arthur had exclaimed when told.

Georgie and I go for a ride every morning and we have just returned breathless from that day's journey. Arthur holds his arms out to our son but not long enough for Georgie to scramble down and enter the embrace. My husband is wearing a velvet jacket in burgundy and a bright yellow cravat and his mood is extravagant as he bends down and kisses me on the lips before ruffling his son's blond locks and calling him 'a fine little fellow'. I shoot a glance towards the door, half expecting some visitor to be accompanying Arthur. His good moods mostly coincided with the presence of guests. He is a good host, making every guest feel as if the event was arranged just for his or her benefit. And how well he always speaks of me and our little son. Were it not for those happy boasts in front of strangers, I might never realise how highly he prized us.

But there is no one else in the room; even Nanny is elsewhere, talking to Cook about Georgie's lunch. 'Your work must be going well.' I smile up at him. 'It makes me so happy to see you in such good humour.'

That causes a frown. 'Don't watch me like this, Louisa. It makes a chap nervous, always being watched and clucked over, his every mood and manner examined. Suffice yourself with the boy while he's too young to defend himself.'

I look away, out of the window, trying not to cry. There was no reason to; Arthur was just teasing.

'I'm here to talk about little Jane. She is upset, you know.'

Slowly I turn and look at him, resting my chin lightly on my son's fair head. 'Why is Jane upset?' I make it sound like a quiz. 'Jane, Jane, Jane?' Georgie claps his chubby hands. 'Jane is a little busy mouse scuttling around on her busy way.' At this Georgie squirms out from my embrace and down on the floor and makes to scuttle back and forth just like a mouse, his hands like whiskers beneath his tiny nose. These days there is nothing bruised about him; his eyes are shaped like mine, but the colour is all his own: a clear amber, an unusual shade of light bright golden-brown that I had last seen on a piece of the stone itself in the window of a jeweller's in London. And he has grown sturdy, my boy, with strong legs and chubby little arms – 'like strings of sausage,' I said to Arthur the other day.

'Where is the poetry?' Arthur had lamented, but he had been laughing in the old indulgent way. 'Where is the beauty in that simile? Strings of sausage. I ask you.'

Now I pick my son up and kiss that whole plump arm from the wrist all the way to the shoulder, pretending to bite, sending him dizzy with giggles before letting him go.

But there is nothing indulgent about Arthur now. He is like an April day: sun one moment, dark clouds the next and you never know when to expect the change.

'I tell you that Jane is upset and you seem to find it amusing. Sometimes I just don't understand you, Louisa. She's giving serious thought to moving away. She feels you disapprove of her, although God knows how anyone could disapprove of such a sweet little creature. She tells me you don't seem to trust her with the child. Why, Louisa, when playing with him gives her such pleasure? Why should you deny her that? A possessive mother is a very bad thing.'

'*Child*, tell Papa your name.' I grab Georgie as he scuttles past, a mouse still.

'And now she tells me you deliberately sabotaged her flower arrangement.'

'I did not sabotage it; I released it.'

'I must say you're in a very queer mood. Jane has made herself invaluable to me over the past few years. There is no one who understands the business side of my life as well as she. It started out as a kindness to her, employing her, but I don't mind admitting that now it is I who have cause to be grateful, as does Mama. She is *not* one of the servants, Louisa.'

'Arthur, you know very well that I would never treat any of the *servants* with anything less than respect; I abhor rudeness to staff.'

The colour rises in Arthur's cheeks but he only says, 'All she wishes is to be of use.'

'And I'm sure you make great use of her, my dear. As for Georgie and I, I'm afraid we think her so tiny and quiet that mostly we can't seem to find her. But she knows everything that goes on in the house. Maybe that's how she can make herself useful, as a spy.'

Arthur's cheeks turn purple above his golden-orange beard. Golden-orange and purple; a successful combination in the garden but disastrous on the face.

'And may I remind you that we have guests for luncheon. Sir Hugo and Lady Glastonbury.'

'And Viola, Viola is coming, is she not?'

'Yes, yes, of course.'

Georgie is attempting to balance a bright yellow brick on top of his brick castle and topples the whole edifice. His eyes grow huge. His little mouth opens and he lets out a piercing howl. I kneel by him on the floor. 'Don't cry. It was a good thing. Look, look, Georgie, the princess managed to escape. See,' I point at the rubble of bricks, 'she's gone. By now she will be back home at the castle all safe with her mother the Queen and her father the King.'

Georgie stops crying and gets to his feet. 'Where?' he asks, starting to look all around the nursery.

'You know that Sir Derek's friendship is important to me.' Arthur squats down by our side, his tweeds straining round his heavy thighs. Georgie wriggles free. 'Louisa, why are you doing this to me? Why are you being difficult when I most need you? I need my sweet Louisa. Where has she gone?'

We are on the floor, eye to eye, and something small and tight loosens within me. He smiles, a little sadly, and straightens, his hand held out. I allow him to pull me to my feet. 'I'm sorry, Arthur.' Before I know it my eyes brim with tears. 'I get these black thoughts; they scare me. I behave badly, I know I do. And I love you so much. You're so good to me. You've given me,' my gesture takes in the room, the golden child within, the pretty dress I am wearing, the pretty woman he thinks me to be, '*everything*.'

His lips move downwards in concern but not before I glimpse the slight smile in his eyes. 'There, there, don't upset yourself.' He pats me on the cheek. 'Just try and be more mindful of my needs in the future. You know how I have only now got my confidence back after that dreadful fallow period. It's something altogether new to me, not being able to work, feeling that the fire has cooled and fearing, dreading, Louisa, dreading, that it might have died for good. I'm not saying that this had anything to do with your presence in my life, although the tensions you create at times can be very wearing. But without my work, Louisa, I might as well be dead. Dead, do you hear? And now I am feeling better, you seem at times to go out of your way to upset me. It's not what I expected, Louisa.' Following his little speech he walks to the door. His steps are light. He turns in the doorway and his face has relaxed. 'Don't forget our guests. They are asked for twelve o'clock. It would be a nice surprise for me to see you there on time and with a smile.'

I dress for luncheon, weighed down by guilt. According to my husband, I create tension, upset the equilibrium of the household, endanger his art. I stand in front of the glass and stare at my wretched reflection. Was it really so? Had my uneasy presence stopped him from working? I, who loved him? I, who wanted to understand his work? What kind of a woman did that make me? An ungrateful one, and a failure. I had set out to be his love, his friend and his inspiration; mine would be the calm spirit reigning in his house, making it a haven of solace for his tumultuous soul. I would be the softness where Lydia had been harsh; the quiet light

172

where she had been blinding. Instead, I am just another shrill voice in the cacophony around him. How had I got it so wrong? At times he called me sharp and crass; at others a moping dragging thing. But he is the moody one. Of course, with Arthur the cause and the justification is the artistic temperament. I raise my hands to my throbbing temples. Thoughts rush round my head colliding with each other. It was wrong of him to lay the dark clouds at my door. I was mostly even-tempered. Maybe not inside, but I took great pains not to let him know. It is as if, when looking at me, he sees himself reflected – his bad temper, his despondency, his petulance – and thinks it is me.

'Your husband has recommended an excellent teacher for Viola,' Lady Glastonbury is saying.

'Teacher, Lady Glastonbury, what kind of teacher?'

'For Viola's painting.' She looks across the table at Arthur, her smile approving, warm, grateful. 'He has arranged for wonderful Monsieur Grandjean to come to the house two afternoons a week. Derek has had a little studio built just for the purpose.'

'Yes, Arthur, you have been most helpful.' Viola is sincere but as always her eyes seem to be laughing as if at a joke of which only she is aware. I want to see what she sees through those merry eyes, but I'm too big – galumphing, Arthur says, in jest of course. Sitting there at the table I have a vision of myself galloping across a field with a net held high, like an inept butterfly catcher, chasing Viola's elusive jokes, and I begin to laugh. Everyone turns to look at me.

'Is something amusing you, Louisa?' Lydia's question is phrased like a reproach.

'I'm sorry.' I make my face placid, my voice soft. 'I'm afraid I wasn't paying attention. I was thinking about something that . . . that Georgie said.'

'Why don't you join me for my lessons?' Viola asks me. 'I would love some company and I believe you have an eye. I have admired your flowers on many occasions.'

Lydia's face assumes a look as if the maid had just spilt gravy down her best silk frock. 'Are you sure it's not Jane's arrangements you've noticed?'

Viola turns and looks at Jane Dale who sits so quietly at her end of the table. 'I'm sure Jane has excellent taste but I believe I am thinking of Louisa's flowers, the colours she uses. I myself would never have thought of putting such combinations into the same arrangement but when Louisa does it it looks like it is the only way.'

'I would hold you back,' I tell her. 'I haven't picked up a brush or a piece of charcoal since I was a girl at school.'

'You will be fine, Louisa. And anyway, mine is a very small talent, really a facility more than anything.'

'Don't do yourself down, Viola,' my husband says. 'Claude Grandjean tells me your watercolours of the gardens at Horton Hall are quite charming.' He spears a piece of mutton on his fork as he looks at me. 'Why don't you take Viola up on her invitation, Louisa? It would do you good to get out of the house. There, I think it's a capital idea.'

'Don't you think it's enough with one artist in the family?' I ask, but I feel happier suddenly.

'I don't know that we shall consider you an artist quite yet, Louisa,' Arthur says, but he is smiling, well fed and benevolent.

'Then yes, if you are sure, Viola, I should love to join you.' I turn to my husband. 'And, Arthur, I shall have a much better understanding of your work as a result. I might be of real use.'

He wipes his mouth. 'You're getting ahead of yourself, Louisa. One step at a time and then we shall see.'

I don't know what gets into me at times; I drop my knife and fork on to my plate, the heat rising in my cheeks. 'Why do you always have to slap me down, Arthur, the moment I feel some enthusiasm?'

Arthur is angry, throwing words at me over his shoulder as he strides off towards the studio. He tells me I put on a performance to embarrass him in front of his guests. I note that he says *his* guests. I follow him, anxious to explain that it is hurt that makes me say those things, not spite, and that the last thing I wish to do is to embarrass him. 'Arthur dear, wait.'

'I've said my piece.'

I catch up with him and place my hand on his sleeve. He

halts. If he were a statue I would name it *Impatience*. 'Yes, speak.'

I let my hand drop. 'No, you go. It's nothing.'

I am alone in my room, reading by the open window, when Arthur steps inside, having knocked first. He has made an effort to wash the paint from his hands and face and his hair is slicked down and wet still. But for the beard he looks like a little boy who knows he has upset you but is also aware that he need do very little to be forgiven. I try to remain stern.

'Louisa.' He steps towards me, both hands outstretched. 'Louisa, my temperamental little wife.' He takes my hands and smiles down at me, amused and loving. My head spins with this sudden turnaround. 'I should be more understanding of my little girl's moods and fancies.' His smile is rueful. I smile back at him and my cheeks turn hot as he takes me in his arms and waltzes me round the bedroom singing:

Dance little doll, dance while you can,
Dance little doll while you're young,
For soon you'll be old and so heavy.
Dance little doll, dance while you're young and lovely,
Because soon you'll be old and have no one to dance with.

In his light I felt as if I was painted bright. I look at myself in the glass after he has gone. 'Why, Louisa, you're quite the beauty.'

When you touch Arthur he is always warm; even in winter with the fire cold in the grate. But he is wanted in so many places. He is constantly on the move, and I'm left shivering in his shadow.

Viola is making good progress, delighting Monsieur Grandjean with her neatness and her delicate colours. My work pleases him less.

'Too much colour.' He peers over my shoulder at the easel. 'Too much wildness. This is crudeness, Madame. You go over lines and use these colours as if they were oils. But these are watercolours; *water*, Madame. They should be applied with the light hand. Look at Miss Viola, how delicate is her work, how right for a lady to paint.'

175

I can see from Viola's profile that she is trying not to laugh. 'But, Monsieur Grandjean, this is what I see.' I point out at the gardens. 'How can I paint it otherwise? Look at the borders out there and you'll see that I'm right. Those plants might look so neat, so groomed and staked, but look again and you will see how they struggle to get free from the wire and how they clamber over the edges of the borders in their eagerness to escape.'

Monsieur Grandjean sighs and shrugs. I don't believe he's paid to work too hard with us. He contents himself with saying that my eyes must be very different from his, if that is what I see when gazing out at the immaculate gardens of Northbourne Manor.

Viola and I take tea together after the lesson. It pleases Arthur that I have become friends with Miss Glastonbury and it surprises him. He would deny it, of course, but I know he asks himself why would someone as jolly, as well connected, as spoilt for choice as Viola Glastonbury choose his poor Louisa as her companion.

'Your landscapes *are* strange,' Viola says. 'What a frightening world you see. And yet beautiful too.' Her smile turns mischievous as she asks, 'So what about me, how do I look through those strange eyes of yours?'

I pause to study her; teasing because I know her face well enough already. 'Pure,' I say finally. 'Good and kind. And beautiful.' Viola laughs but she is blushing. 'Yellow,' I add, 'and bright pink and orange.'

'Yellow and pink and orange? You're mad!'

She is laughing still, but I look back at her, serious. 'Don't say that.'

'Oh Louisa, darling, it's only a figure of speech.'

'I know. But sometimes I wonder.' I look up at her and she returns my gaze, steady and kind. 'Oh Viola, do you ever feel so sad, so heavy with sorrow, so sick of being you, that it's all you can do not to fall to the ground and slip deep into the earth?'

'No. No, Louisa, I don't.' She leans forward across the table with its pretty embroidered cloth and puts her small soft hand on mine. 'Who makes you feel that way?'

'That's just it; I do. It's all me. But there are times too when I feel as if I have special gifts, as if I can see and hear and understand the world like no one else, or I would, if only I could catch the

176

thoughts that race through my mind. But they move at such a speed all I ever catch is the echo. I run, Viola, I run and sometimes I get so close that I see the very gates of heaven about to open before me. But I never get there in time.'

Viola keeps her hand on mine. 'I think you live in an unkind household.'

I stare at her. 'But Arthur is the kindest man. Although I know he doesn't always seem that way. And he's given me my son. No one loves you the way your child does. It makes me weep sometimes, when I look into those eyes of his and know that I'm the most precious thing in this world to him and he to me.'

'Why should that make you weep?'

'Because what if we should lose each other? And because my love is destined to last whereas his will weaken as his world grows. With each year and with each new door he opens it's bound to weaken; that's nature's way.'

Viola has withdrawn her hand and is pouring us both another cup of tea scented with rose petals. She dries the petals herself and mixes them with the ordinary leaves from the grocer in the village. 'You have a bleak view of life.'

'It's what I see.' It's my turn to lean close and take her hand. 'Do you know, the odd thing is I wouldn't want to swap. That's what I mean when I think I might be mad; I can hate myself and feel a sadness so profound I fear nothing can banish it, yet I am glad I'm me because I feel that one day that view will be my very saviour. Oh, I know that sounds contradictory.' I look away, laugh to lighten the mood. 'I have no idea how I shall accomplish this. I was never any good at music. I've tried my hand at poetry but my work made me blush and giggle with its earnest pretensions. I do love to paint, but look what happens: my work does not delight the eye and inspire the soul.' I look at her and burst out laughing. 'It repels.'

'It doesn't repel me,' Viola says. 'But maybe if you want an audience you need to learn from men like your husband and our monsieur how to please.'

'But I never know what I am *meant* to do and that's when Monsieur Grandjean gets impatient with me. It's as if I'm following

177

some rhythm in my head towards a clear goal and then, when I look at what I have achieved, I see the faulty proportions and the childish lines and lack of detail and I understand the poor man's frustration.'

'Maybe you should concentrate on your drawing skills for now,' Viola says. 'You have the heart for the work; all you need is for your hand to catch up.'

I tell Arthur what Viola has said and he agrees with her about the need for me to pay more attention to my drawing techniques. 'Even a hobby is worth taking seriously,' he says. 'And if you are intent on improving you have to heed the advice of those who know better. Unless of course you belong to the school of thought so fashionable in some circles that all that matters is expressing yourself with no more skill than a child let loose with his brushes.'

'No, no, of course I want to learn. But Arthur, don't you feel sometimes that the essence of a thing can get buried under too much attention to its exact appearance?'

'I don't think I follow you, Louisa. Surely it's by the skilled and artful portrayal of your subject that you shall reach its essence. Or maybe you are an admirer of Surrealism? Maybe you yearn to follow the style of Señor Dali? Or maybe you believe that you will understand a person better if you paint him with one eye and four ears and a mouth the size of a cavern?'

'I don't think I've seen enough examples of that kind of work to have an opinion,' I tell my husband. 'But from your description I suspect the answer should be no, I don't.'

So I tried to follow the advice of those who know so much more than I.

'But it's not right,' I say one day. I had enjoyed the approval but could no longer deny how hollow it rang within me. I am looking at the small painting of Viola that I had produced and brought back for my husband to see.

'What's not right? It's not a bad likeness, not a bad likeness at all, considering you're still a novice. I've seen many a student, less quick to learn than you, who has gone on to do very pleasing work. Did I not say so just the other day, Jane?'

178

I had not noticed her sitting at the small desk in the window alcove. Jane is as quiet as a mouse, Arthur always says. In my experience mice are not quiet in the slightest. They pitter-patter across the floors and squeak and squeal as they fight over crumbs of food. And if you have not heard them their droppings show that they have been in even the most unexpected places.

'Louisa is a credit to you,' Jane says. 'Better be careful or before you know it she will be stealing your commissions.' Her laugh, I have often thought, has a musical quality to it and I think Arthur has noticed too because he turns and laughs with her, although he says, 'I think I shall sleep soundly for a while yet.' Arthur hands me back the sketch. The room descends into silence. Silence, Arthur is fond of saying, is his favourite sound. I asked him once how silence, the absence of noise, could be described as a sound. I knew that absence can be a stronger currency than presence. If Georgie is with me in the room I might pay less attention to him, knowing he is close at hand, but when he is elsewhere I miss him and worry about him and wonder what he is doing. I had tried to explain to Monsieur Grandjean that such thoughts led me to paint the things he could not see in the scenes before us. I had tried to explain the presence on my canvas of hard hands training wire round the rambling rose and a bird caught in the mesh of the fruit-cage, a wing broken from its attempts at flying free. But Monsieur Grandjean had put a large charcoal X across the things he said only I could see and had told me to start again. So now I was painting the pictures he and my husband wished me to paint, garnering praise at last and only, it seemed, because I was no longer true to myself.

Monsieur Grandjean has decided to return to his native country. Arthur is absorbed in work on his Island canvas, so when a friend of his suggests his son, just out of the Slade, to take the Belgian's place he agrees.

I find a very different teacher waiting in Viola's studio at my next lesson.

GRACE FOUND NOAH stretched out on the sofa in the library, feet on the armrest and his fair head resting on a tapestry cushion. He looked comfortable and not so different from the boy she had once known. Sleep took years off people; it was letting go, she supposed. She picked up a magazine and dropped it on the floor deliberately. He stirred and turned round, lifting his head. His hair was messy and damp from sleep and his eyes were pained.

'Finn used to look just like that when he woke up; all puffy and long-suffering,' she said.

'I don't suppose that ever stopped you from waking him?'

'Not really.' Grace brushed his feet off the sofa so that she could sit down. 'I don't know why she isn't telling, but I'm pretty sure she knows who Forbes is. She is forgetful and sometimes she comes out with something that seems to be several steps to the side of what we were talking about, but that's when we're in the now. Take her back to the past and she is as clear as a bell. Something she said just now makes me think he might even have been her art teacher. Although why she would keep that quiet, I do not know. Have you ever seen any of Louisa's paintings?'

Noah straightened and yawned, showing white even teeth with several black fillings. 'My mother has one, only because it's supposed to be of my father and Aunt Lillian. I just remember it being weird, as if a child had painted it. I don't think it was much more than a hobby; women like her did that kind of thing, you know: piano, watercolours. I expect she found it a bit difficult to hold her own with Grandpa being who he was.'

'Self-obsessed and insensitive, you mean.'

Noah sat up. 'What brought that on?'

Grace had turned pink. 'Sorry. It's just that listening to Louisa – well, I don't think he was quite as lovely as you think.' She raised her hand. 'And before you say anything . . .'

'I wouldn't dare.'

Grace pulled a face. 'She is not complaining. She's not poor Marjory getting her own back, she's just remembering.'

'If she had such a trying time with Grandfather, why don't I know about it?'

'Did you ever ask? Anyway, she probably didn't want you to have to take sides. It's generally both easier and safer to talk about important matters with comparative strangers.'

'She knows I'm doing the biography. Why has she not wanted to give her side of the story?'

'Because you're not doing her story, are you; you're doing the big boy. And she adores you and wants you to have your little fun. And, unbelievably, she retained some affection for her husband and is glad that he is celebrated. She's not a selfish woman.' Grace looked him up and down. 'It's uncanny how like your father you are to look at, at least judging by the photographs on Louisa's mantelpiece.' She handed him a small notebook. 'I have made some notes of the things she's been telling me; just in case you'd find it useful. You need patience when you listen to someone that age. I'm patient. It comes with the job. The job I had, that is.'

'The job you should and could still have if you weren't quite so keen to send yourself to hell before anyone else gets the chance.'

Grace, who had been walking towards the door, swung round and looked at him. 'Hell. You think it's hell for me, not doing photography?'

'Well, isn't it?'

She shrugged. 'It's empty; I suppose that's a kind of hell.' She turned in the doorway on her way out. 'Oh, and has she ever mentioned Viola Glastonbury to you? Her family were friends of yours. They used to own Mrs Shield's development.'

Noah shook his head. 'No, not really. Why?'

'They seem to have been very close, Louisa and Viola, that's all.'

Mrs Shield was feeling left out. Grace, looking through some old correspondence of Arthur's passed on to her by Noah, could tell from the way she circled the table humming a little ditty. She craned her neck and peered over Grace's shoulder, giving a groan of pain. She made several comments about Grace always being busy. 'You're like your father. *He* was always busy with something or another, even when there seemed to be nothing to be that busy with. Not that I'm complaining, I never did. I'm a busy person myself. And I know I'm very fortunate to have you here for your holidays.'

'Not *all* my holidays, Evie. I'll stay until you manage on your own but then I've got things to do, lots of things.' But she remembered that moon-face peering round the door of her father's study, hoping for an invitation to enter. She remembered sitting in her room with a group of friends and Mrs Shield bustling in with a tray of cocoa that no one wanted, lingering just in case she was needed, before disappearing back to that chill corner of the house where the leftover people go. It was Mrs Shield's peculiar tragedy, wanting so much to be needed that in the end she became the needy one.

'But I'm really enjoying us spending some time together,' Grace said, feeling guilty. 'It's been ages. And it's a help to me too, you know, being able to bunker down for a while.'

'That's the point of family,' Mrs Shield said, cheeks pink with pleasure, 'providing refuge. So have you found out anything more about your picture?'

Grace shook her head. 'I thought of driving up to London just for the day to fetch it so I can show it to Louisa; see if that jogs her memory.'

'Tomorrow is my little party. You haven't forgotten, have you? You did say you'd cook. I don't think I could manage on my own yet . . . although I would have to try and do my best.'

'Of course I'll do it,' Grace said. 'Although I can't see why you

182

thought it was a good idea to arrange a dinner party just when you've broken your ribs.'

'I thought it would be nice for everyone to meet up. I've got Percy coming, and Elsa, and poor Marjory of course, and Noah. I did ask if he thought Louisa might like to come but he said she never goes out. I was quite relieved, I have to admit; old people can be very hard work.'

Grace had decided on the menu for Mrs Shield's party: scallops, followed by duck in morello-cherry sauce, then cheese. Mrs Shield would protest that men need something sweet to finish off their meal, but Grace, a reluctant cook at the best of times, decided the best she could do was a box of mint chocolates. The small market town was full of women just like her, walking back to their cars, squinting against the rain, no hand to hold the umbrella, gorilla arms trailing heavy carrier bags. Oh, Nell Gordon, she thought, if you could see me now I would be obligingly as you described: a love lost, a promise unfulfilled, a talent squandered . . . What else can I add to that impressive CV? Oh yes, dottily seeking Forbes. Her face contorted, her eyes shut tight squeezing out tears that mingled with the drops of rain running down her cheeks. 'It isn't fair, you know, Jefferson,' she mumbled. 'You make me love you and then you leave me, twice, and you're still not content but you send me a picture to fall in love with too, by another man I cannot find. So what hope have I of ever getting free of you?' She opened her eyes and realised that she was providing entertainment – sad old woman talking to herself – for a group of giggling teenage girls all topknots and dangly earrings and jackets like puffed-up frogs. She was right outside the Lion and Lamb Antique and Tea Shop and she escaped inside. Putting her bags of groceries down on the floor, she stopped to admire a white enamel bucket with *Soiled Dressings* painted in large black letters. It would look good in her kitchen, she thought. And she could not resist leafing through some old magazines from the 1940s, full of brave good cheer, recipes and handy tips for making the rations go further. She was tempted to buy a tin box containing a primus camping stove but rightly decided she would never use it and passed on by. There was a glass-topped display table with silver and enamel boxes and some cigarette cases. One she especially liked: a plain silver case that looked long enough to take filter tips. She asked if she could take a closer look and was told to go ahead, the glass top lifted right up. She picked out the case, thinking it probably dated from the late 1920s, early 1930s. She would have to check the hallmark with a magnifying glass to be sure. There was quite a dent in the side, she noticed. That should bring the price down to affordable. She opened the case and saw that there was an inscription. It read *Forbes Forever*.

'I stood there, mouth open, heart beating,' Grace told Noah at the dinner table. 'I know Forbes is not that uncommon a name, but still . . .'

Percy said that unfortunately scallops didn't really agree with him. Used to, but not any more.

'I'm not usually given to flights of fancy but I can't help feeling that this was some kind of sign.'

Noah finished his scallops and leant back in his chair. 'A sign?'

'You know, as in *find me*.'

Noah was quiet for a moment and then he said, in a voice so low that only Grace, sitting next to him, could hear. 'The most preposterous idea's just occurred to me. Think if my upright old granny and your Forbes were lovers? I know there was some kind of major drama back before the war. That could be it and it would explain your feeling that she knows more than she's letting on.'

Grace nodded slowly, taking it in. 'You could be right.'

'And how is our young celebrity?' Percy said in the loud voice of the slightly deaf. 'I hear they want you on television next?'

'I think you've got that wrong,' Grace said. It had been too much to hope that the subject of those wretched articles would not be brought up. But at least he did not sound as if he was feeling sorry for her. She smiled as she said, 'There's no television.' Just then she caught sight of Mrs Shield. Her moon-face was blushing red as Mars and she refused to look at Grace as she busied herself with clearing the plates, grimacing from the discomfort of her damaged ribs.

'Evie,' Grace used her mildest voice, 'do you know anything about a television programme?'

The pile of plates had to be rescued by Percy. Mrs Shield sat down again. 'Oh dear, I quite forgot in all the excitement of our little party, but there was a call for you, when you were out, from a very charming young man putting together something for *The West Bank Show* . . .'

'*South Bank*,' Grace corrected automatically.

Mrs Shield perked up. 'There, you know it. They would be so pleased if you could come on the programme and speak about . . . well, I don't exactly remember what, but it's to do with your award. A new shortlist, I think they said. Anyway,' she paused and, not quite looking at Grace, added quickly, 'I said I was sure you'd be only too happy. He was so grateful, Grace. You should be pleased to be so highly thought of.'

Noah was covering his mouth with his napkin but it was obvious he was laughing. Grace shot him a mean look before getting to her feet, saying to the table in general, 'If you'll excuse me, I have to go and slice the duck with a very sharp knife. Care to come with me, Evangeline?' Mrs Shield got up from the table clumsily, supporting herself on the back of her chair. Grace felt instantly ashamed; in the topsy-turvy world of ageing, she had the power to turn her stepmother into a chastised child. It was not a power she wished to have.

In the kitchen, as she deposited a stack of plates in the sink, Mrs Shield tried to make things better by saying how everyone seemed to think Grace appearing on television very exciting. 'And I sort of led that sweet young man to believe that you would do it. He'll be terribly disappointed.'

'Evie.' Grace took her stepmother's hands in hers. 'Look, I hate to be awkward.' Mrs Shield's sandy eyebrows rose in a question. 'All right, so that's not strictly true, but this time it's for a good reason. I know there seems to be a feeling that being on television is one step from entering the gates of heaven, and had I been working still and been asked to talk about my work then I might have leapt at the chance. But it's not my world any more, and to the programme makers I'm just a warmed-up old scandal they think might add spice to their recipe. It's the difference between appearing at the fair as the juggler or the bearded lady. You do understand?'

185

Mrs Shield gave Grace's hand a little pat and made an effort to smile. 'Yes. Yes, of course I do. I just think you're a little particular. But that's probably to your credit.' And she added, so quietly Grace could hardly hear, 'Some of us would be glad to be asked to appear at the fair in the first place.'

After dinner the talk turned to Noah's book. 'It's about time someone did your grandfather that honour,' Percy said. 'This part of the world has an unfair reputation for being stuffy. My own boys keep going on about it. "It's so dull, Dad. So middle class and boring." Middle class, perhaps, but boring? People need to be reminded that it was these pleasant lands that produced a great artist like Arthur Blackstaff. They don't make them like that any more, no they don't. I credit him with firing in me my lifelong interest in the fine arts. Without him as an example I don't believe I would ever have even thought of picking up my brushes.'

'I didn't know you painted, Percy,' Noah said.

'I'm strictly amateur, dear boy, just an amateur, but it's given me great pleasure over the years. I know there is a view that would say why bother when your work is never going to amount to anything. But I believe there's something to be said for endeavour. I don't wish to be pompous, but I think I'm a better person because of my little hobby. Art ennobles the soul, even when the art in question is far from perfect, I truly believe that. And, as I see it, art should be uplifting, beautiful, and that's what Arthur Blackstaff believed. I heard him speak once. I was a young man but I never forgot. "I deplore *isms*," he said. "*Cubism, Expressionism, Surrealism* . . . there is no *ism* in *beauty*."'

'Hear hear,' poor Marjory said. 'Some of the things they call art these days . . .'

Grace, fearing a conversation about unmade beds and piles of bricks, pretended not to hear. Instead she asked Percy, 'But beauty in whose eyes? I admit it; I have problems with Arthur Blackstaff's work. Oh it's all there, every detail correct and present, every colour true. Everything is spelt out and speaks to me not one word.' She turned to Noah. 'I hope you don't mind me being so blunt.'

'Isn't it a bit late asking that *now*?' Elsa interjected mildly. Grace grinned at her.

186

'Are you sure you are the best judge, dear?' Poor Marjory's voice came clipped from smiling lips. 'Arthur was one of our greats.'

'You can think what you like, Grace,' Noah said, 'but I don't agree with you. How much of his work are you actually familiar with? Have you seen the Island canvas, for example?'

'No.'

'Well, you should.'

Marjory's face, pink-powdered and rouged, took on the alert look that Grace knew meant she was about to say something unpleasant. 'Wasn't there some drama at the time of its unveiling?' she asked, proving Grace right. 'One of the old people told me. You know how the villagers like to gossip.' Seemingly oblivious to the embarrassed hush around the table and the clenched set to Noah's jaw, she went on, 'I know he was no angel, there was the matter of his young women . . . but I don't really see that as an excuse. I know my children are always saying that I was a saint to put up with Malcolm the way I did, but I never saw it that way. No, he had his little ways, but I knew my duty.'

'Poor Marjory.' Mrs Shield shook her head. 'You are the bravest woman I know.'

Marjory murmured a protest that sounded just like agreement. 'No, no, well there have been times . . .' She straightened her back and patted the side of her candy-floss hair. 'Of course adultery is a mortal sin whatever the reason for it.' She paused and glanced sideways at Grace. 'But best not to go into that.'

'Oh please don't worry on my behalf,' Grace said. 'I have no shame.'

'Why do you say things like that, Grace,' Mrs Shield fussed, 'when we all know it isn't true?'

That's when Percy stood up and said that he did not know about anyone else but he was ready for his beauty sleep.

Mrs Shield declared the party a success. 'Although I wish you wouldn't make those little jokes of yours. People who don't know you as well as I do take you seriously. And Noah, what a delightful young man he's turned into. Those wonderful eyes. I never knew his poor father but they say he's the spitting image. It's all very sad. Everybody dying.'

Grace put her arm round Mrs Shield and gave her a little hug, careful not to hurt her ribs. 'Oh Evie, you haven't been going around thinking we weren't; dying, I mean?

Mrs Shield looked puzzled for a moment then her brow cleared. 'You know what I mean, Grace. And dear Marjory; I noticed you two having a little chat by the door and I thought I'd leave you to it.'

Poor Marjory had lingered after the others had gone. 'Now, I can't deny that I was more than a little shocked to read about your . . . well . . . Evie never said a word. And him married all those years and three little girls too. But I want you to know that I believe you've suffered enough.' It was all in her gentlest voice and as she finished speaking she placed her bird-like hand on Grace's arm. 'And *don't* thank me. I *care* about you, my dear. As I always say, there's no changing the past however much one might wish to. There can only be a determination to do better next time. Not of course that there would be a next time. I know you have learnt your lesson. You're in my prayers, dear, every night. As the good Lord says, repent and you shall be forgiven.'

Grace looked at her, at the small triangular face and the clever close-set eyes. 'You're right, Marjory, you can't change the past. Which is fine by me because the particular part of my life to which you are so delicately referring is the one I'd never change, not for anything.'

Marjory had fled into the night cloaked in indignation.

Grace lay in her narrow bed trying to get to sleep counting the ways by which she could murder poor Marjory: tripwire, fire, axe, poison, trap, hole, water, knife, push, stairs, crash, toadstool.

And you, Nell bloody Gordon, don't think I've forgotten you. You're like a great big bluebottle, buzz buzz buzz. Each time I think I'm shot of you, I find a little more dirt has spread. And I bet you're not having problems sleeping. Why should you? After all, journalism is next to godliness.

NELL GORDON: *Following her divorce, Shield ended up living back in London.*

'One, two, three, four, five, six, seven, eight, nine, ten . . .' Grace was doing her exercises by the open window on a chilly spring morning when she saw him walk by on the street below. She stopped her sideways stretches and leant out of the window, calling his name. He didn't turn so she wolf-whistled. Finn had taught her and she had not forgotten. But the sound was drowned by the wind and the noise of the traffic, and he walked on. Grace stood staring after the disappearing figure and then, although she knew it was too late, ran barefoot down the stairs of the building and out on to the street.

Back inside she laughed at herself, not very convincingly. All those years and Jefferson McGraw still appeared, a mirage reminding her of what she did not have.

'It can't have been him,' she said to Angelica on the phone.

'You might or might not have sighted a childhood sweetheart from fifteen years or so ago. You don't actually *care*, do you?'

Grace paused. 'No. No, of course I don't. Well, that's it, I do. Oh hell, Angelica, why am I still so hung up on this one episode in my past? He's always there, nagging away at me in the background like an unanswered question. It's the magic of love untried by reality; it never fails. Seeing him, really seeing him, would give me all the answer I need: yes, he's just another man and I would have been no happier with him than with anyone else.'

'I would probably still be hung up on Tom if he had dumped me instead of marrying me,' Angelica said.

'That was not helpful.'

*   *   *

Grace saw him three more times in the ensuing six months. She began to wonder if she had a problem. She went to see a therapist. The room was cheerful, sunshine yellow: yellow chairs, yellow sofa, yellow walls, yellow curtains, bowls and jugs of daffodils and yellow tulips. You could go mad in that room and still think you were having a good time.

'Why, why do I still think of this man, Jefferson? I mean, it was almost fifteen years ago. I was a child, we both were. It was a holiday thing. I've had several relationships since and I've been married. What's wrong with me?'

'There are no rules governing emotions. There doesn't have to be a reason. Not one to do with sense and logic, anyway. Still, I agree that we have to consider the possibility of you having developed an obsession. Has it occurred to you that this reconnecting with a long-lost love, a teenage romance, is a way for you to cope with the feelings of failure associated with the breakdown of your marriage? In your own view, are you an obsessive character?'

Grace thought about it. How did she live her life? She worked for up to fourteen hours a day, six days a week, seven sometimes, taking pictures, developing, learning new techniques, reading, teaching, because she loved to and because her work was her particular God-given talent and not to be squandered. It was her sincere belief that to squander a God-given talent was a deadly sin. Grace told the therapist that. The therapist said Grace's approach to work might count as obsessional but then again it might not. 'People are very keen on absolutes,' he had added a little apologetically, 'but we live in a fluid world.'

'Document, document, document,' Grace said. 'That's how I deal with that.'

'That's OK if it works for you. What's important is not so much what happens to you in your life, as how you react to what happens. You might feel out of control in a chaotic and ever-changing universe, but you're not actually, because you and only you control how you receive what comes to you.'

That yellow room, the calm voice, the reassuring words; Grace felt better already. But she was impatient for some answers. 'But is it normal to still be hung up on this man or have I developed some kind of obsession?'

'That's for you to work out.'

'That's not really an answer.'

'I'm not here to give you answers; I'm here to help you find your own.'

Grace nodded. 'And what about seeing him everywhere?'

'How do you mean?'

'I keep seeing him. Although it's not him, of course. At least I don't think it is. I have run after him, whoever, a couple of times but I've lost him each time.'

'You used the word *lost*.'

'Yes . . .'

'It's an interesting choice.'

'Not really. I just did: lose him. Anyway, I know it can happen to anyone that you think you see someone from the past, but it happens to me all the time. I don't even know what he looks like these days. Last time I saw him, I mean actually *saw* him as opposed to imagining that I had, he was nineteen; a child, for heaven's sake. He'll be thirty-four now. That's how stupid this whole thing is. No,' Grace prepared to go as she could see from the clock on the yellow wall that her hour was up, 'no, it's an obsession all right and I'll treat it as such.'

She supposed that's what the therapist meant when he talked about helping you to find your own answers.

But she saw him again; this time he was in the park, crouched down patting a dog. She just shrugged and told herself to get on with the day.

'So you see, I'm cured,' she said to Angelica who was over for Sunday brunch. 'I just walked on by.' They had agreed not to spend the whole morning discussing work.

'You look tired,' Angelica said as Grace handed her a cup of tea with an extra spoonful of honey.

'That's the all-time least encouraging remark,' Grace said. 'People joke about that one in sitcoms.'

'When did you last watch a sitcom?'

'Friday. I do watch television, you know.'

'But mostly you work. I'm all for it, in a way. The more you earn the greater my percentage, but I don't want you burning out.'

'I won't. People spending their whole career going from war zone to war zone, they burn out.'

'There are enough people chasing the big stories, the earth-shattering events. The quiet lives of quiet people need their chronicler too.'

Grace liked that answer. It got her off the hook. Right now she was working on her contribution to an exhibition of portraits of twentieth-century London women.

'They've asked me to caption my pictures,' Grace said. 'I don't know if I want that.' She usually preferred her photographs to speak for themselves, but there was a time and place for text. Angelica was good at titles. Grace could come up with a whole series of pictures and have no idea what to call them, but Angelica usually found something spot on, so spot on that Grace sometimes asked for the captions to be left out. 'But I only put down what you said you meant by a certain shot,' was what Angelica usually said when they had such a discussion. And Grace would explain, 'I know that's how *I* said that *I* saw it, but that doesn't mean everyone else has to see it the same way. A photograph should be like life itself, open to interpretation, viewed through a living mind. Otherwise it's just another lifeless thing.

'Look at this one,' she said now, wiping the toast crumbs from her fingers and pushing the proof for the exhibition catalogue over to Angelica's side of the table. She pointed at a picture from the 1930s of a woman standing, surrounded by her four children, on the striped lawn in front of their solid suburban home. 'Maybe she was perfectly happy,' Grace said. 'But all I think is, thank God I'm living now. If now had been then, I'd still be with the Abbots, being slowly suffocated by heartless do-gooders whilst outside, life happened without me. Women like this one had the same big world outside their windows as we do, but they couldn't get out there. Think about it; think about the wasted lives of women, generation after generation. They weren't heard, they weren't seen. God knows what passions and talents they might have harboured that were never given vent and space to grow. We all know that, but looking at some of those faces for the first time I actually *feel* inside me what it must have been like. Look at her; look at that blank expression, those lips set tight as if they were holding back a scream. I look at her hand resting on one daughter's neck, and I feel she wants to squeeze. She's thinking if I have to brush that hair into a perfect little parting with a tiny bow like the two princesses wear one more time, I shall go mad. If I have to listen, one more time, to my husband saying yes, I did have a good day at the office, thank you dear, I shall claw his eyes out. If I have to listen to one more Ovalteenie, or read one more article about how to make my home a perfect haven for my tired family, I shall slit my throat.'

'I don't see that at all,' Angelica said. 'I'm thinking what a nice-looking family. I envy that woman. Look at her, the adored centre of a happy family. No pressure to go out and fight in the workplace every bloody day. No commuting on filthy underground trains. She's got a husband and she knows he'll stay put or he'll probably lose his chance of promotion at work, not to mention his Rotary membership. There would be lots of other women living the same kind of life so she wouldn't be isolated. She'd have had a cleaner and maybe even a cook. In the afternoons, if she wasn't having tea with a friend, she might do some gentle shopping, no lugging heavy groceries obviously, but a new hat or some gloves.'

'So should that picture be captioned or not?' Grace wanted to know. 'Because my caption would read: *Woman in gilded cage on the verge of breakdown*. And most likely that's what people would then see. Yours would say something like *Mrs Charles Phillips and her happy brood in front of their comfortable Wimbledon home*. In both cases we would be steering the viewer in our particular direction. With some pictures and in some circumstances, that has its place. But then it ceases to be a partnership and the picture has no life beyond that one view.'

'So I'll tell the gallery you won't caption your pictures. *Now* can we go to Harvey Nichols?'

Grace enjoyed shopping with Angelica who tended to buy what Grace secretly hankered after – the soft pink things, the velvet stuff, the nipped-in-at-the-waist and lace-trimmed items; everything that turned Angelica into a golden goddess of Boho chic but made Grace look like a Grenadier Guard in a frilly shower cap. 'Simple lines in grey or navy,' Mrs Shield always said as Grace grew up. 'Nothing fussy or pink.' She was right. Grace had substituted black for navy but otherwise she had stuck to her stepmother's advice. If you opened her wardrobe you would find three pairs of black straight-legged trousers and two black jackets: one linen, one in a wool and cashmere mix. There was a knee-length black leather pencil skirt, one white cotton shirt, two black T-shirts, four white ones, a black poloneck jumper, two black V-necks, both cashmere, and one red cotton sweater for the days when she wanted to make out that she did not always wear black and white. She compensated for the lack of variety in colour by indulging her love for soft fabrics. She wore her cashmere jumpers as armour. Cashmere spoke. It said, *Don't fuck with me.* Her underwear was pretty routine. If *it* spoke, Grace supposed it said, *All right, so fuck with me then but don't expect me ever to wear a thong.*

Trailing behind Angelica on a shopping trip – watching as she tried clothes on, holding up the jumpers she pointed at – Grace's yearnings for pinker fluffier things were satisfied by proxy. Maybe this time she had an especially longing look in her eyes because Angelica thrust a jumper into her hand and gave her a shove towards the changing rooms. 'Try it on.'

'It's baby blue.'

'I can see that.'

'It's got little puffy sleeves and a frilly neck.'

'Yes, Grace, it has.'

'I'll look like a Beatrix Potter animal.'

'Don't be stupid. You're a very good-looking woman.'

'Jemima Puddleduck was a very good-looking duck but she still looked jolly silly in that blue bonnet.'

'You don't look like a duck and that's not a bonnet. Come on, I can see you like it.'

Grace did as she was told and tried on the jumper. As she expected, she looked stupid although she appeared from the changing room still wearing it, just to prove her point. 'Wow,'

Angelica said. 'Wow, wow, wow.' She paused, head tilted. 'Actually, maybe not. No, you're right, it's not your kind of thing, is it?'

Grace was about to say, *told you so*, when she saw him, Jefferson McGraw, across the shop floor, standing by the till, a heap of women's clothes in his arms. This time it really was him; not a delusion or a fantasy but the boy she had loved the summer she was eighteen, the boy who had so nearly been the father of her child; a man to whom she probably meant nothing. She stepped closer. 'Shut your mouth,' Angelica said.

'It's Jefferson.'

'I thought you'd stopped that.'

'No, really.' Grace's voice was shaking and she paused, took a deep breath and tried again. 'It's funny, isn't it?'

Angelica looked over to the till. 'Hilarious. He's cute, whoever he is.'

'Jefferson.' Grace stared as he handed the clothes to the assistant and watched as he smiled that big guileless smile she had captured in countless photographs.

'So don't just stand there.' Angelica gave Grace a little shove in the small of the back. 'Go up and say hello.'

'I can't do that.'

'Why not, for pete's sake?'

'I just can't.' Grace took her eyes off him for a moment, turning to Angelica. 'You're right, it can't be him. I mean, what is it with us and retail? The first time I met him I was coming out of a fur shop.'

'Don't stall.'

Grace sighed, pulled back her shoulders and . . . 'Where is he?'

'I expect he's gone where all good phantoms go, up in a puff of smoke.'

'It *was* him.'

'So run after him. He won't have got very far, unless he flew.'

Grace gave her a look and then she ran for it. She was still wearing the angora jumper. The store detective stopped her as she reached the escalator. By the time she had convinced the floor manager that she had not intended to steal – 'Please, put yourself in my place; would you wear *this*?' – Jefferson, if it was him, had vanished.

'After Tom and I divorced I kept seeing him everywhere,' Angelica said to Grace who stood by the escalator with a look on her face as if she had missed the carnival. 'I even saw him in the breadbin. Well, his head anyway.'

Grace relaxed and smiled at her. 'You're right. It could never have been him; he looked too much like himself.'

'I'm sure that makes sense, to someone.'

'And what would he be doing at Harvey Nichols of all places, and with his arms full of women's clothing?'

Angelica winked. 'He's *your* friend.'

For a hallucination, Jefferson McGraw had strong powers. There was Grace's flat for a start. She returned that afternoon to find it had changed. Instead of being on just the right floor above street level, it was now far too high up. If Jefferson were ever to walk by, he wouldn't be able to see her sitting reading by the window. Old Mrs Blenkinsop with her bald patch and her velour lounging suit would be clearly visible as she sat by her ground-floor window smoking her pipe, but Grace, far up there, would be as indistinguishable as one pigeon from another. The phone was too far from the bedroom should he – who was not Jefferson, who had forgotten all about her, who did not know where she lived – decide to phone. Should he appear on her doorstep unannounced, the comfort-sag in the sofa and tea stains on the armrests would not say cosy but slut. She stood in the middle of the room, her hands to her face, thinking she must be going mad. There was nothing for it but to kick some furniture. She started with the sideboard that Mrs Shield had given her for her thirtieth birthday. She moved on to the pine coffee table. (What had possessed her to buy pine?) And finished off with three high kicks to the side of the sofa as she hummed some show tune she had not even been aware she knew.

She mixed herself a mug of whisky and hot lemon and went to bed early that night, her toes aching . . . and her heart.

The day she had moved into her new flat she had walked along the busy street, smiling at the unconcerned strangers in her path,

196

people who might or might not smile back, but who basically did not give a damn what she was doing as long as she did not take their parking space or queue jump at the bus stop. She had listened to the hum of traffic, the roar and singing of engines, the calling of sirens; she had drawn in the cool fume-filled air: she was back and she was free.

For a while, after her marriage ended, she had been angry – at Andrew and herself, for failing. There had been sadness too, but it had come in such manageable gulps and sniffles it could hardly count as suffering.

And her work was going well. Lately she'd had to pass on commissions to colleagues because she had too much work herself. And then, when all seemed to be going so swimmingly, the sightings had begun.

'Do you know what I like best about living on my own?' Angelica said. 'Being able to fart in bed.'

'So don't move in with Whatshisname.'

'His name's Nick. Can you at least try to remember?'

'I don't know if I want to. It's like naming your car; next thing you know you endow them with feelings.'

'That's so funny, Grace. But seriously, don't you ever miss . . . you know . . . having someone?'

'No,' Grace said. 'I'm not very good with possessions.'

It was just over a week since her hallucinatory experience on the second floor of Harvey Nichols and her flat had begun to return to normal. On Monday morning she got up early to catch the light of a fine London day, that special light of the sun fighting through the pink-edged orange haze of pollution. One of the big photographic magazines was running a series of special features on the theme of the Family of Man. Each week featured the work of a different photographer. Grace had been asked to contribute to the Christmas issue. The lead-time was about four months so she needed to get on. None of the shots she had taken the previous week had been exactly what she wanted, what she had already seen in her mind's eye. Although there is no need for an artist's hand to hold the camera, there should be an artist's eye behind the lens; and it seemed that her eye had got tired lately, letting

197

down the equipment. But this morning she was wide awake, the way you are when you're in love and have the energy and curiosity of a puppy or a young child.

For a photographer, Grace travelled light. As often as not she would use the Leica M4. It had no inbuilt light-meter and no flash; with the latest equipment she could shoot for as long as her eyes could see, although obviously some light was better than others. But she did carry three lenses. For portraits, the Hasselblad camera was still the best, but it was not one for informality, more an acquaintance to invite along respectfully; it had none of the easy camaraderie and go-anywhere style of the Leica.

This Monday morning she wandered the streets in search of a picture. One would present itself eventually but, as is common with hunting, you had to be patient. She took some colour shots but knew none of them was strong enough. As the morning wore on, the haze lifted. She reloaded with black and white.

More and more she thought how much of what mattered came down to something as simple as distance. Show a picture of a crowd at a funeral, getting them all in, every single person there, and watch the punters walk on by. Come in tight on one weeping pain-distorted face and hear the plucking of heart-strings. God had not only given us the Dumb-chip to protect us, Grace thought, but myopia as well. Part of the photographer's role was to provide the glasses.

From a distance the street was busy with busy people. A little closer you could see the beggar slumped on a filthy sleeping-bag, a raggedy mongrel on his lap, his dirty hand outstretched. You noticed his pallor and the sores on his face and neck. A young woman comes towards him. She has a spring in her step and her soft brown-leather boots shine. Her face is an immaculate oval of clear skin, her lips are glossy red, her smooth hair bounces off her shoulders. They look a different species; the beggar and that woman. A young man swooshes past on a skateboard, a can of Coke in his hand. A dog leashed to an elderly woman wags his tail at the raggedy mongrel and sniffs a greeting. It seems a better day for the Family of Dogs than for the Family of Man. Grace watches and waits. The young man on his skateboard passes the other way. Without slowing, he raises the can to his lips. The next moment he's collided with a lamp-post and fallen flat on his behind. The young man begging raises his head. The glossy girl meets his gaze and then they both laugh. Different lives, same laughter. She had a picture.

The next day, developing the film, Grace saw him again, Jefferson McGraw, at the edge of one of her shots. Angelica suggested she see a grief counsellor. 'Don't be ridiculous,' Grace said. 'Whatever it is I'm going through it can't be grief, not over a love affair that ended fifteen years ago.'

'Grief lasts as long as there are people willing to pay hourly fees. Anyway, didn't you tell me yourself that the reason you found it so difficult to get over the death of your mother was that you were too young to remember what she was like. It's the loss of a dream you're grieving over.'

Grace had not expected such understanding. 'I never knew you could buy a heart at Harvey Nic's,' she said.

But Angelica herself was in love. She had reached the mellow stage when the all-engulfing flames of passion had died down to a manageable warm fire, but had not yet been doused by the cold water of realisation that life with Nick was much the same as it had been with Tom and Derek.

'You are so sane, so cool-headed and firm, but when you meet a man you disappear into the nearest phone box as Wonder Woman and emerge in your mother's pinny. I don't get it, Angelica.'

'Of course you do.' Angelica looked at Grace, all wistful smile and sad eyes. 'No woman is a prophet in her own heart.'

'I *think* I understand what you are saying, sort of. I just wish you'd stop trying to please these men whose nature it is to remain displeased, whose very lifeforce seems to spring from discontent.'

There had been no way of pleasing Tom, because in his eyes how could anyone fool enough to love him be worthy of respect? And then there was Derek who fell in love with an independent career woman in killer heels and pillar-box-red lips, only to wipe down her lips with a damp cloth and hand her some comfy flats the moment she was his. That was before running off after the next woman with a bright-red come-hither smile and stiletto heels. And now there was Nick. Angelica always hoped things would change for the better. Hope saved lives, hope was the greatest gift given to mankind, but hope was also a knave. Hope makes us carry on. Hope makes life possible. Hope, Grace thought, was what made her stomach lurch whenever she glimpsed a tall loose-limbed man with dark auburn hair or heard a male voice speak in a soft East Coast accent. Another name for Hope was Dumb-chip. But this time, as it happened, the Dumb-chip was not so dumb after all.

NELL GORDON: *The rekindling of an old love affair led to renewed heartache.*

She slipped on a leaf. It can happen in autumn if the leaves have fallen suddenly and not been cleared and rain has followed, turning them to a soapy mush. She was coming out from the dentist who had told her that she was lucky her teeth were as white as they were but also that if she did not stop chewing tobacco they would soon be as yellow as an old dog's. 'What about polishing?' Grace said. She did not like the thought of giving up the tobacco. You needed both your hands for the camera so cigarettes were often not an option. But she needed tobacco in some form or another. She imagined that it kept her alert. Grace had a horror of inertia, ever since those days, as black and still as a forest mere, that had followed her miscarriages. *The universe rewards action. The roots of evil grow in sloth.* She repeated such little mantras to herself daily to kick herself into action and to keep going. And then there was nicotine which did its part.

She had had two cavities and on her way home she was walking without attention, her tongue teasing the outline of the fillings. She stepped on the leaf and lost her foothold, falling face down on to the pavement, her hands busy protecting the Leica. She lay there hurt and dizzy until someone put out a hand and helped her to her feet. Blood was trickling from her nose and forehead. She felt sick. A voice said, 'Are you all right?'

'Yes,' she said, still unable to focus, still bleeding. 'Absolutely spiffing, thanks very much,' and she hobbled off hanging on to the railings for support. 'Shall I call an ambulance?' the someone called after her. Grace just raised one hand in the air, waving off the suggestion. She knew there was a café just yards away. She

201

would sit down. Have a cup of tea. Check in the mirror to see if her nose was broken.

Stars of gold and red shot across her blurred vision. Later, because it amused her, she took a photograph of a brilliant night sky and called it *Pain*.

She had washed the blood off her face and hands and was sitting at a table by the window with her pot of tea for one, a jug of milk and the miniature pot of honey she carried in her handbag, when she noticed someone walk past outside, stop, walk back, walk off again only to return, stare in through the glass at her and enter.

'It's not?' the voice said. Grace was too sore to bother turning her head. 'Grace? Grace Shield.'

Soft male voice, East Coast American. Now she did look up. 'Jesus!'

'Not exactly. Have another guess.'

Grace stared at him. 'Jefferson?'

'That's it. Can you believe it? How long has it been?'

'If you are real and not a hallucination, sit down and order some tea.' She was trying not to stare at him while she worked out how she felt; there were too many emotions running through her all at once for one to stick right away.

Jefferson McGraw sat down opposite Grace at the table in the café by the dentist. 'You look a bit bashed about. Are you OK? Grace, can I take you to see a doctor?'

'No, it's all right. It's just I was wondering if I was unconscious or something.'

'You don't seem unconscious.'

Angelica had once said that if Grace ever did meet Jefferson again she would wonder what on earth she had seen in him. Angelica had been wrong. Grace scrabbled in her bag for her cigarettes, offering him one. He took it and offered her a light in return. She inhaled and gave him a pale smile. He grinned back, the wide-open smile she remembered so clearly.

'How about that?' he said. 'Of all the people in all the places . . .'

'Good,' she said.

'What?'

'A hallucination would have come up with something a bit more original.' For a second coming something a little more startling is usually required.'

'I like clichés,' he said, just as he had back when they were lovers. 'They're so true.'

She must have hurt herself quite badly, because for no reason her eyes filled with tears. She turned away and pretended to blow her nose, actually wiping her eyes. Jefferson shot her a concerned glance as he moved his hands from the table to his knees and then he raised the right one to the back of his head in a stretching yawning movement as if about to scratch an itch. As their eyes met he lowered his hand to his side. Next he placed it on his hip in 'Hello, sailor' fashion before turning the fist around to inspect the nails. He raised it again, this time to scratch his ear. Grace knew how he felt. You spend most of your life perfectly comfortable with your hands, then comes a moment when they take on a life of their own, popping up everywhere like the snout of an over-excited dog.

'You never ordered,' Grace said. 'Shall I get you some tea?' She realised that she was staring, and quickly looked over at the waitress. He said he would love some. Grace wondered how anything could seem so impossible and so normal both at once; she, him, together, on an autumn day in London. She chatted on, the words coming faster and faster as she avoided his gaze. 'You won't believe this, but I've been seeing you. Of course it can't really have been you . . . can it? So what are you doing in London? You don't live here, do you?' Now she looked straight at him, he was sitting, back to the window, askew in the chair, long legs crossed, playing with his packet of Marlboros. The sun appearing from behind a cloud picked out the auburn glints in his hair. He always had understood the importance of lighting.

'I'm over visiting clients. We've opened an office over here. I come over about once every two months. So it probably was me you've been seeing.'

'Animals?'

'Pardon me,' he said.

'Your clients.'

'No, no, I wouldn't say that. They're rich, most of them, I suppose, but that doesn't make them animals.'

Grace's forehead was throbbing and her nose felt as if it had grown two sizes. 'Aren't you a vet?'

'A vet?' He laughed. When she did not laugh with him he checked his watch. Her gaze followed his. She knew that hand: average size, long square-tipped fingers, clean nails bitten right down. And that hand knew her, every inch of her. She felt the heat in her cheeks and looked away. 'It's almost lunchtime,' he said. 'I think you should have something to eat.'

'I'll dribble.'

'You never used to.'

'I've been to the dentist.' She opened her mouth wide.

'Have some soup,' he said, glancing at the menu. Then, 'Are you sure you shouldn't go see a doctor? Head injuries are not to be trifled with.'

Her eyeballs felt as if they were being slow-baked in their hollows. She blinked and blinked again. 'What is to be trifled with?' she said, feeling suddenly and unaccountably sad. 'Life, death, people, feelings, head injuries, pets, livers, hearts? Really, when you think about it, there's very little that can be trifled with. Or you could say that as life is essentially impossible – I mean, who would believe it – there's everything to be trifled with. I'll have a chicken sandwich. I'll chew on my good side.'

'Not feeling dizzy, wanting to throw up?'

'No more than usual. It's just having seen you all those times and then us bumping into each other like this. It's like fearing being mugged or getting cancer; we fret, tell ourselves that it's bound to be our turn next but when it is – our turn, I mean – we stand there, amazed, aggrieved, our hands raised skywards asking, "Where did that come from? Why did this happen to me?"'

'Mugging, cancer and me; that's nice.'

She smiled into her cup and then looked straight at him, holding her gaze steady. You could barely see it but he flinched and then he flushed pink. He gave her an uncertain smile. He had filled out a little, especially round the jaw. It suited him. His mouth was as firm as she remembered and still stretched impossibly when he smiled, and his bright-blue eyes had that perky watchful look that she had loved; the look of a puppy told to lie still, watching, waiting, ready for action at the first sign of anyone willing to play. And there she was, as angular as ever, same straight hair falling to her shoulders, still pale but with more freckles from more years in the sun. And her skin was not as young as his. She had crow's feet from all that squinting into the lens. Still, she imagined that to a passer-by they looked good together, although she might come across as a little stern, someone who would give that easy-looking guy a hard time.

'So what do you do, if you're not a vet?'

He looked puzzled for a moment then he sat back, laughing indulgently at the boy he used to be. 'Of course back then I wanted to become a vet.'

'You were going to open a wildlife clinic where people could bring in injured and sick animals and have them treated free of charge.' She could hear the faintly querulous tone to her voice, the voice of someone who had been told the restaurant was all out of wild strawberries and knew they must try to be adult about it. 'I really loved that about you.' She should not have said that because now they were both embarrassed. Whatever would she come up with next? *Oh, and then you cheated on me with that pink-bubblegum girl and broke my heart, leaving me alone and pregnant, although I miscarried of course.*

Grace became dogged, the way she often did when in a tight spot. 'I never thought you would change your mind about being a vet. You were passionate about it.' There was that reproachful tone to her voice again.

This time he noticed it too. 'You sound as if I've let you down.'

All the times she had thought of him on seeing an injured animal on the road. She had to smile then as she remembered all those long-ago fantasies of her turning up at his practice with a little crushed body in her arms, him striding towards her and relieving her gently of her burden. And it had been a good match: she took pictures of suffering and he relieved it. She blushed just thinking about it now. Why could she not just have masturbated like a normal person?

'Actually, I'm a lawyer.'

'A lawyer! So you wouldn't have healed that poor little animal, you would have sued it for dripping blood on your corporate carpet.'

'What animal? Which carpet?'

'Oh, never mind.'

He asked her, 'What do you do?'

'Photographer.'

'So one of us stuck to our youthful passions.'

She lit another cigarette before remembering to offer him one. 'Thanks. Actually, my wife thinks I've given up.'

Of course he was married. It was entirely to be expected. Even Grace had been married, for a while. 'Children?'

He nodded, looking proud, as if he was about to haul out a wallet full of snapshots. 'Three girls.'

And our boy. But all she said was, 'Three girls, goodness. And what about their mother?'

He cleared his throat, not quite looking at her as he answered. 'Actually, you know her. It's Cherry. We got married.'

Grace thought about it. 'That's good,' she said finally.

He looked relieved. 'You think so?'

'I do. At least you didn't break my heart over some passing fancy.'

He had always been touchy-feely, quick to empathise. Now he leant forward and, in a quick gesture of sympathy, put his hand over hers as it rested on the table. 'I didn't really break your heart, did I?'

Grace withdrew her hand and gave him a straightforward sensible look as she lied, 'Of course you didn't. We were young. I was upset at the time, but a broken heart . . .' She inhaled on her cigarette and smiled through the smoke. 'It's the usual inflation of words: a cold is the new flu, a headache is a migraine, a man doing his job is a hero and England's collapse at cricket is a tragedy.'

She could see that he did not quite believe her and that he was concerned. His face, although conventionally handsome, owed its particular charm to its mobility, the way feeling was translated into expression. She had not realised until years later, when she did fashion shows of models whose faces looked like still photographs even in life, that she had shown precocious skill in capturing that liveliness in those early photographs of him.

'And you,' he glanced at her bare left hand, 'are you married, children?'

'Divorced. No children.'

'Did you not want any?'

'Yes, I did.'

'I'm sorry.'

'Don't worry; you did your best.'

'How do you mean, I did my best?'

'Did I say that? What I meant to say was, it was *for* the best.'

'Oh.'

'How long are you over for?'

She stubbed her cigarette out and almost immediately reached for another. He raised an eyebrow but lit it for her and said, 'I go back in two days' time.' There was a pause. 'Are you busy tomorrow?'

She nodded. 'A job. King's Road. Advertising. It could take most of the day.'

'I've got a partners' dinner in the evening. So what are you shooting?'

'The woman who is strong yet vulnerable, outgoing while possessing an aura of mystique, happy-go-lucky yet ambitious to get to the top, independent yet yearning for love, the woman who wears Whispers panty-liners.'

He laughed, but he asked, 'You don't mind doing that crap?'

'Not at all. And it's not crap, it's work. And the money it brings in is what gives me the freedom to do my own stuff.'

'You're so yourself, Grace. You always were.'

He looked so beautiful and so serious that she said gently, not teasing, 'But who else would I be?'

'You know what I mean. Most people act out all these different roles. You don't. It's very relaxing.'

Smiling, she shook her head. 'I used to, but I've come to think it's best to leave being someone else to others; they tend to be better at it.' She looked at him, her head tilted, a small smile on her lips. 'When I first knew you, you cared so much; about your wild animals and your woods. You invested everything you did with this intensity, as if you lived your life in bold letters.'

Jefferson tried not to look flattered, and failed. It was that open face of his. 'I still care,' he said. 'That's one thing I've learnt: you can make yourself interested in almost anything as long as you go in deep and with enthusiasm. I quite see now how someone can dedicate their entire life to the study of a particular kind of ant. There's no subject that doesn't stretch to accommodate your interest if you approach it the right way. Anyway, the law is fascinating. Maybe not the initial study but the practice and the principles.'

They both glanced at their watches. It was time to go and they rose from the table in perfect synchronicity. They shook hands as awkwardly as children, but as he turned she kept him back, just for a moment, raising herself on tiptoe and giving him a kiss on the cheek. 'Goodbye then, Jefferson McGraw.'

That night she phoned Angelica. 'What do you do when you have just come face to face with a romantic fantasy?'

'Celebrate?'

'And when it's unobtainable?'

'Get drunk?'

'You're not being helpful.'

'All right then; live the rest of your life unfulfilled and yearning for what can never be, and knowing that your dream is real, out there, but always out of your reach.'

'That's it. That's better.'

'Or, assuming it's a guy, you could fuck him senseless and damn the consequences.'

'That too is a tempting option.'

But alone, away from the phone, she stopped being flippant. What kind of freak was she still to be in love with a man who she had loved and lost when they were both no more than children?

He called her two months later. He was back in London.

('Dangerous,' Angelica said.

'It's OK. We both know that nothing can happen.')

Liar, liar, pants on fire. Well, they might as well have been, the speed with which the two of them undressed. Quickly, quickly, no time for regrets. Illicit lovers live in mean time; time is their enemy. Come on down, every second counts. Don't answer the phone. Stay a little while longer; you've been gone for so long.

She could not possibly sleep. How could she when he was lying there beside her? He was a miracle. If a miracle occurred, did you turn over and go to sleep? She could not have enough of him. Proudly she listened to him inhale and exhale; look at him, he *breathes*. Every moment they were together was to be savoured. Precious, precious seconds. Tick-tock, tick-tock, tick-tock . . .

But she did sleep eventually and when she woke it was seven o'clock and he was up and dressed already. He perched on the bed looking at her with a mixture of helplessness and determination, as if he had no choice but to cross the field of fire. 'Last night changed things.'

'Call me a silly deluded thing,' Grace said, 'but I already thought spending the night making passionate love and mumbling over and over that you love each other kind of did.'

He rolled his eyes. 'And you're just the same sweet soppy creature that I remember. I know I state the obvious but someone has to. So what do we do now?'

She smiled dopily, too happy, too close to the night before to worry.

'I really think I love you, Grace,' he said. But he did not look happy about it.

She pulled him gently down towards her. 'I really think I love you.'

'That makes it pretty serious.'

She nodded.

209

'I can't leave Cherry.'

'I didn't ask you to.'

'No, you don't understand. This is not some cheating-husband bullshit. I really can't. She's not well. She . . . she's got a problem.'

I could have told you that fifteen years ago, Grace thought, but she didn't say it.

'She never really took to New York, to our life there. And why should she? We don't have that much in common.' He looked away as he said, 'She got pregnant that summer. The summer you were over.'

Well, *snap*!

'I had been dating her for two years. Then she told me it was over and she went away. I was pretty cut up for a while although if I was honest with myself I knew we weren't that good together. I had some fixation on her.' He smiled wryly. 'Boys are like that. I met you and you were everything she was not. I really liked you, but you scared me too. I know I talked a brave talk back then but I was a seriously square kid. You were so different from my mother, Cherry, most of the women I knew. That's what was so good, and that was what drove me back to her, to what was familiar, unthreatening. Once I was back with her I knew pretty soon that I'd made a mistake but by then it was too late. By the way, she thinks I'm a pretentious little prick, and she's probably right. But she really doesn't have a lot of interests. She's not a stupid woman. But she has her views and beliefs and she's not prepared to move outside, not ever. And I've been busy working, being the husband I thought she wanted rather than the one she actually needed. I didn't pay enough attention to her, to what she really wanted.' The look on Grace's face made him laugh. 'Don't look so surprised. We guys can work these things out as well as the next woman when pointed in the right direction; in our case two years of couple therapy and a spell in a drying-out clinic for her. A while ago she got drunk at lunchtime and wrapped the car round a lamp-post on her way to fetch the girls from school. I can't stop thinking, what if they had been in that car with her? She spent six weeks in hospital. They sent her away with stronger painkillers and more sleeping tablets. We've got a housekeeper now. Cherry's

210

been back to the clinic but she's drinking again. It's a miserable sordid story and I'm greatly to blame. I've thought of leaving but, apart from feeling partly responsible for her problems, there are the girls to consider. If their mother was OK and we shared custody, I reckon they'd get over it, cope like most kids do. But she is not all right. I'm scared that if I did go, she'd lose it altogether and what would that do to the girls? I couldn't leave them with her, so I'd take them and they'd probably end up having visits with their mom in an institution – not a good scenario.'

As she listened, Grace had tried to picture life in the Upper West Side apartment. All she saw were gothic images of a puffy prematurely aged Cherry reeling round the perfectly decorated rooms with a vodka bottle in her hand, her bubblegum-pink lipstick smeared across her lips and chin. Did she feel sorry for her? Not yet she didn't. She could not forget the way Cherry had sailed back into Jefferson's life, reclaiming him as carelessly as she had discarded him a couple of months before and with even less regard for the girl who had picked up the pieces while she was away. To this day she wondered if Cherry would ever have bothered if it hadn't been for her seeing someone else making such a good thing from what she had thrown out. Jefferson was gazing at her as if she held the answer to the unanswerable. She took his hand and kissed it then held it to her cheek, looking up at him. 'You said it yourself. You have no option but to stay.'

He was examining her cameras, turning them over in his hands, holding each one up to his eyes, peering through the lens. 'Actually,' he said, handing them back to her, 'I'm a hopeless photographer.'

'That's all right; I'm sure I'm a pretty useless lawyer.' She grinned at him. 'Then again, as the man said when asked if he played the violin, "I don't know, I haven't tried."' She placed the Hasselblad in its box and held on to the Leica.

'The way you touch those guys, the way you look at them, it's like you're in love.'

She did not reply. Instead she said, 'The Leica is good for sneaking up on people. No mirrors shunting up and down. And at

211

the moment of exposure you see the entire motif. The Hasselblad is for *The Moment*. The Leica is for the moment.' She signed the different emphases in the air with her finger.

He liked her fashion shoots against the backdrop of a polluted urban wasteland, pictures she had done years before. 'The message is excruciatingly obvious; I was a lot younger. But they're good shots.'

'You don't want to be too subtle,' he said. 'People don't get it if you are.' He told her that he still wished he could take those complacent citizens from their lit-up, centrally heated, air-conditioned homes with their three-car garages and show them the desert they were helping to create. 'Myself, I'm just the most eco-friendly guy you could hope to meet. I turn the tap off *while* I brush my teeth. I bicycle. I recycle. I eat organic so I expect I shit organic too. I drink coffee from humanely picked coffee beans. I spend a set amount of hours each week giving free advice to environmental organisations. Do I make a difference? Like hell I do. Do I carry on in spite of that? Sure I do.'

'Of course. It's the fun of being human; you just carry right on although you know damn well it makes no difference.' She was still preoccupied with distance. She showed him some more fashion shots taken in the Seychelles. It had been early morning on Bird Island, a place easily confused with paradise.

'For man there are no predators. The sea is a liquid-blue embrace, the wind wraps around you like a soft shield against the heat. The sky is alive with birds: humble-looking sooty terns, the rare tropic bird with its quill tail, and the white fairy tern, a perfect beauty across a night sky. Those white birds lay their eggs in the branches of the trees. The baby birds hatch precariously, and they stay there on that same branch waiting for their parents to feed them. From far away it looks as if the branches are covered in white candy floss. Up a bit closer, you think it must be singing fruit. Get closer still and you see it's baby birds, from tiny to almost fully grown. The adult birds can only feed their young on the wing. It's when you're at touching distance and happen to shift your gaze downwards that you realise that, for every ten fluffy baby birds decorating the tree, there is at least one who has slipped and fallen to the lowest branches or even to the ground beneath. Once that low down they can't be fed. But they don't know, so they just sit there, stock still, patiently waiting for the food that never comes. The ones on the ground seem to be of a darker colour. Get right down, look closely, and you see that that darkness is the ants eating them alive. "Just look at that," one of the models said, standing on the terrace of the restaurant, pointing at the trees. "Isn't that just the cutest sight?" Well it was, from where she was standing. So it beats me how people always talk about having to see the wood for the trees; that way how can you learn to treasure each and every single plant for its unique contribution to the wood? If you see only the wood, you'll never miss a tree when it is felled. It's more comfortable at a distance, of course it is. In fact it's a godlike state.'

'Perhaps distance is His problem – God's, I mean,' Jefferson said. 'Perhaps that's the answer to the age-old question of how He can allow such misery on earth. He means well, the very best, but from where He stands it all looks pretty good: there's air to breathe (apparently it looks prettier from up there, the more polluted it is), we have the oceans and the lakes, the mountains and the streams, woods, plains . . . "Take a look at that," He says to a visitor, pointing at the far-away earth. He is proud. Why shouldn't He be? "You remember when I did the work?" He says to his friend. "I was flat out and so exhausted I had to rest all Sunday. But I knew I had done a great job. It's a beautiful place; oh, is it beautiful. There's everything anyone can need: air, water, food. The way I ordered nature, I'm telling you . . . genius. And look at them, I call them my children, see them milling about? How they have grown and multiplied. Actually, in that respect they have outdone all my expectations. I'm telling you, things must be going pretty well down there."' Jefferson stopped and shrugged, palms up to the heavens. 'Could be as simple as that.'

'So will you still love me from a distance?' she asked, although she was sure his answer would be a resounding yes.

Instead he shook his head and sighed. 'I honestly don't know. Earth might look better from afar; but me, I'm a close-up kind of guy. I might not have the soul to love from a distance.' He took her in his arms, kissing her hair and the lids of her closed eyes, her cheeks and her lips. 'Let's not worry about that. It's here and now that matters. But whatever happens this will never be just another affair.'

Disappointed as she was with his answer, she could not help smiling. He was an intelligent man, a successful lawyer, yet he spoke his soap-opera lines with all sincerity and she loved him all the more for it, although she could not resist teasing. 'This is bigger than both of us,' she mumbled.

He replied, unsuspecting as ever, 'I know, darling, I know it is,' and there was a catch in his voice that made her feel instantly ashamed of making fun.

She shot a whole roll of black and white film just of him. At first, when she pointed the lens at him, he looked awkward, the way most people do, but soon he loosened up and enjoyed himself. 'I always knew how to photograph you,' she said. 'Oh, I'm so good.'

'Oh yes, oh yes, my darling, you are.' Their eyes met and they burst out laughing. 'But really,' he said, 'you have turned from gawky Grace to graceful Grace. When you work, you move with such delicate precision and you always know exactly where you are going.' She blushed, pleased. It was her quiet embarrassment; being big and strong and often clumsy and answering to the name of Grace.

They sat together on the sofa, talking, as lovers do, of everything, as long as it was to do with them. 'I was such a fool back then,' he said.

'And now?'

'And now I'm older and a wiser fool.'

'See, apart from you having become a bloodsucking leech of a lawyer instead of a man who treats wild animals for free, you haven't changed that much. You're a romantic who cheats on your women. You're a loyal friend. You're vain about your good looks but you still won't pay for a decent hair-cut. You're capricious and you're thoughtful. You're always in a hurry unless you're making love. You have the ego of a small-size town but you love the success of others and dislike talking about yourself, and, my darling, you still mouth clichés with the innocent wonder of someone who's just woken up to this world.' At that he laughed, his dark head thrown back, his throat exposed where it was soft and white. She slid her finger across, just below the Adam's apple. 'Cut or kiss,' she said.

He had a week. They made the most of the time between his meetings and her jobs by the simple trick of not sleeping more than an hour or two each night. Lying next to him in the early hours of the morning and able to touch him, just like that, as easily as if she was still dreaming, was a great and wholly unexpected happiness.

The morning he was due to return to the States she wanted him to go as soon as possible. She perched on top of the dirty linen basket watching him shave. He was naked. He had been curiously shy at the start of the week, covering up as if she might find his nakedness offensive, but now he moved around as easily as if he were alone, or showing off.

She had made breakfast – toast and soft-boiled eggs – although she ate nothing herself, but just kept downing mugs of sweet milky tea. He ate his own egg and hers, but when he looked at her she saw he had tears in his eyes that he wiped away quickly with the back of his hand.

Go, she thought; go so I can start grieving. The days ahead would be strewn with burning coal and lined with barbed wire and there was no other way than through; so, she reckoned, the sooner she could begin the sooner she would be out the other side.

'I've got time for another cup of tea,' he said.

'No. No, you don't.' She got to her feet. 'The traffic can be dreadful at this time of the morning.'

He looked a little surprised. 'But I'll be going against the traffic. Anyway, the car won't be here for another ten minutes at least.'

'Better get going then,' she said.

'I'm screwing up your life again, aren't I?'

'Yes. But I wouldn't have it any other way.'

He looked at her. 'Would you move to the States? You could work over there just as well as here.'

Her heart skipped a beat as if it was already celebrating. But she shook her head. 'No. This is my home. Everything you see I've built for myself. I took nothing from my husband in the divorce. And it's not so easy to start again, even for a freelance. I've built up a reputation here, I have my contacts; people who know my work

215

and trust me. And there's Mrs Shield, and my friends. I might end up hating you, leaving it all behind to sit around in some cabin waiting, waiting for you.'

'What's with the cabin? It could be a real elegant condo or a cottage in the Hamptons.'

'Wherever . . . waiting for you to turn up and dreading for you to leave? What kind of imbalance would that bring to our relationship? I would become someone else, some dependent, clinging, frustrated version of the woman you love. And,' she put her arms round his neck and looked him deep in the eyes, 'I still don't entirely trust you. This time, if I'm going to have my heart broken I want it to be on my home ground.'

'You can trust me,' he said. 'But I don't blame you for not knowing that . . . yet.'

She sat on the bed and cried at the sight of the crumpled sheets. She lay down and rested her head on the pillow that smelt faintly of him.

She took a picture of the bedroom. It became the first of a whole series of shots where absence spoke strongest. A child alone outside the school gates, a woman alighting from a train on to a deserted railway platform, the same woman keeping to one side of a double bed.

'Have you ever suffered from depression?' Noah asked Grace. 'And I'm not talking about feeling a bit down.'

Grace looked at him, wondering where that question came from. 'Depression is the absence of the Dumb-chip,' she said. 'And yes, yes, I have. It was deathly. I saw the world as an ugly place filled with darkness and malice and life as utterly pointless. Then the Dumb-chip kicked in and now I find the world miraculous and each and every life as something sacred, occasionally even my own. I don't know how long it'll be until sanity returns.'

'That's what I like to see; a positive outlook.'

Grace lit a cigarette. 'Don't get me wrong; I prefer it when the Dumb-chip's in. Without it you see clearly and that is unbearable.'

'Call it illness or unbearable clarity of vision, but I wonder if Louisa suffered from depression way back. There are letters from Arthur to friends, entries in his diaries. Something was going on and it must have affected his work.'

'Well, did it?'

'What do you mean?'

'You know his work. Did it go through some kind of sea-change?'

Noah scratched his head as he paced the room. 'No, not really. The Donald Argyll biography hints at some personal problems way back in the early 1930s. Of course Argyll's book only goes up to the Second World War. I've been studying Arthur's work from that period but I can't say that I see any reflection of trouble there. Part of me, the professional part, the one who wants some money and a few decent reviews, wants to explore this further. But then there's the good-grandson part. Talk about selling one's granny.'

'No.' Grace shuddered. 'Let's not.'

He stopped his pacing, reaching out and taking her hand, and he looked at her as tenderly as he had once, long ago, when she fell off her bicycle and ended up weeping inconsolably for the mother she had lost five years earlier. 'Was it worth it, Grace?'

She paused again before answering, 'I still don't know.'

Louisa was in the garden seated on the wooden bench beneath the
copper beech. She turned her head as Grace approached. Her face,
a construction of bones draped in ill-fitting skin, lit up with a smile
of such sweetness that Grace reached for the camera she no longer
carried. 'Autumn's coming.' Louisa patted the seat. 'Sit down and
have a chat. I adore my grandson but I do find it difficult to have a
proper conversation with him. Do you have that problem? Maybe
it's men.'

Grace put her hand to her mouth, disguising her laughter as a
cough. 'Yes, I think it probably is.'

'The gardens are lovely, don't you think? I shall miss them. Of
course Arthur did not approve of my taste. He thought all the
colour vulgar and he disliked what he saw as the lack of order,
but I put my foot down. "I'm in charge of the gardens," I told
him.' She chuckled, then added, 'of course we haven't been able to
keep them up the way they should be for a long time now.'

'These colours,' Grace made a sweeping gesture towards the
herbaceous borders, 'these colours that Arthur didn't like are the
colours of my painting.'

'I never was very good at what you call the nitty-gritty of
gardening. And once something was in the soil I liked to leave
it there. I liked seeing what's going to happen next to the shape
of a flower or a shrub, or the colours of the leaves. The gardener
always wanted to move and replant, to bring some in and put some
out, but I told him to let things be, to let them find their own way;
to grow or die. Arthur always said I was the most passive woman
he'd ever met. He was right, of course. I just never felt the urge to
change things. I'm happy to watch what's there.'

'I can understand that,' Grace said. 'When I worked as a photographer I did pose pictures, obviously; portraiture especially is all
about posing, about composing the picture. But what I liked best,
what really interested me, was to catch the fleeting moment.'

'Lillian was born about this time of year,' Louisa said. 'Lillian.
Now there's a happy creature. Strange but happy. I miss her. She's
in Tanzania, you know.'

'I know. You told me.'

Louisa

OLD LYDIA HOBBLES INTO the nursery on Jane Dale's arm. She bends so low over the crib I fear she might topple and crush my baby. The sing-song talk she addresses to her granddaughter makes me giggle, although I'm still exhausted, floaty with the pain and exhilaration of birth – imagine, Lydia Blackstaff cooing like a dove. They don't stay long. Outside the sun is shining but the heavy curtains are drawn across my windows. In the twilight I see the door open slowly, inch by inch, letting in the light from the landing. It's Georgie. He looks so big now I've held a newborn baby again, my golden boy with his sturdy little limbs and his thick flaxen hair; but not too big to cry. I can see that he's been crying; his eyes are puffy and pink-rimmed. Nanny told me that he had been frightened – 'very worried' he had said in his solemn way. Jane had told him that once there was a new baby in the house, the old one – in this case Georgie – would have to grow up quick smart because there was only room for one baby even when the house was as big as this one. After that Georgie had had nightmares, awful dreams where the baby grew larger and larger until it took up all the space that should have been Georgie's, and finally he was squeezed out altogether, alone outside. 'And I looked in through the window,' he had wept to Nanny, 'and all I could see was a big fat baby cheek. I couldn't see you or Mama anywhere.'

I hold my arms out to my little boy. 'You come here.' He rushes to me and I hug him close and feel his hot damp cheek against mine. I stroke his curls and whisper in his ear that everything is fine and no one could ever take his place.

'Where is he?' Georgie wants to know.

'Who, Georgie?' Then I realise and I smile at him. 'You mean the baby? Well, the baby is a she. Look over there, in the crib.'

Georgie looks and then gives vent to one of those sudden bursts of hilarity that annoy his father almost as much as his sudden bursts of tears. 'But she's so little!' he shouts, bouncing up and down on the bed until being dragged off by Nanny. 'She's not big at all.' He jumps up and down on the floor in his excitement.

Lillian should have been the boy in the family: that's what Arthur says every time he sees her. There is nothing of her pale moon-struck mother or brother about her, none of our reproachful presence. For a while Arthur seems content. He picks up his son and throws him high in the air, catching him with strong sure hands. He makes me laugh with silly jokes and stories of his days as a young man sharing a loft with his poor artist friends and hiding the generous allowance from his mother so as not to be different from any of the others. He tickles the baby's plump little stomach. He lights up our days, making us feel warm and strong, and full of hope. But soon he has to move on, leaving us alone out there in the cold.

I engross myself in caring for my children. I try to make friends with Jane Dale, and I wait, wait for him to notice me again. But, like fruit left untasted in the bowl, I grow bruised and then plain bad. Arthur says my bad humour goes before me like a foul smell.

'You complain that I avoid you. Of course I avoid you. Why should I risk my good humour and my peace of mind on a sour, bitter woman? You become my sweet funny Louisa again and I will want to be with you more, don't you see?'

Why was I never enough? What was it about me that the people who were meant to love me had such problems doing so? What was it about me that those people who said they loved me behaved as if they did not? I stand for hours staring at my reflection. I do not realise it at the time but Jane is watching me through a crack in the door.

What she sees she describes later, in detail, to both Arthur and

Lydia; she claimed they ought to know so that they could help. I know what she said.

'There she was, stark naked, with all that hair falling down her back . . .' Lydia interrupts to say how she is always saying I should have it cut, my long hair, my inelegant outmoded hair.

'Mother!' That's Arthur speaking. 'Jane is trying to tell us something.'

'She was like an animal; no, a crazy woman, screaming, cursing.'

'It's the quiet ones you have to watch.'

'Mother, will you let Jane finish.'

'"What's the matter with you all?" That's what she kept screaming over and over again, even though there was no one in the room . . .'

'Well, thank God for small mercies. Just imagine what the servants would have made of it. It would be all over the village.'

'Mother!'

'It was as if there were people there that only she could see. It was eerie. "What's wrong with you all?" She said it over and over again but there was no one there. I closed the door and left her, in front of the glass, stark naked, weeping like a baby.'

Arthur comes to see me. He tells me what he has heard. He is hurt, he says. He feels that I'm being most unfair. Do I not realise that he needs peace right now with the exhibition coming up? 'Really, Louisa, does it always have to be about you? Now, I know things aren't as we had hoped between us, but you're my wife. We shall both have to make the best of things. I'm not an insensitive man, as you know. In fact, I sometimes think that I am too sensitive for my own good. I understand the burden you carry from your unfortunate early life. The ghosts of your parents haunt you still. Suicide is indeed the greatest betrayal. That's why, however distressed I myself might get at times, I would never contemplate such an action. So you need not worry on that score, I can assure you.'

I look at him, wondering if his words are calculated, if he knows the distress they cause. 'Arthur,' I say, 'until now I had never thought it the slightest possibility that you, of all people, should

221

wish to take your own life.' I look down at my quiet hands folded in my lap and then I face him again with a smile. 'But thank you, my dear, for your assurance.'

Georgie has turned into a whiny boy, Arthur says, always clinging to his mother and glaring at the world through those amber-coloured eyes. He runs to me or Nanny whenever his father takes the trouble to pay him attention. I get cross with Arthur for complaining about our son and I tell him that people are not possessions that can be toyed with for a while and then put back in the cupboard until the next time you feel like having a game. For someone who never tires of pointing out the faults and weaknesses in others, Arthur takes these remarks of mine very much to heart. He protests. Next his eyes are full of hurt like Georgie's when he got smacked once for running out on to the road. Finally he storms from the room.

My little daughter . . . she is a strange one, of that there is no argument. Nanny shakes her head in wonderment. 'It's not natural, a child that young who doesn't cry. Look at her screwing up her little face and glaring at us.'

Only rarely did she cry and then it was from rage, not pain or sorrow. Lillian is bold. You see it in the way she pulls herself up to stand, as she takes her first step at only ten months, her straight dark brows knitted together in concentration. When she falls over she labours to her feet without a whimper, her tiny mouth clamped shut. But she has a temper, that little one, banging her tiny fists on the floor as if to punish it for her tumble. I love my daughter and I'm amused by her, but there is none of the visceral closeness I have with Georgie; rather, there exists a detachment, as if we, Lillian and I, have yet to work out the connection between us. She is so much her own person, with not a trait for which to thank or rebuke me. She looks at us all with her clear-eyed gaze, as if secretly we amuse her. She is the only one in the household who is unperturbed by Arthur's rages. The only time she seems to mind is when he upsets Georgie. She adores her brother and treats him a little like her pet. And she is fond of me; I know that from the way her cross little face brightens when I hold my arms out towards her and the way she moves just a little closer when there are strangers around. I enjoy those moments when she shows her need of me. Mostly she does not seem to need anybody, but if she does – if she is hungry or wants a toy from a high shelf or a toddle in the gardens – then Jane will do nearly as well as I, and Nanny of course, or even the stern-faced whiskery old Grandma.

Arthur tells me that I should get out of the house, have some interest outside him and the children. 'Look at Jane,' he says. 'She cares for us all and yet she is always out and about in her free time. It would do us good to have to manage without you now and then.'

'He thinks I'm boring,' I tell Viola.

'Do you think you are boring?' she asks.

'I wonder about it,' I say. Then I smile. 'But I think Jane, with all her activities, is duller still.'

But I resume my painting. I don't know that I'm very good at it, but I do know that when I'm at my easel I don't need to ask who and why I am.

'I was right, was I not?' Arthur says, pleased and mellow, stroking his beard, twinkling at me. 'You just needed to get out and about and enjoy some activity of your own.'

I fear I shall never understand my husband. Our new teacher William Fenton is so pleased with our progress, Viola's and mine, that he has suggested we hold a small exhibition. A friend of his owns a gallery in Guildford. 'It would be the ideal venue. Lewis is especially keen to help new artists.'

'I don't think so,' I tell William at first. 'We're just lady amateurs.'

'Do you believe that? Is that how you feel? Like a lady amateur?'

I look up from my easel. 'No,' I tell him. 'When I paint I am alive.'

And Viola is game. I tell Arthur of our plans, expecting him to be proud. My dream is for him to speak to me with seriousness, to discuss and engage the way he does with his friends. If I prove myself, even in a small way, he might. That's what I hope. But unaccountably he is angry, accusing William Fenton of taking advantage of his pupils. 'Can't you see? Can't you see that he and this friend of his are trying to gain from your connection with me? Oh, you are so naïve.'

'I think William believes I have talent.'

Arthur shakes his head. 'Oh, Louisa, I'm not saying you don't produce some very pleasing little pictures . . .'

'It's been a while since you saw any of my work.'

'Maybe, maybe, but I doubt there has been such progress as to justify exhibiting. No, my dear, I fear you're taken for a fool.'

But some days later he tells me he has a surprise. 'I have asked Donald Argyll down for the weekend to look at your work. We have the business of my next show to discuss anyway. If he thinks well of it then I am prepared to admit that I was wrong and I will personally organise a small exhibition for you. Although I think that here at home, with our friends and neighbours invited, would be most suitable.'

Donald Argyll owned the fashionable gallery in London through which Arthur sold his work, and his opinion was much relied on. 'He is a fierce critic,' I say.

'You have nothing to fear, Louisa. What Donald abhors is pretension: callow youths with their talk of Modernism setting themselves out to be great artists. You make no such claims. You are simply a young woman keen to share her husband's world, and with a pleasing little talent of her own. He will be able to tell us – I feel I am too close to be an entirely reliable judge – if this young man is justified in raising your sights.'

'Should you not take a look yourself first?'

'If you wish, dear, if you wish.'

But he is busy in the next few days and there is never quite the right moment. By the time Donald Argyll arrives I feel shy and foolish for having listened to young William Fenton. Mr Argyll is charming, however. He compliments me on the children and on the excellent luncheon. Then they withdraw to the studio to look at Arthur's work in progress, his great Island canvas. Much later, when the light is fading and I believe with some relief that they have forgotten all about *me*, Jane fetches me from the nursery saying that Mr Argyll is ready to look at my work.

With the help of William Fenton and Viola I had chosen five paintings to display. I had placed them in the morning room: one on my easel and the others propped up on chairs. (I had felt it presumptuous to replace the paintings already on the walls with my own offerings even for a day and Arthur had not suggested it.)

Mr Argyll walks around the room. Arthur is not with him. I watch him, alert to every flicker of emotion. My heart beats faster and my palms turn clammy as I await his pronouncement. He does not keep me long.

'My dear Mrs Blackstaff, I must ask you why, when you have so many duties to which you are so eminently suitable, would you wish to pursue the difficult path of the artist?'

The heat rises in my cheeks and my eyes start itching, but I look straight at him with what I hope is an easy pleasant air. 'I never set out to. It was just something to bring me out of the house. But gradually it began to take me over; yes, there's no other word for it. I tried to pretend otherwise, I am aware of my limitations, but this,' I gesticulate towards the easel and my picture upon it, 'is what I am happy doing. When I paint I feel most myself. And then Mr Fenton, our teacher, told us that he thought we were ready, Viola Glastonbury and I, to put our work before an audience. He believes,' I hesitate then I push back my shoulders, 'he believes that I have a talent.'

'Does he, now? Then let it rest there.' Donald Argyll turned on his heels, about to leave the room. 'I shall make no further comment.'

Arthur had come in and now he too was inspecting my work. I tried to read his expression; he noticed and turned away, but in the short moment when his eyes met mine, I saw it: dislike. I felt close to tears and tried to compose myself, turning to the window, looking out across the garden.

'No, Donald,' my husband's voice was even. 'We asked you here to give your honest view. You would not do Louisa any favours allowing her to labour under false illusions or allowing her to make a fool of herself.'

I blanch at his choice of words and dread what will follow, but all I can do is wait.

'Very well. I would not go as far as to say that what I have seen is entirely without merit, Mrs Blackstaff. There is a naïvety that can be quite charming in its place. However, were I to judge your work against that of true artists, your husband being one . . .' here Arthur inclined his head in recognition of the tribute '. . . then I would have to say that everything about it speaks of a negation of the skill and care that is the hallmark of the professional artist. May I also add that I find some of your work, mainly the canvas entitled *Mother and Child*, lacking in good taste as well as the basic skills in drawing, composition, perspective and colour.'

'It was for the best.' Arthur wants to comfort me. There is no sign now of the anger I had seen in his eyes when he first saw my pictures. Maybe I had been mistaken; I was upset. 'I fear you would not have taken my word alone but that you would have suspected me of some underhand motive in wishing to keep your work from a wider audience. This is why I called on Donald to give his opinion. Surely it is better we are spared the humiliation of a public exhibition? And don't forget, there would have been far more interest paid than is usual for the efforts of an unknown lady artist because of who I am. Believe me, he did us both a kindness. Now, no one is suggesting you should not go on enjoying your lessons, only that you should see it for what it is: a pleasant pastime. And can I also say that you have been a little neglectful of your duties at home of late.'

I stop going to my classes. I try to explain to William Fenton and Viola. William's jaw clenches and his dark eyes flash with anger; how young he is, I think. 'That pompous old fraud. That . . .' I put my hand on his arm and as he glances down I wonder if he thinks, as I do, what a large strong hand mine is, what an unladylike hand. 'Louisa, I implore you to take no notice. Don't let them take this away from you.'

I smile at him. 'You speak as if there is a conspiracy. I don't think I'm important enough for that. No, this is my choice. I simply respect the work of real artists too much to wish to waste time and paint and canvas playing at art. Mr Argyll would have said if he had seen anything of real merit in my work.'

'He is one man.'

'One who happens to be our foremost critic. And don't forget my husband. He did not disagree.'

'Your husband . . .' William paces the small studio, a frown on his handsome young face. I wonder if maybe his mother was Italian, Spanish perhaps; he has the colouring: olive skin, and those fine dark eyes. He turns and looks at me and I can see that he is trying hard to remain calm. 'All I can say is that they are wrong.'

'Oh, William, you are very kind, but I can't dismiss their opinions like that. I respect yours, of course I do . . .'

'But not enough to trust it above theirs?'

I pause. 'No. No, maybe not.'

'You love your painting,' Viola says. 'Does that not count for anything?'

'I told you; it counts for everything. I have too much respect for art itself, I love it too much to keep on producing inferior work.'

William looks surprised. He is not used to me speaking like this, my voice raised. Viola knows me better by now, but she does not agree with my sentiments. 'I think you are wrong. I think that in every sense you are wrong.'

'What would you say if I told you that I do not find your husband's work all it's made out to be?' William's look of sullen defiance makes me think of Georgie and I can't help smiling.

'I would say that you are entitled to your opinion,' I tell him.

'And you, what do you really think of it? If you tell me you think him a great artist then I shall not try to persuade you further.' William takes a step back, a look in his eyes as if he had won the argument.

I look back at him, keeping my gaze steady as my heart beats faster. 'I believe my husband is a fine artist,' I say.

William does not take my hand when I offer it to him. Young men break my heart with their earnestness and their futile passions.

'You were right,' I say later to Arthur. 'I was a fool for ever thinking I could be anything other than an amateur, and an indifferent one at that.'

'No, not at all, my dear,' he says, taking my hands in his and lifting first one, then the other to his lips, kissing each and every one of my fingers. 'It's never wrong to strive. What's wrong is not to accept when one has reached one's limitations. And you know how stern, how uncompromising Donald Argyll is. He was asked to judge you alongside professional artists, men of note. Had he seen your pictures in the context of a lady's accomplishments his judgement would have been made accordingly.'

'You mean it would have better befitted the crime?' I try to smile.

He laughs. 'No, Louisa, not at all. What I'm saying is that the fault is not with your work but with your aspirations.'

A few weeks later he returns from a couple of days in London and tells me that he has talked again to Donald Argyll. 'He asked me to give you his regards and to tell you that if you feel a need for a creative outlet you should consider textile work. He told me, and this is praise indeed from a man like Argyll, that you have an interesting way with colour.'

'Could he not have said that at the time?' I mumble but I do not make an issue out of it. His other comments made it quite clear what he thought and so did Arthur's reaction. He had been ashamed at the poor quality of my work; that's why he had looked angry. I think that was what affected me most . . . that my husband thought my work so poor he was ashamed. But my failure as an artist had served the purpose of bringing Arthur and me closer together. I could not have enough of my husband when he spoke to me in such a good-natured interested manner; as if we were truly friends and confidants. How could I have been so ungrateful, so unfair, the way I had almost hated him lately? Look at him, so handsome, so gentle and caring. I step towards him and put my arms round him, resting my cheek against the rough tweed of his coat. He quickly frees himself with a shrug and a small laugh.

Of course he had his moods and his tempers. But I had known that when I agreed to marry him. He had told me himself, as he knelt before me in the wet grass that had quite destroyed his white flannel trousers, that he was a tricky fellow. That's how he put it: 'I'm a tricky kind of a fellow, given to all kinds of moods and tempers. I want you to know what you're taking on, Louisa my darling, my solemn Madonna.' He said I reminded him of medieval panels of a stern yet serene Mary, staring out at the world and its pain and sorrow with unblinking eyes.

I store away the good moments and, during the bad, indifferent days, they sustain me.

I'm expecting once more. I wish I were not. I fear the pregnancy will destroy the new closeness between us. After Lillian was born Arthur confessed that he did not much like the way a woman's body changes in pregnancy. 'Of course I know it's not your fault,' he added, 'it's nature's way, but I would be lying if I said it was attractive.' And I know that he is jealous of the love I give my children although he will never admit it. He is a good man at heart and he wants his children to have a good and loving mother. The problem is that he also wants a wife who loves only him.

When John is born it is obvious from the moment the cord is cut that something is wrong. The midwife shakes her head and tuts before catching my eye and trying a wan smile. Later my new son's father and grandmother bend over the crib and stare down him, finding nothing to say. They don't stay long.

'You'd think they'd ordered beef and been given tripe,' Jane says to Nanny. They are just outside my open door but she doesn't bother to lower her voice. I can hear Nanny rebuking her, saying this is no time for glib remarks.

I know he will not live. And I know why. He will not live because his own mother wished it so. I had wished it from the moment I knew of his existence. I had railed against every extra inch on my waist and every vein showing on my breasts; oh, I hated the child growing inside me for keeping my husband out of my bedroom and alone at night I had whispered poison. 'I don't want you, do you hear? You're ruining everything.' I wished the life from my baby through the days and weeks of red rage, through the orange weeks of smouldering resentment and the charcoal months of bitter melancholy. And I was heard. Now I gaze down at my transparent child, and I weep. 'Be careful what you wish for because one day it might come true.'

Georgie tells me that today the baby is 'very well, it seems'. I had held John in my arms only moments before and had seen no improvement in his tiny waxen face. I whispered, 'I love you,' even as I knew I was too late. But I also know that Georgie is trying to cheer me up the best he can, so I nod and smile and say yes, maybe he is right, maybe John is better this morning. 'Lillian wanted to come and say hello but when Nanny told her she could go for a ride in the big wheelbarrow she did that instead.'

'That's fine,' I tell him. 'Not everyone likes little babies the way you do.'

'But you and I, we like them very much.' He climbs up on my bed to sit next to me. After a moment he clambers on to his hands and knees and peeks over the edge at the baby in his crib. 'If you promise to get well I shall show you my toys,' he says.

'That's a good kind boy,' I say.

'He is looking at me but he won't smile. Why won't he smile at me?'

'He is too little. He hasn't learnt how to yet.'

Georgie tugs at my sleeve. 'But he's staring. It's rude to stare. *You* look.'

I lean across the bed and I have to clamp my hand over my mouth to stop the scream.

JEFFERSON STOOD ON Grace's doorstep on a fine mid-winter day, a shiny brown leather suitcase in his hand. She stared at him as if he was a photograph come to life. 'You haven't muddled up the days, have you?' he asked as he stepped inside. 'You *were* expecting me?'

She shook her head, then changed her mind and nodded. She kept her distance and he didn't encroach. 'Are you OK?' He lifted his hand and traced a smile in the air. Now she took a step towards him, walking into his arms.

Later, after he had had a shower and something to eat, she tried to explain. 'You leave and go back to your family and it hurts; it really hurts, here.' She frees one hand, bashing her chest with her clenched fist. 'I toss and turn in bed. I wake up sweating, my heart racing from all the devils chasing my sleep. My work suffers because wherever I point my camera I see you. My mind is not on what I'm doing, only on what *we did*, what *we* will do. I am a poor friend because while I listen I am only thinking of you. It's hopeless, this love; it sucks the life out of me.'

'Do you really mean that?'

'Yes, but it's worth it as long as you will still love me when all that's left of me is a little desiccated gnome with a Leica dangling round her neck.'

'As long as that Leica keeps dangling I know you'll be all right.'

'I don't ever want to use emotional blackmail, you understand? I just need to complain a little and for you to say you understand how hard it is for me and how much you admire me for coping so wonderfully.'

'You say it so much better than I could ever hope to do. And don't hit me. No, darling, of course I understand. But has it occurred to you that it's not that easy for me either, being apart from you?'

'For you it's different. You've got your children; all that family activity.'

231

'And you have your work, which you love as if it were your family, and you have your stepmother and lots of friends. Now,' he kissed her briefly on the lips, walking her backwards towards the bedroom as he spoke, 'now, do you think I could take you to bed?'

'You're selfish and insensitive with a one-track mind and the answer is yes.'

They were down in Northbourne walking in the rain. Jefferson had wanted to see where she had gone after she left Kendall, where she had grown up. 'You're at an advantage,' he had said. 'You know exactly where I come from. You even knew my parents.'

'I was disapproved of by your parents; that's slightly different.' He opened his mouth to protest and then clamped it shut and smiled. 'Good boy,' Grace said, smiling back. 'Not trying on the bullshit. Anyway, as it would prove complicated, in fact impossible, for me to introduce you to my parents, I'll show you Mrs Shield.'

To Mrs Shield she had said only that a friend from the US was visiting and could they come for lunch. 'Stay the night,' Mrs Shield had offered before trying to find out about Jefferson. Grace would only tell her that she knew him from her summer in Kendall and that they had kept in touch.

'He isn't that boy you were so broken up about?'

'No, no, of course not.' Grace had come a long way from the days when she could not tell a lie.

'The one who changed your mind about going to Cambridge.'

'He didn't change my mind, I did.'

'Ha! So it *was* him.' Grace just sighed, shifting the receiver from one ear to the other. 'What's that, dear? You disappeared. Anyway, *he* had one of those funny Christian names that sound like a surname. I remember at the time thinking how very odd Americans must be to look at a tiny wee baby and say, "I know, let's call him or her Anderson or Harrison or Maddison . . . and as for Ladybird . . ."'

'Well, his name ain't Ladybird,' Grace had reassured her. 'Jefferson is a good friend. I thought you might like to meet him, that's all. But there's no point if you're going to be asking questions all the time. He wants to see the area so if we could stay the night it would be great. But we'll be off first thing the next morning. We have to get back to London.'

There was another reason for Grace not wanting to linger at Mrs Shield's. She just knew that there was a limit to how long she could sit in the same room with Jefferson and not be found out as a woman who adored him. In his presence she was not entirely herself. There she was now, sitting so primly on the very edge of the sofa in the beamed and floral sitting room of Mrs Shield's little cottage, her eyes as moony as a heifer's and her smile smug and greedy both at once. And there she was giggling and talking in a girly voice. Mrs Shield was no fool. She kept shooting Grace meaningful little glances. 'You might as well be semaphoring,' Grace hissed at her when Jefferson excused himself to go to the bathroom.

'And so might you, my girl.'

Grace meant to frown but it turned into a big grin instead. 'I'm happy, Evie. I sit here knowing that at any moment now he'll reappear through the door and that simple fact is enough to . . . don't laugh . . . to make my heart sing.' Grace was crossing and uncrossing her long legs as she spoke, inspecting her newly painted, already chipped nails, as fidgety as a five year old.

'Oh Grace, you have got it bad.' Mrs Shield moved right up close on the sofa. 'But dear, just don't get hurt again. There's been enough of that.'

Grace smiled and then she sighed. 'I don't know that I have much say in the matter.'

Touching Grace lightly on the shoulder, Mrs Shield said, 'Remember that you *do* have a say in how you take what comes your way.'

'I saw a shrink once and that's exactly what she said.'

'All shrinks, as you call them, say that.'

'And you would know.'

'I know everything,' Mrs Shield said.

'I like her,' Jefferson said the next morning, after they had managed to prise themselves away from Mrs Shield's bear-like embrace. As they drove off down the short drive Grace wondered how it was that, when you said goodbye, her stepmother

233

always managed to look half the size she'd seemed when you arrived.

'I'll tell you a secret,' Grace said, 'I like her too.'

'Why is it a secret and why, when you speak of her, do you call her Mrs Shield and not "my stepmother" or her first name or even Mother?'

'Childhood stuff, inevitably. I spent years after my mother died secretly waiting for her to come back. I had not been allowed to see her at the hospital but I had overheard my father telling Aunt Kathleen that she was "disfigured beyond recognition". I clung on to that phrase, thinking it had been a case of mistaken identity; all my favourite books back then were big on mistaken identity. I had it all worked out: the memory loss, the years of aimless wandering. When she didn't come back I started blaming it on Mrs Shield, telling myself that my mother knew her place had been taken by someone else. Oh, I was a muddled child, and cross. I called her Mrs Shield as a way of spiting them both, her and my father, and to keep my distance, I suppose. But I grew older and stopped thinking my mother might come back. I got used to Mrs Shield. I grew fond of her; I even remember the exact moment of recognition: I was sitting at the kitchen table at The Gables, doing my times tables, and she was making my tea. I looked up at her and there she was, the way she always was at five o'clock when I got back from school, standing by the stove in her ghastly pink frilly Doris Day apron. And I loved her for it, for always being there. I wanted to make her happy in return so I decided that I was finally going to call her Mummy. But when it came to it I just couldn't. I tried Evie and that's what I call her to her face, but I had grown used to Mrs Shield.'

'I'm the antithesis of always being there,' Jefferson said quietly.

Grace took her left hand off the wheel, raising it to his cheek, holding it there for a moment. 'Yes, you are. But that's all right; my expectations have gone down since childhood.' He laughed but he squeezed her hand hard.

Once they reached Northbourne, Grace parked the car on the verge outside a large white-rendered 1920s house, the kind that would have looked more at home in the London suburbs than in the country. 'That's where we lived, that's The Gables.'

234

'Nice house.'

'Mrs Shield loved it. It was a real wrench for her to leave but the place had got too large. It's funny how we talk about a house getting too large, as if it had changed overnight in some teenage growth spurt, emerging suddenly with all the curtains too short and not a single piece of furniture that fits.'

'And you, did you mind her selling up?'

'I suppose I do have a certain sentimental attachment. All those happy childhood memories. I could show you the spot under the large rosebush where Finn and I buried our pets, until eventually the little bodies were stacked so high we had to take our funerals to the lilac hedge . . . only kidding. And look, there's the oak, just over there, from where I fell and broke my arm when I was ten. And you see that little shed in the corner, that's where I locked Finn up and forgot, going off to stay the night at Noah's house, so Mrs Shield called the police and reported him missing . . .' Grace turned to him with a radiant smile. 'Such happy days.'

'Sounds as if you were a truly revolting kid.'

'Oh I was; everyone said so.'

He pulled her close. 'I was really angry with my parents when they sold up,' he said. 'I knew I was being selfish, and illogical too as I had left home about ten years earlier, but I still gave them a hard time. It was absolutely too much for them to cope with: six bedrooms and that large yard, and all my poor old mom had ever really wanted was one of the neat and modern handy little apartments on the outskirts of town with a view of the river. But I behaved as if it was their duty to remain the same – same them, same home, same rituals – just for me while I was free to move on and change as much as I wanted.'

'It doesn't matter how old we get, in the relationship with our parents we're all arch-conservatives. Still, I really didn't mind Mrs Shield selling The Gables. I was perfectly happy there, but I always thought it rather a dull house. Anyway, the really big wrench was leaving Kendall. There I could stroke a wall and think, my mother touched this exact place, my handprint is resting on hers, she walked these stairs, and cooked my dinner in that kitchen; you know the kind of thing. After that I stopped being too attached. Maybe once you've been pulled away roots and all, it gets easier the next time it happens. Actually, I wanted to live in Noah Blackstaff's house. He was this kid I hung out with. His father was dead. It's actually his grandparents' place but he stayed with them in the long holidays. The old people still live there, in that large, wonderfully gloomy old house down the lane. *And* Noah had the ghost. It wasn't his father or anything, but any ghost was better than none, in my opinion. And he wasn't even that interested. It just seemed unfair. He had Northbourne House, a ghost and a famous grandfather. The old boy's an artist; a bohemian, for heaven's sakes. Of course, Arthur Blackstaff is a very Home Counties bohemian; just enough cloak and wide-brimmed hat to fit the image to a tee at the same time as riding to hounds and knowing how to eat soup properly. Looking back, I think he was always pretty conservative – you know, the kind of guy who would pat you on the back with a "Bad luck, old chap, there but for the grace of God" if you told him you had syphilis, but would blackball you if you had Aids.'

'You have a different definition of conservative round here.' Jefferson kissed the top of her head. She loved that he was tall enough to do that; it was nice, sometimes, to be allowed to be small. 'I have to admit I've never heard of the guy.'

'He used to be all the rage, as Mrs Shield would say. Mostly with the kind of people who aspire in vain to a set of ancestors for their walls. No, I'm being unfair; there's more to him than that. In his day – strange expression, that – he managed to be both popular *and* highly regarded by the critics.'

'I take it you're not a huge fan?'

Grace shrugged. 'It's ages since I saw any of his stuff, but no. His are the kind of paintings that shout *this is a horse*; oh, it is so exactly like a horse, every detail is right, every horsy inch of it, and yet . . . yet I don't *feel* it. But take Picasso's bull. I know he started off with every detail of that animal, every muscle and sinew, but when he had finished he was left with just a few lines that just screamed bullness.'

'I don't really get Picasso.'

'You haven't seen enough, that's all. When you have you'll fall in love with him, I promise.'

'I'm in love already. There's no room for Pablo. In fact I believe that right now I'm experiencing the very essence of inloveness. So, who's the ghost?'

'Was. It's not been seen for ages.' Grace lowered her voice to not much more than a whisper. 'She walked the gardens at night, keeping to the shelter of the trees. She was tall and slender in her flowing white robe and her hair rippled like moonshine all the way to her waist. Only one person saw her face, an old poacher, and he said she had the face of the Madonna. He swore off poaching after that, and never had another drink.'

'My darling, are you making all of this up?'

'No.' Grace looked up at him and shook her head. 'Not a word.'

'But no photographs, I suppose, of the ghost?'

'No.'

'As a matter of interest, has anyone ever captured a ghost on film?'

'Some say they have. But looking at the pictures, you can't tell for sure. It could be a wisp of steam, a trick of the light or just jiggery-pokery. I think mostly you have to content yourself with trying to catch a spirit. If I have caught the spirit of a subject of one of my portraits, then I will have done well.'

'I can't even take a decent snapshot. Truth is I've never been that interested in trying.'

Grace turned round and raised her arms, cradling his face in her strong hands, looking him straight in the eyes. 'You know something?'

'What?' He looked back at her, unsure suddenly.

'Don't look like that,' she exclaimed. 'So stricken.' She kissed him on the lips and on the tip of the nose and on each cheek, tanned even now, in mid-winter. 'I was just going to say that you're allowed not to be fascinated by the same things as I am.'

He smiled, a little embarrassed. 'Yeah, sure. But I feel like I should know more, that's all. I want to share in your kicks.'

'Lots of people don't get it. I have friends who never even take a camera on holiday because they feel it comes between them and the experience. For me, it's the opposite. To me, everything is floating, unreal, until I've got my shots.'

'You sound like a druggie.'

She laughed. 'I've got a habit, that's for sure. But it's a way of working things out too, little things like life. We all need that: some kind of black box explaining what's actually going on. When I'm behind the lens I see differently, I see more. Things begin to make sense even if the sense is just me taking a picture. Of course, there's the fact that I'm bloody good at it – photography, that is. I mean, who doesn't like doing something they're good at?'

'Maybe then you'll understand my choice of career. When I strapped the leg of an injured rabbit once, I made such a hash of it the poor bunny ended up being carted off for an amputation. Working as a defence lawyer on my first big case, on the other hand, I saved a guy's arse – said arse having been headed firmly in the direction of the electric chair.' He paused. 'Though if you ask me, I'd say the rabbit was the better man.'

They went for lunch at a place some fifteen miles from Northbourne. 'Worth it?' Grace asked as they arrived. The sun turned the old brick of the house a red-pink, ivy clambered up the walls between the leaded windows and just yards from the porch was the river where a swan made its regal progress, seven grey cygnets in her wake, through a noisy group of ducks making way like courtiers. 'Worth it,' he said.

After lunch they went for another walk. Jefferson was carrying the Leica. He looked through the lens then he asked Grace, 'What should I be thinking about if I were to take a picture right here?'

Grace stopped and looked around. 'I tend to think in terms of three components.' She pointed to a woman standing on the small bridge some ten yards away. 'You see her? OK, so she is our first component. The backdrop of the bare branches of the trees reaching into the river and the old barn is our second component. But there is more to come, I reckon. I'm never quite sure why I know this, but I'm usually right. There's a third component and it will make my picture. She's waiting for someone? You sense her impatience in the way she paces up and down a tiny area of the bridge. And the little smile that plays at the corners of her mouth; again it's as if she is expecting something good. So we wait and see if I'm right. You have to be both patient and ready to move fast, which is why,' she

238

said by way of an apology, 'I got into the habit of chewing tobacco.'

'I'm sorry I made you give that up.' Jefferson was looking at the woman on the bridge.

'No, you're right, it's a disgusting habit.'

'It wasn't the aesthetic aspect; you're my girl, yellow teeth or not.' He leant across and gave her a quick kiss. 'It's your health I'm thinking of. Cigarettes are bad enough, but that shit you chew . . .'

'Which is why I don't do it when you're around.'

Jefferson looked at her. 'When I'm not around?'

'Look, take what you can get.' Grace took the Leica from him and pointed it at the woman.

'Won't she *mind* you staring and pointing that thing at her?'

'She won't notice. She's in her own world.'

'And what about her privacy?'

Grace lowered the camera for a second and turned to look at him. 'What about it?'

'It's that easy, is it?'

'It has to be if I'm to go on working. Look, she's frowning now and she can't stop glancing at her watch. Before, she was gazing out across the water; now she's looking over her shoulder at the road. Who do you reckon she's waiting for?'

'A guy?'

Grace nodded. 'Perhaps.'

But they were wrong. A woman in her sixties came round the corner, bent low as if she was walking against a strong wind. She was pushing a baby in a buggy. Her steps were quick and full of purpose, her sturdy legs were clad in thick navy tights under a pleated plaid skirt in grey and beige, and on top of that she was wearing a green quilted jacket. Her face was broad and her short grey hair sprang back from her forehead as if trying to get away. As she walked she kept looking over her shoulder. The woman on the bridge relaxed into a smile as she ran towards them and up to the buggy, lifting the child into her arms and kissing him and holding him close. The older woman looked uncomfortable. Her stern expression softened only once, when the child grabbed at the young woman's hair, getting his tiny fingers caught. She laughed as she gently untangled him. The boy pulled back in her arms, his gaze locked into hers, and then he too laughed and Grace got her picture.

Later she showed Jefferson the finished photograph. 'If you wanted an illustration of true happiness,' she said, 'that picture is it.'

'And what if, after we left, that old woman took the child away again? What's your truth then?'

Grace thought of that vexed line, *the camera never lies.* The look on that young woman's face when she held the child in her arms was one of pure joy. But there had been a prequel of anxious waiting; there had been the furtive manner in which the older woman had looked around her all the while. Maybe, as Jefferson said, the child had been taken away again. Maybe he had been pulled screaming from his mother's arms and strapped back into the buggy while she had to stand by, helpless, her eyes filled with pain and longing, as she was parted from her child once more.

'Truth is such a slippery beast,' Grace said to Jefferson. 'Have I captured a moment of joy, or just an interlude in suffering?'

'What about a happy moment in sad times? After all, that's what life's like for most of us.'

His dark hair shone. His eyes were intensely blue underneath arched dark brows. His chin was firm and his upper lip was a perfect Cupid's bow. He stood waiting for her on the high street, leaning against an open-topped sports car. Grace, looking at him through the lens, smiled approvingly; he was the picture-perfect romantic lead in countless women's dreams. 'Say orgasm,' she said and closed the shutter.

She was playing with stereotypes; comforting, dangerous stereotypes, beloved aids of the propagandist. She wanted to see how much of the personality you could obliterate simply by concentrating on the stereotypical elements of your subject.

'I want you to pose as the Each and Every Lover,' she had said to Jefferson. 'You shall be the hero of every romantic novel, every Hollywood film. If I get it right, whatever makes you uniquely you will not be seen. I would like to be able to place the photos side by side and for no one to notice that they are all of the one man. My aim is to obliterate you.'

'You will have to. Or I will have a hard time explaining what I'm doing in your photos.'

'C'mon, what are the chances of anyone who knows you back home seeing my pictures in some small gallery over here, or even seeing it's you? Anyway, if the shots work out, you won't be yourself; you'll be my creation, my wishfulfilment.'

'Aren't we just talking disguises?'

'Oh no. There will be no wide-brimmed hats or false beards. All I'll be doing is giving our common prejudices a helping hand. And if you confound me and remain you, then I won't show them.'

The only thing Jefferson did not like doing was nothing. He was really bad at nothing. Other than that he was easy-going. He did not protest one bit when she made him put on a check shirt and a Barbour jacket she had borrowed from a photographer friend. He was perfectly happy to pose some more, chin held high, pipe in hand, legs sturdily apart and feet planted firmly on the fake soil imported into the studio she shared with four other photographers, a black Labrador at his feet. He made a great fuss of the Labrador, borrowed from the same friend who had lent the jacket, and this delayed the shoot as the Labrador – whose name, inevitably, was Bertie – got over-excited and peed on Jefferson's green gumboots.

She took some shots after they had made love, of him dozing in bed on rumpled sheets, a faint flush to his cheeks. He was fine about that too, once she had reassured him that he had been lying demurely on his front.

For some of the pictures Grace rigged up the camera to include the two of them. 'Gee, darlin', I wish we could always be like this,' he said as he sat at the kitchen table, wearing a navy V-neck sweater over his shirt and tie, a plate laden with apple pie before him. Grace, in long blonde wig and a floaty floral frock, hovered by his side, ready with the jug of cream.

'In yer dreams, honey-pie,' she drawled as she reached for the remote switch and the shutter clicked.

The final picture in the series was shot the day before he had to return home. 'There is not a woman born who's not a sucker for manly tears,' she said. She posed him at the corner of Kensington High Street and Old Church Street with a bunch of wilting flowers in his hand. It was dusk. He had done a lot of walking that day, as there was a tube strike and he had to get to a meeting in the City, so he was tired already. Looking at him standing there, with the bunch of dying anemones in his hand, he seemed as forlorn as if he had been waiting half the day. 'She's not coming,' Grace said. 'That's what you have to keep saying to yourself: the love of your life is not coming. She's gone to Timbuktu and will never ever return. Or she's died. Yes, I think she's dead. You're waiting for your one true love but she's lying dead in her smashed-up car not one mile from here. You don't know it yet, but the sirens you heard some fifty minutes ago were the emergency vehicles rushing in vain to her aid.' At that he looked so upset that Grace almost put the camera down to wrap her arms around him and tell him it was all right. But she took the picture instead.

242

Louisa

I HAVE MY OWN sitting room upstairs. It's been fashioned out of what were two small bedrooms. Arthur feels that I need somewhere just for me, somewhere quiet. I sit by the open window in my new quarters. It is warm for early September and the leaves have not yet begun to turn. I can see the children playing on the lawn, disappearing and reappearing in and out of the mist rising from the river. When Jane looks up at the window I raise my hand and wave them towards me. 'Children, come up and see your mama,' I mouth.

After John died I was not at all well and Lady Glastonbury suggested I see someone. As it happened she knew the very man, Sir Charles Granger, eminent in his field and no stranger to royalty either, although the last was whispered only in confidence. He had recently retired from his London practice to dedicate himself to the running of the excellent Harvey Clinic only fifteen miles away in Basingstoke.

I do not like Sir Charles. He tells me he is there to help me, but he never looks at me directly and he speaks over my head to Arthur and gives *him* the tablets I am to take. I ask Arthur what the pills are for. 'They're to give you a rest.'

I need a rest even though I have done very little lately other than sit in my room, so I take the pills. I take two in the morning and two after my evening meal and I feel more and more tired, too tired to think. But I try to look awake when the children come to see me in the afternoon. I tell them stories.

Georgie wants to hear about the time his mama travelled with her friends to Germany and how they all went down a deep dark mine.

The mother had soon had enough of fairy-tale castles and ginger-bread houses. She was bored with the gentility of the spas. She wanted the boys and their little friend, a quiet girl with no mother or father of her own, to see something different. They passed the men seated by the roadside eating bread and cheese and sausages. Their faces were as black as Negroes'. Jack said the men were lucky because they were allowed to eat their supper without first washing their hands and faces.

The children wore brown smocks over their sailor suits. Jack was cross. He said that his smock would not show up the black dirt the way his blue and white sailor suit would. His mother ignored him. It was her way. She didn't waste her breath on arguing. She told you how a thing was but if you had an objection after that you might as well not have spoken. This was the reason for her calm and peaceful nature.

As they were lowered into the pit, Jack said it was the most exciting moment in his life. Maybe, he said, they would find treasure down there.

They arrived in the magic underworld and saw what the mother had wanted them to see; that it was nothing but a prison where men lived out the precious daylight hours in darkness, where the ponies wore blindfolds to keep them sane and where one solitary bird sat caged and silent.

The little guest, who was not a brave strong girl like Lillian, began to cry. Jack liked to argue about anything and everything but even he could not find a reason why he should want to be one of those men now.

When they were back up in the sunlight the girl who had cried asked, 'What have those men done that they are made to work down there?'

'Done?' the mother said.

'Have they been very bad? They must have been.'

'They have done nothing wrong. Good people can be given bad lives and bad people can be given good lives.'

'But that's not fair!' the girl wailed. 'That's not at all fair.'

'No,' the mother said. 'No, it is not.'

The girl followed behind the others, walking slowly, feeling the ground beneath her feet, scratching at the soil with the toe of her black polished boot. If what the mother had said were true, she would never again feel safe because whatever she did, whether she was good or bad, there was only a layer of soil and rock between her and the underground.

'That's a strange story to tell young children,' Jane says. She has come into the room without anyone noticing.

'They like it.'

Jane says, 'If you say so,' and means, 'I don't think so,' but she keeps her smile in place as she picks Lillian up from the rug on the floor. 'However, in my experience what children like and what is good for them is seldom one and the same.'

I want to tell Jane to put Lillian down and leave us all alone. I want to tell her to stop telling Arthur lies about me in that soft voice of hers, but I'm too tired and anyway she would go straight to Arthur and he would accuse me of being unkind.

Jane takes the children away. At first they protest and say they want to stay but by the time she has promised them a game they skip ahead of her through the door.

Arthur suggests a small dinner party to show the world that I am well again.

The guests smile and chat but I can see their thoughts. It's not difficult; I have lived amongst these people for long enough to know that what they said about others they would sooner or later say about me. *Poor Arthur. His splendid beard has turned grizzled; worry of course. How attentive he is of his wife. Such a stony-faced woman. Prematurely aged. She was never exactly a beauty, in spite f those fine eyes, but now she is downright plain. You get the face you deserve.*

Jane was at the dinner. When had she stopped being shy? When had she become so sure, so at ease, and when had these people started to treat her as their friend?

'What's the matter with you?' The party is over and Arthur is angry. He had troubled himself, arranging the dinner party, and what had I done in return? 'You sat at the table showing as much life and interest as a mechanical doll.' Was there anything I could be bothered with these days, anything at all? His eyes are narrow with hurt; his strong hands flap helplessly. What had happened to his Louisa? 'I loved you dearly. I thought you were different from the callow young girls I had come across. *I* saw your beauty when no one else did. I admired your serenity, your sweet temperament, your honesty. Even when that honesty presented itself as gaucheness, rudeness, even then I defended you.' He paces up and down the floor, and with every step I hear those words: 'I loved you dearly.'

I want to put my hand out but I can't reach. He gives me another look full of hurt and disappointment and, as he leaves, stalking off, stamping on the floor with his heavy-soled shoes, I stand with my hand half raised and tears falling down my face.

I dream that I live in a place in the sun where my children play beneath the blossoming orange trees, but what warms me most is that, in my dream, Arthur loves me still.

One day Viola arrives in her brand-new motor car. 'We are on our way to paint the sea,' she announces. 'William is outside.'

Arthur says I should go. 'It'll do you good. Remember how you used to enjoy playing around with your paints and brushes?'

'You make me sound like a child, Arthur,' I say. If I made him cross he does not show it, not in front of Viola. I can never tell if he likes her. I know he disapproves of her habit of dressing in slacks, but I also know that he enjoys telling people his wife is a close friend of the daughter of Sir Derek Glastonbury. Viola follows me up to the nursery and kisses my children and laughs at Lillian who frowns with furious concentration as she attempts to thread a huge needle with yarn. 'She's been at it since she got up,' Nanny says. 'And she won't let me help.'

I look at my children and I want to hug them both close, squeeze them to me, never let them go, but I stay by the door.

On our way downstairs Viola tells me that William is angry with me for giving up on my classes. 'You must allow him to persuade you of your worth. I thought I was only capable of the most commonplace little things, competent, pretty, but nothing more.

But you should see how he has brought things out of me: colour . . . boldness of line. You must reconsider, Louisa.'

'I'll come out with you both today, but I don't think that I will come to any more lessons, although I'm glad to hear you are making such progress. I always thought that, of the two of us, you were the artist.'

'I don't think that is what you really believe. It might be what you wish to believe to make your life easier.'

I stop at the bottom of the stairs and put my finger across her full pink lips. She looks straight at me and I feel the colour rise in my cheeks. Slowly she raises her own hand and puts it across mine, imprisoning it. Now her eyes are easy, smiling. Then she lets me go.

I sit in the front next to Viola who is driving the Lagonda. William Fenton sits in the back holding his tweed cap down on his head first with one, then with both hands. He shouts against the wind, 'Louisa Blackstaff, I want you back!' I can't remember the last time I laughed like that.

The waves are tipped with light and overhead the gulls circle, laughing at us sorry earthbound creatures. I lie down on the warm sand and close my eyes. Viola lies next to me and I feel her fingertips touch mine. The sun warms my face and penetrates the thin skin of my closed lids, filling my head with soft yellow rays. The grey mist that had shrouded my heart and mind for so long turns transparent, liquid, and in that liquid a tiny quicksilver fish stirs and flaps its tail, reaching the surface and the sunlight.

'And now to work.' I open my eyes and look up into William Fenton's smiling face. He is just a boy, a laughing, kind, talented boy who believes in himself and in the goodness of the world.

I say to him, 'William, I'm done with painting; I told you so.' But I allow him to pull me to my feet and lead me to the edge of the water. Viola follows, barefoot and laughing. 'There,' William says. His feet are bare too and his trousers are rolled up at the ankles. 'Behold,' he makes a sweeping gesture across the horizon, 'the beauty of creation.' He turns and takes a step back into the water, his eyes, like the sea, reflecting the sun. He is smiling and he waves his arms about as he speaks. 'Come on, Louisa Blackstaff, you must do your part. You must create your own beauty. It's a sin not to when you know how.' He attempts to look stern. 'Think if God had given up halfway. Think if He had got bored or discouraged after He had created the mountains, and never got round to the sea?'

I take a step towards him, not caring that my shoes are getting wet. I reach out and take his hands in mine. 'But, dear William, there is a difference, can't you see? I'm not God.'

Viola has brought a picnic. When we have finished with it, William lies down on the sand, his panama over his face, and soon he is snoring. Viola and I glance at each other and then we laugh, hands across our mouths, trying to be quiet, not to wake him. I look at her: olive complexion flushed with peach, smiling eyes, a small hand with its palm padded like a child's. A soft mouth. Our eyes meet. We stop laughing and Viola leans across and her lips brush against mine.

We sit side by side looking out across the sea. I believe I have never been happier.

William is asleep still. 'You will return to our lessons, won't you?' Viola asks me.

I have been looking at the horizon, thinking how much is out there that I will never see. 'What's the point? Even if you and William are right and I have some talent, I shall never be able to paint the way I want to. For that I would have to be very brave, crazy or,' I laugh, 'a man.'

'You're brave.'

I shake my head. 'No, that I'm not.'

'So be a man. Smoke cigarettes and strut and preen and admire yourself greatly.' She draws a heart in the sand, smiling as she tells me, 'At my school there was a teacher with whom I imagined myself in love. He was tall and straight and fair like you, although his eyes were not such a dark blue. His name was Forbes.'

'What do you see, Louisa?' William asks. In front of me, between me and the sea, he has put up his easel. I look at Viola, and at the empty canvas before me. 'Hope,' I say, 'I see hope.'

*　　*　　*

It's late, the sun is setting. William says it is time to go. Viola and I glance at each other. 'I'll drop you at the station, William, and you shall have to take the train back. Louisa and I want to go on.'

William sulks and protests that then he shall have to walk the three miles from the station at Northbourne to his house, but Viola just laughs and tells him the exercise will do him good. 'When you get home,' I tell him as we part, 'could you please call my husband and tell him that I will not be returning until the morning.'

Viola pulls up outside the front door. I remain in my seat, gazing up at the house. I had never noticed before quite how meanly proportioned the windows are. I turn to her and whisper, 'I can't go back.' She takes my hand and lifts it to her cheek. She kisses my upturned palm, then gently, and in turn, each finger. I pull free and grab her by the wrist. 'It would have been kinder if you had never come for me.'

Tears fall down Viola's cheeks. I kiss each one away; I don't care who sees.

My children ask for a story.

Snow White lay alone in her coffin of glass, neither dead nor of the world. Men came from far and near to gaze at her perfect silent beauty. Her eyes were open but, although she could see the young men bending over her coffin, she could not feel the warmth of their breath. She saw the branches of the trees move above but she could not feel the breeze against her skin. She could see the birds but the sound of their singing was distorted by the glass and sounded like no song to Snow White.

Then one day a young prince came past in his motor car and when he saw the coffin of glass he stopped and stepped out to take a better look. And he saw how beautiful Snow White was and he loved her. He lifted the heavy glass lid and bent down and kissed her and as he kissed her the warmth returned to her cheeks and the breath came strong and calm from her lungs. He picked her up in his arms and lifted her out of the coffin of glass into the sunshine and the birdsong and the soft gentle breeze.

The children clap and cheer. I keep the true ending of the story to myself.

Gently, tears falling from his eyes and down upon the face of his beloved, the prince lowered her back into her glass coffin because they both knew that was where Snow White had to stay.

*　　*　　*

Arthur has finished his Island canvas. He says it will be his finest work to date, a rebuttal of the degenerate tendencies pervading the world of the day, a triumphant affirmation of Beauty as the true and noble goal of Art. During its creation, our third child had been conceived, born and buried, yet he has scarcely deviated a line from his initial sketch. The canvas will form the centrepiece of a grand new exhibition at the Argyll Gallery but first, that was the plan, there would be an unofficial unveiling at our home. The planned date for this has had to be postponed because of the mourning period. Arthur told me at the time that this was a great disappointment. I believe he looked to me for sympathy.

I, too, have been busy. During the day I look after my children, I garden and oversee the running of the house. I have had no need of Sir Charles's pills although I have been careful to remove them, each time, from my breakfast tray and to retire, as for a nap, when expected, mid-morning and before dinner. In the early morning, as soon as the sun has risen but before the household is awake, I creep up into the attic, to the small room at the back with the north-east-facing window, and I work.

The moment has come for the unveiling. Arthur strides ahead of the guests; he struts as proud as a sergeant major. He halts outside the morning room then pulls open the double doors.

Silence. Then noise breaks out across the room and flows down the hallway. Lady Glastonbury grabs her husband's arm and someone pushes a chair beneath her. I stand at the back, unnoticed. I feel nothing. Not triumph, not pity. Inside me there is a void. Into that void all feeling is drawn, soaked up, gone.

Crude. Offensive to good taste and refinement. Perverse. An affront to art. The work of a deficient.

The colours scream as they are dragged across the canvas. My painting speaks of friendship turned to love and love turned into hatred. There are pitter-patter mice with big velvet eyes and ears that are bigger still. There is a house with all the windows shut and a sea that melts into the horizon. On the beach, with the women, two young children play. I do not know to this day what offended them all most, that there was love or that there were children watching that love.

All of it, my world, my picture, propped up against the wall beneath my husband's great work.

Arthur faces his guests. 'Ladies and gentlemen, something appears to have gone wrong.'

The question many of Grace Shield's friends asked themselves was how she, an independent, free-spirited woman who had made her way in the competitive world of photography, could have meekly played the role of 'other woman' during a six-year relationship.

Grace opened the back door and Pluto waddled out, wheezing, bug-eyed, weak old bladder fit to burst. She followed him, barefoot on the morning-damp lawn, still in her dressing gown. She leant over the gate, feeling the spiky wood against her chest. She was watching the road. There he was, turning the corner by the fire station. He was too far off for her to distinguish any features, but it was his walk, loose-limbed and easy, that gave him away. She raised her hand in a wave and, with Pluto puffing at her heels, walked back into the kitchen and put the bagels in the oven and the kettle on the stove. She left the door open with the bug-screen shut tight. It was going to be another hot day. She glanced at her reflection in the small mirror above the fridge. Her hair was damp from the shower, her cheeks were pink and laughter lines fanned out from the corners of her eyes. I'm just so smiley these days, she thought. I hardly recognise myself.

'Honey, I'm home.' He said that each day as he returned from the shop with the papers and every time she laughed, not because it was especially funny but because he looked so pleased with his little joke.

She went to kiss him but tripped up on Pluto who was intent on getting there first. 'Breakfast's nearly ready.'

As usual he commented on near enough everything in the paper and as usual she listened to only half of what he said. What took up most of his interest this morning was a proposed housing development on land that was known to be a toxic dump in an old whaling town some fifty miles down towards the mainland side.

253

'So, the big guys say, do you folks want a roof over your heads or not?'

'You're a lawyer,' Grace said. 'Help. Offer your services to these people.'

He looked up at her and smiled. 'Oh, so you were listening. Well, maybe I shall.'

Was he getting old already? But he was only just forty. Yet there were times, like right now, when Grace looked at him expecting that hum of energy when his whole body radiated enthusiasm, and got instead a glimpse of weariness. She leant across the table and put her hand on his. 'Are you feeling all right?'

He straightened in the high-backed wooden chair and grinned at her. 'Of course I'm all right. I'm always all right. I shouldn't have had that second whiskey last night, that's all.'

'You go read your paper on the porch.' She planted a kiss on the top of his head, drawing in the warm scent of his hair. 'Smells nice.'

'It's that new shampoo I bought. It's French. It says on the bottle they've used real vanilla essence.' He bent down and scratched Pluto behind the ear before getting up from the table with the paper in one hand, his half-finished mug of coffee in the other.

She grinned at him. 'What?' he said, self-conscious all of a sudden. 'What?'

'Nothing,' she said, but she smiled at the way he had of telling you the exact contents of his shampoo, the details of a meal he'd had out, or the exact ratio of wool to cashmere in his new sports jacket. It was as if by sharing each small thread of his life he tied the two of them closer together.

In a while she would bring him a fresh mug of coffee. She liked spoiling him in little ways like that. She liked thinking of him dozing in the rocker while she pottered round the kitchen, her heart filled with love, her brain gingham-wrapped. She put away the milk and the carton of juice and wondered at the way American appliances were so huge, so 1950s-bulky, compared to the ones at home. And those top-loading washing machines where you could watch the water pouring in. It was all about confidence, she thought, confidence in unlimited space and unending resources.

* * *

They always went for a walk after breakfast and then again last thing before bed at night. She liked the sound of that, saying it to an imagined listener: *we always* . . .

On the way to the beach they walked down Main Street, Jefferson holding her hand as he hurried along, his blue gaze fixed at some point far ahead. Grace pulled at his arm. She liked to take her time. She liked looking through lace curtains and half-open blinds and the shutters of the shabby-grand old houses.

Every day, as she put on her trainers ready for their walk, she felt that same current of excitement. Jefferson said she had got it all wrong; it was Pluto who should be wagging his tail and rushing to the door. But she knew what it was all about. It was going somewhere together openly, no sneaking around, no looking over the shoulder. It was about the way the most mundane experience became heightened to something noteworthy just because he was there. Ordinary days became gilt-edged.

They walked along the beach and the sun played with the many colours of the sands that flowed grain by grain towards the ocean. Above their heads busy terns flew back and forth between their nests and the sea, the returning birds carrying their silvery catch crosswise in their bills.

'Did you know,' Jefferson said, 'that the tern can cry out and still not drop its catch? It makes it such a superior bird, don't you think? Such a clever pretty bird,' and he raised himself on his toes, his right arm in the air as if he was trying to stroke one of those graceful curved wings.

Being in love brings out the mother in a woman and the boy in a man, Grace thought, as she pulled out a tube of sun cream and smothered it across his burnt forehead and the bright-red bridge of his nose. Jefferson, shifting restlessly from foot to foot, had been in the middle of drawing their initials in the sand with a stick he had stolen from Pluto, and as Grace patted the last of the cream into his cheeks he returned to his work, finishing off with X for a kiss.

They took a detour through the town on their way back, nodding hello to at least seven people. They stopped at the

255

bookshop. That shop surprised them every time, the way the aisles stretched back impossibly until it seemed the place defied the laws of nature, with the inside being larger than the exterior. Pluto was welcome and off his lead he just curled up right by the cookery section, as if he knew that was of interest to him. Jefferson and Grace, too, had their routines: he picking out book after book, checking the covers, the writing on the back, the author photograph; Grace choosing one book and reading it until he was through browsing. This way she already knew the first twenty pages or so of pretty well every one of the great American classics. So far she had enjoyed four enough to buy them and read them all the way through to the end. At the checkout they chatted to Mary who owned the store and worked there every day including Saturdays. She smiled as she looked at them. 'You know,' she said, 'it is truly uplifting to see a couple like y'all. You're just so nice to each other, so loving in everything you do and say. I tell you, I get enough couples in here bickering and glowering, needling and snatching. But seeing you two gives me hope.'

Maybe, Grace thought, they had no right to, but they walked out of that shop feeling pleased with themselves all the same, like a couple who had made it through the rough and the smooth and emerged not just together but wanting to be that way. Although they had no right, that was how it felt, and that was how they looked to the outside world. And what, Grace thought, was life but a series of perceptions?

Usually ten minutes was the most Jefferson would ever nap, but that day after lunch he just slept on and Grace did not have the heart to wake him. They played music in the afternoons and left it on to sweep them off to sleep. Today it was Verdi: *La Traviata*. It usually was. 'I listen to them all,' Jefferson had said some time back, with that slightly self-important air he had when he was trying to impress her. 'Bach, Beethoven, Chopin, Debussy, Richard Strauss, Stravinsky, but I keep returning to Verdi; Verdi and Mozart . . .' Grace had given him a look. 'Oh all right then, and Dolly.'

Violetta, in her aria, was begging her lover's father to remember her kindly when she'd gone. Grace listened as she looked at

Jefferson sleeping, and she thought that life did not get much better than right there. She picked up the camera. She looked through the lens then went across to the window and opened the curtains a fraction. She gazed at him through the lens. He was lying on his back, one leg pulled up at an angle, both arms up above his head. His face was smooth in sleep but although the room was cool his hair was damp with sweat. He often woke up damp with sweat these days. He said he was dreaming. The way he looked tired even after a long night's sleep and the way he had been sweating, she thought his dreams must be the most exhausting part of each 24-hour day. 'Did you run?' she had asked him the other morning, holding him tight. He nodded. 'Were you frightened?'

'Not really. I just knew I had to keep on going.'

'What did you think would happen if you didn't run?'

He had looked at her with a child's all-knowing, all-questioning eyes. 'That I'd stop. That's what scares me; having to stop.' But for now he was sleeping soundly and, if he was dreaming, these were peaceful dreams.

The afternoon was turning into evening and their neighbours, Rob and Melissa Walker, were expecting them for dinner at that strangely early time that Americans like to eat. Grace had to wake him.

Rob taught English and history at the local high school. Melissa was, as she put it herself, 'a full-time mom'. They were good people, gentle and bright, but Grace wished Melissa would not always look at her so pityingly when it came to the subject of children. This evening, though, she asked if Grace would consider photographing the two Walker babies. Melissa wanted proper portraits, she said. 'I'll pay you the going rate, of course.' Grace told her there was no need for that. 'It will be fun,' she said. 'I don't usually do babies. However sweet-looking, they are too unformed, their features are suggestions still. But your two do have good faces.'

'So Jeff,' Rob said, 'have you ever come across a guy named Tim Hubbard? He's a veterinarian too, got a small-animal practice on 47th and 3rd. No? I suppose I thought all you guys kind of knew each other, like a vets' fraternity type-thing, getting together over the issue of the Upper East Side's overfed pooches, that kind of thing.'

'Speaking of which,' Melissa said, 'is Pluto all right? He's been sounding kind of wheezy lately. I know he's always wheezy, but isn't he getting worse? Not that I'm in any way implying that you wouldn't be taking care of that dog, you being a professional . . . but we've known him for so long, that's all.' She turned an apologetic smile on Jefferson.

'He's fine,' Jefferson said firmly. 'I listened to his chest only this morning and he's good.'

Grace stifled a giggle, feeling guilty for playing games with nice Rob and Melissa and enjoying it all the same. 'You did too, my darling,' she said, reaching across the table and stroking his cheek. 'You even warmed the stethoscope first. He does that. They might have fur but they don't like a cold metal thing on their little chests any more than you or I would; that's what you say, isn't it, dear?'

He smiled back but he seemed a bit tense. 'Are you all right?' Grace mouthed. It was exhausting at times, she thought, having all the sums of your happiness adding up to just one person.

'I just love your accent, Grace,' Melissa said. 'How long did you say you've been over here?'

Grace changed the subject. 'Is it true that Clarissa James is marrying Alec FitzWilliam? I mean didn't he leave school just last summer?' Clarissa was a colleague of Rob's at the high school. She was a keen amateur photographer so she and Grace had gone for some walks together in the weeks before Jefferson's vacation. But once Jefferson had arrived Grace had not got around to seeing much of Clarissa. It was one of the things Grace found confusing about love. It was supposed to have the power to turn you into a better person – a more tender, universally caring one – and sometimes it did; yet often it made you plain selfish, forgetful of friends, of everyone and everything that did not belong to the tiny universe inhabited by two people in love.

As Grace had hoped, Melissa turned her attention to the budding scandal, away from the mystery of how two people could have been married for twenty years and still behave like lovers. 'I hear his parents are just furious,' she said. 'And is *she* going to see him

258

through college? She'll have to. They're threatening to cut him out of the trust fund and they're a very wealthy family.'

'I'm encouraging them, the family that is, to leave the boy's share to the local rabbit sanctuary instead,' Jefferson said. 'I mean, if they really are cutting him off, the money might as well go to a good cause.' Grace took the chance, when Rob got up to get some more wine and Melissa was fussing over the stove, to whisper to Jefferson, 'Honey-pie, you're going too far.' He stroked a loose strand of hair from her forehead, smiling, teasing, loving. 'C'mon, give me a chance here. I'm a small-pet vet. Some of my best friends are rabbits.'

Melissa and Rob were back in the dining room. 'You know,' Melissa said, smiling, hand on her hips, her head tilted as she looked at them. 'You two even look alike. Has anyone ever said that to you before? Same-colour hair, same-shape eyes, same square chin. You even have a dimple right there,' she pointed to the tip of Grace's chin, 'although his is deeper. You look at them, Rob. Don't you think I'm right?'

Later on, over coffee – decaf because there was nothing else in the house – she asked, 'Have you ever thought of combining your work? I was thinking how neat it would be if you took, like, those before and after shots of the little creatures.'

'Like Tom with balls and Tom without them,' Jefferson said. 'Remembrance of things past, that kind of thing.'

Grace looked hard at him. He was getting tired, that was obvious, although she could not see why when he had slept most of the afternoon. Maybe he was coming down with something. 'It's not a bad idea,' she said. 'But I'm not sure most owners would be too keen on having shots reminding them of such painful times.'

'No, no, I was thinking of it like a portfolio thing. Like plastic surgeons have. To advertise your skills, you know the kind of thing. I mean, you two are so great together.'

'I don't know, Melissa,' Grace said. 'We're both kind of possessive about our work. We like to keep things separate.'

It was not even half past ten when Grace got to her feet, pulling Jefferson up from the sofa with her. 'No stamina,' she said. 'But we've had a great time. You must come over to us soon.'

259

They walked the few steps home hand in hand, and the evening was warm but overcast and quite still.

Jefferson fell into bed like a traveller after a long journey and was asleep within moments. Grace lay awake listening to his soft breaths and Pluto's wheezing ones, and she wondered what was different because something surely was. Then she realised it was the ocean. It was quiet; the constant roar of the breakers had silenced to a sound too soft for her to hear. It was the absence of sound that had disturbed her.

Usually Grace watched Jefferson return to his wife and family with heavy-hearted acceptance that this was how it had to be. There were those first few hours of gut-wrenching pain to get through once the door had closed behind him and she felt as empty as if her insides had walked right out with him. And there was the constant nagging fear that something might happen while they were apart: an accident that she would know nothing of until it was too late, because she had no right to know, not even to know if he was dead or alive. But the pain and fear would ebb. She would remind herself that she was far from unhappy living on her own and that there were times when she could not imagine living with anyone, not even Jefferson. She would think sacrilegious thoughts, like maybe Cherry being sick was not the reason for Grace and him not being together all the time, but that secretly they both suspected that their love was the kind best protected from the everyday and that therefore this full-time love in a part-time relationship was all they dared take on. But eventually her emotions would settle like the sea at night. She would return to a contented equilibrium: in love, busy, achingly lonely at times, but doing all right until the next time they met up.

But this time it was different. This time as he turned round having closed his suitcase, he had a pleading look in his eyes. The last time she had seen a look like that was when Angelica took Michael to a birthday party. The little boy had stood with them in the doorway, surveying the large hall teeming with noise and movement, the pushing and shrieking and giggling of a mass of little boys and girls, and he had turned and looked up at his mother with an expression as if to say, 'Don't make me do this.'

But he was a brave and proud little boy so after that look he had straightened his shoulders and joined the fray.

Jefferson, bag in hand, straightened his shoulders and walked out of the bedroom. She followed behind, her lips clamped shut on a small calm smile, her heart thumping. Grabbing hold of him, clinging to his arm and weeping, 'Don't. Don't leave. Stay with me and give us a chance, please', was not an option.

Bollocks! Grace, dreaming her past, heard the words as clearly as if Nell Gordon was in the room. Nell Gordon, that smug cultural regurgitator, that second-guesser of other people's lives, who flattered herself that she understood it all because she knew the 'truth', when every sane person knew that there was no such thing, just a flock of perceptions, as similar and different, as ever present and elusive, as the birds in the sky.

Bollocks, bollocks, bollocks. There she was again. *And you're telling me I distort the picture. That little scene of domestic bliss was one big lie, wasn't it?*

Grace was tired but she still could not sleep. She was not averse to the idea that there was such a thing as telepathy and, if there was, maybe Nell Gordon was tossing and turning in *her* bed.

What kind of day were you having when you decided to deconstruct my life, eh? Bad, I wouldn't mind betting. A dearth of interesting material and you with a deadline and probably little Tristram's birthday party to organise and at least three launches to attend. Do you have a file marked Subjects For That Desperate Day, that day that comes in every journalist's life when there's inches and inches of empty columns to fill and nothing to fill it with? And I sympathise with you, I really do. You're not some tabloid hack. You're a serious writer on the arts pages of an important broadsheet; you can't just make up some natty little piece about the vicar and the golf-club secretary. But Nell, why me? I who, after the furore and the applause, after my own personal chariot ride between triumph and disaster, withdrew into what my father used to call a becoming silence? Why pick on me?

But all right, it had been a game that first summer they spent together on the Cape. She and Jefferson had wanted to act out what might have been if, that other, long-ago summer, he had chosen Grace. They had wanted to let their love, poor sinner that it was, out of the shadows and hold it up to the light. They had wanted to have people walk by and say, 'There go Grace and

Jefferson,' as if such a couple really had a right to be. So they had pretended to their neighbours. So they had lied. They had played house, watering the plants on the porch of the little cottage at the edge of town, just steps from the beach and the roar of the ocean. They had given Pluto his morning bowl of warm milk and wheat as if that was how they had always looked after their dog. So what? They never lied to themselves or each other; all they had done was dip their toes in a dream.

That time – four weeks in a borrowed house on the Cape – was the longest they had together in their six years.

A year earlier Jefferson had left his Manhattan law firm to take up a post teaching law at Redfield College, New Hampshire. Cherry had been going through an especially bad patch and he thought that moving back to small-town New England might help her. And for a while the drinking stopped. Jefferson drove her to AA meetings in another town, near enough to reach in half an hour, far enough away from the tittle-tattle tongues of neighbours. But come February she was a regular instead at that town's only karaoke bar. The call came one evening from a man named Dwight, who asked for her to be collected as she was hogging the mike again, and there had been complaints.

He phoned Grace in London. 'What am I doing?' he groaned. 'What am I doing with my life?' This was her moment; the moment when he was weak and she could make him come to her and stay. 'Grace, Grace, are you there? Can you hear me? I was saying . . .'

'I'm still here. And Jefferson, my darling, you're being good. You are staying because your wife is sick and would get sicker still if you weren't there. You're staying because if you left, your children would not just lose you, they would most probably lose her too. Now just don't ask me my opinion too often because it's possible that I shall not always be this good myself.'

'I don't know that either of you are *exactly* good,' Angelica had said. 'I mean, you are committing adultery.'

Grace, who had been sitting at her kitchen table resting her forehead in her hands, looked up at her with tired eyes. 'I know, Angelica, I do know that. But how good do you want me to be?'

'No, how good do *you* want to be?'

'Don't ask silly questions. Like most people, I want to be good but I also want my own way.'

So when a friend of hers, an American photographer called Dylan Lennox, had suggested a house swap, Grace had called Jefferson up to say she had the chance to spend the summer not more than two hours' drive away. She had been working all year so she had money to fall back on and there were at least two famous writers, both known as reclusive, living on the Cape whose portraits were always sought after. 'I think by now they're bored with being out of the limelight and dying to have someone hunt them out.'

The plan had been for Grace to spend the summer in the house on the Cape and for Jefferson to visit when he could: the odd weekend and the annual week he 'walked the trail with a couple of the guys'. Then came their stroke of luck: Cherry had announced her intention of taking the girls to visit her parents in Florida. She was tired of the rain, she said, and the way people kept sneaking looks at her when they thought she couldn't see. Jefferson was happy. The girls would be fine with their grandparents to help care for them. They were excited about going away, especially as they had been promised a trip to Disneyland. Jefferson made up some story about extending his walking tour while he had the chance, saying, because he thought it would please Cherry who watched *Oprah* a lot, that he felt some quiet time communing with nature might help him find his spirit. Cherry always said he did not have one, and if he did, it was buried so deep it might as well not be there. To Grace, Jefferson said that was unfair; his spirit just ran and hid when Cherry was around.

Cherry certainly did not suggest that he come with them. Without him she was her parents' princess once more, free from any adult responsibilities. 'You're always watching me, as if you're just waiting for me to do something wrong. I sometimes think that's what makes bad things happen; you watching and expecting the worst.' Then she went off on her holiday.

That's how Grace and Jefferson got their time together in the cottage on the Cape.

Louisa

VIOLA HAS BEEN SENT away. Arthur tells me, stone-eyed, that I am entirely to blame for her banishment. I weep and beg him to at least tell me where she has gone but he refuses. 'You should have thought, perhaps, about the consequences for your friend before you decided to flaunt your perversion to the world.'

I put my arm up across my face, trying to shield myself from the words. But he goes on. *Betrayal. Depravity. Moral corruption. Bad seed. Inherited weakness.* Then he leaves me weeping on the floor.

I beg him to let me see my children, but he refuses.

Sir Charles has told him they are best kept away. He shows the doctor my painting. 'I don't understand why,' I say. 'He won't like it.'

'You might think this amusing, Louisa, but I assure you there is nothing amusing at all about your situation. I am working hard on your behalf to make sure that when you come out of this, you will still have some friends.'

'Have you heard from Viola?'

'No, and I don't expect to.'

'And you're sure she left no message for me?'

There is a pause before he replies, 'No.'

'I don't believe you, do you hear? You are lying.' I realise that I am shouting but I cannot stop myself. 'You're lying, do you hear? She wouldn't leave without a communication of some kind.'

*　　*　　*

I am better. There is no storm inside me now. But still Sir Charles is not satisfied. 'Mrs Blackstaff,' his expression is stern, 'were you aware, at the time, what effect your . . . exhibition,' the word is bracketed between two raised eyebrows, 'would have on your husband, on your friend, Miss Glastonbury?'

'*Your* friend Lady Glastonbury's daughter.'

'Were you aware, Mrs Blackstaff, of the harm you were doing?'

I am too exhausted to explain or to try to please. It would have been easier, of course, if I had possessed the gift of dissembling. A few tears on the great man's country tweeds, a helpless flapping of hands and murmured expressions of grief and regret might have helped my cause.

I want to see my children, so for his next visit I try to think of an explanation that might satisfy him. There would never be time for the whole truth and he would never accept that I was proud, still, of my work.

'I mourned my baby. You see, I killed him.' (Sir Charles jots down *probably delusional* in his small black notebook.) 'No, you don't understand.' I put my hand out, touching his lightly. He shies away. For a week now no one has actually touched me or allowed me to touch them. No caresses from Arthur, no sticky kisses from my small children. I yearn to be touched.

'Voices are telling you that you killed your child?'

'Yes. No, not voices, not in the sense that you mean. I'm talking of an inner voice. You have an inner voice, don't you, Sir Charles? An inner voice that tells you the truth?'

'We are not talking about me, Mrs Blackstaff.' He is writing in his book; his hand, pale and stubby-fingered with a covering of silky black hair across the knuckles, moves fast across the page.

He can upset my calm like no one else. I feel the heat rise in my cheeks as my heart pounds, harder and harder, until I fear it will burst free from the confines of my ribcage. Numbness spreads from my shoulder down my left arm. I have to stand up. 'Stop that writing,' I shout.

'There is no need for aggression, Mrs Blackstaff.'

I sit back in the chair and try to turn my thoughts inwards, towards far more pleasing images than that of Sir Charles with his long face where every feature pulls downwards, but I know something bad is happening. *I* hear what I say but *he* seems to hear something different.

'It was the only way I could find relief. When I paint it's as if the work itself is the answer to all the questions. The accusing voices cease.' I look at him, searching for some glimmer of understanding in his eyes, but there is none. 'My husband turned away from me when I needed him most. In the past I have made excuses for him, but no more. To him I was always in the wrong. I never got it quite right, Sir Charles. What was it about me that I never got it right? I thought I might go mad, asking, asking myself that question.' Sir Charles scribbles away in his notebook. *Subject exhibiting signs of paranoia, mentioning being in conflict with the rest of the world that in turn is colluding against her.*

I am desperate for him to understand 'Then there was Viola.' I feel my jaw relax into a smile and my eyes soften as I speak her name. 'She was a rock. She *heard* me. She melted the ice around my heart.' I lean towards him, willing him to look me in the eyes, but his gaze keeps slipping off my face.

'I admit that I knew I was causing mischief by showing my work the way I did, the night of the unveiling of my husband's great canvas, but I'm afraid that at that moment I did not care.' I realise I'm speaking loudly again, so I lower my voice. 'I don't often get angry, Sir Charles. And I'm not proud of what I did. But I had to do something. You must understand, Sir Charles, that I had been in prison and I had to get out. I didn't care whether or not the sun rose in the morning or set at night. I did not care about eating or dressing or even washing. And the worst of it was that when I lost John I lost the others too. Or so it felt. Even when they were in the same room with me I heard their little voices as if in the distance. I wanted to reach out and hold them but it was as if an invisible wall was in the way. Then, suddenly, it was not there any more, that wall. I could not stop talking, running, hugging my children; oh, it was as if I was living all the life I had missed out on.' I look up at him. 'But, Sir Charles, I am quite myself now.'

'I see,' he says.

But to Arthur he says much besides. They stand not more than a foot from my door talking as if neither of them cares that I might hear. Sir Charles speaks words like *persecution mania, suppressed grief, hysterical temperament* and *moral insanity.*

I knew that I had hurt Arthur gravely but I still expected him to speak up in my defence. 'You failed to tell me, when I first treated Mrs Blackstaff, that both her parents were suicides.' It is Sir Charles speaking still.

'She comes from bad stock. I should have realised. But I was young. She was a dashed handsome woman, Sir Charles. Ah well, there's no greater fool than a lovesick fool, what?' Their voices trail off as they move down the corridor.

I get up from my chair and follow them. In the past I have complained of feeling invisible but now I'm glad of it as I listen, unobserved, at the top of the stairs.

'I never considered that she might be seriously ill. Is it something I have done? You must tell me the truth. I can live with it. I have to live with it. I am not a man to shy away from my responsibilities.'

'My dear fellow, of course you're not. And you must remember that you have nothing at all with which to reproach yourself. There is obviously an inherited weakness and a moral weakness too, I am sorry to say. The death of your younger son greatly exacerbated the problems already there. Your wife is calmer now. The mania has subsided, as has the severe melancholy which it followed. However, I believe a period of supervision and treatment is desirable. Of course I could attempt to treat her in your home but in view of the presence of two impressionable young children I strongly recommend that Mrs Blackstaff be admitted to the Harvey Clinic. It's an excellent private facility and she will be under my direct care. We have recently introduced a treatment pioneered by my esteemed Hungarian colleague, Doctor László Meduna, whose belief it is that there exists a biological antagonism between the illness grand mal and psychosis. I have found the treatment most effective when undergone by patients such as your wife.' There is a pause. In the silence I hear the beating of my heart, so hard, so loud I think they must find me out at any moment but they don't even look up.

'You're right,' I hear Arthur sigh. 'The wellbeing of my children must come before all else; there can be no question of

268

anything other. I cannot allow them to be further exposed to their mother's . . . their mother's perversion, but an institution . . .' From my place above I see how he rakes his hair with his strong fingers; fingers that, not so very long ago, travelled across every inch of my body as he whispered, 'Let me worship at your shrine.'

How comical that sounded now, how very comical; and I can't help myself, I burst out laughing; and although I'm quick to cover my mouth, it's too late: they've seen me.

My husband's face is an upturned plate. 'My God, Louisa, what are you doing?'

I can't stop laughing.

'I'm afraid that you have no choice,' Arthur tells me. 'You can agree to go or you can be sectioned. I'm sorry to sound harsh but, whether or not you can see it now, we all have your best interests at heart.'

'The children; I can't go away, they need me. I'm not ill, Arthur. I admit I have been acting somewhat out of character and I'm sorry, sorry for embarrassing you and . . .'

'Louisa, it's not a matter of saying sorry. You're not well, which is why no one is blaming you. But you need looking after in a way that we can't manage here and, quite frankly, I don't think that you are a suitable person at present to be looking after our children.'

'Arthur, don't say such things. I'm their mother; I love them.'

'You said that you had asked yourself many times in the past months whether they would not be better off without you. Sir Charles told me that you yourself had expressed doubt about your suitability to be in charge of young minds.'

'I didn't mean it, not like that. Please, Arthur, you must not take the confidences I have given you and turn them against me like this. I have doubts, but we all do, don't we?'

Arthur shakes his head sadly, as sadly as an actor in a tragedy. 'Don't make this any more difficult than it has to be, I beg you, Louisa. This is not a punishment. You are going to be looked after by people who understand your problems and as soon as you're strong enough you will come home again. Then you can spend as much time with our children as you like; once you are your old self.'

'I don't want to be my old self, Arthur. I will die if I have to go back to that.'

'Louisa, listen to yourself; you're hysterical, irrational. No, really, I cannot be expected to put up with this.' He rises from the chair. At the door he turns with a look of deep reproach and leaves.

'Your mama needs a rest,' Jane tells my son who is weeping in her arms. Her voice is light and briskly cheerful. 'She has had enough of naughty little boys and girls and needs to spend time on her own. And you, young man, must not be selfish and stop her.'

I am already in the car. I want to scream at her not to say these things to him but I sit there, saying nothing, doing nothing as the motor moves off. I see my small son waving and tears fall down his cheeks. Lillian is happy with her new doll and does not need either comforting or explanations. *Why now?* I'm sure she is saying to herself. *Why should I want to understand them now?*

I know from the smell of camphor that it's time for another treatment and I steel myself for what is to come. There is no point in begging for them to let it be, to stop. The treatment is doing me good, so they say. And this is not a bad place. There are locks but they are seldom used. We are even allowed to stroll freely in the grounds, though if we are found outside the perimeters we will be locked up.

The feelings of panic and terror that the camphor induces before the blessed fit takes over are hard to bear, especially when you know what to expect. And I do know. I have been here for three months now. I have not been allowed to see my children in all this time. I tell Arthur and Sir Charles – I tell them all, the doctors and the nurses – that if only I could see my children I might not need any further treatment, but of course they won't listen. When you are well no one notices you and when you are sick no one listens.

The door to my room opens and Sir Charles comes inside followed by two nurses. 'Now, now, Mrs Blackstaff, let go of the bed and let us get started. You know it has to be.'

'It's for your own good,' the young nurse says but she looks unhappy. Mostly the staff are kind.

I doze and in my sleepy state I think of them, of Georgie and Lillian, and how comfortable, how picture-perfect they looked having their tea with Jane Dale by the sitting-room fire. The curtains had not yet been drawn; it was only four o'clock but already it was getting dark. I used to dread the darkening evenings but lately they have become my friends. The doctors are surprised at how strong I am. But you have to be, to walk twelve miles in one night.

I am coming home. There they are, waiting at the door, my husband and my children; my family. I am crying as I step out of the car helped by the chauffeur. Jane Dale appears behind them on the front steps. She looks so young although we are almost of an age. She is wearing a soft green dress that clings to her tiny figure. Lydia is not there, nor Nanny. My mother-in-law departed this life while I was away. Arthur came to see me at the clinic to break the news in person. He did not visit often; it was not judged to be in my best interests, he said. But he did come to tell me about Lydia having passed away and about Nanny having left. When I cried he thought I wept over his mother and, more tenderly than he has spoken to me for a long time, he said that I must not upset myself, that she had had a 'good innings'. But it was for Nanny I wept. She had been my ally.

My husband kisses me on the cheek, gingerly as if he is afraid I burn. 'Welcome home, my dear.'

Lillian allows herself to be embraced before running off to play with the new puppy. Georgie refuses to come near me, clinging to Jane Dale's arm. She is smiling, not at him, not at me, but to herself. I kneel in front of my son and put my arms out but he just fixes me with those eyes I love so well and refuses to leave Jane's side. I look up and meet her gaze and I see the triumph before she turns away to arrange a more suitable expression. 'Kiss your mama, Georgie, and say welcome home,' she tells him but she keeps her hand on his shoulder.

I get to my feet. 'It's all right, Georgie. I can have my kiss later.'

'He thinks I abandoned him on purpose,' I say to Arthur once we are alone.

'Of course he doesn't.'

'But I didn't; I always watched over them.'

Arthur gives me a queer look. He really does think I am crazy, but I cannot tell him or my children that I had been there, in the garden after dark, looking up at their windows, catching a glimpse of a fair head or a dark one, or a small hand opening the curtain to look out long after the lights had been turned out. Nor can I tell him that, because of those night vigils and what I saw, the mere presence of Jane Dale makes me feel mad enough to satisfy even Sir Charles. But I don't want to go back to the clinic. I want my children, and for that I need my husband and my sanity.

'Georgie was a little difficult for the first few weeks of your absence. It didn't help that he had a fever for a while. We did not want to worry you but we were concerned. He kept saying that he wanted to go out in the garden to find you. But he got well and he settled. Nanny did not have a good effect on him. But luckily we had our little Jane. No, the boy's a little cross now, but he'll forgive you.'

'You say he settled, but I suspect he simply gave up.' I take off my hat and run my fingers through my newly shorn looks. 'Is Viola back?'

'Viola is still on her travels. Please don't give me cause for anxiety the moment you return.' I heed the warning in his voice.

With me from the clinic comes a list of instructions as to what I should and should not do. I should have complete peace and rest. I should have plenty of fresh air. I should *not* be allowed to exert myself in any way nor must I be exposed to any undue excitement. I should occupy my time with gentle tasks like gardening and flower arranging. If I insisted on picking up the pencil or the brush, my work should be scrutinised daily for any signs of a disturbed mind. Some visitors would be allowed and, if the improvement in my mental state continued, excursions could be considered under supervision, and later on my own. The children should of course see their mother but they should be discouraged from forming too close a bond as the illness could return at any time.

It takes a week before Georgie will come near me. I had waited for him, forcing myself to be patient and to let him take his time. I was sitting in my parlour with Lillian on my knee, reading her a story from her red book of fairy tales. I knew that he listened outside every afternoon and the previous day he had come as far as the doorway. Then my patience was rewarded. I see him there, walking in, one finger in his mouth, keeping close to the walls as if crossing the room could be dangerous, and then, with a dash, he is at my side, pressing up close. 'Oh Georgie,' I tell him, 'I love you so much.'

I garden and I walk. I play with my darling children, but, as yet, I see them only briefly before breakfast and again at teatime. Arthur assures me that if I continue to make progress I shall see them as much as I could possibly want. 'You will be begging Jane to take them off your hands, you'll see,' he smiles. I look at him and I find it impossible to equate this affectionate if slightly distant man with my enemy of only months before. I thought the wounds inside me would never heal but I am beginning to think I might have been wrong.

Georgie sneaks into my room, making me laugh with his furtive little glances over the shoulder and his tiptoe walk. But I stop laughing when I hear that Jane has said he must not come to me without checking with her first or I might get ill and have to go away again. 'You don't want to make your mama ill, do you Georgie?' He is puzzled; that's how he puts it himself: *puzzled*. How could he make me ill just by being there? Especially when I am always so pleased to see him.

I hug him close and tell him that of course I shall not get ill from seeing my own lovely children. But when Jane comes looking for him I cannot contain my anger. I tell her that she is to stop feeding my children such nonsense. 'I will not tolerate your constant undermining of my relationship with my family. In fact, Jane, I believe you are a most destructive force in my life.' I surprise myself with my frankness, but my voice remains level, polite, conversational. I watch as Jane flees dissolved in noisy tears.

Arthur comes up to my room. I expect him to chide me for upsetting Jane. Instead he sits down beside me and takes my hand. His cheeks are flushed and there are tears in his eyes. 'I did what I thought was best.'

'What do you mean? When?'

'The clinic. Sir Charles is one of the best in his field. You frightened me, Louisa. Your moods. For weeks you're like a sleepwalker who no one, nothing, can wake. The next you are in the grip of some mania. And then your painting, this fantasy . . . of you and poor Viola. What was I to do? There were the children to consider.'

'What do you want me to say?'

My husband kneels before me, burying his face in my lap. I feel his tears through the thin silk of my dress. I watch the sun set behind the large oaks, and with a sigh I raise my hand, pausing in the air before resting it on Arthur's curly head.

Jane Dale has left. She is working as secretary to Donald Argyll and in her letters she tells us she is very happy in her new position and that she finds London 'exhilarating'.

For my birthday Arthur gives me a pearl necklace. And there is something else. He looks awkward as he hands me the parcel. 'She came here to see you before she left. I told her you were to have no visitors. She asked me to give you this. I'm afraid I waited, until now . . .' I get to my feet and walk to my room. There I sit down by the window and unwrap my gift. It's a silver cigarette case. I read the inscription: *Forbes Forever*.

I return to the drawing room for now but when everyone sleeps I go to my husband's studio and pick out what I need. I work that night and every night for a fortnight, contenting myself with the electric light. Each morning, in the early hours, I clean the brushes and hide the palette, hoping he will not notice what is missing. Thankfully Arthur is a messy worker. I store the canvas at the back of the gun room.

When finally I'm done and the paint is dry, I wrap my picture and write her name on the parcel, care of her parents at Northbourne Manor. I ask Jenkins our gardener to deliver it. To this day I do not know if it reached her.

NELL GORDON: *There exists in photography a vast grey area between legitimate documentation and voyeurism, between art and exploitation. This is where Grace Shield stepped with her prize-winning photographs of the very private experience of dying.*

Grace had expected the house on the Cape to disappoint when she returned the following summer, for it to have shrunk unbecomingly and for the whitewashed walls not to be the soft chalky white of her memory but a shabby shade of undecided. And the view from the bedroom would surely turn out to have been workaday rather than sublime. But as she opened the back door with the big old key and walked inside, it was all as she had remembered, right down to the smell of beeswax and salt; only Pluto's chewed wicker basket with his red and white crochet blanket was gone. She had known Pluto would not be there. Dylan Lennox had written to her in the mid-winter to tell her that the old pug's heart had given out one cold morning on his favourite stretch of the sands and that he had buried him, wrapped in his favourite blanket, under the maple. In fact there had been five identical blankets, all made by Dylan's mother, an expert craftswoman who had hoped for grandchildren and got a wheezy old pug instead. 'Don't tell him,' Dylan had said at the time of their first stay in the cottage. 'He thinks it's always the same ones.'

Grace left her cases by the door and walked through the house, through the pale blue and moonshine-yellow sitting room out on to the wooden floorboards of the open porch, up the narrow wooden staircase to their bedroom. She sat down on the bed and stroked the worn patchwork quilt. Next she lay down, closing her eyes, smiling to herself as she imagined him there, next to her.

He called that evening and every evening but he could not say for sure when he would be able to join her or for how long. She moved through the next weeks in a restless way, never quite still, never really at peace. Most mornings she woke with a start in the middle of some dream she couldn't quite catch and leapt out of bed eager to get the day under way, eager to work. She was not there just to sit waiting for her full-time love and part-time lover, she had things to do. But this restlessness was a problem. To get the shots she wanted, that she expected of herself, she needed to think deep and look hard. Instead her thoughts were all surface, insects skimming a pond, too light to reach the murky depths where the interesting stuff was to be found.

And something was up with Jefferson. She had seen him only three times since last summer. There had been a week in London in the autumn, a couple of days in Paris early in the new year and then four days in New York just before Easter. He had cancelled the trip to London planned for May, just two weeks before he was due to arrive, and his reason, pressures of work, had not convinced her. But she knew he still loved her; she trusted him absolutely.

'No you don't,' Angelica had said at the time. She had rushed over with a box of Kleenex and a bottle of vodka. 'You're stupid, but not that stupid.' Angelica was single again and from the way she talked you would have thought it the only way for her to live; unless you knew her well, that is. She poured them each a half tumbler of vodka. 'Now come on, Grace; you don't have to be brave with me.'

Grace had looked up at her with swollen cried-out eyes. 'I'm not brave. I'm bawling my heart out.' She wiped her face with the cuff of her sweater. 'But not because I think he doesn't love me. I've waited too long for him to waste time doubting. I'm sad, that's all, sad not to see him. And I'm worried about him. The last time I saw him, over in New York, I was shocked at how thin he was. I couldn't stop staring at him and then I felt even worse because he covered himself as if I had made him ashamed of his body. His body was beautiful; he was just too thin. He said it was stress, that's all. Too much work, that kind of thing.'

'Men shouldn't be too thin. Then again, when they are it's less of them to dislike.'

'Aren't those man-hating remarks rather passé?' Grace said.

'Mark my words,' Angelica said, 'the pashmina might come and go but hating men will never go out of fashion.'

Grace had looked at her. 'In your working life you're exemplary; hardworking and professional, but to your private life you bring the consistency of a schizophrenic.'

Grace kept asking Jefferson, over the phone, in her e-mails and in her letters, if he was sure he was well. If he should not see a doctor. If he had put on weight. When he phoned to cancel his visit to London the first thing she had asked was if he was sick. She had stood there, the receiver away from her ear, her hands clammy as he shouted down the line that her fussing was enough to make anyone feel ill. What was happening? Some things were a given; he never yelled at her, she never begged for his time or wept in his sight.

After that she knew to keep her concerns to herself while feeling further away from him than at any time since they had met again six years ago.

Mrs Shield could not understand why Grace had to go away a second summer. 'What's wrong with your own country? And Finn and the boys might visit. Than you'll miss them.'

'Finn might always visit but he never does. Anyway I like the States. I was born over there. It's good to keep in touch with my roots.'

'Roots, my foot,' Mrs Shield said. 'You're hiding something.'

'My roots.'

'Don't be silly, Grace. What is it?'

'If I *were* hiding something, telling you about it would kind of defeat the object.'

'Very well, Grace. Have it your way.'

'Oh, Evie, that's what I'm trying to do.' Her expression softened. 'I'll phone and write lots, I promise.'

She had been in the house on the Cape now for two weeks and still she had not seen him. 'So when is your husband due?' Melissa asked again as they had coffee in the Walkers' back yard with the Walkers' bonny babies toddling about their feet.

'Soon,' Grace said, thinking she knew just how Jefferson had felt being nagged.

She walked alone for hours each evening along the beach where they had walked together. She had never shied away from the possibility of their affair ending, but she had never doubted that their love would last, until now.

She had just returned from one of those walks when the station wagon pulled up. At first she assumed it was some tourist needing a place to park but when the front door – the one no one ever used – rattled, she got up and walked round to see who it could be. By then the person calling had made their way to the back and next thing she heard steps like hail on the wooden floor. 'I know you're there. Just come on out and face me, you tart.' It was a woman's voice.

'What the hell?' Grace hurried towards the kitchen.

'It's Cherry McGraw. How many people d'ya know who call you a tart?'

'Cherry.' Grace faced her in the small hallway. Her heart was pounding but she kept her voice light. 'Only you, as it happens.' She reckoned Cherry was allowed the 'tart', assuming she had found out about Grace having an affair with her husband.

They stared at each other. Grace thought she would not have recognised her if she had passed her in the street. When last they met, Cherry had been a sunkissed dainty little thing, all soft curves and pert features. The Cherry glowering at Grace across the kitchen was baked to a terracotta brown; her body, once so neatly packed, looked loose and the delicate features had lost their definition as if painted on with too much water. Then again, Grace thought, I'm seeing her through jealous eyes.

She started as Cherry laughed the kind of lean-back, hands-on-the-hips, mouth-wide-open laugh favoured by Joan Crawford in so many films. 'I never could understand what he saw in you back then and you certainly haven't improved . . . God, what a mess.' Cherry threw her head back and laughed some more.

'Different minds think alike,' Grace said but she automatically put her hand to her hair. It would be a mess, piled up any old how and fastened with a chipped old clip.

'And this place.' Cherry made an exaggerated play at looking around. 'So this is his little lovenest. Pigsty, more like.'

'I wasn't expecting anyone. Had I known you were coming I would have lit twenty scented candles and chucked the shag-pile rug by the fireplace.' Grace thought she should not have said that. After all, Cherry was the injured party here and as such was the one entitled to the rude remarks. She noticed that Cherry's nails were perfect, filed into neat ovals and painted a ladylike pink. Grace hid her hands, red and stained with development fluid, behind her back. 'So what can I do for you?'

There was another Joan Crawford laugh. Quite right too; it had been a stupid thing to say.

'Now, let me see.' Cherry was marching back and forth between the table and the back door. 'Oh yes, not fucking my husband would have been a good start . . . notice I am speaking in the past tense. As it is, you can have him.'

Grace stared at her. 'What do you mean, *I can have him*?' Cherry was playing some kind of game, it was obvious. Grace felt as if the warmth was retreating from her body, down past the forehead and the lips, pausing in the throat, down again past the chest and the stomach. 'You have to excuse me.' She sank down on the small bench by the wall. Cherry was smiling at her like someone about to grant you your most foolish wish. Midas would have seen that smile just before everything around him began to turn into cold hard gold.

'I mean exactly what I say.' Cherry was quite calm now; her fists had unclenched and the tension left her shoulders. When she spoke again her voice was normal, conversational. 'You can have him. The arsehole is dying.'

Cherry had kept him in the car, like some cumbersome delivery. 'It's OK, dear,' she crooned, waving to the figure slumped in the passenger seat. 'You can come out now; she'll take you.'

As Grace gave a little yelp of distress, Cherry turned to her with a smile that was almost motherly. 'Don't get upset now. I mean, isn't this what you've wanted all these years, my husband? OK, so he's not – how shall I put it – he's not quite the hunk he was. The hospital gave him a wig although he refuses to wear it. It's been worse. But I agree, white is not a very flattering shade for him.' She shrugged. 'So he's all yours, although I can't help thinking it's just a little bit pathetic, don't you think; a grown man allowing himself to be bundled off like . . .' her eyes narrowed but the smile remained like a sweet wine turned sickly '. . . like some . . . thing surplus to requirement. Still, they say all men are babies. And stop snivelling.'

'I'm sorry.' Grace rubbed her eyes. 'I don't, as a rule.'

Cherry ignored her and carried on talking. 'Of course he tried, rather belatedly, to be a man, refusing to come inside. He said he didn't want to add to the pressure on you.' The smile gave up the fight against the hatred in her eyes and faded. 'It doesn't seem he trusted you to pick up the pieces. And I wouldn't blame you if you refused to take him. He'll need a lot of care. And it will get worse, that much we know.' Her tone was brisk as if she was going through the care instructions with a pet minder. 'There'll be a lot of that . . . you know . . . embarrassing stuff. And I never had you down as the nursing kind. More of a career girl, aren't you, Grace?' Grace could smell the alcohol on her breath. She hung back as Cherry opened the car door and poked her head inside, saying in her brisk matter-of-fact voice, 'There, you're all right. Didn't I say she'd have you?' She backed out again, stumbling slightly as her heel sank into a soft bit of ground. The lawn was full of those; old holes dug by Pluto to hide his treasures, but never quite filled in.

'Good old Grace,' Cherry said, wobbling on her heels as she hit another hole. 'Always there, panting for a crumb of love to come her way.'

'I expect you're standing on a bone,' Grace said, her eyes wide and fixed on the man in the car who was her lover, who was Jefferson like she had never wished to see him.

Cherry looked down for a moment, moving an inch to the side. 'What are you babbling about? What bone? What the hell are you doing, having bones lying round the yard? Are you renting from the Addams family or something?'

Grace giggled. Leaning back against the sun-warmed bark of the maple tree, she could not stop. Then Jefferson got out of the car. He moved slowly like someone with a stiff back but he walked all

281

the way up to Grace, taking her in his arms, holding her tight, whispering, 'I'm sorry, my darling, I'm sorry.'

'Sweet.' Cherry spat out the word as if it was a bad prawn. 'Now, if you'll excuse me, much as I'd like to hang around here watching my husband make out with a gawky brunette, I'd better be off.' She paused, gazing at Jefferson, summing him up, before saying, 'You see, *I* have a life.' She opened the back of the car and grabbed a small suitcase, dumping it on the ground before getting in and driving off, whipping up the gravel with the back tyres.

'What's going on? Jefferson, for God's sake, what's going on?' There was a whine in Grace's voice – she could hear it herself – as if she was eight years old and someone had played a mean joke on her.

'Let's go inside,' he said and picked up his bag.

'It's not true, is it?' Now she was pleading. 'I know I've been worried, but you kept saying you were OK. You are OK, aren't you?' She walked alongside him into the kitchen, babbling her questions, and then she burst into tears.

He sank down on a chair and took her hand. At first he would not look her in the eyes. 'I'm sorry, Grace, but I didn't *know*, at first.'

'What didn't you know?' She held her breath, eyes closed, as if when the answer came she could avoid it.

'About the cancer.' His sigh was so heavy she half expected it to fall with a thud to the floor instead of drifting off into the ether. 'And this kind, bronchial carcinoma, it moves fast. I've had chemo. It didn't work. I don't want any more. I want to be left alone.'

'You're way too young for lung cancer. They must have got it wrong. Have you sought a second opinion? Angelica has a friend who's a cancer specialist at Mount Vernon. It's one of the best places. I'll call her.'

He was shaking his head. 'No, Grace. I've had second and third opinions. And it is rare, I've been unlucky.' He smiled at the understatement. 'But smoking and asbestos; that'll do it. You remember that summer I worked in Greg's Building and Hardware? I handled asbestos all the time. You remember how I used to come in from the back covered in dust? That was asbestos. It was used everywhere in those days, especially on the farms.'

Grace stared at him. Pictures and questions collided in her head until she put her hands up to her ears and screamed, 'No, no, no, no, no!' She sank down on her knees before him and wept.

'How could you not have told me? It was cruel. I knew something was wrong. I pleaded with you to tell me. Couldn't you see how unfair you were being, keeping such a thing from me? You even cancelled your trip. I don't understand; didn't you need me?' She pulled out a tissue from her pocket and blew her nose. 'Your wife knew, your family, your friends. And me . . . am I so irrelevant?'

'Grace, please.'

'Don't "Grace, please" me. And if Cherry hadn't taken matters into her own hands, what then?'

They were sitting on the porch watching the world go by, two lovers side by side; picture-book nice, but for the fact that one of them was not going to survive the year. Grace kicked back against the wooden plank floor, sending the hammock swinging. He was trying to explain. He had been ill for some time but had refused to consider that something could be seriously wrong. Finally a friend on the faculty staff had, quite literally, taken him by the hand and brought him to see the college doctor. Several examinations had followed; hours and days spent waiting for results, hoping against all his instincts that the news might be good. It never was. 'I had a scare, years ago, when I was barely thirty. They sent me off for a brain scan. The daffodils were out all over the hospital grounds. I remember thinking that by the time I next walked past them, in an hour or so's time, I might have been given a death sentence. When I was told everything was fine I waited for the relief to surge over me, but I just felt numb. I walked outside and the sun was shining. There were the daffodils and that's when I got happy. I did what everyone does at such times; I told myself that never again would I worry about the little things, the trivia, but that from then on I was going to live for the bigger picture. Of course things returned to normal pretty quickly.' He smiled and the smile was such a poor imitation of his usual wide grin that Grace had to look away. Jefferson, a little more distant already, as people are who are preparing to leave, stroked her hair absentmindedly. 'We're so damn ungrateful, aren't we? And stupid. God must despair. Well, of

283

course He must. He gives us these gifts of insight and we hold them in our hot little hands for a moment or two before dropping them and forgetting we ever had them. Anyway, I kept remembering that walk in the sun amongst the daffodils as I sat waiting in some reception area or another, and later, when they put me in more private spaces reserved for those whose misfortune brings them special privileges, I went over that miraculous moment when I got my life back, over and over, pretending that it would happen like that again. But there's no miracle in the pipeline this time. They gave me the option of treatments while telling me that none would make me well or even significantly better. I have excellent insurance,' he smiled and shook his head, 'the doctors wouldn't let me go without trying at least some of their best, their latest and most promising treatments, but in the end they had to.'

'You're not explaining why you didn't tell me. When were you planning to? At your funeral?' She slapped her hand over her mouth. 'God, Jefferson, I'm so sorry. I didn't mean to . . .'

He took her hand and put it to his cheek. He looked at her, smiling.

'It's not funny, it's not funny,' she wailed.

'It is, just a bit.'

They sat in silence for a while. Then she had to ask again, 'Why, even if you didn't want to travel to London, didn't you ask me to come over to you? We could have met in Boston, anywhere.'

'Grace, I was ashamed. Well, look at me.' He faced her, flapping his hand at his chest, agitated. She had to look away for a moment; it was her heart he was breaking with that flapping hand. 'I wanted to tell you. More than anything, I wanted to, but, Grace, I could see the way Cherry and the girls looked at me, with a mixture of pity and . . . distaste. Day by day it was as if I lost a little of myself to the illness. Everyone treated me differently. People didn't see me any more; they saw my illness, this terrifying, ugly illness eating me alive.' He put his hand on hers. 'I spoke to you on the phone, I read your letters and wrote mine to you, and I was still me, I was still,' he looked down, an embarrassed smile on his lips, 'I was still this handsome, sexy fellow who could look after *you* – not that I ever did.'

'But I would have had to have known, sooner or later. When, Jefferson, if Cherry hadn't taken matters in to her own hands? And when did she find out about us?' In the turmoil of emotion one other question nagged at her. Why had he led Cherry to the house, gone along like an obedient child and allowed her to invade their home with her hatred and spite? But she said nothing; this was not the time.

'I suppose it was some kind of deathbed confession. I just wanted everything out in the open. I don't know how I could have been so naïve, so stupid, but I imagined that she might understand. I'm ashamed to say it but I even thought she might be grateful to me for staying with her all these years.' He shook his head. 'Unbelievable as it sounds, I thought she owed me some *care*. Grace, how could I have dumped myself on you now?' He looked away. 'Don't you think I know how I was never there for you?'

She tried to silence him, putting her finger against his lips that were chapped and hot, but he moved her hand away gently and carried on. 'You know it's true. My record is appalling. I dumped you back then. I lived my life and never once got in touch to ask after you. When we meet again, I help myself to you like a greedy child to a bowl of strawberries, helping after helping, but where have I been when you've needed me? Then, when Cherry tells me to get the hell out of her life, I let her drive me here to you.' He gave a bitter little laugh. 'I'm not allowed to drive any more. Now how pathetic am I?'

'You tell that so well,' Grace said. 'But, actually, you've got it all wrong. Do you want to hear my story?' He gave a small shrug.

'When I was not much more than a child, inexperienced, thinking it was beyond me to find someone to care about, I met a boy who was the most beautiful thing, inside and out, that I'd ever seen, and I loved him without question and for a while he returned that love and I discovered sides to me that I had not known existed: tender and loving and womanly. I lost him, but I never lost what loving him had taught me. The years went by and I met him again and now we were grown up and we loved each other and, because of that, my life when it isn't sad is wonderful.'

*   *   *

285

While he napped Grace unpacked his bag. He hadn't packed himself, that was clear. She had always found it touching the way he took such care of his things: shoe trees in his shoes, sweaters carefully folded, jackets hung on good hangers. Here his clothes had been just stuffed into the bag any old way, with no thought to what they would look like at the other end. At that moment Grace hated Cherry – for that, if nothing else.

'Did Cherry never suspect about us? All this time, did she really have no idea?'

'She says she didn't and I believe her. She's never been very good at hiding her feelings. My biggest mistake was to overestimate my importance to her. God, what a self-regarding fool I've been. I told myself that I was thinking of *them*. But I was thinking of myself just as much. I couldn't take feeling that bad about myself. If I left and she went to pieces then it would be *my* fault and I couldn't stand that. I needed to feel good about myself. Oh, I was a good guy, all right; I didn't run out on my alcoholic wife, I just cheated on her. And you, who I profess to love more than anything, I hurt you instead because it was the easier option. Because you were strong and never made a fuss. And the irony is that I was most probably wrong about Cherry anyway. She's as tough as anything. If I had left, maybe she would have been forced to pull herself together. You and I could have had so much more time if I hadn't been such a sanctimonious idiot.' He looked as if the pain of dying was nothing compared to the pain of that wasted time. She bent forward and took his hand. 'Leave the obsessive pondering, the self-hatred and the what ifs to me; I do it so much better. *Your* job is not to die. Once you haven't, then we can plan our future. And don't think we're not alike you and I, because we are, more than you know.'

He squeezed her hand. 'But I am going to die, and soon, Grace. We should not waste time pretending otherwise.'

'That's giving up. It's not fair. You don't have a right to. You're to make a miracle recovery and live on to become a monument to the power of love. That's how it's meant to be.' She tugged at his hand so that he was forced to turn and look at her. She looked back at him as if she was pleading for her own life. 'That's how it should be.'

Cherry phoned once. Grace picked up the phone in the kitchen. 'Jefferson, please,' Cherry said. Their conversation was brief.

'She's moving to Florida. She's having some papers sent over for me to sign so that she can go ahead and sell the house.' He smiled ruefully. 'When she wasn't blaming me for her problems, she blamed them. She had to be perfect. They never understood who she really was. Now she's moving down to live on their doorstep.' He looked at Grace. 'I've been terribly stupid, haven't I?'

'No. You've done what most of us do; given a lot of your best and a little of your worst. Don't beat yourself up over it. Humankind was not placed on earth to get it right, only to try. So what about the girls? When will you see them?'

'I asked her that. She told me they didn't wish to see me. It seems that she has spared them no detail of their father's transgressions.'

'And of his illness?'

'That she didn't say.'

Grace kept bumping into Melissa, on the street, in the shops, on the beach. How were they? Was it her imagination, or had Jefferson lost weight? And wouldn't it be nice if the four of them got together real soon?

'Everything is fine,' Grace said, speaking with the conviction of a robot. 'We'd love to see you but right now . . . well, you know.' Melissa looked a little more hurt each time. Grace wished she could explain: 'I'm not ready for everyone to know our unhappy ending.'

When Joy, the specialist nurse, came round on Monday morning, Grace stopped her on the way into the bedroom. 'He's mad to refuse chemotherapy, isn't he? If he goes along with the treatments on offer, there's a chance that he'll make it, isn't there? I mean, look at him; I know he's thin, he always was quite thin but he doesn't look like someone dying.' Grace's eyes bored into Joy's, her shoulders tense, her voice eager. Then she relaxed a little, even managing a smile as she answered her own question. 'No, of course he doesn't. You'll talk to him, won't you? Now, which hospital do you suggest?' Grace drew breath and Joy put a hand on her shoulder. 'Let's have a cup of coffee, shall we,' she said.

She sat Grace down at the kitchen table and explained matters, calmly and gently. She said there was a good chance that with chemotherapy his life would be prolonged by a few months but that that was the best they could hope for. Jefferson would have had all the options explained to him. If, as sometimes happened with this type of cancer, his lungs got congested he would be offered palliative radiotherapy on an outpatient basis. He would have received counselling. He had made his decision. Grace looked up at her with hollow eyes inky-ringed from lack of sleep. Joy leant across the table and put her hand over Grace's. 'I know it's not what you want to hear, but really I don't disagree with him.'

'He should want those few extra months. Believe me, we've not been spoilt with time. No, I'll talk to him. I'll make him change his mind.'

Joy looked at her and the pity in her eyes frightened Grace more than any words.

'I'm not going into hospital,' Jefferson said. 'What would be the point? Another few months of life spent away from you. No, not unless you feel you can't cope with me here.' He slipped in the last sentence in that kind of careless way Grace knew meant he was terrified of her answer. So she put her arms round him and told him that she was there for him for as long as it took, that she would cope, that for him she could cope with anything.

He was wearing a polo shirt the exact blue of his eyes and the breeze from the great saltmarshes blew across his face and smoothed his strained features. They were walking slowly, making frequent stops for him to rest and catch his breath. 'It should be easy, catching it,' he said, trying to smile as he leant against the upturned hull of an abandoned rowing boat. 'Seeing the damn thing never seems to get further than halfway down my throat these days.' Grace had been about to take a picture of him but she changed her mind and put the camera back in the deep pocket of her old tweed jacket. She had got greedy for pictures of him; they would have to see her through a lifetime without him. In the late nights and early mornings when he slept, she worked in the small darkroom poring over the negatives, choosing which shots to print. Once the printing was done she spent hours studying every feature, every expression the way she could not with the real man. He got edgy if she was always close. He didn't like what he called her 'anxious looks'. But at night alone in the darkroom she studied his face and smiled when he smiled and hurt when she recognised a twist of discomfort at the corners of his mouth.

'It's all right taking pictures,' he said now.

'I know. The light wasn't right, that's all,' she lied. They resumed their walk.

He said, 'Don't go queasy on me, Grace.'

She looked sideways at him. 'What do you mean, queasy?'

'The day you stop taking my picture is the day I know I'm just a care package.'

'I just want lots of pictures of you to . . .'

'To remember me by; I know. But you like to work too and don't tell me the slow dying of a man does not make an interesting subject.'

Grace started opening her mouth to protest, closed it again, shook her head and smiled, placing her hand gently on his shoulder. 'No, no, I wouldn't tell you that.'

He grinned back. 'And there is the being-remembered factor and the having future generations poring over the pictures and saying, "So that was Jefferson McGraw dying so gracefully, with such style and such panache."' Then he started to cry. He cried and she hugged him and this time her eyes were dry.

The nights in the darkroom got harder as she saw the changes in his face that she had been too busy, too shy, too scared, to notice during the day; the pain etched around his eyes and mouth and the growing weariness of his gaze. 'You see him every moment of the day,' Joy said. 'You won't notice every little change. And that's no bad thing.'

'I see it in the pictures,' Grace told her.

He got up for lunch. They even had some white wine with their shrimps and French-style bread. The sun was streaming through the open door and windows, bathing the kitchen in a warm bright light, the kind that fooled you into thinking life was good.

But by the afternoon he was fretting about his children. He had called Cherry's parents but they refused to say where their daughter and grandchildren could be found. 'Haven't you hurt them enough?' his mother-in-law said.

'But the girls, I need to see them.'

'You should have thought about that before you cheated on their mother.'

'I did think about them, and Cherry; that's why I didn't leave.'

'So now they should be grateful?' Grace could hear her laugh, sharp and theatrical, although she was a couple of feet away from the phone. Like mother, like daughter, she thought.

Jefferson contacted his colleagues at his old law firm, asking them to find out what could be done. 'Grace, I might never see my daughters again.'

He called his parents-in-law once more. 'I'm real sorry, Jefferson, but I've told you: Cherry and the girls don't want to hear from you right now. I know you're sick, and I'm sorry.'

'What about the girls? Haven't they got a right to see their father before he dies?'

'Now, don't you go exaggerating like that, Jefferson. The girls are fine and we just don't see the need to drag them through all this . . . unpleasantness.'

'That's what she called it,' Jefferson said to Grace, 'an "unpleasantness". All I can say is that it's becoming one of my greatest regrets that I won't be there to see my mother-in-law come to meet *her* "unpleasantness".'

'You should call the police or social services or something. You have a right to see your daughters, you know that; you're a lawyer. And they have a right to see you. How will they feel if they are made to stay down there and never . . .'

Jefferson finished the sentence for her. 'Never see me again. Quite.'

'They wouldn't let me see my mother after she died. It was the worst thing they could have done because it made it so much more difficult to let go. No, I'd call the bloody FBI if I were you. In fact, I'd have Cherry stuck in chains and thrown into prison without access to vodka *or* that bloody pink lipstick.'

* * *

290

'What the hell are you doing, barging in like that?'

'I just thought you might need a hand.'

'Get out! For Christ's sake, do you have to follow me even into *here*?'

When he came out of the bathroom she saw he had been crying. 'I'm sorry; I thought you were having a bath,' she said.

'No, I'm sorry for yelling at you.' He wouldn't look her in the eyes as he passed her. 'I'm meant to be your lover.'

'You *are*.'

His jaw was working and his cheeks were fever-pink. 'Then your idea of a lover is pretty different from mine.'

'I want to know about this exhibition you're meant to be working on. Have you got anywhere?' He had come down to the kitchen. She was cleaning the windows. She had cleaned them the day before too, and the day before that.

She put the cloth down. 'You know I haven't. I just haven't *seen* anything. Nothing really fires me; hardly surprising.'

'You'll just have to try harder.'

'Somehow that damn exhibition just doesn't seem very important right now.'

He slapped his hand down on the kitchen table. 'That's just dumb. It's real important. Look at me. Have you thought how it makes me feel, thinking I'm messing up your career as well as having you run around like some damn nurse picking up after me, wiping my arse . . .'

'You're not messing up my career and I haven't wiped your arse.'

'The time will come . . .'

'And then it'll be a privilege.'

'Not for me, it won't. Look, Gracie, I'm the one dying here. That's enough of a burden. Don't make it heavier by adding guilt.'

'I've *been* out, you know that. I've taken some shots: the usual, laughing kids, newborn bunnies.'

'You should travel.'

'Don't be silly.'

'OK, so you don't want to leave just at the moment. That's fair

291

enough, I accept that. But I'm right about one thing; you can't press a pause button on your life while you wait for me to die.'

Grace couldn't take any more of that kind of talk so she got to her feet and tramped out of the door, slamming the bug-screen behind her. She did not go far, staying in the garden, breathing deep, looking up into the sky that seemed weighed down by the mass of working birds, holding her hands over her ears to shut out the noise of all that *life*, hating God.

Then she thought, what am I doing wasting time that I could spend with him? And she went back inside. He sat where she had left him, staring at the wall, his food untouched. When he heard her come in he turned and smiled at her. How could he still smile like that, like a child smiling at the future because they had not seen enough to fear it? She went up and wrapped her arms round him, but not too tight; his whole body was tender these days.

'What's the title of the exhibition again?' he asked.

She kissed the short soft hair on the top of his head. 'You don't give up.'

'No.'

She sighed and went to sit down opposite him. 'Would you believe, *A Celebration of Life*?'

He laughed. It was a big, genuinely amused laugh. '*A Celebration of Life*. OK. Let me think about it. Actually, I'll do the thinking in bed.'

They went upstairs together and she stayed with him. She had brought the rocker up from the porch and placed it by the bedroom window. She sat there often, reading, or trying to, or just watching him.

'Honey, I've thought.' He used a silly voice and was looking at her with the old perky look in his eyes. 'Use *me*.'

'Use you?'

'Use *me*. Make me your model for the exhibition, for your celebration of life. C'mon, you know you want to. I can see it in your eyes sometimes, that hungry glint like a lioness who's just spotted a plump and lonesome antelope. Work is your other love. I stopped being the jealous type when I was told I had three months to live. So enjoy. Use me. Combine us, if you like. I'm dying. You can't change that. You're a photographer; it's your job to document. So do your job. I'm a fading lens-louse; it's my job to be photographed. Catch me while you can. Let me do *my* job.' He was smiling, talking brave, being flip, but he could not disguise the pleading in his eyes. Next he was looking at her, serious, thoughtful. 'I like the idea of being part of this exhibition. You said it was important; big London gallery, that type of thing?' He grinned again. 'I mean, I have my standards. I wouldn't go wasting my dying on any old hick-town exhibit, but this will be good. Even the title is great.' He made a sweeping gesture as if describing his name in lights. '*A Celebration of Life: One Man's Final Journey.*'

Grace looked at him. 'That's not funny,' she said, but she was smiling too; it was a while since she had seen him so . . . well, so alive.

'It's bloody funny. But *I'm* serious. Come over here.' He patted the side of the bed. 'Comfortable? So, I'm sick but I'm not blind. I'm changing. It's like one of those speeded-up nature films when they show a bud grow and open, blossom, wilt and die all in a matter of seconds. So I might not make a very convincing flower but look at me.' She did and to her shame she was already weighing up the possibilities in her mind, framing her pictures, thinking light and backgrounds. She had to look away. What's wrong with me? she thought. What kind of freak am I?

He grabbed her hand and put it to his eyes. 'It's kinda interesting. Don't tell me that for you, as a photographer, it isn't, the way the journey marks my face with each passing day, because I won't believe you. I know you, Grace. And I like the irony; a celebration of life. Or maybe there's no irony. Maybe dying is the ultimate celebration of life.'

'And that's the kind of pseud's statement that I love you for,' she said, trying not to cry. Every day she saw the distance grow between them, the distance between the one who was going, and the one who would be left behind. It was his journey and all she could do was watch him go. 'Jefferson, I'm sorry to be making this about me . . .'

'That's all right, sweetheart; familiarity is comforting for the sick.'

'I don't know if I can do it, that's all.'

'I know it's tough watching me dying,' Jefferson said. 'Not as hard as actually *doing* the dying, but tough nevertheless. That's why I want you to use the camera. It'll help you and actually – far more importantly – it'll help me. It will be something we *are* doing together. Anyway, I've told you before, I like to watch you work.'

Grace got up and fetched the Hasselblad. 'I shall take a shot of you now because you are looking particularly gorgeous.'

'Ah well.' He struck a pose, hand to the back of his head. 'Death becomes me.'

He was asleep on the porch, his head tilted backwards, the skin tight over his collarbone, half his face in full light. Careful not to disturb him, she set up a white cardboard reflector on his shadow side, but a flock of terns, flying by so low she could distinguish the faint rose hue of their under-plumage, woke him. Still woozy, not quite focusing, he smiled at her as she pressed the shutter.

Saturday morning and just getting out of bed made him so out of breath he had to lie straight back down again. Every gulp of air sounded like it had to fight its way down into his lungs, and when Grace laid her head on his poor chest every breath rattled; but he pointed at the camera on the bedside table. She shook her head violently. 'I'm calling Joy,' she said. It was his turn to shake his head. He pointed again at the Leica.

'Don't chicken out on me now,' he whispered. 'This isn't pretty, but we're doing good work, remember, not Hollywood schlock.'

She sighed and got the camera. Blue eyes faded like an old shirt that had gone through the wash too many times, white close-cropped hair, a complexion tinged with a grey that no sun could disguise, grooves and lines; a man who was still young. So this was to be her job now: documenting the disintegration of the man she adored. She looked away, blinking, fixing a breezy smile.

She took ten shots and with each one she got more absorbed in her work until he was simply a part of the scene: a bed with the bedclothes tossed to one side, bright light from the sea, a rose in a vase, closed eyes, open mouth, a nose set in deep furrows, hands clasping a sheet. She knew these shots were good. When she went downstairs to phone Joy she felt sick; as if she had pigged out on her favourite food or spent more money than she could afford.

Joy was over within the hour. She said the patches weren't enough and put him on a subcutaneous drip, showing Grace how to check that it was clean and not blocked, telling her how to manage it.

'That's it,' he said. 'I'm going into hospital. I'm not having you care for me, not like this.'

'Would he be more comfortable in hospital?' Grace turned to Joy.

The nurse shook her head. 'Not really. This is a bad day. I'll get Doctor Howard to call in later.' She turned to Jefferson. 'You might well be off the drip again tomorrow.'

'I'm not staying here,' he insisted.

Grace sat down next to him on the bed. 'Go into hospital then, but I won't be able to work there. It just won't be right; the hospital light, the institutional aspect of it all. It just won't work.'

Out of the corner of her eye she could see the look on the nurse's face; surprised, suddenly disapproving.

Downstairs Grace said, 'It's as if he's ashamed of being sick, and I can't bear it.'

'It's hard being the one receiving all the care. It's easier dealing with us professionals. The patient knows we get paid. You, he can't pay.'

'He's trying to.' And Grace explained about the photographs. 'I know he doesn't want to go into hospital. He says he does because he can't bear thinking he's a burden, so I talk about the photographs; nothing else convinces him that he is not.'

Joy listened and then she said, 'I suppose I can see his point.'

'But?'

'Well, to be honest with you, Grace, I find it harder to understand how you can do it, take all those pictures. I'm a nurse. I see people dying all the time and I have to stand back from the person and do my job. But he's your husband.' She looked away. 'I shouldn't have · said that. We're all different.'

'That's true.' Grace sighed. 'In fact, there are times when I wonder whether I'm part of the same species.'

'If you feel that way, don't do it. You must have plenty of snaps of him by now and you can find another way of making him feel less beholden.'

Grace looked at her. 'Do you know, the worst of it is I don't want to.' She got to her feet and walked over to the window, looking out at the maple tree. She wondered if they, any of them, would be there to see its leaves turn.

Grace made another call to Jefferson's old law firm, asking if they had managed to get in touch with Cherry, if there had been any progress on the court order forcing her to give him access to his children. 'He needs his daughters. Please do this for him.'

Jefferson slept and while he slept Grace went for a walk. Autumn was approaching; the growing surf told her so although the air was warm and the terns remained, leaving only for their fishing trips to that point on the horizon where the sky melts into the sea.

'Stop posing.' Grace laughed. He was sitting up in bed with the rose she had picked for his breakfast tray stuck behind his ear. A little earlier she had been in to change his morphine patch. He hated her doing anything of that nature, saying, 'I'm not your patient, I'm your lover.' But there he was now, fluttering his eyelashes, tossing his head, trying to make her laugh. 'OK, Carmen,' she said, grinning at him. 'Do your worst.'

'See,' he said, looking inordinately pleased with himself. 'You're OK,' he said.

'No!' She lowered the camera.

'Don't look so stricken, my darling Grace. You're not a hypocrite? I'm a man who has to ask for help to go to the toilet, for Christ's sake. Can't you see how much better it makes me feel to think I am of some use?'

She looked at him and then she smiled. 'There are moments when you are in control of your equipment, and your subject. Then the camera ceases to be something mechanical, a piece of machinery, and becomes a part of you; your extended eye. It's a good feeling. In fact, it's a great feeling.'

Jefferson sighed, not the heavy sinking kind, but a contented sigh that rose like a tiny feather propelled on a breath. 'And it was my doing just now. I gave you that feeling.'

'Oh yes, you gave it to me.'

There were times when he could not bear to be touched. 'And I've told you, stop looking at me like that.'

'Like what? Please, like what?'

'Like you're expecting me to drop down dead any moment.' Before she had a chance to say anything he changed his expression from disgruntled to smiling. 'Of course that's exactly what you are expecting, but it makes me uneasy, that's all. I feel like I have to hurry up and oblige.'

Grace looked at him and did not smile back. 'That was cruel.'

'It was a joke.'

'It was cruel.'

He put his hand out, willing her to let him take hers. 'I'm sorry. Forgive me. Dying puts me in a bad mood, that's all. And I want you around; all the time, just not hovering, anxious and un-Gracelike. Go fetch your camera, my darling. I feel a heroic air coming on.'

'You're an idiot.' But she did what she was told.

'Look at you; you're making love to me with that camera.' Then he paused before saying, 'I've got ugly?'

'No.'

'But I look so old. A couple of weeks ago I was forty. Yesterday, looking in the mirror, I thought, I'm giving late fifties a run for its money. So tell me, my dearest love, how old am I today? And please don't give me the one about you're only as old as you feel.'

Grace sat down at the foot of the bed. 'To me you are always beautiful . . .'

'Peleease. Don't give me that bullshit.'

'. . . *and* never more so than now because . . . because each day I see it more clearly; your soul.' She raised her hand. 'No, don't snigger. I'm serious. Until . . . well, until I got to watch someone, you . . .' She paused.

'. . . dying.'

She smiled weakly. 'Yes . . . until then, I didn't believe there was such a thing as the soul, not in the sense of something outside the physical body something that wasn't just the bits of DNA and brain chemicals and whatever that makes our personality. But I know now that I was wrong. The soul is there, a separate entity that will go on after our physical presence has ceased.' She put her hand lightly on his cheek, on the flesh sunk back against the bones. 'I can't say that right now it's much of a comfort because I'm selfish and I want you, all of you, with me, where I can feel you and speak to you and hear you . . . but it will be, won't it? It is for you, isn't it?'

'If you tell me you have captured my immortal soul on camera then I am comforted. Not enough to stop me being angry at dying when I'm only just forty or desperate that soon I shall not see you again, but comforted to a degree. So you see,' he smiled, 'we've done a good job.'

'I love watching you work. You're all precision, like a ballet dancer.'

Grace shot him a quizzical look. 'Ballet dancer? Me? Hardly.'

'All right, maybe ballet is not quite the right word, but you *are* different when you're working, and I like it. You act differently according to which camera you're using, too.' He looked pleased with himself for having made the observation. 'With the Leica you're all loose and easy, like you're hanging out with an old buddy. You keep it with you all the time. With the Hasselblad you're reverential and, as soon as you've got your shot, you put it away.'

One morning when he was too tired to sit up, he asked her, 'How's my soul today?'

'It's good.'

'And the bone structure?'

Grace put the camera to her eyes to hide the tears.

He was lying on his back beneath the thin cotton sheet, palms facing skywards in the pose of a sleeping infant. His breathing was rapid, as if he had been running, but his face was peaceful. The lace curtains at the window softened and diffused the fiery light of the hot afternoon, leaving him to sleep. She had not been able to protect him or to make him well. So she did what she could do and caught his suffering humanity on rolls of film. The bed framed his sleeping form and the window was reflected on the white wall behind. The camera was raised to her eye but she lowered it again as, for a moment, she could not hear his breath. But no, there it was again, rapid, shallow, telling her he was with her yet; for a little while longer he was there and hers. In a moment she would go and lie down next to him, hold him and tell him how much she loved him. Beg him to stay a little while longer. She heard a faint cough. He opened his eyes and looked straight at her: alert, alive. She adjusted the focal length, determined the shutter speed and the aperture. Then his chest shuddered, sending a fine spray from his lips, and his eyes widened. She did not go to him, not straight away. She took her picture first. By the time she reached his side and took his hand, he had died.

NELL GORDON: *As Al Alvarez said, 'A great work of art is a kind of suicide.' So, are Grace Shield's award-winning photographs art? And if they are, did she commit professional suicide in the process?*

Every minute of every hour of that flight back to London gave its sixty seconds' worth. She sat strapped in her seat, suspended between two continents, with nowhere to put down her grief. Were she the type to go mad, she thought, she would have done so on that flight from Boston.

Once home, she went straight into the darkroom and developed the last roll of film. She did not sleep that afternoon or the night which followed. She spread his dying days across her kitchen table and gazed upon them. Each picture told her, in its different way, why she had loved him: his smile, his eyes, warm and full of interest in the world, even after he knew that his stake in it was diminishing by the hour. The way he tried to hide his fear from her, making her laugh. She sat there at the kitchen table, not sleeping, not eating, studying those images.

Angelica came over. She used her key to let herself in. She took one look at Grace, shook her head and proceeded to view the photographs.

She said, 'They're beautiful.' And she gave Grace two sleeping pills and helped her to bed.

Grace slept for twenty-two hours. When she woke, she found Angelica had returned and was sitting at the kitchen table, the photographs laid out in front of her. She looked up as Grace staggered through the door. 'Sorry, I forgot; you should only take one of those pills. Still, you got some sleep.'

'I did. Now I want to know if I'll ever wake up again.'

'Here.' Angelica handed her a mug of strong Indian tea. 'It's your best work to date.'

Grace drank greedy gulps, leaning against the doorpost. 'Can you see his soul?' she asked.

A couple of days later Angelica phoned to say, 'Everyone loves the pictures.'

Grace was feverish in her need to have her beliefs confirmed. 'They saw it, the spiritual side, the . . .'

'Sure. They're great pictures. Harrowing. Could win prizes.'

'I don't think it's what I want. They're private, as private as birth and death . . .'

'Death, at least, used to be a very public affair: relatives, friends, priests, servants, dogs . . . that's why they weren't so damn scared back then.' Angelica must have been on her mobile because she was round at Grace's flat just three minutes later. Taking Grace by the shoulders, she jerked her close. 'Do you know what I see? I see great shots and first-rate work. Star-quality work. Of course it's spiritual, of course there's soul. But you know how it is. People see what they see. Really, Grace, I know you're in a tough place right now . . .'

Grace couldn't help a smile. 'What's this about "tough places"? I'm the one who's been watching American television.'

'Look.' Angelica let go of her shoulders but took her hand instead, leading her to the sofa. 'I know you're going through hell right now. You've just lost the man you thought you loved.'

'Try the man I *know* I loved.'

'Whatever. You're in shock. You're grieving. But you've taken some truly great pictures here. You've told me yourself that it was his idea you should do it. His idea that you should put them on show. You're honouring his wishes. I don't see a problem.'

'You're full of it, Angelica.' Grace sat down, as stiff and heavy as a woman twice her age. 'It helped him to think he was doing something for me, for my career.'

'There you are. Honestly, what's the point of no one seeing them? Who will that help? I know how hung up on him you were.' She caught the look Grace gave her and said quickly, 'All right, all right, you loved him.' She pulled a chair out. 'Sit down.'

Grace did what she was told. Then she grabbed a cigarette from the packet on the table. 'But I wanted to do it. Can't you see, in the end I really wanted to take those pictures, for me?'

Angelica found some matches. 'But, Grace, you did your best work while he lay dying. You composed your shots, worked out your light and your shades, your planes and your angles. Look, I don't doubt you loved him, but your work is who you are. Why deny it? Why waste it?'

Grace inhaled on the cigarette, rubbing at her forehead, then she looked up at Angelica. 'I was taking his picture when he died. I had my lens pointed at him, thinking about the way the light was falling, of the shadows cast; I was adjusting the focus and while I did all that, while I did all those things that I do to take my great pictures, he died and I did not even notice. So, do what you like.'

Grace walked up to the podium, her steps drowned out by the sound of applause. She accepted her cheque for thirty thousand pounds and said her thanks.

She asked the cab to drop her by the Albert Memorial. She wanted a walk. She passed a drunk on a seat in the park and gave him her Leica. Back home she transferred the cheque to a charity for the blind.

Grace told Mrs Shield that she was going back to London 'just for one night'. Mrs Shield opened her mouth to speak, but Grace got in first. 'I know you need me here a bit longer. And I'm having a nice time. The country isn't all bad. I'll be back tomorrow; promise.'

Mrs Shield put both her hands to her large chest. 'I'm not healing as fast as I had hoped,' she said, giving Grace a sideways glance under her sandy eyelashes.

'I know, Evie.' Grace stifled a smile. 'It's a bummer, isn't it?'

Mrs Shield inclined her head. 'A bummer, yes indeed.'

How many antique shops can there be in the Chelsea Embankment area? Lots, Grace thought, as she traipsed along Royal Hospital Road, her painting wrapped in a pillowcase. But no one had recognised the picture as having been theirs although several dealers had expressed an interest in acquiring it.

She nearly missed the small shop on the corner of Tite Street. There was no sign that she could see and the window display was as sparse as if had been someone's home and not a shop; a Lalique bowl flanked by a pair of stark silver Art Deco candlesticks and the sign on the door saying *Antiques* was easily overlooked. Inside there was more Art Deco: lamps, bowls, a couple of hand mirrors, and a few pieces of furniture from a much earlier period. A gilded birdcage hung empty from a hook in the ceiling. There were some decent watercolour landscapes and, on the far wall, an oil. Her heart raced as she moved closer. When a woman appeared from the back and asked, 'Can I help you?' all Grace could do was point.

The woman looked at the painting. 'I'm afraid that's not for sale.'

'It's by Forbes.' In the picture a young boy, six years old perhaps, with flaxen hair cut in a pudding-bowl and dressed in a bright golden-yellow sailor suit, sat sideways in a chair, one leg drawn

303

up beneath him, a toy train dangling from one hand. His face, a small triangle with huge almond-shaped amber eyes, was a study of the kind of boredom that only a child feels; so intense it hurt. The chair was faded red and a blue and white patterned shawl was thrown across its back. A little girl, a couple of years younger, knelt on a green and red rug, ministering to a doll with only one arm. She was engrossed in wrapping the doll in a small piece of peacock-blue velvet, paying no attention to the boy in the chair. He too was looking down past her; they each acted as if they were alone in the room. The walls were painted in melting shades of green. The picture glowed with light.

'I know who painted it, his name is Forbes.'

The woman looked at Grace. Then she looked at the painting Grace herself had brought. 'If you wouldn't mind waiting a moment.' She disappeared behind the curtain and Grace could hear her calling, 'Come out here, will you, dear, there's someone I think you should meet.' Grace read the signature in the bottom left-hand corner of the second picture. It said *Louisa Blackstaff.*

Noah helped his grandmother out of the car, supporting her as they walked the few steps to the shop. Inside, Viola Glastonbury, hunched over a walking-frame, was waiting. When she saw them, she let go of the frame and took a step forward, her left hand outstretched. Louisa held it in hers and the two of them stood silently gazing at each other. A smile, like a note hit and held at perfect pitch, lit up Louisa's face. 'Viola, there you are. I dreamt I couldn't find you.'

'Your pictures were never for sale,' Viola said to Louisa. 'Then this young man came along. Oh, he was determined; he had to have the painting. "For his special friend," he said. He was so eager, charming and handsome,' she turned and smiled at Grace, 'and he talked about you with such love. I was never going to let it go, especially not that one, but then he told me that you were from Northbourne, that you knew them all, that you knew her.' She looked at Louisa. 'So I let him have it and, my dear,' she put her hand over Louisa's and held it there, 'I've been waiting for you ever since.'

They were drinking tea in Viola's little sitting room at the back. 'Rose petal,' Louisa said, lifting the china cup to her lips. Grace looked at her shaking hand that was beautiful still, inky veins laid like ropes just beneath the surface of the paper-thin skin, strong long fingers; the hand that had painted her picture.

Noah stood by the window, staring out at the tiny back garden. When he turned round his cheeks were flushed and there were tears in his eyes. 'How can you ever forgive me, all of us? What kind of a family have we been to you, we who should have cherished you? And why didn't you tell *me*? Why didn't you make me take notice?' He took a step forward and knelt down by her side, taking her hands in his. 'Why did you allow him to win?'

'Oh Noah, my dear, how like him you are at times; all storms and thunder. Tell me exactly how what happened to me is your responsibility.'

'I didn't *see* you.'

Louisa smiled and shook her head, slowly, painfully. 'But, dearest Noah, *I* saw *you*. I lost your father, my Georgie, but I had you.'

'But you gave it all up. Your work,' he glanced at Viola, 'your friend . . . It seems that between you and Grandpa it was you who were the better artist, yet you allowed yourself to be intimidated, trampled . . .'

Louisa interrupted. 'In the end it was my choice. Whether it was the right one is another matter. I was there when my children grew up.' She turned to Viola, 'But my dear, how I missed you.'

Grace and Noah stepped out into the back garden, leaving the two women to talk. 'It is the usual story,' Grace said, kicking a stone into the tiny pond. 'The wasted lives of women.'

Noah looked at her, a small smile in his eyes. 'Well, Grace, you said it.'

MERRICKVILLE PUBLIC LIBRARY

It was Sunday morning. It was going to be another hot day, but as yet it was pleasant enough with the sun filtered through the early-morning haze. Grace was strolling through Kensington Gardens, towards Hyde Park, a Leica round her neck. She was on the way to the gallery where she was helping to hang the paintings for Louisa's retrospective. Later on she was meeting Noah who was coming back from Canada for the opening.

She was walking along Rotten Row when she stopped and looked intently at the path in front of her. She knelt down, the camera raised to her eyes. Next she took a few steps back, on her haunches, Cossack style, and focused the lens on the pile of horse dung and on the butterfly, its gold and orange wings fluttering as it clung on to the steaming heap. A moment later, at the sound of a car horn, the butterfly was gone, but by then Grace had her shot.

Standing up she smiled to herself, *You know, Nell Gordon, you never would have got the butterfly.*

MERRICKVILLE PUBLIC LIBRARY

ACKNOWLEDGMENTS

My warmest thanks to Jo Frank and the team at A.P. Watt and to Alexandra Pringle and Martin McCarthy and the team at Bloomsbury for all their wonderful work and advice. Also to Garlinda Birkbeck, Peter Claaesson and Alf Weihed for our conversations about photography. To John Cobb for all his help. Harriet Cobbold, Jeremy Cobbold, Lars Hjörne and Anne Hjörne for reading, advising and listening, and to Sally Montemayor for her help with absolutely everything.

A NOTE ON THE TYPE

The text of this book is set in Galliard, a relatively new type face designed by Matthew Carter and introduced by Mergenthaler Linotype in 1978. Carter based his design on a face created in the late sixteenth century by Robert Granjon. This elegant face has a comparatively large lower-case x-height, which makes it easy to read in all its weights and sizes.

A NOTE ON THE AUTHOR

Marika Cobbold was born in Sweden and is the author
of four novels. *Guppies for Tea*, selected for the WH
Smith First Novels Promotion and shortlisted for the
Sunday Express Book of the Year Award; *The Purveyor of
Enchantment, A Rival Creation* and *Frozen Music*.
Marika Cobbold lives in London.